ONE ORDINARY DAY IN LIAVEK...

"Hello, Silver," Snake said. "What can I do for you?"

"I'm not Silvertop," the Margrave said, and he knew he sounded foolish. "I'm Koseth."

Snake nodded. "And I'm His Scarlet Eminence."

"Blast it, Snake! This may be Silver's body, but I *am* Koseth!" He scowled at Snake, took her face in both his hands, and kissed her with ferocious intensity.

"Well!" she said, a little gruffly. "I'm convinced. You're the only person in Liavek who'd try that and expect to live." She grinned. "How is it that you're wearing Silver's body?"

Koseth flung himself into a wicker chair. "I woke up in it. I assume he woke up in mine. Some poor fool certainly did."

Snake pointed a finger. "You haven't checked?"

"I tried. Someone seems to have kidnaped me."

LIAVEK

The PLAYERS of LUCK

edited by
Will Shetterly
and Emma Bull

ACE FANTASY BOOKS
NEW YORK

This book is an Ace Fantasy original edition, and
has never been previously published.

LIAVEK:
THE PLAYERS OF LUCK

An Ace Fantasy Book/published by arrangement with
the editors and their agent, Valerie Smith

PRINTING HISTORY
Ace Fantasy edition/June 1986

ACKNOWLEDGMENTS

The editors would like to thank Professor Elmer C. Birney of the University of Minnesota for improving our acquaintance with camels; Fred Haskell, for telling us the name of the other doorkeeper; and Melissa Pierson, the copyeditor of this book, for reasons that would be obvious had there been no copyeditor.

For Susan, Beth, Terri, and Val,
who make it possible—and fun.

CONTENTS

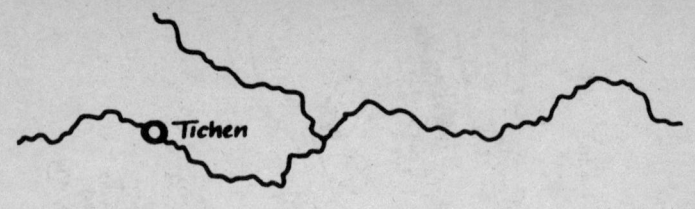

Tichen

EMPIRE of TICHEN

THE GREAT WASTE

SILVERSPINE

Trader's Town

Liavek

Ombaya City

Hrothvek

Saltigos

Crab Island

THE SEA OF LUCK

N

Gold Harbor

Ka Thow

Ka Zhir

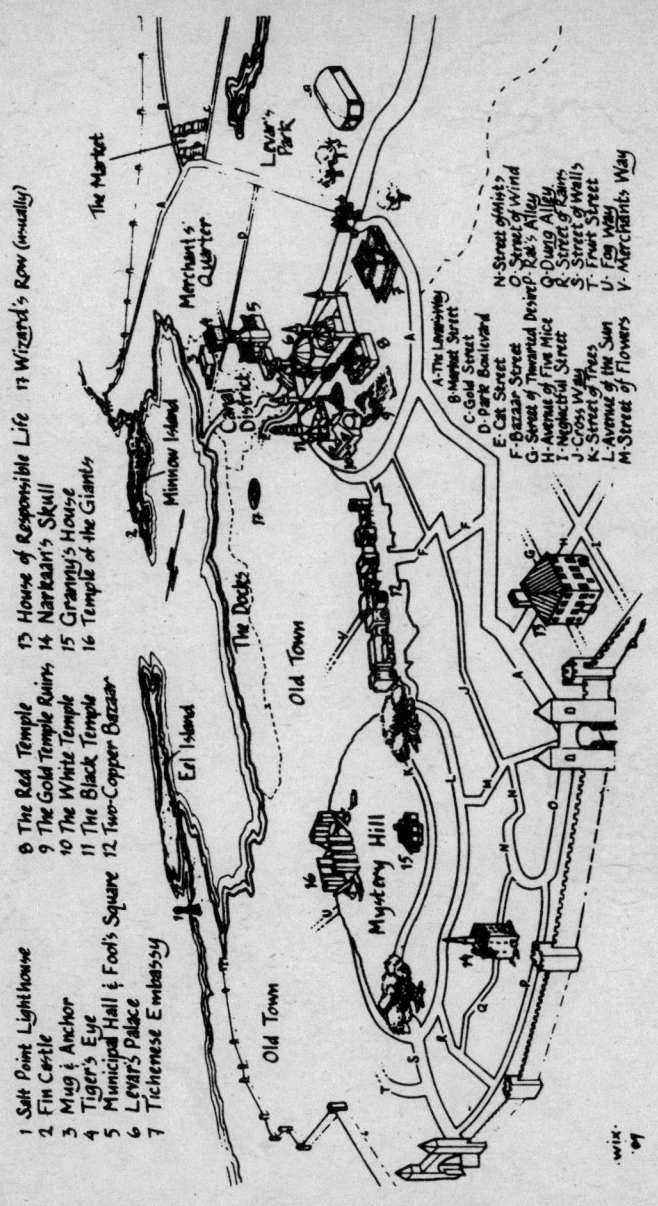

1 Salt Point Lighthouse
2 Fin Castle
3 Mug & Anchor
4 Tiger's Eye
5 Municipal Hall & Fool's Square
6 Levar's Palace
7 Tichenese Embassy

8 The Red Temple
9 The Gold Temple Ruins
10 The White Temple
11 The Black Temple
12 Two-Copper Bazaar

13 House of Responsible Life
14 Narkain's Skull
15 Granny's House
16 Temple of the Giants

17 Wizard's Row (usually)

A—The Levee Way
B—Market Street
C—Gold Street
D—Park Boulevard
E—Cat Street
F—Bazaar Street
G—Street of Thwarted Desire
H—Avenue of Five Mice
I—Neglectful Street
J—Cross Way
K—Street of Trees
L—Avenue of the Sun
M—Street of Flowers
N—Street of Mists
O—Street of Wind
P—Rat's Alley
Q—Dung Alley
R—Street of Rams
S—Street of Walls
T—Fog Way
U—Fruit Way
V—Merchants Way

wix '84

A Happy Birthday

by Will Shetterly

———◆———

EARLY ONE MORNING in the month of Fruit, The Magician
stood on a tower that rose over Liavek's Old Town. A late
summer breeze bore the smells of the sea, and mingled with
the tang of brine were the traces of smoke from cooking fires,
the aroma of pot-boils simmering and bread baking in brick
ovens. The breeze also brought the cries of seagulls and a
healthy murmur of conversation, curses, greetings, laughter,
bits of song—all the noises that a successful center of trade
and art should produce in early morning. The City of Luck
gleamed in sunlight reflected from tiled roofs and painted stucco
walls. A slight smile touched The Magician's youthful features.
If there was something of wistfulness in that smile, there was
contentment, too.

A new sound came from behind him, of light footsteps on
the stairs. A new smell joined those of morning: a hint of copper
and jasmine. Then a woman's body pressed against his back
and her arms embraced him. He felt her stand on tiptoe to kiss
his neck, then heard her say, "You're being rather flashy this
morning."

He shrugged, a little embarrassed. "I've never seen Liavek
from this height."

"I thought you were advertising for clients. Liavek's never
seen a tower on Wizard's Row."

"Well, not in a few generations, anyway. Besides, it's only
visible to magicians."

He felt the woman nod. "It's beautiful."

1

"The tower?" The golden cylinder was half again as high as Mystery Hill, usually the highest point in Liavek.

"No, my vain love. The city." She moved to his side, and he put his arm around her. After a moment, she lifted a hand and said, "Here." She held a box wrapped in silver cloth.

He raised an eyebrow.

She smiled. "Don't pretend you'd forgotten, Trav. You just felt like waking well before noon. You just felt like expending Rikiki knows how much power raising a tower that only people like us can see. Right." Slightly off-key, she sang:

> On each birthday, for the hours
> Mothers labored giving birth,
> Folk receive from unknown powers
> Luck, a gift of unknown worth.

> On each birthday, wizards wrestle
> With their birth luck to invest
> Birth luck's power in a vessel
> Granting magic on request.

> On each birthday, sad folk wander
> Hoping luck will alter fate.
> Happy folk who will not squander
> Happiness stay home and wait.

> Happy birthday, happy luckday,
> May kind fortune follow you,
> Luck's capricious, luck loves patterns.
> May my gift shape luck for you.

She thrust the box at him. "Happy birthday."

With a laugh, Trav set the box on the wall and quickly unwrapped it. Her present's nature was obvious when the first corner of the box was revealed. The sides and bottom were teak, but its top was a tessellated inlay of ivory and rosewood. "It opens?"

She nodded, and her wiry bronze hair bounced about her face.

"Thanks, Gogo. How?"

With a smirk, Gogo slid one of the side panels. The game-board tilted up, and shah pieces lay beneath it in felt-lined beds. Each had been carefully carved and painted, so their living models were easy to identify. One set of pieces stood on bases of enameled Liavekan blue and the other on Tichenese yellow.

Trav moved his finger across the rows. He touched the figure of a small girl in long robes. "The Levar, dressed as she was on her last official birthday."

"Who else for shah of Liavek?"

He tapped another, a middle-aged man in the red robes of the Faith of the Twin Forces. "And His Scarlet Eminence, the Levar's Regent."

"Of course. Who else for sultana? His reach extends to the limits of the board. I think he'd be flattered."

"I do, too." Trav touched two others, one of himself and one of an old woman who wore her white hair braided about her head. "The Ka'Riatha and me. That's very flattering, but you could've used yourself for a wizard."

"I could've used half a dozen folk. But you've been The Magician for nearly three hundred years; you have to be there. And Granny's the link between the old city of S'Rian and the new one of Liavek."

Trav's finger brushed over the two Liavekan towers, one being the Levar's palace and one Fin Castle, and rested again by a stocky, older woman in a gray uniform and a blue cloak sitting on a racing camel. "City General D'genli for one warrior." He touched a man astride a white horse. The man's red cape helped identify him, as did two flintlock pistols in his sash, as did two dark scars on either side of his face. "And dear Count Dashif for the other. An interesting choice."

Gogo wrinkled her lip, then said, "Admiral Tinthe would have been more appropriate, but a ship would've taken too much space on the board."

The soldier pieces were a miscellany of Liavekan inhabitants: a ship's captain with a shaven head, a white-robed priest of the Church of Truth, a red-haired Levar's Guard, a gaudily dressed entertainer of indeterminate sex, an elegantly dressed noble carrying a walking stick, a street musician playing a cittern, a slender girl in clothes too large for her, and a tall, attractive woman with a whip coiled about one shoulder. Trav paused by the last. "That's the woman from the Tiger's Eye? Who are the rest?"

"Just folk who caught my eye."

Trav nodded as he scanned the other pieces. "The Emperor of Tichen for the opposing shah; his daughter for sultana. I agree. For wizards, the Guild of Power's Old Teacher and Young Teacher." He touched the latter. "Someone new has taken the Young Teacher's part."

"Yes. Djanhiz ola Vikili. They say she's more impetuous than Chiano Mefini, but more powerful, too."

Trav laughed suddenly and pointed. "King Thelm and Prince Jeng of Ka Zhir for Tichenese soldiers! You do have a wicked wit, my love."

She grinned. "Just because they don't know they're pawns—"

"It's a little frightening to see Liavek's opponents laid so neatly out."

"Isn't it consoling to see our defenders?"

"Not really. Well, I suppose." He kissed her and said, "Thank you. I suppose we should go below before my magic fades." In spite of his words, he made no move toward the stairs. "I wonder who'll take part in the next game between Liavek and Ka Zhir?" He glanced at the figure of the Levar's Guard, then looked from the set of playing pieces to Liavek below them. "And I wonder if Tichen's Old Teacher has a similar shah set?"

Bejing Ki, Old Teacher of the Guild of Power, flew over the sands of the Great Waste in the belly of a large red bird made of wicker and painted cloth. Her apprentice, a nomad boy named Chiba, sat before her, peering through the red bird's eyes and guiding its flight with levers that controlled the angle of its wings and tail. Bejing's power had lifted the bird into the air above Tichen, but the former Young Teacher, Chiano Mefini, had designed it so well that Chiba's power was sufficient to propel it forward. The Old Teacher's thoughts were free to drift or plan as the Old Teacher pleased. She tried to anticipate her actions in Liavek and found she could not.

A cluster of images continued to return to her. She heard Chiano whisper his story, and she saw him gasp and die when he finished. She thought of The Magician, and how weak he would be in less than an hour. Chiano had said that today was The Magician's birthday, when the thing called power by the Tichenese and birth luck by the Liavekans would flee whatever vessel Trav had invested it in and return to his body. And while he labored to reinvest his luck before his birth hours ended, he would have no magic to use on other things. Every spell he had ever cast would have failed. Trav, The Magician of Liavek, would be as defenseless on this day as any wizard can ever be.

Chiano Mefini had been her sister's son. The Old Teacher had loved him as much as if he had been her own.

Someone would pay.

A very small girl in a clean, unbleached tunic ran through the Canal District of Liavek's New Town. No one chased her, and she did not seem to chase anyone else, so most people smiled and stepped aside for her. A few frowned and muttered about "children today."

Far ahead of her, two men in the gray of the Levar's Guard walked toward the municipal hall. Both wore light wool capes of Liavekan blue, thrown back from their shoulders since the morning had already begun to grow warmer. One was a tall, stocky man with his hair tied at the nape of his neck; the other was slimmer and shorter with reddish hair, though his complexion was as dark as any Liavekan's. The girl's black eyes widened when she saw them and she tried to yell, but she was too tired and too far away. Her calls of "Rusty! Rusty! Wait for me, Rusty!" disappeared among the sounds of the street.

The two were about to turn onto the Street of the Dreamers when a dog ran into the red-haired man's legs. He tripped into a rack of costly clothing set beside a shop called Master L'von's. An old man ran from the shop at the sound, then stopped. "I suppose you're trying to flush some damned Zhir counterfeiter from the ladies' undergarments, Lieutenant?"

"No, I—" Rusty pointed toward the dog, but it was gone. "I tripped. Sorry."

"'S'all right." The man and the guards set up the rack again and brushed dust from the clothes. "Nothing hurt but the reputation of the Gray Guards, eh?"

Rusty winced and shrugged. As the man went back into his shop, Rusty said, "Two days counting baubles in a ship that stank like a dragon had died in its hold, just because the Navy's too incompetent to sink a captured pirate. Then our replacements relieve us an hour late. Now this. I swear I—"

The girl ran up to him. "Rusty, Rusty! You gotta come help!"

Rusty squatted to catch her in a hug. "Sessi! What's happened?"

"I was playing ball, and the ball rolled into a street, and it disappeared!"

He laughed. "That's odd, little sister, but it's hardly a catastrophe."

"Yes, it is! It was Kolli's favorite ball, and he won't like me anymore if I've lost it."

Rusty nodded. "All right, Sessi. We'll go find it. Where'd the ball disappear?"

"The ball didn't disappear, Rusty. The street disappeared."

The two Guards glanced at each other. The stockier one scratched his scalp. "Wizard's Row, huh? Want some help, Rusty?"

"No. It's probably there now." He stood, touched his forehead in salute to his friend, and began to walk away with the girl. Suddenly, he spun and said, "Stone! What's today?"

"I dunno. Rainday, I think."

Rusty nodded. "Lost track on that inventory job. Tell Captain Bastian I'm taking the day off!"

"She won't like that."

"Tell her it's my birthday present. I'm going to help Sessi find her ball, then I'm going home to hide for the next five hours."

At mid-morning, 17 Wizard's Row was a square, two-story structure of yellow brick. Its front door was oak, with brass fittings which included a large gargoyle's head with a lolling tongue. Two very dark men and a very tall woman approached wearing dusty, hooded robes of the clans of the Waste. One reached to pull the gargoyle's tongue and it snapped at his hand. The man stepped back, glancing in surprise at his companions.

The gargoyle said, "Go away. We're busy today."

The man hesitated, then said nervously, "We've traveled far. We want to see The Magician."

"Want all you will," the gargoyle said. "But want somewhere else."

The shorter man, who stood to one side, moved suddenly for the handle. The gargoyle's head swung toward him. It began to step out of the oak as though it had only been lying in a pool of water, but the woman touched the gargoyle's neck with a carnelian ring. The gargoyle halted immediately, a bas-relief of a beast with its chest and front claws lunging from the door.

"How long will that hold him, Young Teacher?" said the shorter man.

"Long enough," said the woman, pushing on one of the gargoyle's paws. The door swung silently open.

A dark hall lay beyond, with light splashed at the far end from another room. Djanhiz ola Vikili, Young Teacher of the Guild of Power, remembered what she had learned when she had invaded this house under Chiano Mefini's direction: 17 Wizard's Row was inhabited by the guard they had just passed, two cats, and two humans: Trav The Magician and Gogo. The guardian at the door, whether demon, god, or eccentric magician, was now trapped by a spell which could check earthquakes and tidal waves. Protective spells hid the three intruders from the cats' senses. The hours of The Magician's birth had begun, so all of Trav's power and training were turned to reinvesting his birth luck before those hours ended. Only Gogo remained to face the combined skill of three sorcerers of the Guild of Power.

The taller man completed a simple illusion so that passersby would see The Magician's door closed. Djanhiz nodded her approval. The shorter man said, "Done," and Djanhiz felt a mystical tether about her waist, linking her to the street like a diver or a climber. If the house suddenly traveled away from Wizard's Row, her companion's spell would snatch them out of it.

Rumor held that others had entered this house uninvited. None had left of their own choice. Some, it was said, had not left at all. The three Tichenese walked slowly down the hall, using every sense to search for traps. Djanhiz found many, and since The Magician's would have failed when his birth-time began, these had to be Gogo's. The Young Teacher's respect for her increased with each guardian spell she unraveled. Half of The Magician's reputation might have come from Gogo's efforts.

At the end of the hall, Djanhiz peered into the open door of a small office. A short, slender woman in a green shift sat facing a slim man who lay on a wicker couch, his body covered with a light sheet for warmth or ritual purposes. The Magician's eyes were closed, as if he slept or meditated. Gogo's lips moved as though she were singing, and her gaze remained focused on The Magician. Neither gave any sign that they were aware of the three intruders.

The shorter Tichenese whispered, "Why is she here? Investiture is private."

Djanhiz said in her usual speaking voice, "You don't see it?"

"No," the man admitted, with a hint of shame.

"How old is The Magician?"

"Two centuries, at least."

"And does he have some artifact of power to keep him alive when his age returns to his body with his birth luck?"

"He must, if he has lived..." The short man glanced at Gogo, who still chanted silently. "He trusts her? Another magician?"

The man's voice went loud with surprise, and Djanhiz laughed. "Obviously. Perhaps he pays her so much that he thinks she cannot be bribed. Perhaps she is so powerful that he does not expect an enemy's spell to bend her will to learn his weaknesses, and perhaps she is so determined that he thinks torture could never break her will. Perhaps they love each other so much that they trust each other without other considerations. It is very romantic, isn't it?"

The taller man spoke for the first time. "Yes."

"And it is a shame that they are our enemies," said Djanhiz. "Yet Liavek's growth must be at Tichen's expense. So we must check that growth with a few careful prunings."

She touched Gogo's back with the carnelian ring.

As Rusty walked up Healer's Street with the girl's hand in his, he said, "You play up here often?"

"Uh-huh."

"You shouldn't."

"Uh-huh."

"'Course, I suppose that's why it's so much fun."

"Uh-huh. Look! It's there now! Wizzer's Row!"

"Of course. If you'd gone back on your own a little later, it probably would've been there."

"Uh-uh. It's 'cause you're in the Guard, Rusty."

He laughed. "Right, kid."

This section of Old Town was never as busy as other districts of Liavek, for most of the trade was across the Cat River in New Town, by the docks and in the Merchant's Quarter. Old Town's life centered on Temple Hill and Mystery Hill, and in the bustling old market between them, the Two-Copper Bazaar.

But Wizard's Row almost always seemed deserted, or so Rusty thought. It was never the same, but it was usually quiet, often mysterious, always awesome. Some of the buildings were so common as to be unnoticeable. Others were constructed in impossible ways, and some of impossible things. One house seemed to be made of living birds who flew about in a pattern that always shaped a house, though the style and size of the house shifted with the flight of the birds.

"Where's the ball, Sessi?" He wondered if his nervousness carried to her.

"I dunno." She began walking down Wizard's Row, peering into every yard. "Maybe it went to see someone."

"I doubt that." He spotted a battered white ball in front of a gate midway down the street. "That it, Sessi?"

"Yaaay, Rusty!"

He released her hand and they ran for the ball. He laughed again, forgetting his nervousness. As they came close to it, Sessi said, "Rusty, look!" He glanced where she pointed, at a house unharmed by the flames that surrounded it. His foot came down on the ball. He fell, barely catching himself, and the ball scooted into the nearest yard. Looking up from the ground, Rusty saw a brass gargoyle on the door and the number seventeen above the lintel.

"I been here before," Sessi whispered.

Rusty set his hand on her shoulder. "Yes. The Magician's. He sent you to live with Mom and Dad, thinking they had no children."

"I like him. He's got cats."

"I suppose so," he answered, and the conversation suddenly seemed very strange. "Well. Let's get the ball and go, hey?"

"Sure, Rusty." The girl ran along the flagstones. She reached for the ball, then straightened up, leaving the ball where it lay. "Something's funny about the door."

"I'm sure it is, kid." He grabbed the ball.

Sessi stood before the brass gargoyle. She reached out to pat its nose, and before Rusty could stop her, her hand passed through the illusion. She gasped. "Something's wrong, Rusty!"

"I know," he said carefully, moving toward her. "It's my birthday. I should be asleep in my own bed. I should not be on Wizard's Row, trespassing on The Magician's lawn. Let's—"

Sessi stepped through the illusion of The Magician's door.

"I hate kids," Rusty whispered. He breathed deeply, touched his short sword with the back of the hand holding the ball, and entered 17 Wizard's Row.

For Trav, several things happened so quickly that he could not place them in order. His thoughts were of investiture, of coercing his birth luck into his favorite vessel. The birth luck struggled against his will, as it always did, but he felt himself close to success. Then Gogo seemed to start, or maybe her abrupt cessation of motion only seemed to have begun with a tiny movement, the slightest anticipation of surprise. Her words ceased, and so did the flow of power from her spell of youth. The sky fell upon him, as if it would crush him into the sofa. His attempt at investiture collapsed. The birth luck returned to his helpless body, but he did not have the strength to try to use it.

The light in the room grew dimmer, then disappeared just as three shadows seemed to appear. His mouth fell open, but he could not speak. He lay motionless. Something in his mind shrieked in fear. Something else said, *This is death. Accept it.*

In the crowded office, the three Tichenese sorcerers looked at the withered thing that was The Magician. "He still breathes," said the short man.

"For a while," Djanhiz said.

"He has all his teeth," the short man said. "I'd think that he would lose his teeth."

"He took very good care of them."

"Ah." They listened to Trav's slow breaths. "I could smother him," the short man offered.

"No," the tall man said.

"No," Djanhiz agreed. "We are not murderers."

The short man looked at her in surprise, then covered his surprise and said nothing. The tall man spread his fingers wide before them. "Our hands are hardly clean."

"No," Djanhiz agreed. "Nor am I proud of this. But I will be proud of success." She glanced at The Magician. "I wonder if he still lives because his birth luck is within him? Or if it is only that death has not yet recognized its opportunity?"

"Does it matter?" said the smaller man.

Djanhiz shrugged. "No. He cannot live much longer. We will wait."

• • •

The hall was dark, lit primarily by light reflected from a far room. The illusion of the closed front door remained inside the house; either the magic that created it also blocked light, or it preserved the illusion *very* thoroughly. Rusty walked in, wanting to tiptoe in hopes of leaving undisturbed and wanting to stomp so the residents would know he did not come as a thief or an assassin. He opened his mouth to call Sessi's name.

Movement toward the middle of the hall proved to be the girl, huddled against a door. Her motion was the bringing of her finger to her mouth for silence. In spite of himself, he obeyed as he came up to her. He reached for her shoulder to grab her and take her away when he heard Tichenese voices from The Magician's study.

That was not odd. Many Tichenese lived in Liavek, and many visited for reasons of politics or trade. The Tichenese embassy was not far from here. Rusty had spent a year in Tichen; he respected the people and their culture. He also knew enough of their language to be surprised when a woman said, "Chiano Mefini failed the Empire, but we will not. Indeed, The Magician's death restores glory to his name."

"Perhaps," a man said. "What of the woman?"

"We will let her live. Perhaps she will inherit The Magician's title. It will be good for the head witch of this little nation to have known failure at Tichenese hands."

"And now?"

"Now we wait. I've completed a spell to ensure privacy. No one, wizard or other, will be able to enter the house until one of us leaves."

Happy birthday to me, Rusty thought.

Danger or caution or surprise had left him unable to do more than listen. Still considering the implications of the woman's words, Rusty mimicked Sessi's gesture and prayed she would understand to be silent. He tugged Sessi's shoulder. She shook her head, but when he tugged again, she began to follow.

Halfway to the door, a floorboard creaked loudly under his sandal.

Three people in bulky robes raced into the hall. One whirled, pointing back into the study and saying to another, "Very well. Kill The Magician."

Rusty pushed Sessi toward the door. "Run!" Would anyone's departure cause the woman's spell to fail? If so, Sessi could bring someone back. . . .Rusty felt her ball still in his hand, so he flung it hard down the hall at the head of the Tichenese returning to The Magician's office. It hit and the man fell, and Rusty praised his birth luck.

Rusty spun to flee and something seemed to envelop his legs. Sessi stopped before the door, crying, "Rusty!"

"Go on!" he shouted at her. He drew his sword, knowing that steel was useless against wizards. "Run, Sessi! Get help!" The woman who seemed to be the Tichenese leader walked toward him. She smiled grimly as she raised a carnelian ring.

He slashed at her hand. She dodged, laughed, and said something quickly, and his sword arm was caught in whatever held his legs. Watching the ring approach his chest, he yelled again, "Run, Sessi! Get out! Get help!"

At the edge of his vision, he saw Sessi leap through the illusion of the closed door. The spell dissolved, and the hall brightened with admitted sunlight.

The tall male Tichenese ran past them to catch Sessi halfway down The Magician's walk. She screamed and kicked in his grasp, and he carried her back with difficulty.

The Tichenese woman turned her hand to touch Rusty's chest with her palm rather than the ring. "What have you gained, Liavekan? A moment of time and nothing more." Casually, she tapped Sessi with the ring as the tall man passed by them, and the girl stiffened in his grasp.

"Damn you—"

"No," the woman said, touching his lips with her finger. "You've been nuisance enough. I'll restore my spell about this house, and then—"

A small red bird glided through the open door.

The Magician wrestled with the question of what had happened to him, to his house, to Gogo, to Gogo, to Gogo. . . . Something in him said, *Live! For her, live!* And something answered, *How? I'm old, old.* . . .He tried with one supreme effort to raise himself and he felt pain in his chest.

He relaxed then, and the voice that said, *Die now, Trav, die gracefully, for it's time,* was pleased. It said, *Yes. Accept this. It's been a good life.* And the voice that said, *Live, Trav! Live for her, for yourself, for your city!* was pleased. It said, *Yes. Save your strength. Relax. Breathe shallowly. Think. You are*

The Magician of Liavek, Trav Marik. Survival is success. Survive.

As Rusty watched, two tiny things leaped from the stiff red bird. They landed on the hall tiles, becoming an old Tichenese woman and a nomad boy, both dressed in dark blue robes. The boy immediately ran to pick up the bird, which seemed to be a toy of lacquered paper. The three Tichenese in desert robes bowed very low to the old woman, the tallest man first placing Sessi carefully on the floor. Rusty thought the old woman must be their leader, come to view their success.

He began to wonder if this was true when the young Tichenese woman said, "Teacher, this is not your concern. I—" The old woman gestured for silence, then turned slightly away to accept the toy bird from the boy. As it began to shrink even smaller in the old woman's palm, the young woman snapped her carnelian ring toward the old woman's side.

Rusty grabbed the young woman's wrist with his free left hand. She exhaled loudly, almost a bark, in frustration or annoyance.

The old woman placed the red bird in her pocket, turned, and smiled at them both. For a moment, Rusty wondered whether he had done the best or the worst he could do by acting.

The old woman flicked her hands as if flinging water from them. The three Tichenese in desert robes disappeared. Tiny things like black beads lay where each had stood. The nomad boy gathered the three beads and presented them to the old woman. She nodded to Rusty and suddenly his limbs were free. "Thank you," she said. Before he could reply, the woman and the boy entered The Magician's office.

Power coursed suddenly about Trav, as though he were immersed in a pool of the raw essence of magic. His eyes opened. Cool air filled his lungs. He smelled foreign scents, perfume and sweat. He sat up, starting to reach out about him to learn where he was, and then he could see. Shapes resolved themselves in instants. Gogo sat before him with an expression of desperate relief.

He caught her, or maybe he threw himself into her arms; he could not tell. After a moment, he looked around his office

and saw they were not alone. An old woman watched with
something like cold approval on her face. She wore a silk robe
of a blue that seemed darker than black, and after a second,
Trav recognized her. He released Gogo to lean forward in a
deep bow, bringing the fingers of both hands to his forehead.
"Bejing Ki, Old Teacher of the Guild of Power. I would never
have expected mercy from you, though I thank you for it."

The woman's face wrinkled into a smile. "Trav The Magician. This is not mercy; this is an attempt to restore honor.
You must forgive me."

"If you will explain what has happened," Trav said carefully,
"I think I will forgive anything."

"Explanations later," Gogo said. "We have an investiture to
complete."

The old woman lifted both eyebrows. "You hope to succeed,
with so little time remaining?"

"He is The Magician," Gogo replied.

Trav set his hand on Gogo's. "And I have friends."

In the hall, Sessi suddenly leaped up, crying, "Rusty,
what—"

He caught her. "'S'all right, Sessi. I think. C'mon,
let's—"

A short, scowling, dark-haired man in a green tunic stood
by the front door. The man touched both hands to his forehead
and bowed low. "He says you're owed an explanation, too. I
don't think so. Come."

"Who's he?" Reluctantly, Rusty sheathed his short sword.

"The Magician, of course. Owes me an explanation first.
No matter. Come."

The man opened one of the many hall doors, gesturing them
into a sitting room, then brought refreshments and left again.
Sessi whispered, "That's the door thing."

"The servant?"

She nodded, then began to feast on honeycakes and lem-
onade. A gray and white cat hid under her chair, as though it
had not decided whether it approved of these visitors. A cream-
colored cat climbed onto Rusty's shoulder, where it purred
contentedly, occasionally drooling a bit.

The sullen man opened the hall door again and the old
Tichenese woman and the boy entered. Rusty stood to salute

in the southern fashion and the two bowed. "An explanation soon," the woman said. The gray and white cat brushed against her ankles and she smiled.

Half an hour passed while Rusty and Teacher Ki talked of Tichen and Liavek and the importance of free trade. Sessi and the boy found a shah set. Ignoring the board, they improvised some game with its pieces, and bits of their conversation occasionally interrupted that of the adults: "An' the whip lady says, 'Hi, Master Emperor, I like sausages and beans a lot!'"

Trav, Gogo, and the scowling man returned. Trav made introductions: "Mistress Gogoaniskithli and Master Didieskilor . . ."

"Gogo and Didi will suffice," Gogo said.

"For her," said the scowling man.

". . . Lieutenant Lian Jassil and his sister by adoption, Sessi Jassil . . ."

"Hi," said Sessi.

". . . Mistress Bejing Ki, Teacher of the Guild of Power, and Chiba of the Tilandre clans."

The Old Teacher nodded. "I owe all of you an apology, I fear." She opened her hand, showing three dark beads. "These hold the souls of my Young Teacher, Djanhiz ola Vikili, and two of her aides." She glanced at Trav. "How much shall I tell before these outsiders?"

"Enough to explain what has happened."

"Very well." The three beads disappeared and the woman laced her fingers in her lap. "Some time ago, the previous Young Teacher, Chiano Mefini, laid a trap for The Magician. It failed, but in the course of events, he learned several of The Magician's secrets. The Magician allowed him to live, after he took a vow on his life and luck never to reveal those secrets."

"A vow which he seems to have broken."

"Not by choice, Trav The Magician. There are factions in the Guild of Power, as there are factions in any group. Djanhiz led the most radical of those. When Chiano returned to Tichen in disgrace, he gave up the title of Young Teacher, left our guild, and turned his attention from the study of magic to the study of science. Djanhiz had accompanied him to Liavek, and she knew that he had learned more about The Magician than he had said, so she forced a spell of compulsion upon him and he told her all he knew."

"It was not his fault, then."

"Perhaps not. Perhaps he thought if he had been more careful, he would not have been trapped by her. He escaped from the trap she had left him in and came to me. After he told me what had happened, he willed his death."

"I am sorry."

"As am I. Still, I came to preserve our honor, if I could. You needn't worry about your secrets, Trav The Magician. My apprentice and I have both taken the same vow that Chiano took. So long as Liavek and Tichen are rivals, we will be your opponents, but we will not use Chiano's knowledge against you."

The Magician nodded. "Thank you. What of the three who attacked us?"

"I will take them to Tichen, where they will have a choice. They will each bind their luck forever into a thing of my choosing, and they will accept a magical compulsion to never tell what they know of you. If they do not, I shall transform them into beads again and throw those beads into the ocean."

"I see."

Rusty said, "You both seem rather trusting, for enemies."

All the magicians in the room stared at him and he said, "Um, I mean—"

Trav said, "Please. Rivals."

Bejing Ki laughed. "You are not a magician, Lieutenant Jassil. You wonder what honor is among magicians? I will tell you this. We may have too much power for any human to wield. Even young Chiba could, with time and great effort, call tidal waves or hurricanes. There are not many in the world of our power, but there are enough. If wizards did not accept constraints, a war of magicians could destroy the world. You understand?"

Rusty nodded slowly.

"I can think of no proper reward for your part in this, Lieutenant Jassil," the old woman said. "But gold is usually appreciated." She drew a purse from the pocket of her robe and gave it to him. "As for your adopted sister, you may tell your parents that Bejing Ki will sponsor her at any of Tichen's universities, when she is of age."

"Thank you." The explanation seemed to be at an end, so Rusty stood and took Sessi's hand. "I don't think we deserve your gifts, or if we do, it's only because I was too stupid to stay in on my birthday, but—"

"Your birthday?" The Magician said.

"Yes. Every fourth of Fruit. Thank the Twin Forces the next is a year away."

"Today is the third."

Rusty stared. "But all the coincidences!" He hesitated, then said, "The secret that these people learned was that today is your birthday."

The Magician nodded.

"I won't tell anyone."

"I know."

"Then I was affected by your luck, not my own? That's incred—"

"No," said Gogo. "I can still feel birth luck in this room, and Trav's birth hours have ended."

Rusty looked at every face in the room.

Sessi smiled shyly. "Do I get a present?"

Before the Paint Is Dry

by Kara Dalkey

COLOR CAME AGAIN to the Market of Liavek as the street merchants returned from their naps, unrolling their bright silk booth awnings and laying out their wares on patterned carpets. The sun was already hidden behind the taller buildings, making the Fruit-month heat a little less intense. In the distance, the eerie drone of conch-shell trumpets from the tower of the Black Temple called those of that faith to prayer, over the clatter and din of the merchants and the bellows of obstreperous camels.

Strolling with easy, long-legged strides, Aritoli ola Silba looked at booths of Ombayan fruit, Tichenese porcelain, and brass Zhir lanterns. A warm wind redolent of cinnamon, garlic, and sweat tousled his shoulder-length, wavy black hair. He was pleased the woman on his arm had chosen to wear pale gold that day, as it did not clash with his green silk blouse.

"'Merchant Councilor Tafiya Mielo'" said the woman, her amber eyes flashing above a brilliant smile in a ginger-hued face. "I like the sound of that. Such an impressive tone it has."

"I am sure you will wear the title well, Tafi," said Aritoli. "Do you intend to keep running your import company while you are a councilor?"

"Of course. Merchant Councilors are expected to have interests to defend while in office. The Lord Councilors don't give up their estates and heritage when selected for the Levar's Council, do they?"

"True, they certainly do not. Though to hear First Lord Ezvi ola Thinoli speak of it—"

"You listen too much to rumor, Ari. It isn't true that he

19

doesn't approve of Merchant Councilors. Ezvi's been perfectly polite to me. Oh, look over here. I want you to see these."

Aritoli glanced over at a display of what appeared to be clumps of string on wooden frames. As he tried to make out what they were, he became aware of someone on his right, staring at him. He turned and found his way blocked by a small, thin man with challenging brown eyes.

"Master ola Silba, so-called Advisor to Patrons of the Arts?"

"I am." Aritoli narrowed his eyes and studied the man a moment. "Freneza, isn't it? Student of the Shatter-Eye School of so-called art?"

The small man's nostrils flared and his eyes blazed, but he maintained his composure. "The very same. I have news for you, Master ola Silba, of myself and my school which I think you may find interesting. If you care to hear it."

"Certainly, sir. I always appreciate the opportunity for a good laugh."

Freneza bared his teeth and growled, "You may think you're the talk of the town now, you bed-hopping fop, but wait until you read this!" He pulled out from beneath his plain, stained brown tunic a rolled-up copy of the *Cat Street Crier*. "In this paper, it is announced who was assigned to repaint the Council Chamber mural. Yes, that's right—the project you've been trying to grab for one of your trite, traditional paint-daubers. Well, Master Artist-Hater, guess who was chosen? Me! Freneza of the Shatter-Eye School! Despite all your scoffing in your filthy little gossip-sheet columns. Put that in your bed and fuck it, ola Silba!" Flinging down the paper like a dueling glove, Freneza stalked away.

Aritoli stood stunned for a moment, then slowly bent down and picked up the *Cat Street Crier*.

"What a dreadful little man," Tafiya said.

"Tafi, do you know if this is true? Has Ezvi mentioned it to you?"

"I recall Ezvi mentioning something of that sort, but what of it? You aren't going to let that artist's taunts upset you, are you?"

"You don't understand, Tafi. My recommendation for artist for the Levar's Council was the most important opportunity of my career. My reputation could suffer severely for this."

"I'm very sorry, Ari. Is there something I can do? Shall I speak to Ezvi for you?"

"No, Tafi. There's no need for you to be involved. With

any luck, it is all a mistake or a sick joke on Freneza's part. But I must find out for certain. I'm sorry, Tafi, but I must part from your charming company for today." Motioning to a foot-cab runner, Aritoli helped Tafiya into the seat and paid the runner for her fare home.

"Oh, but Ari! Must you go now? There was something I wanted to show you—"

"I am sorry, Tafi, but my mind will not be at ease until I sort this out. Another time, I assure you."

"Tomorrow?"

"Very well. Tomorrow. Afternoon. I promise." Kissing her hand warmly, Aritoli took his leave and called another footcab for himself. This he took directly to the source of the offending information—the offices of the *Cat Street Crier*.

Said offices were located, with typical Liavekan logic, slightly east of Cat Street, roughly halfway between the Fountain of the Three Temples and Wizard's Row. The footcab let Aritoli off on Kit's Alley, where a white stuccoed archway led him into a small courtyard filled with flowering shrubs. Aritoli scarcely noticed their perfume as he entered another archway to the left. Passing by two printing presses that stood idle, he proceeded up a set of stairs and through a beaded curtain into the office of the publisher.

In the center of the room, a round, balding little man sat on a floor-cushion at a low desk, idly puffing on a hookah as he gazed at the papers scattered on his desk. As Aritoli strode toward him, the man looked up with a quick smile.

"Ah, Aritoli! We had not been expecting your next piece for days yet. Please, come sit. Would you like some kaf?"

"I regret, Fatar, I am not here to deliver a manuscript. I am here concerning this!" The advisor waved Freneza's paper under the publisher's nose.

Slowly taking the paper in hand, Fatar frowned at it in confusion. "What? Our latest issue? What concerns you, Ari?"

"Is this copy genuine?"

"It would appear to be."

"And that article about the Council mural, is that genuine?"

"Yes, we received the information from Chancellor ola Thinoli's secretary yesterday afternoon. Say, weren't you involved in that project? Is there some problem with the way we presented the news?"

"The problem, my dear Fatar Shimuuz, is that it is news to

me! This is the first I have heard that the assignment was awarded to the Shatter-Eye School!"

"Dear me, that does seem a bit short-sighted of the First Lord."

"Short-sighted? It is a slap in the face, I tell you! How could he select an artist from a school that throws paint at canvas and dares to call it art! And when I have offered the names of the finest artists in Liavek! It is an insult! An outrage!"

"Ari, calm yourself. Aren't you taking this just a bit too personally?"

The advisor took a few breaths, then sat, sighing, on a cushion. "This assignment was important to me, Fatar. I was virtually assured that one of my recommendations would be selected. Now, to have it snatched out from under me and given to . . . to . . ."

"Yes, a disappointment, to be sure."

"Perhaps I should speak to Chancellor ola Thinoli."

"A good idea, but not possible currently. We wanted to get a statement from him and learned that he was away on a diplomatic mission to Gold Harbor, date of return unknown."

"How convenient," murmured Aritoli.

"As to why the Shatter-Eye School was selected, perhaps it has changed direction since the Church of Truth became its patron."

Aritoli sat up. "Church of Truth? Those sorcerous white-robes who teach that 'reality is illusion' or some such nonsense? When did this happen?"

"Not long ago, from the sound of things. Let me see, in our article here it mentions a Sister Vanta who has become headmistress of the school."

"What would those half-mad mystics want with an art school?"

"How would I know?" Fatar shrugged. "Perhaps you should talk to this Sister Vanta yourself."

"An excellent idea, Fatar. Have you any idea what would be the best time to call on her?"

"Well, I assume she keeps an ascetic's hours. Dawn to dusk, you know."

Aritoli glanced out the window at the setting sun and knew that what had to be done would mean enduring the worst. It meant getting up early in the morning.

• • •

Aritoli cursed his curiosity as he stood shivering outside a rickety wooden building in the Canal District, on a street incongruously named Paradise Alley. Trying to keep his eyes open, he peered through the morning fog until he saw it—a shingle painted with an abstract eye, hanging from the second story.

He tightened his grip on his walking stick, a black cane with a raven's head of gold in which his luck was stored. Dealing with sorcerous priests could be touchy business at best. He sincerely hoped his magic would not be needed. Pulling his cloak tightly around him, he went inside.

The ground floor of the building had apparently been a shop. But now the walls and floor were bare, only nail holes and dents showing where furnishings had been. The wooden slats and beams were gray with neglect.

Next to a door at the far end of the area, in marked contrast to the pale decay around him, stood a large, brightly dressed man. His ebony skin gleamed and muscles rippled across his bare arms and chest as Aritoli approached the door.

"Do you have an appointment, sir?" said the doorman in a deep, cultured voice.

"Ah, as it happens, my good man, no. But I'm sure Sister Vanta will see me."

"I'm sorry, sir. I can let no one pass who does not have an appointment."

"Do you know whom you address, sir?"

"Yes. You are Master Aritoli Montanija Galifavi ola Silba, Vavasor of Silversea and Advisor to Patrons of the Arts. And I still cannot let you pass."

Aritoli rested his hand lightly on his coin purse. "Surely you would not let protocol interfere with important business?"

"Important business is generally conducted by appointment. And gold will not pave your way through this door."

"Indeed?" Aritoli paused, impressed. "Are you sure we couldn't make some . . . arrangement, perhaps?" He stroked the doorman's upper arm.

"I prefer the talents of women, sir." The doorman removed Aritoli's hand, nearly crushing it in the process.

Wincing in pain, Aritoli growled, "Since you refuse to be civil, how would you like to spend the day as a camel?" He allowed a magical cascade of light-motes to fall from his fingertips, just for effect.

"Not much," replied the doorman, fingering an enormous belt buckle at his waist. "How about yourself?"

Blast it! thought Aritoli. *They're even hiring wizard door-men these days.* He was about to despair of ever entering when a voice came from behind the door. "Who calls at this hour?"

The doorman replied, "It is Master Aritoli ola Silba, Sister Vanta. Shall I send him away?"

There was a pause, then the door opened to reveal a dark-haired woman wearing a floor-length, hooded white robe, tied at the waist with a white cord. Knotted onto one end of the cord was a small, spherical construction of sticks and string. Her left hand idly toyed with the sphere as she spoke.

"Have your critiques become so unpopular, Master ola Silba, that you must now do them unannounced?" Her voice was low and hollow, and her deep-set eyes seemed slightly vacant.

"I came to offer congratulations, Sister Vanta, for your ex-cellent good fortune on the assignment of the Levar's Council mural. Also, there are some matters I believe we ought to discuss, if you are willing."

"We are not yet open for the day. But since you have already disturbed my meditations, you may as well come up." Beck-oning Aritoli to follow, she turned and ascended a staircase behind the door. With a smug nod to the doorman, the advisor passed and went on, up stairs that groaned beneath his feet.

At the top was a long room, mostly bare. The floor and walls were splattered with all colors of paint, and a few easels stood empty.

"Come into my office," said Sister Vanta. She led him into a room which contained only one wooden chair. "Please, sit down."

"Have you no desk or chair for yourself?"

"I have no need of one. Now, what is it you wish to say?"

Aritoli sat, feeling more than a little uncomfortable. "Well, as you might imagine, I was quite surprised that Freneza was chosen to paint the mural. I decided it was time I learned more about your school."

"I understand that our work is not to your taste."

"It may be that I lack sufficient experience to judge."

"There are those who would say so. What is it that you do not understand?"

"For one thing, your emphasis on deviation from realistic representation of your subject."

"Of course. That is our intention. Reality is an illusion. There is no need to create an image of an illusion. It merely perpetuates the lie."

"I see. And there is no discipline—"

"Discipline, as you call it, is merely a tool for the repetition of illusion. We have no need of it."

"But all that is left is chaos."

"Yes." Sister Vanta smiled.

Aritoli paused and scratched one side of his moustache. "And the sorcery?"

"Is a means to an end."

"What end?"

"The end of illusion."

"I . . . see. And is the mural also to benefit from this 'means to an end'?"

The priest's smile vanished and her eyes grew wary. "Do not concern yourself with the mural. You could not possibly understand it. Do not attempt to."

"But your words intrigue me, Sister Vanta. Understanding is, in part, my reason for coming here. I believe I must see this mural. Perhaps tonight, or some other time when I will not inconvenience Freneza at his work."

"That would be ill-advised, Master ola Silba. Unenlightened as you are, the mural would no doubt disturb you."

"Then what of the unenlightened council members who shall sit beneath it? Clearly, if I am to gain enlightenment, I must see more examples of your school's work. 'Reality is an illusion' . . . I take it this is a tenet of the Church of Truth? It sounds . . . fascinating. Please tell me more."

"Master ola Silba, I can see you will accept neither my advice nor our philosophy. I suggest we part company before we waste any more of each other's time."

"Ah, but time itself is an illusion, is it not?"

"In that case, we should not give it credence by appearing to spend it. Good day."

Aritoli wandered the Merchant's Quarter for the rest of the morning, attempting to clear his mind. Sister Vanta had impressed him—not pleasantly. He was certain that Freneza's mural would not be what it seemed.

But what to do about it?

He was still contemplating this as he was shown into Tafiya's study at midday.

She came out from behind her cluttered desk and rushed to take Aritoli's hands. Drawing him into the center of the room, she said, "Ari, darling! Earlier than expected! You are, as one of my caravaneers would say, like a mirage in the desert that turns out to be real. Come, sit."

Tafiya guided him to some plush cushions, where he sat, setting his walking stick aside. "'Like a springtime breeze, you ease my mind of winter's burdens,'" said Aritoli, kissing her hand.

"That's from one of Nimelli's poems, isn't it? The Tichenese can be so romantic when they aren't being stuffy."

"Er, yes. I believe you said you had something to show me?"

Tafiya smiled ecstatically. "You remembered! Yes, I'll go get it now. I'll have my maid bring you tea while you're waiting." She rushed off, whispering directions at a servant.

Aritoli settled back on the pillows, trying to put this morning's interview out of his mind. But as his gaze wandered about the room, it fell upon something that immediately reminded him of Sister Vanta. On a small side table of carved bloodwood sat a familiar construction of sticks and string. Aritoli picked it up and examined it closely. The maid placed a pot of apple and herb tea before him and left before he was aware she was there. In another moment, Tafiya returned, carrying a bundle of white velvet that clearly had an easel and canvas beneath it.

Aritoli sat up, unsure of what to expect. "I had not known you were a collector, Tafi."

"Not a collector, my dear Ari. I've become an artist. And this is my latest and, may I humbly say, my best piece. I wanted you to be the first to see it."

Aritoli shook his head ruefully. "I can never escape my profession."

"And you love it. You needn't do anything more than tell me what you think."

Aritoli sighed. "Very well. Let us see this masterpiece."

As Tafiya removed the cloth, Aritoli stared at the painting in disappointment. Her "masterpiece" was a still life of flowers, done in a painfully primitive style. "Well?" Tafiya prompted.

"You are an excellent businesswoman, Tafi."

"But a terrible artist, eh?" She gave him a wry smile. "Well, at least you're honest." She covered the painting with the velvet once more. "My tutor says I've a long way to go, too. But I enjoy it, and with practice I expect I'll get somewhere."

"Undoubtedly. Tafi, what is this object I found on your table?"

"Oh, that's what I was trying to show you at the Market. It's a shiribi puzzle. My company imports them from a village somewhere west of Ombaya."

"A toy? How odd. Sister Vanta wore one this morning."

"Sister who?"

Aritoli told her what he had learned from Fatar Shimuuz. "I went to congratulate her and to learn more about the school."

"Ah. Well, it's not surprising she had one. A retailer of mine told me he had sold a large number of the puzzles to the Church of Truth."

"Indeed? What would the white-robes want with a child's toy?"

"The retailer said they'd adopted the shiribi puzzle as some sort of holy symbol. And it's hardly for children. It's actually quite a sophisticated mind-teaser. Here, I'll show you how it works."

Taking the puzzle from him, Tafiya tossed the sphere between her hands. "Seems solid enough, doesn't it? Now watch." She found a particular loop of string and lifted it off its stick. The sphere immediately fell into a jumbled pile on the floor. "The puzzle is, of course, to put it back together."

"Order into chaos," Aritoli murmured, finding the symbolism obvious and disturbing. "But reassembly is possible?"

"Naturally." With the ease of long practice, Tafiya connected strings to sticks as Aritoli watched closely. Before long, she again held a sphere in her hand.

"I see."

"You seem concerned, Ari. Is the puzzle important?"

"Perhaps. It's . . . oh, I don't know, Tafi."

"Poor dear. Sad enough that you lose the mural assignment without becoming burdened with more worry. Well, if my artistic talents do not interest you, is there some other way I may distract you?" Tafiya reclined on the pillows beside him.

Aritoli gazed at her and smiled.

"What a lovely evening!" said Tafi as she leaned over the marble basin of the Fountain of the Three Temples.

"Indeed," agreed Aritoli. The cool wind blew a fine spray

off the plume of water that rose from the ancient fountain's central pillar. "In truth, Tafi, if I had known you had such a passion for long walks, I would have begun exercising long before I began to keep company with you." He smiled but found himself eyeing the vast, bare façade of the Church of Truth with disquiet.

"My mother was an Ombayan trader," explained Tafi.

"Ah, yes. Ombayan merchants are legendary for the distances they will walk to a good market. And your father?"

Tafiya laughed. "He was some Farlander my mother took a brief liking to."

"I see." Aritoli felt a tugging on his sleeve and looked down to see a wide-eyed little girl, perhaps eight years of age, dressed in rags. Just behind her stood a slightly older boy, looking equally bedraggled.

"Please, sir," lisped the little girl, "give us a coin."

Aritoli smiled paternally. Beggar waifs were common as pigeons near the fountain, but the Guard usually cleared them out by this hour.

"Please, sir?" the boy begged softly.

Aritoli rested his raven's-head cane against the basin wall and began to open his coin purse. Suddenly, the boy snatched the walking stick and he and the girl dashed away toward an alley beside the Church of Truth.

Cursing, Aritoli ran after them. His long legs gave him some advantage, and he had nearly caught up to the waifs when he suddenly felt something tighten around his throat. He staggered and fell, feeling as if he were being strangled. His hands clutched at his neck but found nothing there. Sorcery, clearly, but the boy held his cane, his magic source, too far away for the advisor to dispel the attack. He felt himself suffocating as the stranglehold tightened.

Then he heard Tafiya shouting, "Drop it, brats! Give me that cane. Now off with you, before I have you put in the orphan's home!"

In moments, Aritoli felt the walking stick pressed into his hands. He pulled on its power with all his remaining strength to break the strangling spell. There was a bright flash and the constriction was instantly gone, though he still felt weak and sore. He was somewhat surprised that the spell broke so easily.

"Are you all right, Ari?" Tafi gasped beside him. "Do you need a doctor?"

"No," he coughed. "I'll . . . be fine. Just . . . home. Help me home. It's . . . not far."

Tafi managed to help Aritoli stand, and with her support he staggered the three blocks to his townhome.

His manservant Maljun, a stately man in his late fifties, raised his brows as the pair entered. "What happened, Master Aritoli?"

Aritoli did not answer until, with a great sigh of relief, Tafi eased him down on the divan in his study.

After listening to the advisor's explanation, Maljun said, "How very peculiar, sir. Not long ago I heard a pounding at our door. When I opened it, I found this nailed to the lintel." The manservant held out a small square of canvas on which was painted a crude but recognizable portrait of Aritoli. But in the portrait, he had a white scarf tied tightly around his neck.

The advisor took the portrait and examined it. "Execrable execution," he muttered.

"If you can make such a pun, you must not be too badly hurt," said Tafi. "But what does it mean? Is someone trying to kill you?"

"I think not, Tafi. The spell was too easily foiled. It may have been intended as an annoyance. Or a warning."

"Shall I summon the Guard, sir?" asked Maljun.

"No, Maljun, there's no cause to bother them over a petty matter like this. You may retire for the evening. I shall be all right."

The manservant bowed and left the study. Tafi frowned. "How can you call this a petty matter?"

"Because I didn't wish to alarm him," Aritoli said softly. "And there isn't, in truth, much that the Guard could do. This is a sorcerous attack, and I am sure by now no traces remain in this portrait of the spell it contained. No evidence."

"But surely we can figure out who's responsible. You clearly have an enemy somewhere."

Aritoli gave a humorless chuckle. "My dear, those of my profession always have enemies. Legions of them. That fellow Freneza, for example."

"Could he have done this?"

"I doubt it. The incident seems too well thought out to be his style." Aritoli examined the portrait closely but found no hidden signatures. Holding the canvas in front of a lamp, he looked at the way the light passed through the different thicknesses of paint but could discern no patterns or symbols. With a sigh, he said, "Whoever sent this seems to wish to remain anonymous." Idly, he ran a finger along a faint scar on his left cheek.

"You think this means a duel?" Tafi said, noting his gesture.

"Eh? I hope not, Tafi."

"Why? You've won duels before."

"Ah, but this would be a duel of sorcery, not steel. My magic concerns light and color only—the stuff of illusion. I could not possibly win such a duel."

Tafi was silent a moment. Then she said, "If the attack was magical, perhaps there is a magical clue in the portrait."

"Yes, that is a possibility." Aritoli picked up his walking stick and drew power from it again, just enough to send a shimmer of light over the surface of the painting. As he did so, the light coalesced into a small pillar over the center of the portrait. The light spun and twisted. Then, just before dissipating, it resolved into a recognizable shape—a white-robed form, whose hood was dark and empty.

"All right, let's look at the problem one more time," said Tafiya tiredly.

"If you wish." Aritoli picked at his breakfast of cold spiced fish. The first rays of the rising sun slipping through the eastern window of his study did little to cheer the room. Neither he nor Tafiya slept well during the night, disturbed by the revelation of the clue.

"Ola Thinoli chose the Shatter-Eye School to do the mural because, we believe, he wanted sorcery in it, and the White priests are known to be excellent magicians."

"Correct, so far."

"Now, the Church of Truth wants to be sure you don't see the mural, so they stage an attack to warn you to keep away."

"Also correct."

"Could it be that the school has done this out of spite? Because of the criticism you've given them in the past, wouldn't they want to keep you out of this project?"

"I wish that were all, Tafi. But I would expect them to want to gloat over their victory, as Freneza did in the Market. They'd want me to see what sort of garbage ola Thinoli was willing to pay who knows how many levars for. No, I'm afraid there is more to this than spite."

"Well, I can't believe ola Thinoli would do anything sinister, when he himself is part of the Council."

"Can't you? Forgive me if I sound paternalistic, but I have lived in Liavek and dealt with its nobility longer than you. They, and the ola Thinoli family in particular, have not been pleased with the rise of merchants to power on the Council. It would not surprise me in the slightest if Ezvi was being that subtle."

"Oh. I see . . . subtle."

Aritoli knew she was trying to find ways to deny the more frightening implications of the event. Part of Aritoli fervently hoped she would succeed.

"Very well. But this doesn't go beyond some petty scheme of ola Thinoli's, then."

"Think again, Tafi. If the Church of Truth is involved, they will use the situation to benefit their own ends as well."

Tafiya crossed her arms on the table and set her chin on them with a sigh. "If the Church of Truth has such powerful sorcerers, why do they care if you see the mural? Could they not make a spell to withstand your magic?"

"Now there is a good question. Perhaps they fear only that I will discover the existence of the spell. A better wizard than I then could be found to break it."

"Hm. So what are we to do? Sit here and cower like frightened mice?"

"No. I still intend to look at that mural."

"Ah, spoken like the brave Aritoli! He who slew the high priest of Irhan—"

"Tafi, I am not particularly proud of that incident. If only the idiot had worn the protections I expected. . . . But never mind. Sometime before the paint is dry on that mural, I will contrive to get a look at it and settle this mystery."

"Ah, you will risk your life to save the Council from whatever surprise the Shatter-Eyes have in mind?"

"No. I will risk my life to see what sort of garbage ola Thinoli has paid who knows how many levars for."

At midday there came a clatter of hooves in the courtyard, and in a few moments Maljun entered the study.

"One of your servants, madame, brought this letter for you." He handed Tafi a folded piece of parchment that was sealed with gold-flecked wax.

Tafiya opened it and quickly scanned its contents. Raising

her eyebrows in surprise, she handed the letter to Aritoli, saying, "I think you'd better read this."

Aritoli read: "To the Honorable Councilor-Elect Mielo; The
First Lord Ezvi ola Thinoli is pleased to announce that those
newly appointed councilors of the mercantile estate are invited
to a preview of the new Council mural on the morning of the
tenth of Fruit."

"That's tomorrow!" said Aritoli. "Could Freneza be finished
so soon?"

"Apparently."

At the bottom of the invitation, Aritoli saw another message
scribbled in purple ink: "My dearest Tafi, much as I would
have loved to escort you to this showing myself, I find myself
unavoidably detained in Gold Harbor. By the way, on no account should you inform that boor, ola Silba, about the preview.
His ill-mannered criticism would ruin the occasion . . . and you
wouldn't want your career to bear such a blot so soon, would
you? With deepest affection, Ezvi."

"Deepest affection, eh?"

Tafiya shrugged. "He likes to pretend he's a ladies' man.
But what do you make of this sudden showing?"

After a moment, Aritoli said flatly, "Tafi, you mustn't go."

"What? People will talk if I don't attend—they'll doubt my
civic pride, or some such."

"Tafi, your very life might be in danger."

"But why would Ezvi or the white-robes want to harm me?"

"It may be nothing personal, Tafi. But it is known you have
associated with me. And you are the newest member of the
Levar's Council. Perhaps ola Thinoli wishes to prove some
point through you. All I know is it may not be safe. Unless . . ."

"Unless what?"

"Unless I get to the mural first. Tonight."

Tafi's eyes glittered. "Excellent, Ari! When shall we go?"

"We? Ah, no, Tafi. I must do this alone. There's no reason
to endanger you as well."

"But if the Church of Truth or ola Thinoli wishes me harm,
don't I have as much right as you to stop them? Don't I have
a duty to protect the Levar's Council? And if you fail, if we
fail, won't my career—and perhaps life—suffer from whatever
spell is in the mural?"

"Well . . ."

"And think, you will look less suspicious with me than you
would by yourself."

"That is perhaps true, but—"

"And there is the chance that, owing to my status as Councilor-Elect, I can get us a key to the Council Chamber. Now what say you?"

Aritoli sighed. "Oh, very well. *If* you can get a key."

"Trust me. Now, where do we meet and when?"

The Fountain Square clock chimed three as Aritoli and Tafiya crouched behind a pillar by the south door of the Councilor's wing of the Levar's palace. They waited until the steady tread of the Palace guard faded with distance, then they silently approached the door.

Pulling a thin metal rod from her soft leather boot, Tafiya said, "Now, let's see if I remember how to do this." She carefully inserted the rod into the large brass lock and wiggled it up and down.

"What? Tafi, I thought you were going to get a key!"

"The Palace Steward wouldn't give me one since I was not officially in office yet. I didn't want to press the matter. Drat! There's a heavy bolt on the other side of the door. I can't budge it."

Rolling his eyes heavenward, Aritoli said, "Allow me." He placed the golden raven's head of his cane against the lock. His hands tingled as his magic flowed into his fingers. Concentrating, Aritoli pressed the sorcerous force through the door, imagining it as an extension of his hand. When he felt his magical "fingers" grasp the bolt tightly, he drew the cane along the lock. The bolt moved aside with it, and the lock clicked open.

"Perfect!" whispered Tafiya, slipping through the door after Aritoli. "What wondrous partners in crime we'd make."

"If I ever lose my standing as an advisor, I'll give it thought."

They tiptoed down a long, dark corridor whose far end was dimly illuminated. Aritoli could barely make out the carving in the wood paneling and the silhouettes of picture frames on the wall. At the far end, another hallway branched off to the right.

"The Council Chamber is down that hall," Tafiya whispered.

"Care to peek around the corner and see if it's guarded?"

Tafiya ducked her head quickly into the branching corridor, then snapped it back, wearing an amused smile.

"Well?" asked Aritoli.

"He's huge. And black as night. And cute."

"Let me guess—does he wear a wide belt with a large buckle?"

"How did you know?"

"By the Twin Forces, we're sunk. I know this doorman. He's tougher than most."

"We're still going through with the plan, aren't we?"

"We may as well. Though I suspect when this is over I may have to take up thievery after all." Aritoli took out from under his cloak a bottle of wine, House of iv N'Bero Vintners 3309, and carefully uncorked it. He sipped it and nodded in satisfaction. Then he opened a small packet of sleeping powder which he emptied into the bottle. After shaking the bottle gently, he handed it to Tafiya, saying, "You remember what to do?"

"Yessir! Executing Plan One, sir." Tafiya winked and saluted, then sauntered off down the hall.

"'Executing' is right," muttered Aritoli. He slunk along the wall and peeked around the corner to watch. By the light of a hanging oil lamp, he saw Tafiya approach the doorman and show him the bottle.

"Compliments of the management," she said, smiling, "For your excellent service."

"And are you complimentary, too, little spicetart?"

"Whatever you wish."

The doorman smiled broadly and uncorked the bottle, taking an enormous swig from it. Then, as he reached out for a kiss, his eyes suddenly glazed over and he slumped to the floor.

"It worked!" Tafiya called out to Aritoli. "He's out."

Aritoli frowned as he came forward. "Worked a bit fast, didn't it?"

Tafiya slapped the doorman lightly and he showed no response. "See?"

"I'm amazed. Ah, well. Let us get this business done." He pushed open the chamber door and they ducked inside. Aritoli lit a lamp on the long Council table. With Tafiya's help he rolled up the canvas curtain covering the mural, then stepped back for a long look.

It was an abstract seascape, as far as Aritoli could tell. Wavelike swirls of green and blue, with a blue-gray "sky" above, marched across the mural. The colors seemed pleasing enough, but the whirlpools within the design gave Aritoli a sense of discomfort—something like seasickness, he thought with amusement.

"Seems harmless to me," Tafiya said.

"No, there is something here." Aritoli could feel the slight pressure, the not-yet-ness of a ritual spell nearing completion. He noticed the lower right-hand corner of the mural was not finished. "But we may have time to do something."

Stepping back, he again let power flow from the golden raven's head into his fingers and cast a spell of magic tracing. Glowing light-motes flew from his hand to the mural and immediately formed an outline of a geometrical structure. A structure both simple and complex, implying beauty, completeness— a summation of imperfections that created a perfect whole. Yet, as he studied the unfinished corner, Aritoli had a curious feeling of being on the brink, as if this glorious structure could fall apart at a single brush stroke.

"Like a great shiribi puzzle," murmured Aritoli. "I was wrong, Tafi. The Shatter-Eye School does teach art, but not a sort that is appreciated visually. Within this mural, Freneza has captured a magical representation of . . . our world. And here," Aritoli pointed to the unfinished corner, "lies the symbolic loop of string, whose movement shall make it all undone."

"I am pleased," said the smooth voice of Sister Vanta, "that you have come to appreciate our ways."

Aritoli turned. She stood in the doorway, flanked by Freneza and the doorman. They each held lanterns that sent glaring light into the room. Sister Vanta bowed to Tafiya. "Welcome, my dear. You are early for the showing, but Ezvi did want you to be among the first to see it."

Tafiya gulped and said nothing.

"I thought painting by lamplight was bad for the eyes, Freneza," said Aritoli. "Why are you here at this hour?"

"I might ask you the same," said the artist. "I've been working late to finish the mural for tomorrow. I was taking a rest when the doorman alerted us to your presence."

Aritoli glanced at the guard.

The doorman smiled. "A valiant attempt, Master ola Silba, but drugged wine is an old trick. It was no trouble for me to feign sleep, then slip away to warn the others."

Aritoli covered his face in weariness and embarrassment. Then he noticed, between his fingers, Tafiya edging along the wall as if terrified. *Perhaps if I distract them, she at least can get away.*

He looked up at the artist. "I must say, Freneza, that I am

impressed with your work. You have tremendous talent. A pity
you lent it to such a dubious tutor."

"This dubious tutor has made the expression of my talent
possible by revealing to me the truth. Now if you will step
aside . . ."

"Certainly," smiled Aritoli, "we were just leaving." He started
toward the door, but the priest blocked his way.

"Oh, no," said Sister Vanta, "you must stay and see the
finishing of the work, that you may truly understand it. Guard,
please make the advisor comfortable. Give him a front-row
seat."

The doorman grinned and offered Aritoli a chair. Aritoli
grinned back and made a break for the open door.

The doorman grabbed his arm, saying, "Now, sir, it's im-
polite to ignore the lady's invitation. I'll just take this so you
won't lose it." He pulled the cane out of the advisor's hand
and set it on the Council table, out of Aritoli's reach.

Suddenly, quick as a flicker of lightning, Tafiya grabbed
the walking stick. She dashed out the door, skirts flying.

"Stop her!" cried Sister Vanta. The doorman frowned and
lumbered down the hall after Tafiya.

Aritoli tried to follow, but Sister Vanta gestured and his gaze
snapped back to the painting. He found his attention captured
by the design, unable to move. Hands grasped his shoulders
and he felt himself guided into a chair. An egg-shaped object
appeared in the priest's hand and she used it to bind him to the
chair with magical force.

"You are afraid," Sister Vanta said softly, "yet there is no
need to be. You will feel no pain. In fact you will scarcely feel
anything. But your mind will become ours." She turned away
and bent to advise Freneza, who was filling in the unpainted
corner.

As the artist worked, Aritoli felt the spell near its completion. The thought that a sorcerous pattern of such beauty was
going to collapse almost brought tears to his eyes. Filled with
trepidation and sorrow, he waited helplessly.

At last Freneza finished and stood back from his work.
Aritoli felt more than saw the priest watching him. She was
right—there was no sudden pain or swift change of mood. For
a moment, Aritoli wondered if her spell had failed.

Then he sensed it. An image formed before him of an enormous shiribi puzzle . . . just after the fatal string had been pulled.

In a constant state of collapse, it was falling, falling, the pieces twisting and tumbling forever into chaos. He moaned in despair.

"Interesting," said Sister Vanta softly. "Each mind chooses its own symbols for chaos. You seem to have accepted ours. Do not fear it. It is the way of things. Let the lies of illusion fall from your eyes. It only distresses you because you cling to lies. It will not harm you if you accept it. It will harm no one. There is no pain in emptiness. Give in to the truth."

Aritoli shut his eyes, but the image remained. He did not know exactly what would happen if he surrendered as Sister Vanta wished, but a strong urge to fight welled up in him. Somehow he had to keep the image from falling, had to put it back together. Could he remember how Tafiya reassembled the puzzle? Aritoli tried to recall each movement of her fingers, imposing that vision over the chaos. Gradually, the falling pieces slowed, and Aritoli began to rebuild the puzzle in his mind.

"It is foolish to cling to illusion," Sister Vanta snapped. "But you will see. These bonds will hold until I return at the showing. By that time your struggle will be over, and Truth will win."

Aritoli heard Freneza and Sister Vanta depart. He tried to move, but still could not. He continued to build the image in his mind, but one piece's movement eluded him. If he could not remember, the game was lost.

A sound in the room penetrated his concentration. "Who is there?" Aritoli demanded.

"It's me! Tafi! I've got your cane. Are you all right?"

"Oh, thank the Twin Forces! My dearest Tafi, you know not what pleasure it is to hear your voice again!"

"I see Freneza finished the m—"

"Don't look at it!"

"Sshhhh! All right, all right, I'm not looking . . . it's kind of hard to see in the dark, anyway. Here. What's happened to you? You're all covered in sweat."

Aritoli gratefully took his cane and began to draw power from it. "I am in the midst of a philosophical struggle with myself. I need your help. But first, drop the curtain over that mural."

"Whatever you say." There was a rumble and a flop as Tafiya covered the painting. "Now what?"

"You must tell me how you solved the shiribi puzzle."

"What? Now? Ari, don't we have—"

"Now! You must!"

"Well I . . . I can't just describe it. It's something I have to do."

"Then do it. Let me watch your hands."

"What? Without a puzzle? That's impossible!"

"I'll give you a puzzle. Come sit in front of me."

Aritoli heard Tafiya slide to the floor before him and at last the advisor dared to open his eyes. With the image of the shiribi sticks still frozen before his eyes, Aritoli poured sorcerous light from his cane to the floor. There, in Tafiya's hands, he projected the image he saw. "Now," said Aritoli, "solve it."

She stared in amazement for a moment, then began to go through the motions.

"Slowly," Aritoli cautioned, making the images of the sticks and string move with her fingers. Still, it only took a couple of minutes before Tafiya held a perfect spherical construction in her hands.

Aritoli reveled in the sight, the wholeness and solidity of the object. Tears came to his eyes. With a surge of magic from his cane, he broke the sorcerous bonds that held him to the chair and he fell forward to embrace Tafiya.

She laughed with relief and said, "We'd better go, before anyone sees us."

"No! We are not done here. I must somehow change the mural so that it's no longer a danger."

"How can you do that if it's harmful to look at?"

Aritoli thought for a moment. "There may be a way. By any chance, did Freneza leave his paint and brushes nearby?"

"Yes. When I watched them leave, I heard him say he'd pick them up later this morning. I'll go get them." She returned with several paint pots under her arms.

"Excellent." Aritoli projected the phantom shiribi puzzle flat against a blank wall adjoining the mural. He then expanded the puzzle and stretched out its image. The lines exactly matched those of the mural . . . except for the lower right corner. Aritoli magically bound the image to the wall so that it no longer required his complete concentration to maintain.

"Now, Tafi, I want you to lift the rightmost corner of the curtain and paint over what is there. It doesn't matter what you paint, or with what colors, so long as your brushstrokes move as I direct."

So Tafiya painted as Aritoli laid down lines of magical force to match those he saw on his projected image, lines that made the mural's broken puzzle solid and whole once more.

Aritoli looked up with a bland expression as the door to the chamber opened. The Merchant Councilors, silhouetted in the morning sunlight, paused at the threshold, surprised to find him sitting there. Sister Vanta and Frenza also feigned surprise as they entered.

First Merchant iv N'Addam, a tall, thin woman in pale silk brocade, spoke first. "Pardon me, sir, I don't mean to be rude, but who are you and what are you doing here?"

"I am Aritoli ola Silba, Advisor to Patrons of the Arts," Aritoli said in as much of a monotone as possible. "I am here at Sister Vanta's invitation. She wished me to come to understand the ways of the Shatter-Eye School. And so I have." He looked at the priest who nodded, smiling.

"Oh. So you have already seen the mural," said the First Merchant.

"Yes. It is a work of genius."

Frenza, who had hovered anxiously behind Sister Vanta since they entered, finally seemed to relax.

"Well, I'm glad you approve, sir," said the First Merchant. "Very glad. Might you do us the honor, then, of performing the unveiling?"

"Of course." Aritoli pulled a rope and raised the curtain as the Councilors gathered around to watch.

Perplexed murmurs filled the room as they beheld Frenza's work. Aritoli heard the artist and Sister Vanta gasp and whisper behind him.

The First Merchant coughed in embarrassment. "Well, I will say it's . . . innovative, Frenza. But I confess it's not what I expected. I'm not sure I could stand to look at those swirling lines and colors for hours at a time."

"Ah, but you see," said Aritoli, "the genius lies beneath. In the flow of sorcerous force that Frenza, with the help of Sister Vanta, placed within. Behold!" Flourishing his cane, he caused the magical design to blaze forth with light.

There came *ooohs* and *aaahs* and scattered applause. Frenza glared at Aritoli with fists clenched at his side. Sister Vanta's face was white with rage. Neither spoke.

"Yes, I see what you mean, Master ola Silba," said the First

Merchant, "but that feature of the mural wasn't apparent until you pointed it out. I'm not sure I'm pleased with the work as it stands. Perhaps if Freneza had made the painted design match the magical one, it would have worked better."

Just then, a heavy man in gaudy silks came forward and said, "Oh, it's not all that bad. Look, I like that cute little fish in the corner."

Aritoli looked and, sure enough, in the lower right-hand corner was painted a small fish—the advisor wasn't certain if it was supposed to be a shark or a minnow, but it was very much Tafiya's style. He glanced at her and she shrugged and mouthed, "You said I could paint anything."

The First Merchant cocked her head, chin in hand, and regarded the corner. "Why, yes, a charming little creature. But it looks rather out of place off by itself. Freneza, could you put more of those fish in the mural—maybe just scatter a few throughout? It would make the mural much more pleasant."

Freneza snarled and said, "No! I do not paint cute little animals! I hate cute little animals! You are all fools! That is not my work. I take no responsibility for it. It's ruined! My mural is ruined and I want nothing more to do with it!" The artist stormed out of the chamber, with Sister Vanta gliding silently behind.

The First Merchant said, "I'd heard that artists were temperamental, but that was uncalled for. What did he mean, 'that's not my work'?"

Aritoli cleared his throat. "He was no doubt referring to the fish, which was a later addition. You see, vandals broke in last night and slightly damaged that corner of the painting. Fortunately, I discovered this early enough to attempt repair. What you see there is the work of your own Councilor-Elect, Tafiya Mielo, who was kind enough to lend her skills at short notice."

Eyes opening wide, the First Merchant said, "Oh. What a pleasant surprise! Tafi, I had no idea you were so talented. Well, a shame about the vandals. I'm surprised our security was inadequate. Still, that bit's good. Say, um...if Freneza wants nothing more to do with this, do you think you would be willing to finish the mural? We'd even give you part of the fee and publicity."

"Why, I would love to!" said Tafiya, beaming. "But first, I must speak to my agent." She pointed a hand at Aritoli, then took his arm and led him aside. It took Aritoli considerable effort to keep from laughing.

"There are still some things I'd like to understand before I touch that mural again. Like what exactly was that spell Freneza painted in?"

"So far as I could tell, it made the mind susceptible to despair, slowly destroying one's faith in reality."

"Do you think ola Thinoli requested such a spell?"

"I doubt it was described to him that way. I imagine Sister Vanta told him it would cause the merchant representatives to become careless in their work. Ola Thinoli would then have proof that the merchants were unfit for the Council. This would make the position of the nobility stronger, and the Church of Truth would have powerful new converts."

"Master ola Silba?" said the First Merchant behind him.

"Yes?" Aritoli turned to see iv N'Addam frowning slightly.

"There remains one slight problem. This mural, and showing, was sponsored by First Lord ola Thinoli. I'm not sure how kindly he'll take to being told about the vandalism and change in mural artists."

"My dear lady, you need say nothing at all to ola Thinoli. Neither I nor the guard saw the vandalism last night. And if you ask the artist Freneza and Sister Vanta, I think they will claim they saw nothing as well."

"Is that so? And just what did you see last night?"

"Oh, it's all rather vague now. I seem to have forgotten. In fact, you might tell ola Thinoli that, if he should ask. My memory of it will probably remain lost forever, unless something happens to remind me."

"I see."

"If he must know about the fishes," Tafiya added, "you could say it's in honor of the new prosperity of our Minnow Island fishermen."

"Yes, that sounds like an excellent idea! And we can have a second, a public showing when Tafi finishes! I say, there hasn't been such an exciting day in Council since that cat was made councilor. Thank you, Master ola Silba." The First Merchant bowed and walked away, smiling.

Turning back to Tafiya, Aritoli saw the man in gaudy silks saying to her, "Oh, that little fishy is so charming, Tafi! Do you do commissions? I know my wife would love to have something like that on the wall of our salon."

"Well," Tafiya replied carefully, "I'd have to think about it." She looked at Aritoli.

The councilor rushed up to the advisor and patted his shoulder. "Oh, don't worry. I wouldn't think of leaving you out of this. You'll get a good finder's fee, I promise you! Tell me when you might want to start work, Tafi, and I'll have you come over to see my home." He bustled off, grinning.

Tafiya raised her brows at Aritoli. "Can you believe this? That little fish has brought me more luck than I get on my birthday!"

"The vagaries of taste—" Aritoli began, then he looked back at the mural and frowned.

"What is it?"

"You know, Tafi, I worried so much about the magic in this 'broken puzzle,' I didn't even think what a 'complete puzzle' spell would do. But that spell remains in the mural. I can feel its power."

"You think the way we altered the spell is responsible for my—our—luck?"

"What would a complete shiribi puzzle symbolize to you?"

"Hmm. A solid structure out of fragile pieces? Unlikely parts creating a pleasing shape? I don't know."

"Nor do I. But so long as it seems good, I don't worry."

Tafiya laughed. "And the Church of Truth will be credited with a spell that reduces some of their beloved chaos. Oh, look! They're bringing in the refreshments. Let's have some breakfast."

As Tafiya led Aritoli away, he took one last glance at the mural. As he did, he could swear that the little fish winked at him.

The Rat's Alley Shuffle

by Charles de Lint

SAFFER WAS SITTING on a flat stone on the strip of land between the salt marsh and the Levar's Highway about a half mile or so west of Liavek. She had her back to the road, her feet in the couchgrass, and her cittern on her lap. The song she was working on was a new one and it was going well, except for the bridge between the verses. She'd tried a dozen different bits and pieces, but nothing fit. It was much more interesting watching the birds in the marsh.

Closer to the sea, black and white oyster-catchers with their long orange bills were feeding among the stones, catching mostly marshcrabs. Four or five terns were hovering over a stretch of open water, slender wings and long tails outstretched as they dropped down to skim the surface. A cormorant flew from right to left across Saffer's field of vision in a straight purposeful line, and she wondered where it was going in such a hurry. Near where she was sitting, a group of ducks were watching her, hoping for more of the bread bits that she'd shared with them earlier.

The song, she decided, should have been about birds. Especially if she was going to work on it here. But this was one of her private quiet places—even so close to the road as it was—and she had to get the song finished. Liavek was noisy at the best of times, unless one could afford private lodgings in the Canal District or a house on the here-now/gone-again Wizard's Row. She lived in Rat's Alley and the only privacy she had there was a box of a room that was stifling at the moment. If only she'd learned magic instead of music, she thought sometimes, invested her luck in a nice little bauble that she could hang around her neck perhaps, things might have been different.

But as it was, it was the month of Fruit, she was always next to broke, the city was too noisy for her to think, and she had a commission from Tapper Tan Burnie that would be delivered late if it wasn't finished today. She was supposed to write a catchy little piece for him, something that prominently mentioned his tavern, The Quick's End, with a tune simple enough for any street singer to sing and perhaps a touch of something hidden in the music to make listeners thirsty.

She played through the newest version of the bridge a couple of times, lightly plucking the cittern's double strings, and frowned when it still didn't sound quite right.

"Duck farts," she told her attentive mallard audience. "That's what it sounds like."

"But coming from you," a voice said from the road behind her, "even farts sound melodious."

Recognizing that voice, Saffer didn't bother to turn around. "What are *you* doing here?" she asked.

"I've come to make you rich."

The ducks swam off as the newcomer came down from the road and gingerly chose a stone of his own to sit on. He gave Saffer a grin and stretched out his long legs. Narrow, spidery fingers adjusted the knot of the scarf tied at his throat. He seemed to be all angles and bony limbs, but anyone thinking him awkward was in for a rude surprise if they sat down to play cards with him.

"Hello, Saffer," he said. "Lovely day, don't you think?"

"Hello, Dumps. How did you find me?"

"I asked Meggy Thistle. 'Meggy,' I said, 'where's Saffer who I plan to make rich?' and she sent me down here. She told me you were hunting tunes—or was it loons?"

"Well, I've found my loon," Saffer said as she laid her instrument down on its quilted bag by her feet.

"Is that the way you always talk to those who mean to make you rich?"

"The last time you meant to make me rich, you almost had us both sent to Crab Isle. We're just lucky it was my brother in the Guard who picked us up and that everyone got their levars back."

Dumps waved off her worry. "Sink 'em if they can't take a joke. Anyway, this time I've got a commission for us that's perfectly legal."

Saffer shrugged and picked up her cittern. "I've already got a commission."

"It'll be perfectly safe—lose my luck if I'm lying."

Saffer shook her head and began her tune again.

"Five levars for you," Dumps said. "And *no* risk."

The tune faltered. "Five levars?"

"Guaranteed."

"No risk?"

"None at all."

"I don't have to get dressed up again?"

"Not so much as a glove."

Saffer gave it a few moments of serious consideration. Her chestnut hair was cut very short at the front, top, and sides, but fell in a long braid down her back. This had come about from one of Dumps's plans of disguising her as a young man for some trick or other that never quite got off the ground. She'd ended up liking the raffish look it gave her—but that came weeks after walking about in a big floppy hat. She ran her hand through the short hair at the top of her head.

"Just as you are, and your cittern as it is," Dumps said, following the motion of her hand. He knew what she was thinking.

"All right," Saffer said. "I'll listen."

"You won't regret this, Saffer. Odd's End, but it's sweet."

"I said I'd listen, Dumps. I didn't say I'd do it. Whatever 'it' is."

"Then listen," he said. "Listen and weep for the beauty of it."

At least one good thing had come from listening to Dumps, Saffer thought later as she was walking down the Street of the Dreamers. She had the bridge for Tapper Tan's commission worked out—she'd just drone for a couple of bars between verses. Tapper Tan had liked both words and music and paid her on the spot. The first thing she did with her new wealth was buy a set of cittern strings at Whistler's Corner, which was dear to her heart for one very good reason: Its goods were cheap. Her purse a touch lighter and the pocket where she'd stuffed the strings a tad heavier, she made her way over to the

Levar's Park where she bought a cup of kaf and a few sticky buns, then sat down in one of her favorite nooks to watch the crowds go by.

When she was finished eating and had carefully licked her fingers clean, she considered putting out her hat for an hour or so. She could always use the practice on her cittern. On the other hand, with her purse still weighty from Tapper Tan's commission, and with Dumps's commission in the offing, she didn't really have the proper air of desperation to do any street singing today. She just wasn't feeling poor enough to put on a proper show. At that moment her friend Kaloo plonked down beside her and settled the whole question.

"My, you're looking prosperous today," Kaloo said.

Saffer nodded. "I finished up that commission for Tapper Tan *and* I've got a new one."

"Don't tell me—let me guess. The Levar's asked you to play for her on her luck day!"

"Nothing so grand. I'm providing the music for a night of private bidding—Dumps arranged the whole thing."

"What'll you be dressed up as this time?" Kaloo asked. "An Ombayan parrot?"

Saffer laughed. "At least I wasn't named after the kookaloo." The kookaloo was a wild songbird that left its eggs in other birds' nests. From someone else, Kaloo might have taken this as an insult, but coming from Saffer, she just laughed.

"Be that as it may," she said, "I saw Dumps at the other end of the park having a most earnest conversation with Coniam—the *wizard* Coniam," she added.

"I know those who're Wizards and those who aren't," Saffer said. Coniam lived at 13 Wizard's Row, and while he wasn't the most powerful magic-worker in Liavek, he wasn't exactly a slouch either. But what business could Dumps have with him? "What were they talking about?" she asked aloud.

Kaloo shrugged. "Who knows? I could ask L'Fertti, but he's not all that mad about cardsharps—especially not dandies like your Dumps. When's this bidding party anyway?"

"Twenty-eighth of the month."

"Can you use a whistle player?"

"Who? Meggy?"

Kaloo nodded. "She's looking for work."

"How is she on Zhir tunes?"

Kaloo pulled a face. "Awful. I don't like listening to all that modal stuff either. Is that what Dumps wants you to play?"

"Nothing but. He says it's to add a little tension to the game, to keep the bidders on a sharp edge. They'll play better—*and* pay better."

"How much better?"

"Five levars for the evening," Saffer said smugly.

"Five . . . ?" Kaloo shook her head. "Oh, that doesn't sound right, Saffer. If it was anyone but Dumps. . . ."

"He's not so bad," Saffer said, but she was beginning to have her doubts again. She didn't like to hear about Dumps being seen in the company of a wizard.

"I have to go," Kaloo said suddenly.

"Me, too," Saffer said. She slung her cittern bag over her shoulder.

"Don't go off in a huff," Kaloo began and Saffer joined her to finish with: "Just go!"

Laughing, Saffer gave her friend a jaunty wave and set off in search of Dumps.

Saffer found Dumps in a tavern that night—the Kondy's Brew off Rat's Alley—and he immediately proceeded to alleviate her worries with two brimming mugs of ale and protestations of innocence that were as preposterous as they were anatomically impossible.

"It's just a luck day party," he finished. "That's all. And Coniam's footing the bill. These're his friends, Saffer—remember friends? They're the sort of people one trusts and depends on."

"What do you mean by a 'luck day party'?"

"Well, it just so happens that each of our five fine—and might I add wealthy—guests were born on that same day, at approximately the same time. Coniam's thinking of organizing a club for them."

Saffer studied her ale for a long moment. Was this still her first, or a second? It was so smoky in here and ale always went right to her head; it was difficult for her to work it out. What she did know was that the more she heard about this bidding party, the worse it was beginning to sound.

"They're friends?" she tried again.

"The very best."

"All born around the same time?"

"So Coniam says. Actually, I think they're more his friends

than each others'. This party's for them to all meet and form
this—"

"Club. Yes. You mentioned that."

"Would you like another ale?"

"I don't think I should. And so they're going to have a
friendly game of Two-Copper Bid, while I play Zhir tunes to
make them tense....This sounds mad, you know that, don't
you, Dumps?"

"I prefer the word 'eccentric.' Poor people are mad; rich
people are eccentric. I read that in *The Cat Street Crier*."

"Yes, well, I don't think I want the commission anymore,"
Saffer said.

"Oh, but you can't back out now—Coniam wouldn't like
it. Not now that I've told you all about it."

"What's he going to do?" Saffer asked. "Turn me into a
frog?" But then, he *was* a wizard and the trouble with wizards
was that they were liable to do anything. "Oh, I don't like this
at all, Dumps. Not one bit. You *promised* me there'd be no
trouble."

"And there won't be. Just come and play some music, collect
your five levars, then tra-la-la, off you go."

Saffer took a long swig of her ale. She was still thinking
about frogs and what it would be like to be one.

"I don't like it either," Dumps admitted. "If I'd known...."
He fidgeted with his ale mug and sighed. "But what's to do?
He *is* a wizard."

"What's in it for him?" Saffer asked. "I mean all this talk
about a club—that's just nonsense. So what's he got planned?"

"Think about it."

Saffer didn't want to because she was feeling somewhat
woozy, but she gave it a try. "There'll be five of them," she
said. "All playing cards, all concentrating their luck on those
cards ... on their luck day... right in the hours of their luck,
the only time it's really potent for anyone who isn't a wizard....Oh, Dumps! He means to bind their luck into a pack
of cards!"

Dumps nodded glumly. "And they're so keen on the chance
to play when their luck's at their best, they can't even see it.
When the night's done, Coniam will be able to use those cards
and no one will be able to beat him. They'll never guess that
he's cheating. In fact, it doesn't even have to be him using the
cards. *Anyone* who knows how to use them will be unbeatable."

That was the worst thing that you could do to someone,

Saffer thought. Steal their luck. And these players, they'd lose their luck for as long as the cards existed. And if their luck was bound into the deck and the cards were somehow destroyed . . . they'd all die. With that control held over them, they wouldn't dare do anything to Coniam if they found out what he'd done for fear he'd destroy the cards.

"But why us?" Saffer asked. "Why would he pick us?"

"Well, he wasn't too happy about my bringing you in— your brother Demar being in the Guard and all— but I know he approached me because . . . well, who could I tell? Who'd listen to old Dumps if he tried to pass around a story like that? I'm like the lookout who cried land once to often."

"What are we going to do?"

Dumps shrugged. "Nothing. I'll run the bidding and you'll play your music and, after it's over, we'll both go home a little richer."

"But those players—what about their luck? What if they come after us when they realize what's been done?"

"There's no way for them to know, Saffer. They're not wizards. The only ones who'll know will be you and me."

"And Coniam."

"And Coniam," Dumps agreed.

"And he's a wizard," Saffer said, "who could conceivably turn us into newts or toads so that we couldn't spread the tale around."

"Or he could kill us."

"Dumps! You promised this would be safe!"

"Or he could just pay us and let us go, because who'd believe us anyway?"

"I suppose," Saffer said, a little mollified. "I wonder what he needs those cards for. You'd think he'd turn his wizardry to a more honest way of making a living."

"Depends on what his luck is. I don't think it's anything useful or he wouldn't be trying this, now would he? I've also heard—just this evening, mind, so don't start on me again about my leading you into danger—I've just heard that Coniam owes a certain Brugsti a great number of levars."

"Brugsti? This just keeps getting worse, Dumps! Brugsti's a thug."

"Agreed. A very rich, powerful, unpleasant-if-you-cross-him-thug. He also happens to be completely resistant to magic—"

"I didn't know that."

"—which makes things difficult if you're a wizard and have decided to renege on your debts to him. Brugsti's paid a lot of levars to a lot of powerful wizards for that immunity, so it's either pay up with him, or get thumped."

"Or worse."

"Or worse," Dumps agreed.

Saffer commandeered an ale from the tray of a waiter going by, gave Dumps a nod that he should pay, and took a long gulp. Was this her third, or her second? It didn't really matter, not when life as a toad was potentially in the offing.

"What are you doing?" Dumps asked her as he paid the waiter.

"I," she announced a little unsteadily, "am going to get levarly drunk. It's the twenty-sixth today, so I'm going to stay drunk until sometime on the twenty-ninth, whereupon I shall sober up—if I'm still all in one piece."

"But what about the commission? Can you still play when you're soused?"

Saffer finished the ale in a second long swallow and regarded him blearily. "I play much better," she assured him and promptly fell head forward against the table. Dumps caught her before her forehead was introduced to the oak slats and propped her back up in her chair. Her head lolled to one side.

"I don't suppose it would help if I said I was sorry?" he asked, but he wasn't really expecting an answer.

When Saffer woke the next day it was late afternoon. She immediately discovered three things. The first was that her head felt as though someone had mistaken it for an anvil. The second was that if she moved very slowly and squinted rather than opened her eyes, the pain would be almost bearable. The third was that she had woken in Dumps's bed with Dumps snoring beside her. She gave him a poke.

"Huh—whuzzat?"

Saffer squinted daggers at him. "What," she began, grimaced, then quickly lowered her voice, "am I doing *here?*"

"You *were* sleeping," Dumps mumbled and began to turn over. Saffer poked him again.

"Did we . . . ?" She'd been a little lax with her Worrynot of late.

Dumps rolled his eyes. "Odd's End, Saffer! I've told you before, you're too skinny for my tastes. Now either go back to sleep or go away."

Saffer thought about thumping him, but decided that in her present state it would probably hurt her more than him. Instead she got up, found she was still fully clothed, grabbed her cittern bag from where it was hanging on the end of the bed, and made for the door. Dumps sat up in sudden alarm.

"Where are you going?" he demanded.

"Out."

"You're not planning a repeat of last night's performance, are you?"

"First," she informed him, "I'm going to look up Marithana and see what sort of a cure she can sell me for this head of mine, and then I'm going to the marsh to look at the ducks."

"But you *will* honor the commission?"

"We'll see," she said maliciously and closed the door. His shouting after her, while it made her head throb more, was still music to her ears. Let him stew a bit, she thought. Serves him right, the rotter, for getting me into this in the first place.

"Fold."

"I'll see your bid and call."

"Fold."

"Fold."

"His lordship has a filled tower," Dumps said as Lord Shin, the Count of Grandeth, spread out his cards. "Mages high." He looked expectantly to Mistress Olna, the Vavasor of Chem's Way, who had seen the count's bid, but she shook her head and threw in her hand. Dumps pushed the pot over to Shin and collected the cards. "Ante up," he said as he began to shuffle the deck.

His lordship was doing very well tonight, Saffer thought, though all five of them would be the losers before the night was out, if Coniam had his way. She was sitting in a corner, playing a Zhir version of an old ballad known in Liavek as "My Love's Left Me and My Luck's All Gone" on her cittern. The irony of its title would be lost on all of them, except perhaps the wizard.

They were using one of the back rooms at Cheeky's for the party. Besides the count and the vavasor, there were three wealthy merchants in on the game. Dumps was the dealer, of course, and she was the entertainment. Judging from the irritated glances that were cast in her direction every so often, she was fulfilling her commission properly, if not pleasing the guests.

Two dancers from Cheeky's had been hired to keep a steady supply of drinks and pastries at each player's elbow. Saffer didn't know either of them and they hadn't bothered to introduce themselves, which suited her just fine. Not present, though certainly watching from a peephole, was the host of the party. After briefly introducing the players to each other, Coniam had bowed out because of other "pressing business."

Saffer sighed as she started up a new tune. It would be at least another hour before the party wound down. Her fingers were getting stiff, though not so stiff that she wouldn't be able to play her own card when the bidders' game was done. Given two days to think about it, she knew that Coniam wouldn't be physically present. And this afternoon, while supposedly checking the room's acoustics, she'd found the chalk markings that encircled the underside of the table, confirming her guess. These five citizens had been chosen because their luck times all coincided with his. At this very moment he was somewhere very near, investing the cards with his own luck as well.

Oh, Coniam was a clever sod, Saffer thought, yes, indeed. It was just too bad for him that he hadn't taken into account the fact that there might be an honest rogue or two in Rat's Alley.

Another hand had ended, one of the merchants being its winner, and Dumps was dealing the cards anew, seven to each player. Two-Copper Bid, Saffer thought. Levar's blood! There was more wealth on that table than she'd ever seen before in one place. They should have called this game Ten-Silver Bid. Each of the players discarded two cards and then the bidding began again. Saffer started up another tune.

"Every cramp in my fingers has its own cramp," Saffer said as she put away her cittern. She slung the bag over her shoulder and wandered over to the table where Dumps was sitting wearily. She flexed her fingers in front of him for a moment. "See?" she said, then added: "Time to pay up."

As Dumps bent down to get at the money box by his feet, Saffer picked up the cards and gave them a quick shuffle.

"Don't touch those!" Dumps cried and snatched them from her.

"Oh, grumpy, aren't we?"

"Don't start, Saffer. Here's your five levars."

Saffer counted them out very carefully, grinning at the annoyance on Dumps's face, then stowed the coins in her purse. Making sure that it was still firmly attached to her belt, she buttoned it shut and gave it a pat.

"One last favor," she said as she headed for the door.

"What's that?"

"Don't do me any more favors."

Dumps looked as though he was seriously considering throwing something at her.

"Sink you, if you can't take a joke," she said and stepped quickly out of the room."

The pounding came at her door at approximately an hour before sunrise—a full half-hour later than she'd been expecting it.

"It's open!" she called out cheerfully.

Dumps stormed in. "You ungrateful wretch!" he cried. "Give me the card!"

"What card?"

"Don't play innocent with me. The Rikiki card that you filched from the deck tonight."

"Oh, *that* card."

"Did you really think you could get away with switching it for one that wasn't a part of the binding? Saffer, he's going to kill me if I don't get it back."

"How? With some terrible spell?"

"He's a wizard, sinkbrain! Get that through that tiny mind of yours."

Saffer smiled. When she was in the room that afternoon she'd made sure that the Rikiki card she was going to have hidden up her sleeve that night matched the pack they were using. After that, with the sleight-of-hand tricks she'd picked up from hanging around with Dumps, it had been child's play to exchange the two when she gave the pack a quick shuffle at the end of the night.

"A wizard without his luck is all he is," she said. "He doesn't frighten me."

"And Brugsti?"

"Well, he's a different matter, but he's Coniam's worry— not ours. Brugsti may be a thug, but he's not stupid enough to come after us because Coniam can't make good his debts. The Alley'd get together and sink him in the harbor."

"Saffer, *please*. Maybe Brugsti won't come after us, but

Coniam can certainly hire a few thugs who will."

"But then he'd never find out where I hid this card, would he?"

"Saffer, don't do this to me."

"All right," she relented. "Tell Coniam that I'll meet him on the docks tonight—ten sharp. We'll work out a deal."

"A deal? Are you mad?"

"No. But I plan to be eccentric some day."

"Saffer—"

"Ten tonight. On the docks. Near Yonner's Netting. He can come alone, or bring his merry luck day club with him—I don't care."

"Saffer—"

"Goodnight, Dumps."

He stared at her for a long moment, then slowly backed out the door and slammed it behind him. The look on his face, Saffer decided, made this all very worthwhile. It was about time he was on the receiving end of things going wrong.

Coniam was prompt—Saffer had to give him that—and very sure of himself. The only person accompanying him to the meeting place was a miserable-looking Dumps.

The wizard was a formidable figure. He was a head taller than Dumps, which made him two heads taller than Saffer. She looked up into his lean features and swallowed thickly at the blaze of anger that brooded in his eyes. He wasn't the sort one would want to meet in a dark alley—with or without his spells. He was also quite rude, Saffer thought, as he came directly to the point without even a few words of preamble.

"Do you have the card?"

Saffer nodded and drew it from her sleeve, being very careful to maintain a distance of more than three paces between them. Unless Coniam was an utter fool, he'd have the rest of the pack in one of his pockets. "Rikiki's here," she said. "What've you got to offer in trade?"

"How does your life sound, child?"

"Melodious as a lark."

"Saffer!" Dumps cried. "Don't egg him on!"

The wizard lifted a hand in Dumps's general direction and the cardsharp immediately fell quiet. "What do you want for it?" Coniam asked.

"Let's see....The use of the cards for one night? But of

course that wouldn't do, would it? Since you've invested your own luck in the pack, it'll only serve you, won't it?"

"How much in straight coinage will you take for it?"

"Well, it depends. You *did* infuse it with more than your own luck, so that should make it worth— But then there's my keeping quiet about it as well. I don't think Lord Shin or any of the others would be all that happy to find out that you've, shall we say, 'borrowed' their luck."

"You are trying my patience, child. You won't say a word about it to Lord Shin or anyone else, or I'll simply have to tell them that it was the pair of you up to your usual tricks. Who do you think the judges would believe if it came to court? A respected wizard, or a pair of guttersnipes from Rat's Alley?"

"Well, that depends," Saffer said, "on whether or not one of those guttersnipes has a brother in the Guard."

"You wouldn't dare—"

"But I already have." Grinning, Saffer tore the playing card in two.

"My luck!" Coniam roared and he charged her, but two gray-clad shapes stepped quickly from the shadows to intercept him. After a very brief scuffle, the two guards had the wizard under control.

"That's one I owe you," Saffer's brother said to her. He was the taller of the pair, not as broad-shouldered as his partner, and his hair was the same chestnut brown as his sister's.

Saffer shook her head. "This is payment for pulling me out of Dumps's last scrape."

Demar shrugged. "Fair enough. This might mean a promotion for us."

"Wouldn't that be grand."

"Try to stay out of trouble now, won't you? Promise me?"

"Singer's honor," Saffer said, crossing her heart.

Her brother and his partner exchanged weary glances. "Go on," Demar said to her, "the both of you. And be quick about it—before we change our minds and run you in as well."

"But, but . . ." Dumps was spluttering.

"What's wrong?" Saffer asked him.

"The five players. When you tore the card in two . . ."

"They're fine," Demar said. "Saffer tore up a fake. The real card's in a very safe place."

Coniam glared at Saffer, but she just grinned back. Her brother took the wizard by the arm and led him off.

"One day . . ." the wizard called back to Saffer.

"Oh, I don't think so," Demar said. He tightened his grip on Coniam's arm. "I'm afraid it's Crab Isle for you, Master Wizard, and I doubt you'll be coming back."

The morning was warm, the sky blue, and the ducks had returned. Saffer was back on her stone between the Levar's Highway and the Saltmarsh, playing a new song to them. She didn't break off when she heard a footstep on the road, just waited for Dumps to sit down.

"I thought I'd find you here," he said. "What're you doing?"

"I'm writing a new song—free of charge—that will make us both famous."

"The one you were just playing? That's the tune you're using?"

Saffer nodded.

"Sounded like duck farts to me."

"Actually, I was thinking of calling it 'The Duck's Fart Shuffle.'"

"Odd's End, Saffer! Sometimes you really make me wonder."

Saffer gave her purse a whack and it replied with a jingle that sounded most tuneful to her ears. "I'm just eccentric," she said, "that's all. Sink you, if you—"

"—can't take a joke."

Saffer laughed. Giving Dumps a poke with her toe, she began to play a jig on her cittern.

Two Houses in Saltigos

by Pamela Dean

DELEON LIKED BEST the plays about the cold places. This was
either a reasonable or an unaccountable preference, as you were
pleased to look at it. The first of his family born in Liavek,
he ought therefore to be, if not fond of, at least accustomed to
its sunny climate, where fire was the enemy and winter brought
only rain, and folk shivered and complained in the month that
to call Frost was an exaggerated courtesy. On the other hand,
he had been conceived in Acrivain in a sharp and uncertain
spring, when the flowers that one's mother said were supposed
to break through the snow and bloom atop it had, in fact, done
just that. This had made his sister Jehane, who was six then,
very happy; and so she had remembered it and told him. And
in the little brownish book he carried sewn in the pocket of his
smock, his mother said just the same; his father seldom noticed
such things.

Deleon, with the ease of long practice, turned his thoughts
from the little brownish book and bent them fiercely upon the
problems of the Desert Mouse. The foremost of these was, in
all probability, its threatening and ridiculous name. But there
was nothing he could do about that. Malion, who had been
there longest, and Thrae, who owned the theater, liked its name.
Calla, because it amused her, liked it, too. Lynno said it sounded
like a place thieves might come to after dark to sell dubious
and not very useful merchandise; Sinati said it might do for a
tavern or even a small pot-boil establishment; Aelim's first
remark to a wondering Deleon, five years ago, had been that

it would do very well for anything other than a theater. But the theater had it, and would continue to have it.

Somewhere in its back passages, somebody started to sing. Deleon immediately shed all thought and resigned himself to a kind of tingling and apprehensive joy. It was Calla, and he was most unfortunately in love with her. She could carry a tune, but her sense of rhythm was uncertain and it was obvious that nobody had ever trained her. She was singing one of the Acrivannish ballads he had translated, but she was taking it too fast. Malion and Thrae had wanted to send her down the road to old Gellirt, who had instructed the other members of the company in the rudiments of proper singing. She had refused to go, maintaining, first, that if she could sing she would be continually made to play simpering fools; and second, that many of the characters, fools or otherwise, who were made to sing in plays were most unlikely, in fact, to be able to sing at all, and would be better represented by someone who was a little shaky at it herself.

The intellectual repercussions of this position had died down three or four days after her arrival, but the emotional ones were still sorting themselves out three months later, and would probably linger for years. Lynno had gotten drunk for the first time in his life because Sinati agreed with Calla. Sinati, whose agreement had been based neither on the merits of the arguments nor on any liking for Calla, had ceased a five years' habit of dithering. She had decided to align herself neither with Lynno nor with Aelim but instead went to live with a young bookseller who had just invested his luck and meant to become a hero. Malion and Thrae, by long experience and natural serenity of character proof against all but the most cataclysmic assaults, had nevertheless been observed, for more than a tenday, to treat one another with a perfect and unnatural courtesy, as though they were one another's distant relations come inconveniently to town. Deleon, hitherto immune to those forces that periodically ravaged the company, had fallen disastrously in love with Calla. And Aelim, during a particularly heated argument about the purpose of drama, had revealed, at least to the keen-eyed, what Deleon already suspected: that he himself so successfully resisted the blandishments of Sinati because he was in love with Deleon.

If Deleon had been head of the company, he would not have hired Calla. She was a skilled player, having been engaged in the trade since she was three years old; she was intelligent and applied her intelligence to her trade, which made her far more reliable than those who depended on a certain moodiness or lack thereof to achieve their effects. He still would not have hired her, not for this company. By her very nature, whatever exactly that was—love, he found, diminished perception, which was dismaying but hardly astonishing—she distressed and ruffled them, individually and collectively. Acrilat knew what, in all innocence, she would make to happen next.

Her voice had been wending steadily closer, and for the first time the words she was singing too fast became discernible. To the delicate and plaintive tune that ought to have told the Acrivannish tragedy of the Second King and the Mountain Empress, Calla sang:

> A knight came down the dusty road.
> All in his horse's mane were twined
> Seven and seventy lively toads
> And forty twinkling newts and nine.

"May these events," said Deleon between his teeth, "not involve thy servant." He had never in his nineteen years set foot in a disorderly house, but it often seemed to him that all Liavek might be so characterized. Liavekans were mad: madder than Kings' Tasters; madder than the mad god Acrilat itself; madder, he finished maliciously, with the ease of someone who long before he became a player had arranged his thoughts as speeches, than their own Levar.

Calla, wearing a threadbare white tunic and an old pair of Sinati's soft boots and carrying a sheaf of papers, came across the platform and sat herself down in the dust next to him. She looked quite sane.

Deleon gazed at her and, as always, felt hungry. She reminded him irresistibly, despite his best efforts to force his thoughts into a more romantic path, of a whole collection of delightful things to eat and drink. Her hair, which she wore long, as women ought to and as many Liavekan women didn't, was the color of strong kaf. Her eyes were the bizarre yellow of green tea that has been brewed too long. Her lips and her palms and the insides of her elbows and the backs of her knees and the heels of her feet were the color of cinnamon bark. The rest of her skin faded, in a series of subtle gradations Deleon wished he could paint, to the color of that peculiar chocolate they sold in the Two-Copper Bazaar. Deleon had stopped putting cream in his kaf since she came; he had always liked green tea; and he had bought a string of cinnamon to hang in his room; but he had been unable to stomach that chocolate. They had made it with goat milk, and it tasted like an unfortunate experiment in cheese over which somebody had spilled a bad grade of sweet wine. The old man who sold it to him, taxed with these deficiencies, had told him shortly that it was intended for cooking, not as confectionery. If you kept it around to look at it grew over itself an unwholesome gray bloom and inspired unwelcome thoughts of mortality.

Deleon was not accustomed to shunning thoughts of mortality. He liked the plays about the cold places not least because so many people died in them. People seldom died in Liavekan plays: though they often seemed to, it was generally a ruse or a mistake, or both. This made for a great deal of hilarity, but gave little scope to his particular talent.

"Deleon!" said Calla, in precisely the tone she used with Thrae's cat when it climbed onto the theater's roof and refused to come down. Her voice, at least, did not remind him of food, or of anything at all; it was hers and brooked no comparisons. "What are you dreaming about?"

"Kaf," said Deleon, smiling on her with considerable satisfaction. A secret love has its rewards, and he reaped them daily. He had not so far chosen to examine in what regards an acknowledged but unrequited love might also have its pleasures. This had never happened to him before and he did not expect it to happen again. He intended to wring the most out of each of its scenes.

"Let's get some, then," said Calla. "I want to talk to you about this play."

"Is it very bad?" They mostly were. Even something like *The Pirates of Port Chai* was beyond the capabilities of the Desert Mouse.

"No, just the contrary. I think we could do it very well if we suppressed Aelim's tendency to make a tragedy out of a drowned spider. But it needs Sinati."

"Don't talk to me about Sinati."

Calla gave him a level and completely opaque look. "Is Aelim suffering?"

"No more than he would over a drowned spider," said Deleon, a little shortly. He had become irritated a month ago at the insistence of the company on assuming that anybody of whom Sinati had chosen to deprive her considerable charms must be heartbroken. "Why does it need Sinati?"

"Isn't she the only one who can do illusion?" asked Calla, with the new-student expression that amused Deleon and enraged everybody else. She knew perfectly well that Sinati was the only member of the company who had invested her luck; the only one who had enough luck to invest. Calla had obviously studied the company for days before offering herself to its employment; what her occasional pretence of ignorance gained her, she alone knew. "Unless," she added, pulling hard on a good handful of Deleon's thick, short hair and almost stopping his heart, "*you* would care to play a simpering fool of a girl with yellow hair?"

"Does she die?" said Deleon just above a whisper, wondering if he were about to do just that. It would be a better way than any he had previously feigned or contrived; but it was beginning to seem to him possible that a world containing Calla might be worth living in after all. She took her hand away and he decided he could still breathe.

"No, but she swoons a great deal," said Calla. "You could practice falling without bruising your elbows." And she laid a finger on the purple patch above his left one, the company's last reminder of *Mistress Oleander*.

"That," said Deleon, feeling the blood rise in his face and cursing the pale skin that would show it to her, "would be useful." He closed his mouth suddenly and stared at her. "Have you spoken to Thrae or Malion?"

"No, I just finished the play last night."

"They cast the characters."

"Well, of course. But if nobody cares to coax Sinati away from her new magician, they must ask you to do it; there's nobody else. You can at any rate decide if you'd like it."

Deleon went on staring; momentarily, the problem she posed occupied more of his attention than her mere bewitching presence. "Just what would you do, my dear, if Thrae gave you a part you didn't like?"

"Tell her so."

"I'd like to be in the audience for that!" burst out Deleon. "In the outside row," he added.

Calla raised her straight, sleek eyebrows at him. "You'd

better have that kaf," she said. "Your wits are addled."

"Yes, all right," said Deleon. "I believe they are."

In the event, they had tea, not kaf, which was expensive these days; and yhinroot tea, not green, which Calla said made her sneeze. Nor did the conversation go as Deleon wished it to. He explained to Calla, as carefully as he knew how, that Thrae had been trained in the very pure and extremely costly school of magical theater. Only her ineradicable penchant for picking up strays and waifs could explain how she came to be burdened with a company so woefully lacking in luck.

Calla interrupted him, possibly incensed at the implication that she was a stray. "Why doesn't Thrae practice magic, then?"

"She used to," said Deleon, who had gotten the story out of Aelim, "but she had only five hours, and the reinvestiture was harder every year. Malion was afraid she'd fail altogether the next time, so she gave it up. *That* story would make a play," he said, scowling. Calla did not look sympathetic to this notion, so he went on. "Sinati says she probably wasn't a good player anyway, and that may be true. But she's a very fine instructor."

"That may be," said Calla. "But—"

"And," said Deleon, "she still has her standards." He picked up the threads of his speech, which he had been prepared for some days to deliver. Quite apart from the unwisdom of usurping Thrae's prerogatives, he explained, it would outrage those standards to suggest to her that someone who happened by an accident of birth to have the required color of hair for a particular part should take that part over someone who could create the color by art alone.

"But that's *all* Sinati can do," said Calla, leaning across the scrubbed wooden table and pinning him with the full force of her great yellow eyes. "She might as well have been a courtesan. *She* never bruises her elbows when she falls down, because it would never occur to her to fall as a real person would."

Deleon put his hand over his eyes. "Don't," he said. "Don't start it again. Don't tell Thrae that characters in a play are as real people."

"I'm not telling Thrae," said Calla. "I'm telling you."

Deleon removed his hand and grinned at her. "Only as a rehearsal for telling Thrae," he said.

Calla frowned at him, putting three straight lines in the clear skin of her wide forehead where the short hairs stuck and curled a little in the heat of the room. Deleon swallowed. *My love is as a meadow of goldenrod,* he recited grimly to himself; *her hair is as the autumn maple and her eyes like the sky above a fall of snow.* As usual since Calla came, the Acrivannish poetry served to show him the inadequacy, not of his taste, but of itself.

"Why won't you talk about it?" she said.

"Look what happened," said Deleon, recklessly, "the last time I talked about it. Sinati's gone."

"Is this the basic obstinacy of your nature," said Calla, "or some Farl—some Acrivannish superstition?"

"What?" said Deleon. It had taken Aelim two years to manage "Acrivannish" rather than "Farlandish." Out of some linguistic and scholarly subtlety he had been unable to explain, Aelim, who stared at you in patient puzzlement when you told him a joke, thought "Acrivannish" a very funny word.

"I was talking to my mother about planting pear trees," said Calla, "on the day of the Marketplace Massacre. Must I therefore never talk about planting pear trees again? Shall we listen now for the sound of pistols?"

"That's absurd," said Deleon heatedly.

"Yes," said Calla, smiling.

Deleon let his breath out and managed to decline the gambit. She could talk circles around him until she snagged him in the noose of his own words and knocked him flat, whereupon he would tell her what she wanted to know: that the moment when he first began to want her, and that other, grimmer moment a day or so later, when he saw Aelim betray himself, still stung. He was not in any case ready to tell her that he loved her; and he would never be ready to tell her that Aelim loved him.

"Show me the play," he said, "and let me decide whether I'll like being a simpering fool with yellow hair."

Calla handed the untidy sheaf across the cups to him.

"Two Houses in Saltigos," read Deleon, "'a play by Andri Terriot.' *Andre Terriot!*" He looked up into Calla's new-student face and told her what she must know already. "He writes for the Levar's Company!"

"Which can afford to send back a play not to its liking," said Calla.

"Well, no doubt. But why send it to us?"

Calla shrugged. "Maybe he's an old friend of Thrae's."

Something in her voice made him look at her carefully. Her cinnamon mouth was turned down at the corner.

"You don't like Thrae," said Deleon.

"I think," said Calla, "that I should like her better did all the rest of you not hang on her like Red priests haunting their temple during a bad harvest."

Deleon went on looking at her. It was the first unattractive aspect she had ever shown him. She put her long dark hand over his where it held the forgotten manuscript. Her touch was warm.

"Read the play," said she.

Deleon read it. Once she had taken her hand away, he was even able to attend to it. The verse was very odd. Many Liavekan plays were in verse, blank or rhymed. The rhymes were often complex, but he had never seen anything so tightly constructed as this. And most Liavekan verse-plays used either the long dactylic line that suited so well the sound of their language, or an iambic pentameter that suited any language. This one used an eight-beat iambic that thumped along ruthlessly like a wagon on a bad road and made everybody in the play sound a little mad. And yes, here was that ridiculous song. The playwright, after the infuriating habit of playwrights, had not indicated any music for it. It did fit very well the Acrivannish tune Calla had been using. The yellow-haired fool would be the singer.

The plot concerned two minor noble courts in Saltigos, the principal members of each of which spent the play in ultimately fruitless strategems to avoid meeting one another. One of these was the simpering, swooning fool. She certainly had a fat part, but even aside from the song Deleon did not much care for it. Her counterpart across the city might do; but, regardless of their relative paucity of lines, the strong parts in the play were those of the two servants who schemed that their employers should meet, to the servants' enrichment and the undoing of the employers. The undoing, as in most Liavekan plays, loomed throughout the play as a very great danger, but in the event was harmless and, to Liavekan tastes, extremely funny. As usual, Deleon found this deliberate thwarting of tragic expectation a grave flaw.

He looked up unsmiling from the last page and found Calla's eyes on him.

"You haven't any sense of humor," she said. "You smiled

four times and chuckled once. I read it yesterday and I'm still sore of laughing."

"You're muddling up your lines," said Deleon, mildly hurt. "Listen closer to Thrae next time. My sense of humor is deficient; it's Aelim's that's lacking altogether."

"Is that why—" said Calla and stopped, regarding him thoughtfully.

So much for Aelim's privacy. "That," Deleon said, over the accelerated thud of his heart, "is why Thrae gives him all the jesters' parts. She's hoping to teach him."

Calla went on looking at him for a short time, much too long a time, and clasped her hands under her chin. "Shall you enjoy the simpering fool?" she said.

When they came back, a stranger in a green robe was pacing up and down the little platform and regarding their dusty hundred-spectator theater as if it were the Fountain Court at the Levar's palace. Even the helpful gloom that three small lanterns made out of the darkness did not cause either the theater or the intruder himself to seem better than shabby.

"May we help you?" said Calla, in her best carrying tones.

The stranger, not starting, turned and looked at them and said something they could not catch. He seemed prepared to outwait them. Calla seemed equally prepared to go away and leave him to prowl about the theater, but Deleon was curious. He was very pleased, as he picked his way across the benches to the stage, to hear her following him.

"May we help you?" he said again.

"Is this the poisonous little mouse, no longer than your finger, that lives at the borders of Ka Zhir?" said the stranger, in his voice a faint echo of the storyteller's chant.

Deleon rammed his knee into the first bench and stood staring, his heart cold and clammy. That was in fact why he had chosen the Desert Mouse. The venomous creature after which some whimsical fool had named the theater had been in Nerissa's favorite story, told them over and over, surreptitiously, by Cook: their mother's most lamentable failing had been a distaste for stories. Cook had called it a foolish tale, as if nobody else cared for it. Had she been wrong, or did this man know a great deal more than he ought?

"Are you looking for someone?" said Calla, at his elbow.

She did not in fact smell like cinnamon or kaf or chocolate, but of the tiger-flowers that grow in Ombaya: a perfume that must have cost her half a levar. Books and scent were the only things she ever spent money on. She wore Sinati's old boots because Thrae did not allow anybody to go barefoot in the theater.

"I'm looking for Deleon Benedicti," said the stranger. His voice was light and unemphatic, as if he were thinking of something else, or talking to himself. The low platform did not give him much advantage of height over Deleon; Liavekans were mostly short. He was neither more nor less dark than most of them; his hair was the usual black, and very badly cut. He had large brown eyes and a hopeful face.

Deleon had abandoned the name of Benedicti seven years ago, replacing it more or less at random with Bennel, a name that gossip bandied about from time to time. Anyone who knew the name of Benedicti was probably best avoided; but anyone who knew it probably knew also to look for a tall, pale, yellow-headed person. There were very few of those in Liavek, and even fewer outside the community of exiles near Old Town, where anybody would seek first. And this man knew Cook's story.

"Who sent you?" said Deleon.

He had not intended this to be an admission of his identity, but the stranger took it so, and smiled. "Your sister says she breaks things."

Deleon experienced a lurch of the heart almost comparable to that with which he greeted Calla's appearance in a room. "I have five sisters," he said.

"Which of them breaks things?"

Deleon was seized with perversity, not least because he sensed so plainly beside him Calla's alert and sympathetic interest. "My sister Marigand," he said precisely, "breaks hearts. My sister Isobel breaks rules. My sister Livia breaks heirlooms, but only when she's in a temper. My sister Jehane breaks her own heart, and would break yours if you had one, being the best of a most hideous family. Are you satisfied?"

"And your sister Nerissa?"

"My sister Nerissa," said Deleon, furiously, "when she was four years old, broke one of the five glass bowls we had managed to bring with us in our flight from Acrivain. Our mother therefore told her that she broke things, and Nerissa believed her. Are you satisfied?"

"She wonders if you are dead."

"And I've wondered if she is."

"She will do better to think you are."

"And shall I do better to think she is?"

"She will be," said the stranger. "You may rely upon it."

What a mercy he had not succumbed to the brisk blandishments of the Tiger's Eye and bought those Tichenese earrings for Calla, who would not have worn them anyway.

"How much do you want?" said Deleon, with as much coolness as he could muster.

"You misunderstand me," said the man in green, in the tone of one who has intended just this. "I am from the House of Responsible Life."

This meant nothing to Deleon, who was prepared to make a malicious joke out of it anyway. The man in green forestalled him. "We are an order of suicides."

Deleon sat down hard on the second bench, and Calla burst out laughing.

"If you all kill yourselves, where is your order?"

There was something in her voice more than mirth, behind the mockery. She sounded as she had in the discussions of singing, however much it might have appeared to Malion and Thrae that she was merely being troublesome. She wanted to know: She had a passionate and serious interest in the answer.

The stranger sat down on the edge of the stage, swinging his feet in their scuffed green boots. "There must be an order to the killing," he said to her, quite soberly. "My name is Verdialos."

"Mine is Calla," she said; Deleon admired the subtle courtesy wherewith, since he had offered no surname, she omitted hers also. "And this," said Calla, without smiling, "is Deleon." She propped one knee on the bench next to him.

"A good death to you," said Verdialos, looking straight at him.

What had Nerissa told him? "What," said Deleon, blessing Thrae's training, which kept his voice steady though his insides were like a welter of custard, "is a good death?"

"I think," said Verdialos, still regarding him steadily, "that you know that as well as I."

"Well, I don't," said Calla briskly, but still with that note of genuine inquiry. "Suppose you tell me."

"How do you regard death?" Verdialos asked her.

"As something to be avoided for as long as may be."

Deleon, relieved of Verdialos's attention, slid his eyes sideways at her. Was that true? He supposed it was true of most people; but would anybody who felt so have indulged in half of the insane things she did?

"And yet it comes as the end?" said Verdialos.

Calla shrugged. "Unless one is The Magician."

Verdialos smiled. "To most of us then. And presumably to you?"

She nodded, and a veil of her black hair slid from her shoulder and lay across Deleon's arm.

"How will you meet it, when it comes?"

"With my back turned," said Calla with finality; and Deleon, incredulous, heard her voice shake. She had made it shake just so as Mistress Oleander's maid; but except for the new-student voice and an occasional demure remark, she seldom employed her arts in private conversation. It was one of the reasons he loved her.

"What," said Verdialos, half mocking and half sorrowful; "so ignominious as that?"

"What do you suggest?" snapped Calla. So she had snapped as Ruzi, the spy and traitor in *How They Came to Eel Island*. He had never heard her do it as herself.

"I suggest," said Verdialos smoothly, "that death may be for you, or for anyone, the best event that ever you saw or heard tell of."

He reminded Deleon of Thrae, teaching Lynno and Calla her theories of playing. She had said these things before; she had said them to Deleon seven years ago and to Aelim two years before that; she would say them again; she could say them when she was too drunk to stand up; she could bring any conversation, start it never so wildly from its point, around to them again, even in her sleep: but this by no means meant that she did not believe what she said. In Verdialos's voice were the same automatic ease and the same underlying conviction.

Deleon sat listening to them, as Calla's questions grew kinder and Verdialos's answers more involved. It ought to be he, not Calla, who was conducting the other side of this discussion. Verdialos had come for him; and come, it must be, from his sister Nerissa.

Nerissa, three years younger than he, with whom he had formed a solid, enduring, and malicious alliance of two against the rest of their family, which so clearly hated them. For they were the last two, the only two born in Liavek, the two whose addition to the requirements of a large family and an even larger network of spies, informers, and less fortunate exiles, had eaten up their father's small and painstakingly acquired income out of Acrivain. Nerissa, with whom, for seven years, he had played a secret game of death. They had drifted from mere childish fantasies of accident, from the state of mind that says, "If anything happened to us, *then* they'd be sorry," to the meticulous devising of ways whereby they might kill themselves. They grew expert at weighing the merits of a painless death against the necessity of making their parents as sorry as possible. They had never found a method that pleased them well enough to be employed. And when he was twelve and Nerissa nine, Deleon had run away.

Listening to Verdialos, Deleon thought that they must be, both of them, minds after the Green priests' own hearts. Just so carefully, with just such artistic thought, did the members of this order plan their deaths. Their motives were other: not to make anybody sorry, but to make order and beauty out of the only event in their lives, said Verdialos, over which they truly had control. It appeared, in fact, that a desire to make somebody sorry was not allowed in the House of Responsible Life, any more than a desire to escape from an unhappy entanglement of feelings, or from a humiliating and irrevocable mistake, or from an ever-present and irritating responsibility. Candidates with those motives were made to wait until they had better ones.

Deleon wondered why Calla wasn't laughing. This was the sort of thing she laughed at. Even he, with the detached and logical part of his mind, could see its classic and lovely absurdity. It ought to make a splendid play, in the best Liavekan tradition. But Calla had fallen silent, her leg pressed against Deleon's shoulder and her eyes on the bench.

"So you see," said Verdialos to Deleon.

"You have my sister?" said Deleon. "She's vowed to die; the manner of her death has been laid down?"

"Yes," said Verdialos.

"Will it be soon?"

"No, not soon," said Verdialos. "She has a cat."

"A *cat!*" said Deleon.

"The responsibility one must not shirk," said Calla, with perfect seriousness, and without looking up.

Deleon, aware of a startled resentment with no discernible cause, frowned at Verdialos. "Did she ask you to find me?"

"No," said Verdialos. "But she told me of you, and after that I was obliged to discover you, if you were not dead already."

"But—"

"We see a great many parents," said Verdialos, "who think their runaway children have come to us. It seems best to us to find those children whom we do not have, that we may dispel wrath and refute the accusation that we have and are hiding them. The Acrivannish are easy to trace."

"So you've come to help me to a beautiful death?"

"If you wish."

"Would you be so obliging," said Deleon, without in the least intending to, "as to give something to Nerissa for me?"

"What is it?" said Verdialos.

Deleon turned up the hem of his smock, considered for a moment, and ripped the hidden pocket out of it. He shook from the frayed blue cloth a little book bound in virulent purple velvet—one ran out of kindly colors after the sixth child— and held it out. It was the size of his two hands, and locked with a minute brass lock.

"This is an Acrivannish custom," he said. "It's how we teach children about love. We don't speak of it. But a mother and father will keep a diary of each child's conception and birth, which they will rewrite as the fancy takes them, and give to the child on his twelfth birthday."

"You ran away on yours," said Verdialos.

"Yes," said Deleon.

"Because of what you read?"

"Yes."

"And took Nerissa's book also?"

"Having read Nerissa's book also," said Deleon, aware that Calla was now staring at him, "I thought I'd better."

"But now, you think, it cannot hurt her?"

"If she's hurt enough to join an order of suicides and plan her death, in sober earnest, as if it were her wedding," said Deleon furiously, "what more harm can be done to her?"

Calla laid a hand on his back. Through the thin cotton of his smock he could feel the warmth of each separate finger. He wondered if he would have forever over the bones of his spine the red imprint of her narrow palm. She was looking at Verdialos.

"The book is locked," said Verdialos.

"Forgive me," said Deleon, "but I think I'll send the key to her by courier."

"As you like," said Verdialos, smiling. "I suggest that you address it to Cinnamon, and take some care that it reaches him. You may remember that your other sisters were given to prying and tattling?"

"Cinnamon?" said Deleon; the resentment grew stronger.

"A Tichenese boy; your cook employs him to do errands."

Deleon fastened on the source of his discomfort. "Did Isobel marry Hanil Casalena?" he demanded.

Verdialos grinned, enlivening his whole thin, dark, unemphatic face. Calla's hand hardened on Deleon's back. "No," said Verdialos. "Some things never change."

That he understood made Deleon angrier. Verdialos reached down from the platform and took the book from him. "I'll give this to your sister," he said. "Will you warn me what to expect?"

"What concern is it of yours?"

"I am her mentor, her advisor. Might this make her wish to hasten the day of her death?"

"I think not," said Deleon. "It's always comforting, isn't it, to have been right all your life?"

"I wouldn't know," said Verdialos, a little anger, a little iron, entering his voice for the first time. He stowed the book in a pocket, and from another pocket pulled a strip of paper, which he held out to Deleon. "If you should want me," he said.

Deleon, looking him straight in his expectant brown eyes, made an astonishing discovery. "No, I don't think so," he said.

Calla leaned past him and took the paper from Verdialos's hand. "If I may," she said.

"By all means," said Verdialos. "I've enjoyed our conversation. Good day to you, mistress. Master Benedicti, good day."

"Well!" said Calla when he was gone. She sat down a few inches from Deleon, her back to the platform, and leaned over to see his face. "I wondered about your name," she said. "The Bennel never lived who'd be taller than your shoulder, and any one of them has more color in one earlobe than you have in the whole of you." She patted his knee. "They don't wear trousers, either."

When Deleon did not answer, she said, "You don't like him."

"I think," said Deleon, not thinking at all, "that I should like him better did not—" and broke off, aghast. Calla seemed unmoved; perhaps she hadn't noticed. "It's hard to hear about my family," he said.

"Did your parents hate you so?" Fortunately for his self-control, she sounded neither skeptical nor pitying, but as if she were verifying some minor statement she had not heard properly the first time it was made.

"No more than the usual, I expect," said Deleon. Without the balance of Nerissa's book, the brownish book in the other pocket pulled that side of the smock down. He was not very neat-fingered, but he could have drawn the last two pages from memory, not just the words but the very curve and scrawl of his mother's untidy writing, the only untidy work he had ever seen from her. She had made eels boiled in broth, a dish heartily hated by every other member of the family as a vile foreign mess, and despised by Cook as fit only for peasants, for his birthday dinner, and he had not stayed to eat it. Cook had never liked the custom of birthday dinners anyway. Liavekans were very odd about their birthdays. Even people who would never invest their luck, and thus never be vulnerable on each subsequent birthday while they reinvested it, often kept the date a deep secret. Eels were bad enough: eels to celebrate a birthday had made Cook, fond as she was of Deleon, suddenly stubborn, and she had taken the maid and gone home for the day. The absence of her sharp eye had enabled him to escape; that, and the fact that the smell of the stew made Nerissa, otherwise his second shadow, sick enough to tell him to go away. He had always hoped that she did not remember that that was the last thing she had said to him.

"Del?" said Calla. It was the first time she had used his nickname, the one bestowed on him by the company. The Acrivannish diminutive was Leyo, but he had never told them.

Deleon shook his head vigorously and stood up. "If I were to play this simpering fool," he said, "how ought I to deliver her three sensible speeches?"

"Three!" said Calla. "One at the most."

"Come out into the light," said Deleon, "and I'll show you three."

• • •

In the event, Deleon did not play the simpering fool. Thrae, who after all had been cajoling and confounding players for the better part of twenty years, went away on the day set for the casting, and returned triumphant not only with Sinati, but with her new magician to do the sets and backdrops. *Two Houses in Saltigos* was mercifully short on spectacle, containing no mountains, seas, deserts, fires, thunderstorms, flying furniture, talking dogs, or vanishing gods at all, but only two walking trees and a modest blizzard. These ought, Malion said to a protesting Lynno, to be within the scope of even the newest magician.

Lynno, of course, was protesting not the new magician's lack of experience, but his presence as Sinati's lover. Deleon wondered if Thrae were losing her touch. First Calla, now this. When he saw the magician, a most unprepossessing young man with a wispy moustache and the body of someone who has sat reading in the same spot since he first learned to spell camel, he understood. Lynno had been a tumbler before he became a player; and Lynno's pride was such that, upon viewing this rival, he would find his estimation of Sinati somewhat lowered. Deleon envied this faculty in Lynno: any lover of Calla's would rise in his own estimation.

The magician, whose name was Naril, was, in fact, amiable, well-read, patient, and possessed of a vivid imagination. He would probably manage their sets very nicely, and for considerably less than Thrae had been paying more experienced people in the field.

The company of the Desert Mouse therefore settled in happily enough to rehearse *Two Houses in Saltigos*. Calla, who had not in fact favored Thrae and Malion with her views of who should play whom, and had been given the part of Bremeno, the young lord who was the counterpart of Sinati's simpering fool, seemed a little absent-minded; but her work was normally so brilliant that she did well enough. Deleon, who had barely accustomed himself to being in love with her, began to experience, at unexpected moments, a desire to snap at her, and chose not to consider in detail what, if anything, she had done to irritate him.

He was playing Bremeno's servant, a part that suited him much better than that of the yellow-haired fool. Aelim was the servant of Lina, the fool in question. This meant that he and

Deleon were thrown a good deal together, running over the
scenes in which only the two of them appeared. Thrae, who
had seen far better than Calla how important their two parts
were to the proper movement of the play, asked them to practice
in private and work out between themselves a number of issues
involving the precise character of the relationship between the
two servants, what regard they had for their own employers
and for their employers' opposites, and whether they ought to
seem very much alike or quite different. Andri Terriot was a
master of ambiguous dialogue.

"This is the best chance either of you has ever had to be an
interpreter as well as a puppet," Thrae told them. Her lined
dark face with its elegant bones looked so smug that Deleon
thought Calla's guess must be right: She *was* an old friend of
Terriot's.

Which was all very well—and in fact, exhilarated both
Deleon and Aelim—but Deleon knew that his presence exacerbated Aelim's nerves just as Calla's exacerbated his own.
He kept as much room as he could between himself and Aelim,
avoiding Calla's brand of careless, affectionate gesture. Every
once in a while, he caught Aelim watching him as he knew he
himself watched Calla; but for the most part, Aelim matched
his behavior.

Nothing untoward happened, and both of them began to
look rather strained. Deleon saw very little of Calla, which did
not help matters as much as he had expected. He began to
wonder, as his store of minor memories of her grew tattered
and dim with much handling, if it would be kinder to Aelim
to give him a hand on the shoulder or a tug of the hair to cherish
from time to time. But Deleon was not demonstrative by nature,
even when he had something to demonstrate; and Aelim was
even less so. Where Deleon suffered whatever gestures of affection the company chose to bestow on him, Aelim had a way
of absenting himself from under a friendly arm, or standing
too far away to have his hair pulled in the first place. It was
probably better to leave him alone.

Rehearsals went along with far less uproar than usual—a
tribute, perhaps, to the unaccustomed excellence of the play.
They had only two major arguments.

The first, a tenday into rehearsals, had to do with the precise date of the first performance, for which the posters must be ordered from the printers in time. Thrae wished to follow their accustomed schedule and open the play thirty days from its casting. Malion quietly but repeatedly said that, because the play was longer and better than those they were used to, they should take an extra fiveday to polish it, and open instead on 27 Wine. The discussion followed its usual course, Sinati agreeing with Malion and Lynno with Sinati, while Aelim, Deleon, and Calla made some attempt to argue the matter on its actual merits and were forestalled by Thrae. She was not, oddly enough, aided by Malion, who generally took up a position opposite hers only in order to flush out those who disagreed with her and put them in their places. He seemed, this once, to be in genuine disagreement with her. It did not help him in the end, of course; but it made Deleon uneasy.

Two Houses in Saltigos would open on the twenty-second of Wine.

The second argument, which was by far the worse, took place on the twenty-first, when they gathered in Thrae's cluttered study to consider the rehearsal just completed. Sinati, scolded severely by Thrae for having produced an uneven and insufficiently polished performance of the scene in which Lina was at last brought face to face with Bremeno, flung her copy of the play down among her compatriots and, most unusual for Sinati, whose normal method of attack was winsome tears, began to shout.

"It's Calla!" she said, at the top of her well-trained lungs. "We've never been over this scene together! She's out all day, and I go home with Naril at night!"

There was a harrowing silence. Deleon, dumbstruck, saw that Aelim was staring at Calla in an astonishment at least as great as his own; that Malion looked blank, Lynno perplexed, and Thrae frankly unbelieving. Thrae might demand Sinati's talents, but she was unlikely to have any illusions about her nature.

"Calla?" she said.

Calla folded her arms across her green tunic and smiled. "I've been undergoing a course of study in the afternoons," she said. "Aelim and Deleon work in the evenings; Naril didn't object; Sinati's just lazy."

"That may be," said Thrae. "But you are negligent, if you employ your considerable energy elsewhere when we are rehearsing a play." Her soft voice bit like the touch of rain in winter. Deleon, flinching, looked away from Calla.

Calla, replying, sounded perfectly composed. "I offered to work in the mornings, if Sinati preferred it. A very little accomodation on her part would have sufficed."

"Mornings!" said Sinati, with a wealth of scorn suitable to Mistress Oleander herself. "I shouldn't think your course of study," she said, as if she were saying, "your hideous iniquities," her lovely face a mask of righteous fury, "would leave you fit in the mornings." And she turned her huge black eyes on the green glass jar of Worrynot that Malion kept on the sewing table.

Deleon, following her gaze with amusement, stared suddenly, and refrained most narrowly from clutching at the pain in his middle. The level in the jar was considerably down. He looked at Calla, who, her mouth slightly open, was regarding Sinati as someone particularly house-proud might look at the carcass of a rat in the kitchen. The Worrynot was probably Sinati's doing. But Deleon considered Calla's green tunic and the uncharacteristic turns of phrase she had just employed. "Undergoing a course of study." "A very little accomodation on her part would have sufficed." A course of study in the House of Responsible Life. Deleon remembered the feel of her hand on his back when Verdialos grinned, and thought he would be sick. He took a step backwards and was arrested by Malion's gnarled grip on his arm.

"Let it finish itself," said Malion softly.

"Sinati, let be," said Thrae, who would have let Calla run a brothel in the cellar and a private college of suicides in the attic so long as it did not interfere with her playing. "Negligence is negligence. Yours is no less reprehensible because you want to be with Naril in the evenings. Why did you not come to me sooner if you and Calla could not agree?"

Sinati's mouth drooped. Deleon, in the detached and logical part of his mind, revised his estimate of her playing ability. "You don't like tale-bearers," said Sinati.

Thrae, her fine gray hair escaping from its jeweled combs, her face stiff, her fists clenched, caught sight of the four wandering players they had hired for the minor parts staring with dropped jaw and speculative or horrified or injurious eye, and let her breath out hard. Malion freed Deleon's arm and chuckled under his breath.

Thrae said, "I will stay here, tonight, with both of you, until we have mastered this scene. The rest of you may go; it was well done."

Deleon went out and drank sweet Tichenese wine, the sort meant for sipping in small glasses, until his head swam and his pulses settled. Malion found him at daybreak, cursed him back to the theater, dosed him with something that tasted worse than the goat-milk chocolate, and put him to bed in the little room the magicians used. He dreamed of the Acrivannish spring he had never seen, and his sister Jehane, the best of a hideous family, picking the golden crocuses and taking them to her big brother Gillo, who laughed and threw them in the well.

The Desert Mouse was full. The posters announcing the play had been of the usual form: they did not boast of the playwright, since most of the playwrights whose work the Desert Mouse presented could not with truth be boasted of. But the bare name of Andri Terriot must have been enough. Aelim came behind the curtain and remarked that the proportion of shabby to splendid had altered for the better; there might even be nobility out there, and there was certainly a number of extremely rich people.

Malion's dose had worked. Deleon had a stinging headache and a feeling in his belly as if he had been hit with a rock, but these were not from the wine. He had slept all afternoon, missing his last private practice with Aelim. Aelim, who in their younger days had been known to knock him down because he stumbled at an entrance, said not a word about this far greater transgression. Deleon wondered what he knew, and how long he had known it, and, in a detached and logical way, whether it hurt him.

The play opened well. Calla played Bremeno, who had been lightly sketched in by Terriot as a serious scholar with a turn of absent-mindedness, as an intelligent and endearing fool, a man who had known the names and uses of every herb in Liavek by the age of twelve (so said Terriot), but did not understand the child's joke about the camel and the empress (so indicated Calla). Deleon, admiring this performance from his servants' spyhole, suddenly realized what she was doing. She was playing Aelim. Deleon got up and walked back of the platform three lines too soon, but was composed again for his own scene, wherein he met Aelim, the servant of Lina, in the marketplace, recognized his livery, and sounded him out.

Aelim was considering bolts of cloth turned from dusty cotton to masses of silk shot with gold by Naril's skill, holding them so that Lina's livery was hidden. He was supposed to put down the one he was holding just as Deleon passed him by, so that Deleon could glance at him, glance again, and approach him. Deleon, closer to the audience and also the focus of their attention, looked abstractedly over their heads in the manner of one who is probably about to miss the opportunity of a lifetime, and saw Verdialos on the third bench, center, intent and absorbed. Verdialos, who talked like a philosopher; Verdialos, who could help you make a beautiful and orderly death; Verdialos, to whom not only Nerissa, but Calla, had spoken at length; Verdialos, who felt responsibility for anyone who might think of killing himself.

Deleon was seized by a disastrous but enchanting impulse, and grimly acted on it. Turning a little too quickly and already hearing what Thrae would say to him about it, he caught sight of Aelim, stopped dead, and proceeded to enact someone smitten with love at first sight. He then recovered his equanimity, settled his cap more firmly on his head, and approaching, spoke, in husky and uncertain accents, the line Aelim was not expecting for perhaps ten seconds more.

Aelim stared at him for about as long as it took the laughter to die down. Then, with the generosity and the care for the theater that Deleon had relied on, Aelim played up to him, admiring in his turn, but cautious; and half relieved, half disappointed, several speeches later, to be presented with a political plot and not a romantic proposition. All their dealings with one another thereafter were laced with the silent language of one servant's courtship and the other's consideration of it, so that any ambiguous proposal on the part of one served as two proposals at once, and any acquiescence likewise. The audience enjoyed itself mightily. Aelim manifested a turn for ironic comedy that Deleon had never seen in him before. That, at least, should please Thrae.

Both of them were on platform, either the focus of a scene or spying around in the background, for the entire portion of the play from then to the interlude. During the interlude, Deleon fully expected their souls to be flayed with the merciless implement of Thrae's tongue. But Thrae had gone forward into

the audience and was talking, with every appearance of ami-
ability and serenity, to a thin, fluffy-haired man with a large
moustache. He was frowning.

"That," said Malion, inserting himself between Deleon and
Aelim as they peered out, "is Andri Terriot. When the play is
done, I shall introduce you."

And having, in his way, punished them as severely as Thrae
would have, he went out to pay his respects to the playwright
whose work they were distorting.

Deleon and Aelim went on looking at the audience. There
was no use in apologizing to Aelim and too much danger in
thanking him. Deleon wondered if Calla had noticed, and what
she thought.

"Rikiki's ears and whiskers!" said Aelim, with more force
than Deleon had ever heard him use. "Aritoli ola Silba's out
there!"

"It must be somebody's birthday," said Deleon, with automatic malice.

"It is," said Calla, passing them in a hurry with the great
feathered fan of Lina in her arms. "Thrae's. Why do you think
Malion wanted to move the opening?"

Deleon's heart battered him like a storm of hail. He wished
this were because of what Calla had said and not merely that
she had said it. He looked at Aelim.

"Terriot," said Aelim to the dusty green hanging on which
Naril had worked such changes, "and ola Silba. And we do
this."

"From what I've heard of ola Silba's preferences," said
Deleon, forgetting in his agitation to whom he was speaking,
"he should like it all the better." He added hastily, "And he's
not a consultant to any patron of *our* art, is he?"

"Who knows where his whims will take him next?" said
Aelim, who had probably heard a great deal more gossip about
Aritoli ola Silba than Deleon had. "A mere paragraph from
him, a line carelessly spoken the next time he judges a portrait,
would be enough, if he chose. He'll see that our interpretation
is not in the lines," said Aelim, "and that it damages the main
story. And he will hate it all the more." There was no reproach
in his tone; he might have been explaining the operation of the
trapdoor to a newly hired player. He looked at Deleon for the
first time. "We had better mend this, in the time we have left.

Shall I insult you, and you spurn me, while Sinati is singing?"

"We can't," said Deleon. "The time isn't enough. It would distract from the conclusion."

"More than it has already?"

"I think so. Better not to thwart the expectations we've built. Let's finish it, Aelim."

There was a protracted pause, during which Deleon looked as steadily as he could into Aelim's grave face, and the entire character of the conversation just finished took on a second and shadowy set of significances. Aelim's face darkened a little as the blood rose under his brown skin, and his forehead grew damp, and he took two steps away from Deleon and sat down, abruptly, on Mistress Oleander's discarded chair of state.

"It's all right," said Deleon. If Calla, for complex reasons of which love was not one, had offered herself to him, would he have looked so? Probably.

Aelim pressed both hands through his short black hair, finer than Calla's, and having in its depths gleams and hints of blue, not red. His voice wavered a little, like a candle in a light draft. "Del, listen to me. Sinati's entirely capable of having taken that Worrynot herself."

"I know. That isn't it."

"Deleon. This is not yourself; this is Thrae's birth luck."

"No," said Deleon. "It's Thrae's bad luck that I did this at opening; it is not luck, Thrae's or anyone's, that has made me do it."

"It would be mad," said Aelim.

"Acrilat will protect us, then."

Aelim made a violent fist and then, very softly, closed his other hand around it. His skin was the color of old wood. "Del," he said, steadily. "Calla says the Green priest is married."

"Aelim, that isn't *it.*"

"She told me to ask you about your parents."

"She doesn't know anything about my parents. Aelim, let's finish this. Let us simply do it. I am very tired," said Deleon, steadying his own voice with extreme care, "of intellectual discussions."

"Indulge me in just one more," said Aelim. "Calla says that, because your parents hated you, you are afraid of love."

"Yes, I am," said Deleon, who had only honesty to give

him, and did not intend to stint it. "But not because my parents hated me."

The ethereal notes of Malion's flute fell lightly into the breathing silence wherein they stared at one another. As he ended, they must enter.

"So," said Aelim.

"Let us go on," said Deleon, "as we have begun."

They climbed the stairs to the upper platform, whence, in their personalities as the two scheming servants, they would witness unseen the final discomfiture of their over-trusting employers. Aelim, for the first time in their long and kindly acquaintance, laid his arm around Deleon as they went. And Deleon, for the first time in his longer and less kindly acquaintance with existence, leaned into the hollow of Aelim's arm and closed his heart to the thoughtful prickings of his mind.

With Aelim's arm still around Deleon they came out onto the high platform with its carved railing, where Lynno held for them a bright but heatless torch of Naril's devising. Lynno's broad and usually placid face was charged with pleasurable curiosity, and he made at them the expression of commiseration appropriate to people who had incurred Thrae's wrath.

When Deleon was sure the audience had seen them, he drew back half a step and smiled, deliberately and dazzlingly, into Aelim's eyes, as the young daughter of Mistress Oleander had smiled at her mother's lover. Aelim, his eyes huge and his mouth grim, turned his own head aside from the audience and touched the hand nearest its devouring eyes to Deleon's hair. Their point made, they turned to lean on the railing and observe, with whatever expression or lack of it seemed best to them, the fated meeting of Lina and Bremeno.

Deleon, settling a smug film of satisfaction over a face that felt like old untended leather, watched Sinati in her golden guise and Calla, her hair tucked up in a linen cap, stand six feet apart and exchange poetic insults. Sinati recited the lines precisely, bringing her voice down hard on each stressed syllable and flinging the rhymed words at Calla as if they were stones. Calla's deeper and more flexible voice rushed over the verses, keeping only to the sense of them and letting the rhyme and rhythm stumble in her wake as best they might. Deleon was struck again by Thrae's brilliance. Neither delivery was what she taught or hoped for; but, set against one another, they

showed up, better than anything else the players might have
done, the fundamental opposition of these two temperaments.
In the pause before the comic turn of the plot, the audience
was perfectly silent.

"Terriot's pleased now," breathed Aelim in Deleon's ear.

"Stew and rot Terriot!" said Deleon, more quietly yet, but
with great venom. "This ought to have been a tragedy. Doesn't
he know it?"

"One day," said Aelim, his insouciant, cunning servant's
gaze fixed immovably on the bright head of the character that
his had betrayed, "we will make it one." And he laid his neat
dark hand over Deleon's thin pale one, on the railing carved
with Ombayan tiger-flowers and little poisonous mice. His
touch was icy.

It was the habit of the company, after they had knelt to the
audience, to climb off the platform and mingle with them. This
was the only neighborhood custom Thrae had been unable to
change after she bought the theater. Deleon did not, as a rule,
mind it much. The audience was apt to consist half of the
players' families and half of the shopkeepers he saw every day,
and therefore to be both familiar and congenial.

Tonight, however, he and Aelim slid behind the dusty green
curtain before Sinati had even stood up, and went side by side
in silence through the crooked halls of the theater.

There was usually a certain vagueness about whether any
given piece of clothing worn by a member of the company
belonged to that person or to the theater. If you were particularly
fond of any item of your own clothing, you didn't wear it to
the theater at all, lest Thrae should decide that Sinati needed
it for her next part and Sinati should then take it home and dye
it yellow. Deleon had lost his only Liavekan shirt that way,
and determined to keep to smocks thereafter. The situation had
its benefits, of course. Calla had worn the Purple priest's robe
from *Mistress Oleander* to her sister's wedding in Fruit, instead
of spending money she didn't have on a dress she would never
wear again. And Deleon had been able to take home and cherish
the black cap she had worn as Ruzi without anybody's so much
as raising an eyebrow.

It was therefore not necessary to comment when Aelim,
having stuck his head outside and ascertained that it was still
raining, left the robe he had worn this afternoon hanging on
its hook and pulled a hooded cloak on over the red livery of

Lina. Then he opened up his worn leather pouch, extracted a large iron key, and held it out on his palm to Deleon.

Deleon hoped it was not necessary to comment on that, either. He took the key and looked at Aelim.

"Penamil will let me in," said Aelim; he rented two rooms from an herbalist who kept late hours. His level and unreadable gaze reminded Deleon uncomfortably of Calla's when she had asked him if Aelim were suffering. "I wish you would think again."

"I'll do what you wish," said Deleon, managing to look him in the face, "and I will see you later."

Aelim turned and went out the door. Deleon sat down in Mistress Oleander's chair of state for about as long as it takes to pull on a pair of boots. Then he jumped up and made for the door. He had had enough of thinking.

"Well!" said Calla behind him.

Deleon turned and leaned against the cold, rough-plastered wall. Calla came beaming into the cluttered room and sailed her linen cap at the mirror that, according to Malion, made you look like a drowned man just rising to the surface of the sea. Because she was careful about such things, the cap did not knock over the bottle of clovewater that Sinati had left open on Aelim's table.

"Verdialos has asked me to tell you," she said, "that he understands that you are no longer in need of his advice or services. I must say you might have dropped a letter to him or a word to me, instead of incurring Thrae's wrath in so spectacular a—*Deleon?*"

She was so quick. He loved her for that also. She came forward, quite sober now, and from a distance of perhaps a hand's width peered at his face as though he were a plant with a disfiguring blight.

"You don't love Aelim," she said.

"Verdialos is right just the same," said Deleon.

"But I asked Aelim to tell you—"

"He told me," said Deleon. "Should I love him for that?"

"You're very well suited," said Calla, in the tone of someone preparing to argue to a standstill anybody who might choose to object.

Deleon stared at her, and his mind presented to him a collection of occurrences and suggested to him how they were related. He thought of his lack of humor and Calla's wanting

him to play a simpering fool who would sing mad Liavekan
words to a delicate Acrivannish tune. He thought of his matter-
of-fact acceptance of his sister's joining the Green priests, and
how Calla had appeared to join them herself. He thought that
she had known Aelim loved him, and must have known that
he loved her. He thought that she believed his parents had hated
him. He thought of how careful she was, in great matters and
small ones. She did not love Verdialos, and she had not meant
to kill herself. But she had hoped to make him think so. She
had endangered the success of the play to make him think so.
Had she in fact visited Verdialos at all?

And because his mind would always prick his heart with
any weapons that it had, he spoke his discovery perhaps less
kindly than she deserved. "You like to meddle," he said.

Calla took two steps backwards and slammed Bremeno's
walking stick down on Sinati's table. "It isn't meddling!" she
said. "People don't understand; they won't see; they won't
think. Not even Aelim, who notices everything. Not even you,
who sit on the back bench in your Acrivannish superiority and
mock at Liavek with every third breath as though it were a
badly written play performed by trained birds."

She stopped and suddenly burst out laughing. Deleon wondered if an excess of plotting had turned her brain. She looked
at him and pulled his hair, hard. "You don't even think that's
funny," she said in despairing tones. "You look as solemn as
a camel while I spout bombast. We should never suit. You
won't connect things; you won't consider things properly; you
aren't interested in understanding."

No, she had not meant to kill herself; but yes, she had visited
Verdialos. She had gone to Verdialos because he would connect
things, and consider things properly, and because he was interested in understanding.

"What," said Deleon, who did understand, but nevertheless
felt meddled with, "ought I to consider?"

"That you love me," said Calla, "only because you know
we shouldn't suit. You loved your parents and they gave you
hatred. Therefore—"

"Wait," said Deleon. "Wait. Let me think a moment."

He pressed his hand over his eyes, and through his steadily
worsening headache set about methodically finishing with his
former life. He had given Nerissa's book to Verdialos; he had

promised himself to someone he would never be in danger of loving in any manner that would cause him this immensity of pain. If he were now to give up his two secrets, the one seven years old, the other less than seven months, there would be nothing left, and he must hereafter find new things to occupy him. It did, also, appeal to his deficient sense of humor to give Calla these secrets as the first and last gifts of the love she disbelieved.

"Calla," he said, from under his hand, "I want to tell you something, but you must promise that you won't—"

"Meddle?" said she.

"That you won't try to arrange matters as they ought to be arranged."

There was a pause, during which Calla shifted her feet twice and sighed heavily once, and Deleon breathed the scent of Ombayan tiger-flowers and considered the way in which his headache throbbed with his heartbeats.

"You ask a great deal," Calla said.

Deleon waited. As he hoped, her curiosity proved greater than her desire for action. "I promise," she said. "Now look at me and tell me."

Deleon dropped his hand. The three creases were back in her forehead and the corner of her mouth turned down.

"I love you," said Deleon baldly, "because I see my faults remedied in you, and yours in me. I think we should suit very well, if I chose to suit with anyone at all. But I don't choose love."

"You haven't *had* love!"

"I have," said Deleon. "That is why I don't choose it now." His mother had written it in the little brownish book: that whatever she and his father might have felt about Nerissa, they loved Deleon and were distressed at his avoidance of them and his championship of that appalling sister. He had read it and run away. "My parents loved me," he said.

Calla looked exactly as Aelim had when Deleon wrote out the Acrivannish alphabet for him and he realized that it was related to the script of Ka Zhir: astounded, furiously intrigued, and painfully delighted. She demanded, "Why haven't they tried to find you, then?"

"Because the Acrivannish are very proud, revengeful, and ambitious," said Deleon, "and because they did hate Nerissa."

"Whom you loved?"

"Whom I championed," said Deleon, "as my fellow in oppression."

Thank any and every god in Liavek that she was so quick. She frowned briefly, but asked him no questions. He clenched his hand on Aelim's key. He might perhaps survive this.

"When I promised not to arrange things as they ought to be," said Calla, "did I promise not to speak to you at all about these things?"

"What you have to say," said Deleon, "say now."

"You say you don't choose love, but Aelim loves you."

"But I know it," said Deleon, "and not knowing it hurt me first. And I do not love him; and loving you hurt me second."

"That's very tidy for you," said Calla very sharply, "but what of Aelim?"

"Aelim knows," said Deleon.

"Then Aelim is a fool."

"Calla, you promised me."

"I know," said Calla. He had never seen her look so angry. "But I promise you this as well. If ever I see Aelim in the House of Responsible Life, I will break my word to you."

"Thank you," said Deleon, who was indeed tired of intellectual discussions.

"This is like one of your plays," said Calla.

"No," said Deleon. "No one will die."

"No," said Calla, "but it might be better if someone did." She seemed to listen to what she had said, in the manner of one running over a set of difficult lines. Then, once more, she laughed. Deleon jumped, and she pulled his hair again, quite gently.

"I am starting to talk like one of your plays," she said. "Let's make an end."

She walked past him and put her hand on the latch of the door.

"It's raining," said Deleon. "Take a cloak."

Calla looked around the room. "I brought a black one, but I don't see it."

"Aelim took it," said Deleon.

"He may keep it," said Calla. She scooped up a voluminous yellow wrapping that Lynno had worn in *The Castle of Pipers*, and went out.

Deleon leaned in the doorway and listened to the sound of

her feet going along Sandy Way and into the Lane of Olives, where it mingled with the tattered noise of the rain and vanished. He had a most ferocious headache and his face was hot. He put his hands up to it and they were as icy as Aelim's had been.

Like Calla, Deleon considered this for a moment, and then stood in the empty room and laughed. He had always liked best the plays about the cold places.

Rikiki and the Wizard
A S'Rian Folk Story

by Patricia C. Wrede

ONCE THERE WAS a wizard whose luck time was three days long. He was the luckiest wizard in the world, and he worked hard at his magic. He did a good business working spells for the people of Liavek. But the wizard was not satisfied.

He bought himself musty dusty books in Old Tichenese and burned sheep-fat lamps until late at night while he read them and practiced the spells they contained. Soon he had a house on Wizard's Row, and the Levar himself was buying spells from him. But the wizard was not satisfied.

He traveled to faraway places to learn their magics, then went into his cellar and invented spells of his own. He became the best wizard in the world, as well as the luckiest. People came from Ka Zhir and Tichen and even from the Farlands just to buy spells from him. The wizard became very rich and very famous. But he was still not satisfied.

"Everyone knows who I am now," he said to himself. "But in a few hundred years they will not remember me. I must find a way to make my reputation last."

Now, the wizard had a daughter of whom he was very proud. She had skin like a flower petal, and long hair that fell down to her feet, and bright black eyes that danced like the sun on the Sea of Luck. She was the most beautiful woman in seven cities, and her name was Ryvenna.

The wizard decided to call on the gods and offer his daughter in marriage to whichever one would promise to make him so rich and so famous that he would never be forgotten for as long as people lived around the Sea of Luck. "For," he thought, "not only will I be as rich and famous as anyone could desire, I will also get my Ryvenna a husband worthy of her beauty."

The wizard made his preparations and cast his spells. He worked for a week to get everything right. But the gods were angry with him, because he had never asked his daughter whether she agreed to his plan.

"Bad enough that he presumes we'd want her," grumbled Welenen the Rain-Bringer. "But giving the girl away without telling her? He acts as if she were a pet dog or a camel!" And the other gods agreed.

So when the wizard cast his spell, none of the gods would answer. He called and called, for two days and for three days, and nothing happened. Finally he resolved to try one last time. He set out the gold wire and burned the last of the special herbs and put all of his luck into the spell (and he was the luckiest wizard in the world).

Now, Rikiki had been at the meeting where all the gods agreed not to answer the wizard's summons, and he had agreed with them. But Rikiki is a blue chipmunk, and chipmunks do not have long memories. Furthermore, they are insatiably curious. When the wizard put all his effort into his last try, Rikiki couldn't resist answering, just to see what was happening. So when the smoke cleared, the wizard saw a blue chipmunk sitting before him, looking up at him with black eyes. "Nuts?" said Rikiki.

The wizard was very angry to find that the only god who had answered his summons was a blue chipmunk. But Rikiki *was* a god, so the wizard said, "Rikiki! I will give you my daughter, who is the most beautiful woman in seven cities, if you will make me as rich and famous as I desire!"

"Daughter?" said Rikiki. "What daughter? New kind of nut?"

"No! She is a woman, the most beautiful woman in seven cities, and I will give her to you if you do as I ask!"

"Oh!" said Rikiki. "Seven cities of nuts! What want?"

"No, no! My daughter, not nuts!"

"Daughter? Don't want daughter. Want nuts! Where nuts?"

But this time, the wizard had decided that Rikiki was no use to him, so he said, "North, Rikiki. North along the shore of the Sea of Luck. Lots of nuts, Rikiki!"

"Good!" said Rikiki. "Like nuts!" And he scurried out of

the wizard's house and ran north. He ran up and down the shore of the Sea of Luck, looking for the nuts the wizard had promised, but he didn't find any. He dug holes in the ground, looking for the nuts. The dirt that he threw out of the holes became the Silverspine Mountains, but Rikiki didn't find any nuts. So he went back to the wizard's house.

"No nuts north!" said Rikiki. "Where nuts?"

"I don't have any nuts!" said the wizard. "Go away!"

"Said nuts north. Didn't find nuts. Want nuts! Where look?"

"Go west, Rikiki," said the wizard. "Go a long, long way. Find nuts. And don't come back!"

"Good!" said Rikiki. "Like nuts!" And he scurried out of the wizard's house and ran west. He ran for a long, long time, but he didn't find any nuts. Finally he came to a mountain range on the other side of the plains. "No nuts here," said Rikiki, and he turned around and went back. It was midday and the sun was very hot. Rikiki let his tail droop on the ground as he ran, and it made a line in the dusty ground. The line became the Cat River. But Rikiki still didn't find any nuts. So he went to see the wizard again.

"No nuts west!" Rikiki said when he got back to the wizard's house. "Where nuts?"

"Not again!" said the wizard.

"Want nuts!" Rikiki insisted. He looked at the wizard with his black eyes.

The wizard remembered that Rikiki was a god, and he began to be a little frightened. "No nuts here, Rikiki," he said.

"Promised nuts!" said Rikiki. "Where?"

The wizard thought for a moment, then he said, "Go south, Rikiki. Go a long, long way south." He knew that south of Liavek is the Sea of Luck, and he was sure that it was deep enough and wide enough to drown a chipmunk, even if the chipmunk was a god.

Rikiki nodded and scurried off. The wizard heaved a sigh of relief and sat down to think of some other way to become rich and famous forever.

Now, the wizard's daughter Ryvenna had been listening at the door since her father started his spell-casting. She had thought Rikiki sounded nice, so she ran out to the Two-Copper Bazaar and bought some chestnuts from a street vendor. She returned just in time to hear the wizard send Rikiki south to drown in the Sea of Luck.

Quickly, Ryvenna opened up the bag of chestnuts. When Rikiki came scurrying out, she said, "Nuts, Rikiki! Here are nuts!" and held out the bag.

Rikiki stopped. "Nuts? Nuts for Rikiki?" He came over and sat in Ryvenna's lap while she fed him all the chestnuts she had brought from the Two-Copper Bazaar. When he finished, he looked up and said hopefully, "Nice nut lady! More nuts?"

"I'm sorry, Rikiki," said Ryvenna. "They're all gone."

"Oh! Fix easy," said Rikiki. He looked at the empty bag and crossed his eyes, and the bag was full again. "More nuts!" he said, and Ryvenna fed him again.

Rikiki was finishing the second bag of nuts when the wizard came out of his study. "What is he doing here?" the wizard demanded when he saw Rikiki.

"Eating nuts," said his daughter coolly. She was annoyed with him for trying to marry her to a god without asking her, and for trying to drown Rikiki. "He made the bag fill up again after it was empty."

"I don't care about nuts!" said the wizard.

Rikiki looked up. "Not like nuts?"

"Nuts aren't worth anything for people! I want gold! I want to be famous! And I want that blue chipmunk out of my house!"

"Oh!" said Rikiki. He looked cross-eyed at the bag again, then said to Ryvenna, "Dump over."

Ryvenna turned the bag upside down. A stream of gold chestnuts fell out, more chestnuts than the bag could possibly hold. They rolled all over the floor. The wizard stood staring with his mouth open.

"Gold nuts for nice nut lady!" said Rikiki happily.

The wizard closed his mouth and swallowed twice. Then he said, "What about my fame?"

"Fame?" said Rikiki. "What fame? Fame good to eat? Like nuts?"

"No, Rikiki," Ryvenna said. "Fame is having everyone know who you are. Father wants to be so famous no one will ever forget him."

"Oh!" Rikiki thought for a minute. "Not forget?"

"That's right!" said the wizard eagerly.

Rikiki sat very still, staring at the wizard, and his tail twitched. Then he said, "Not forget! All fixed."

"You have?" said the wizard, who was beginning to regret sending Rikiki to drown in the Sea of Luck.

"All done," Rikiki replied. He looked at Ryvenna. "Nuts all gone. 'Bye, nice nut lady!" And he disappeared.

"Well," said the wizard, "there's the last of my wishes; that blasted blue chipmunk is gone."

"I thought he was cute," said Ryvenna.

"Bah! He's a silly blue god who'll do anything for nuts. It was very clever of you to get some for him. Now help me pick up these gold chestnuts he made for me; we wouldn't want to lose one."

The wizard bent over and tried to pick up one of the golden chestnuts, but as soon as he touched it, it turned into a real chestnut. He threw it down and tried another, but the same thing happened. Only Ryvenna could pick up the golden chestnuts without changing them back into real ones, and the magic chestnut bag would only make more gold for her. Worse yet, the wizard discovered that whenever he touched one of his gold levars it, too, turned into a chestnut. So did his jeweled belts and bracelets. Even the food he ate turned into chestnuts as soon as he touched it.

The wizard tried to keep his affliction a secret, but it was impossible. Soon everyone was talking about what Rikiki had done to the luckiest wizard in the world. Even people who never bought spells and who had no dealings with magicians heard the story and laughed at it. So the wizard became more famous than ever, more famous, indeed, than he wanted to be. And his fame has lasted to this day, for people still tell his story.

Ryvenna was a clever woman, and she knew that magic does not last. The magic chestnut bag ran out in a year and a day, but before it did she had poured a goodly supply of gold chestnuts from it. She became a wealthy woman, and eventually fell in love with and married a sea captain who was as kind as he was handsome. And she never forgot to leave a bowl of nuts at the door for Rikiki every night as long as she lived.

Dry Well

by Nathan A. Bucklin
Lyrics by Alison Bucklin

> The caravan road to Tichen
> Has ended at Dondar's dry well,
> But throwing the dice yet again
> May lead us alive out of hell.

The tree I called home was solid against my back. The cittern sang like stringed lightning beneath my fingers. A dozen idle listeners clutched at their hats, or pulled their capes around their upper bodies. They didn't see my purposelessness, my weariness with balladeering. They saw only a slender, dark-haired minstrel boy; they felt only my music, and the wind.

> The meadows of Dondar are dry;
> The wind whistles doom to our sleep,
> And thirst whispers, "Here shall you lie,"
> But earth whispers hope from the deep.

And I, in turn, saw something unusual in the distance. Many of the nobles of Liavek walk through the park. The Eminent Pitullio walks in the park, with no guards, and little children run after him and he gives them candy. Count Dashif walks in the park, all by himself, and people stay well away from him.

I rarely saw His Scarlet Eminence, but when I did, he was accompanied by two guards, and he moved fast and silent. At any rate, like the Levar and most nobles, His Eminence never came anywhere near me when I played.

95

First toss gave us meadows of sand,
And fortune is turned into fear;
But Navar holds luck in his hand,
And hope whispers, "Water is near."

Silent and slow gather 'round,
For thirst is a catch in the breath,
And hope is a hole in the ground,
And fear whispers, "Failure is death."

He was approaching. His guards, so alike they might be twins, kept measured pace with him. Around me, heads were turning; I no longer had the full attention of my audience. Strange, that those same people who would wait months for an audience with His Scarlet Eminence would part like a river under a fording-spell when he appeared in their midst. But the line between awe and fear is a thin one indeed. As for me, I had the blackwood tree against my back, my cittern around my neck and under my fingers, my songs in my heart. I needed to fear nobody, and nothing, except my own uselessness.

The sun wheels its watch in the sky,
And waits for its carrion feed.
In chancing, perchance we may die,
But fearing to chance—die indeed.

And we are the wheel Navar spins,
And death is the risk we must take;
But whether he loses or wins,
Still luck whispers, "Life is the stake."

Strange, too, to be singing "The Dry Well of Dondar" when the Levar's Park was so richly blooming. But I play the songs that bring the most coppers. This autumn, especially, I had to think of money for shelter. Last autumn, I had spent perhaps one night a week at the inn called Mama Neldasa's, sleeping the rest of the time in a perch in this very tree and letting the coppers amass in my satchel. This autumn was only a little cooler and rainier, but two nights a week guarding against chill and damp meant that my belly growled its hunger; meant that I wore last year's tight shoes, or walked barefoot in the park and let the mud and grass give me cold after cold; meant that my cittern went without the new strings it so frequently needed, costing me a few discriminating listeners and a major part of my pride.

A pity it was that I could not teach myself to sleep outdoors on damp nights. A greater pity that the gods who controlled the weather did not pay heed to the needs of the park vagabonds. A pity that I had no higher purpose in life than being a wandering balladeer. A pity that His Scarlet Eminence was approaching me, and that my listeners were scattering without paying the last few coppers "The Dry Well of Dondar" usually brought me. But there was nothing to do but finish the song.

> The water is lost in the past,
> And time is the master of all,
> But if Navar's magic should last,
> Then time—for a moment—may fall.
>
> So luck hazards time for a throw;
> A new game, with Navar the dice,
> While water waits silent below,
> And time whispers, "You are the price."
>
> For death waits on time's other hand,
> And luck wins and loses the day,
> For Navar lies still on the sand,
> And time flows like water away.
>
> The desert will blossom again
> With water, the life Navar gave;
> And we take the road to Tichen,
> And flowers will cover his grave.

There was nobody left but His Scarlet Eminence, Iranda the tightrope dancer, and me; the two guards had stepped back half a dozen paces. Iranda is seven or eight years older than I and fair-haired; she is one of my few regular listeners. She does two shows a day about a hundred paces from my tree, and then frequently coils up her rope and comes to listen to me and sing harmonies. I have never found it fair that the folk of Liavek tip her handsomely for her art, and me stingily, and more than once I have let her buy me dinner. Right now she was standing uncertainly a ways off to my right, looking as if she didn't know whether to protect me or not.

"You have a fine touch, boy," said His Scarlet Eminence. "And a fine voice."

More than anything else, I wanted to rest that fine voice for at least ten minutes. I always put my heart into that song; it meant a lot to me. Still, I answered. "Look what you've done! You've frightened away my entire audience. Whom shall I play for until some of them return?"

"Have you ever dreamed of coming to the palace to play for the Levar?" said His Scarlet Eminence in the same tone of voice, hearty but somehow mechanical.

Iranda's jaw dropped. Unconsciously (it must have been), she took a step toward me. I knew what she was thinking: Invite me too, Your Eminence, invite me too!

"No," I said firmly. Iranda's expression turned from amazement to shock. "I do not play music for the love of nobility, and I have no desire to see the inside of the palace." He was watching me through suddenly narrowed eyes. "Actually, I have no musical ambitions at all. Once I dreamed of being a wizard."

Iranda sealed her lips; her right hand was clenching and unclenching, fist to no-fist. I could guess her thoughts: *Liramal, you witling, you're throwing away the biggest chance of your career.* But I couldn't tell her my own thoughts. I knew, because I'd tried. Did she know what it was, to have a trade but lack a purpose? Had she ever spent five years of her life knowing her talents to be ultimately pointless, no matter how great they were? Could she imagine it?

"I have had such dreams," said His Scarlet Eminence the Regent, and this time it was I who was surprised. First Priest of the Faith of the Twin Forces, Regent to the Levar of Liavek, and he had dreamed of being something else? There were ten thousand wizards, but only a few First Priests—and only one Regent. "I invest my luck every year, so it is no lie to say I am a wizard. But I have learned only a slight ability to tell the future, and that only when life and death are involved."

Interesting, finding common ground between the most powerful man in Liavek and the sixteen-year-old waif whose cittern was all that kept him from being a beggar. But I would never be even that much of a wizard, and it hurt to discuss it.

"Yes, it would be a fine life, to be a wizard and cast spells from Wizard's Row. But instead I am a musician, and I play where I choose. Perhaps that is reward enough." And perhaps the Levar would walk in her park some day, and hear me play—on my terms. Not that I really cared.

"Play me one more song," said His Scarlet Eminence impassively. "Then I will leave you." At that his guards stepped smoothly forward and flanked him.

"Here's one I wrote," I said, and played the opening chords to "The Bregas Street Baker." Then I sang:

The Bregas Street baker sells bread by the slice,
He cooks rolls in ovens and stores them on ice,
His wares aren't worth stealing; he never stands guard,
His pies are too tasteless, his cakes are too hard. . . .

After three verses His Scarlet Eminence nodded and threw me a leather coin purse. I broke rhythm just long enough to catch it, one-handed, holding down the chord with my left hand to make it sound like a dramatic sustain. "Thank you, Your Eminence," I said as I dropped the purse at my feet—it was surprisingly heavy—and resumed playing. But he simply walked away.

I wanted to buy Iranda dinner, so she and I walked toward Mama Neldasa's. Besides, a storm was coming up. Dozens of times in the past I had had no coppers at all for a room, and spent stormy nights huddled under my tree, protecting the cittern as best I could with the shelter of my body. I had no wish to repeat the experience.

On a small bench outside a cobbler's shop I sat down to count the contents of the purse. It came to a round twenty levars. Whistling in amazement, I did a fast recount. Twenty levars. Iranda stood by, watching in shared surprise.

The cobbler, a tired-looking woman of well over sixty, called out, "Closing shop! If you are customers, I give you five minutes!" She stood looking over a rack of ready-made shoes, boots, and sandals, staring at Iranda and me.

"I'll be back," I told her jauntily. I dropped the last of the coins into the purse, stood up, and took Iranda by the hand. Five minutes and a few blocks later, with soft mist just beginning to fall from the sky, we stood outside Mama Neldasa's.

Mama Neldasa's had been a second home to me for five years. Mama had watched me grow from a sturdy eleven-year-old, kicked out by the parents who had abused him from birth, through a frail, starving thirteen-year-old—she had given me half a hundred free meals that winter—to my current sixteen-year-old self, accepting everything about his lot in life save its pointlessness. I had played for her customers on Luckday nights each of these five winters, but it was more a friendly arrangement than a business one; my only pay was the coppers that customers left in my old leather hat, and frankly, except during the worst weather I would have made more money in the Levar's Park. Iranda had been here a few times, though she lodged elsewhere.

I pulled open the heavy wooden door and motioned Iranda through. Mama met us both, wearing a matronly smile. "Liramal!" she said. "And your friend. A pleasure to serve you both."

I smiled. Mama had said those words, or similar ones, to thousands of customers, yet they always sounded new and sincere. "And a pleasure it is to be here, Mama. Find us a table for two; tonight we're honest customers."

Mama seated us at a small wooden table near the rear wall. Not far to the left, the inn's famous fireplace roared warmth and camaraderie and security into the room. At the long table between us and the door, a man who sounded like a Tichenese noble argued good-naturedly with a local merchant about the cost of outfitting caravans. I thought of how much easier it would be to outfit a caravan for the trip to Dondar and refill the water bags, replenish the other provisions, at Dondar itself. But it was only idle fancy. The well at Dondar had given water for exactly one hundred years after Navar gave his life to restore it, but since then no wizard of Liavek or Tichen had been able to get anything from it but dust.

The serving boy brought us each a bowl of rich fish chowder, stepping carefully around my cittern where it leaned against the table. Iranda had one spoonful, and then spoke. "I worry about you, my young friend," she said. "Do you have any idea what you turned down today?"

"A chance I don't really want," I said. "If I have a purpose besides playing music, I should be fulfilling that purpose. If I have no such purpose, playing for the Levar won't make me feel any better."

"But, Liramal," she said, "why don't you just play for her

anyway, and put the money she gives you into clothes and cittern strings? Is there a reason?"

"Yes, there is." I put my spoon into my bowl, but left it there. "The Levar is twelve years old. She has a palace, courtiers, people waiting in line for audiences, His Scarlet Eminence to make big state decisions for her, and the admiration of the whole city. When I was twelve years old, or pretty near, I was kicked out of the house with only the clothes on my back. I almost starved before I went back to steal my father's cittern. And then I almost starved anyway, because I could just barely play it and nobody gave me coppers."

I could see Iranda just sitting there, pensive, trying to let it all soak in. "Then you could hardly be expected to speak to her with the proper deference," she finally said.

"Hardly," I said, and dug into my chowder with a will.

"Liramal," Iranda said intently, "it won't matter for a week or two—but be careful dealing with His Scarlet Eminence. He doesn't strike me as someone who changes course easily."

"Why won't it matter for a week or two? What makes you think I'll ever deal with him again?"

"He didn't get what he wanted," Iranda said. "If it's important to him, he'll be back. And Liramal, I know you don't trust anybody's judgments except your own, but I was watching when you and he were talking."

"And?"

"And it was the craziest conversation I've ever witnessed! You started out hostile. Then inside three sentences you were telling him that you wanted to be a wizard. You'd known me for two years before you told me that! I think he was doing something to make you talk—some bought-spell for loosening the tongues of prisoners or something."

"Nonsense," I said. "I often speak freely to customers. Especially ones I don't expect to see again. Why discuss it?"

Iranda was silent for a moment. When she spoke, her voice held the flatness of someone who knows she will not be believed. "He wants something of you, Liramal. He needs you for something, and he wants to find out as much as he can about you."

A purpose. "I'm not afraid," I said. "That is, I'm certainly not afraid of waking up to find myself doing His Scarlet Eminence's bidding. I just don't want to play for the Levar."

The serving boy showed up again, belatedly delivering us two cups of yhinroot tea and a loaf of Mama Neldasa's fine homemade bread. I tore off a corner of the loaf, and Iranda and I sat there for a minute or two, just letting time and our thoughts go past.

Then the storm hit.

A furious gust of wind blew the door open. Mama flung it shut again and barred it. "Nobody's going anywhere until this lifts," she shouted. "You may as well eat."

I could just barely hear her over the wind and rain. A flash of lightning seen through one of the windows cast the tables, the dishes, the tense customers into sharp relief. The thunderclap came immediately afterward. That was close! Rain pelted against the nearest wall of the inn and leaked in rapidly around the edges of windows. The serving boy and Mama rushed around the edges of the room, shuttering windows, lighting candles and lanterns, stuffing rags in the two or three worst leaks. Half-forgotten serving dishes cast eerie shadows on the tables.

Meanwhile, my chowder was getting cold. I dipped a spoon back into it. Two bites later, I remembered what Iranda and I had been discussing. "Hey, acrobat lady. Why won't it matter for a week or two what I think of His Scarlet Eminence?"

I had spoken loudly, firmly. But a sudden lull made it possible for Iranda to answer me in normal tones. "Because this week there's so much going on. It's Calornen's Stone, you know."

Calornen's Stone—I knew of it. But I rarely read the *Cat Street Crier,* or any of its competitors. Reading was a useless luxury for me; knowing the news didn't make me any richer or any happier. "What about the Stone?"

"Don't you know a song about it?" Iranda asked. "Calornen, the Wizard Levar? The stone in the circle?"

Yes, I did know the song. But with firelight flickering across the room from us, with a lantern over our table illuminating everything but the shadows of our faces, with wind and rain battering the walls the way my father had often battered me, Iranda gave me the full story.

A hundred years ago a Levar named Calornen had reigned for seven years. Liavek was thoroughly surprised when their ineffectual ruler let slip that he wore the Stone, the largest diamond ever found, on a coronet because he had invested his luck in it. Calornen became known as the Wizard Levar, though he was scarcely the first Levar to learn magic; and within a year, he was found dead in the palace, and the Stone was missing.

This much I knew; it was in the song.

But unlike "The Dry Well of Dondar," "Calornen's Song" now had a sequel. The Stone had surfaced in Ka Zhir. In a rare gesture of friendship, Prince Jeng had agreed to return it to Liavek; a small sailing ship called the *Praluna* was to carry it across the Sea of Luck, and —if no strings were attached, if no treachery were plotted—the ship's captain would hand the Stone to the Levar on Liavek's docks.

I nodded my head. It wasn't as good a story as Dondar's. But then, it wasn't finished yet.

"Those poor sailors," Iranda said. "Trying to bring their ship to port in a storm like this."

I nodded again. Then I felt a hand on my shoulder and looked up to see Mama Neldasa's fat and smiling face.

"Nobody's going anyplace," she said. "Why don't you play for us?"

So I found a spot in the middle of one wall, wiped some raindrops off my cittern, and began to play.

> The caravan road to Tichen
> Has ended at Dondar's dry well,
> But throwing the dice yet again
> May lead us alive out of hell—

The storm showed little sign of abating, so three hours later Mama led Iranda and me upstairs. I had a usual room when I slept here, little more than a closet under the eaves, with a straw pallet and a candle; but this time, she took us to a far larger room, with a double pallet on the floor, a luxurious embroidered quilt, a rack of gorgeously colored candles along a wide windowsill, and a fine painting of the Levar's palace on the wall by the door. Belatedly, I noticed a jar of Worrynot next to the leftmost candle, and felt a slow flush creeping into my cheeks. Apparently Mama had thought—she'd thought the obvious.

Iranda noticed it too. "Liramal," she said seriously, "any time you want, all you need to do is ask."

I put my hands on her shoulders, trying to keep my voice

steady. "My precious acrobat princess," I managed to say, "I don't need a woman. I need a reason for living."

Iranda shrugged and stepped out from under my hands. "You certainly seemed to have all the reasons you needed, back when you were playing downstairs. Do you have any idea just how purposeful you looked when you were playing 'The Dry Well of Dondar'?"

"It's that song," I said, sitting down on the edge of the pallet and beginning to remove my shoes. The moment was past, and I felt relieved, yet disappointed. "I identify with it, somehow."

Iranda sat down alongside me and removed her slippers. "I think I can understand liking it a lot," she said. "It's a powerful image: Navar, the caravan master, giving his life so that his caravan won't die of thirst. But I don't see what the connection is with you. Why do you identify with Navar?"

"It's not Navar I identify with."

Iranda stopped, her right slipper forgotten in her hand. "Then what in the name of the Twin Forces do you identify with?"

"It's the dry well, Iranda. I identify with the dry well."

Sooner or later, there's always a morning. This one came sooner than I'd expected; apparently I'd slipped into deep sleep in spite of myself. Still, my head had spun for a while first. I could see patterns growing and blooming; yet as fast as I could speak them out loud, they changed.

Yes, it was the dry well I identified with. No, it wasn't the dry well I *wanted* to identify with. I wanted to be like Navar, the caravan master, the wizard. But could I die, to give a hundred starving travelers water? Or would I, in Navar's place, be a well gone dry, a promise left cruelly unfulfilled?

I would never know. Navar had been a wizard and had died a wizard's death. I, who had never known my luck time, would have no such chance. I had been Liramal the minstrel, playing in the Levar's Park, for five years. Liramal the minstrel I would probably be until I died, and the knowledge brought me no joy.

My eyes opened. Sunshine poured in the window. A trickle of dampness along the sill showed that the glass was not watertight, after all. But the candles still stood in formation; the jar of Worrynot, curse it, had not toppled to the floor and broken. I smiled in spite of myself. Liavek might rock in the worst storm of the season, but Mama Neldasa's was solid as bedrock.

Iranda was already up and dressed. "Hey, balladeer boy," she said. "Are you awake?"

I reached for my tunic and trousers at the foot of the bed. "All right, acrobat woman, I'll talk. What do you want me to say?"

"Two points," she said. I pulled my tunic on over my head. "First, purpose. Second, His Scarlet Eminence."

I pulled my trousers on and threw back the quilt. "You mean you think you know what my purpose is?" I asked blankly.

"No, silly," she said. I must have looked hurt. She looked contrite and continued. "Some ideas for where to look."

I put on my shoes and stood up. The floor was steady underneath my feet, and I felt fine. I'd drunk nothing but yhinroot tea all night, but for some reason, I'd expected a hangover. "For instance?"

"There is a man," she said slowly, "called the Vavasor of Fortune Way. I know him, a little. I grew up in Old Town. You can ask him, 'What will be my fortune?' And if he's feeling at all kindly toward you, he'll tell you. If you want . . ." She left it unfinished.

"I've heard the stories," I admitted. "But Iranda, listen a second. There's a difference between a purpose and a fortune. I could know that my *purpose* was to be a wizard, with the same certainty that I know how to play an E7 chord; but unless someone were to tell me my luck time, my *fortune* would be to play the cittern until my fingers fell off."

"Or," she said firmly, "you could go to your mother with some of your new-found earnings and make her any offer you chose, if she would only tell you the day and hour of your birth."

"She would lie. I know. She's done it." I had asked, with all the innocence of nine years, and she had laughed and given me a date, in the month of Meadows; another date, in the month of Wine; another date, in the month of Fog; and a last date, in the month of Heat. And my father had called her a lying halfwitted bitch and struck her hard, so that blood dripped from her mouth and she put both her hands in front of her face. And then he struck her again and she ran out of the room whimpering and bleeding. It was the first time I had ever seen either of my parents strike anybody but me. Later, Father had said all four dates were lies, and I believed him.

"Your father?"

"May the Twin Forces be praised, he is dead." Dead without

telling me my luck time, as he willed it. Men who are bad shots should not duel.

Iranda and I went down to our breakfast, then agreed to meet by my tree in the park the hour before noon. "And just what do you plan to do with the hours of the morning?" she asked.

"Little things," I said. "I plan to get some new strings for my cittern"—Iranda looked suddenly hopeful—"and some polish for its wood." Iranda looked almost joyous. "And then I'm going to speak with the seller of used goods, and see what he thinks it's worth." Iranda's face fell again.

"Liramal, Liramal." It seemed to be all she could say. "I wish somebody could take care of you. I wish you'd let somebody. . . ."

The morning went fast. New shoes from the cobbler we'd seen the previous day; blue tunic and white cotton trousers from a small shop near the Two-Copper Bazaar; finally, new strings and polish at Whistler's Corner. I changed my strings and applied the polish sitting on a three-legged stool in the front of the music shop; then I strode on down the way to the Levar's Park.

It was a fine day for a brisk walk, though puddles and muddy patches bore witness to the previous night's storm. In two miles I saw three separate crowds gathering around three separate scandal-sheet hawkers. Big news today, I thought, and thought little else. When I reached my tree, Iranda was waiting there with a quizzical expression on her face.

"It took you long enough," she said. "Guess what? Liramal, you're not going to have to worry about His Scarlet Eminence today."

"I wasn't worried about him to begin with," I said. "But why not?"

"Calornen's Stone," she said. "It's lost. The ship that's supposed to be carrying it foundered on the Eel Island shoals."

Well, that explained the hawkers of scandal sheets. "And His Scarlet Eminence is off to Eel Island?" I guessed.

"Wherever he is," Iranda said, "he's got a lot more on his mind than one street minstrel who won't play for the Levar."

I glanced toward the sun. It was midday. "Iranda? Shouldn't you be doing your noontime show?"

Iranda looked guiltily at the rope that hung from a hook at her belt. "I should be, perhaps. But I wanted to watch you play today, if it might be for the last time."

She presumed a lot; I had seriously planned on not playing today at all. But I had put on the new strings. "So shall it be, then." I unslung the cittern, tuned it up, and began to play.

There were half a dozen people in earshot as I began with "Pot-Boil Blues." Iranda sang harmony where she knew the words, hummed along where she didn't, and seemed completely caught up in the music. By the end of the song, there were about eight people standing around. I finished, let my cittern hang by its strap, and flung my hat dramatically to the ground. Obligingly, several onlookers tossed in coppers. I bowed.

Then, "The Kil Island Fisheries." "Pell and Onzedi." "Eel Island Shoals," which seemed to earn a disproportionate amount of applause this time, and I understood why. My three-song medley of caravan songs. (Though "The Dry Well of Dondar" was, in fact, a caravan song, I never sang it as part of the medley; it was too special to me.) "Song of the Herdsmen." By this time I had a substantial crowd, and my hat was half-full of coppers and an occasional larger coin. About ten feet away to my right, Iranda listened in a trance.

I was giving my heart to "The Bregas Street Baker" and was only dimly aware of three figures approaching to the rear of my crowd. But suddenly people were moving as though to make way for a noble in a litter. I didn't see any noble in a litter, I only saw—oh. One woman reached to touch his robe, then turned suddenly and ran. I understood her feelings perfectly.

"Minstrel boy," His Scarlet Eminence said when I had quite finished. "I have an errand for you."

"Is this wizardry or is it statecraft?" I returned. I was annoyed; "The Bregas Street Baker" had brought me not a single copper. In fact, there was nobody in earshot any longer except His Scarlet Eminence, his twin guards, and a somewhat frightened-looking Iranda.

"It is an errand," he said.

Iranda was mouthing words at me. I could read lips fairly well, and I understood what she was saying: "Be careful."

Still. . . . "I had planned to play here all day," I said. "But plans can be changed."

His Scarlet Eminence tossed me a leather coin purse, the twin of the one he had given me the day before. I caught it, one-handed, with a catch that was a twin of the previous day's catch, and looked at him, waiting.

"By accepting my wage," said His Eminence, "you have agreed to accept my employment."

"Tell me about it," I said. Suddenly I was trying very hard not to tremble. "Just what have I agreed to do?"

"You will go to Eel Island," he said. "There you will find Zhir divers and magicians trying to retrieve, or pretending to try to retrieve, the Stone from the floor of the harbor. I want you to watch, and write a humorous ballad about it."

I let my breath out all at once. (Interestingly, I'd had no idea I'd been holding it.) "Oh. But, Your Eminence, I have written few ballads. Mostly I just play."

"You are the person I want," said His Scarlet Eminence impassively. "Write a ballad that makes the Zhir look like fools. It will not take you long."

I pondered for a moment. "If someone asks me my purpose in traveling to Eel Island," I said, "do I tell them I plan on writing a humorous ballad for His Scarlet Eminence?"

"Your stated purpose will be to play for the poor folk on the island itself." His face was completely expressionless. "And you will indeed play for the poor folk; but you will watch the divers, and you will listen to everything that is said. You will spend the day there, and you will make a song of what you learn."

So, again, my purpose was to be a musician—or so it was said. But in five years of playing, I'd never really believed that. "Sorry, Your Eminence. I'm going to lean against my tree and play all day, and that's all I want to do."

Suddenly he was standing very near me, well away from his guards, staring me in the eye. "Listen to me. This is a matter of life and death. I have given you money far beyond what you need for traveling, far more than you would earn playing here in one day. I have asked in return that you do only one thing for me. I am not a patient man. *You will do this!*"

"Well—all right, Your Eminence. Certainly, Your Eminence."

"Good," he said, taking a step backward. He appeared relieved, and I was startled to see such a human emotion on his face. "You will leave immediately."

"May I accompany him?" asked Iranda, from somewhere to my rear. Her voice quavered just a bit.

"What you do does not matter," said His Scarlet Eminence, and turned to go. The leather coin purse was at my feet; I had no recollection of dropping it.

The trip to Eel Island was a matter of life and death.

I had known for several days, somehow, that my life as a musician was drawing to an end.

Iranda was worried for me.

And I, an arrogant, insolent street child, had crossed His Scarlet Eminence just yesterday.

The conclusion was simple: Before the end of the day, I was going to die.

I sat, miserable, on the bench in front of the cobbler's. Iranda paced the street in front of me while annoyed pedestrians detoured around us both. The cobbler was nowhere in sight. Distant dark clouds seemed to be blowing in our direction.

"You young fool," said Iranda vehemently, "he said it was a matter of life and death. He never once said that it was a matter of *your* life and death."

"So maybe I'm supposed to save somebody's life," I said. "Do you think that's any better?"

"Oh, for Rikiki's sake," she said. She stopped, but her fists were clenched, white-knuckled, at her sides.

"In 'The Dry Well of Dondar,'" I finally said, "Navar has the job of saving the lives of all who ride with his caravan. He saves them, yes. But the song always ends with Navar lying still on the sand. Sometimes there's no other way."

"Maybe," she said hopefully, "you don't have to do anything special. Just write the ballad."

"So I'm supposed to write a ballad that can save a life," I said hotly. "What next? A chorus that will move the mountains of the Silverspine? A tune that will stop storms in their footsteps?"

"Write it," Iranda almost shouted, "and come back singing it! That's all he asked!"

"Come back singing it? Come back to where? His Scarlet Eminence didn't tell me where or when I was supposed to meet him. He doesn't even know my name. Iranda, he doesn't expect me to come back!"

I could see the effort of will Iranda was making. She took three deep, slow breaths; her fists unclenched. "What I meant," she said, "was that it's better by far if you do what His Scarlet

Eminence says, than if you run and hide. Besides, you already took his money."

I couldn't stay upset with Iranda. In fact, I couldn't remember ever previously being upset with her at all. "Acrobat princess, I'll admit that perhaps I'm frightened of shadows. And I've already spent much of what he paid me yesterday. Very well. I'll go to Eel Island. But can you understand that I may indeed be going into danger, and not punish me for my fears?"

Iranda nodded. "Pick up your coin purse," she said finally. "I think we should go say goodbye to Mama Neldasa."

Mama wasn't in, so I left a two-levar piece to cover what I owed her. Then Iranda and I hopped into a footcab and told the burly young woman between the shafts to take us to the docks.

The dock area was less busy than usual; still, schooners, galleasses, and the smaller yawls and ketches made a colorful clutter around the ends of the docks. Here a young man hawked garlands of flowers, bedraggled but bright from yesterday's rain; there a Zhir sailor caulked leaks in a small boat up on sawhorses; across the street to my left, I heard a voice yelling the availability of the *Cat Street Crier*.

"I think I'd better get one of those," I said to Iranda. "The more I know about what's happening today, the better."

Iranda nodded. Clearly deep in thought, she'd been poor company since before we'd arrived at Mama Neldasa's. I knew some of what was going through her head: If I was in danger, she would protect me. If I were to save a life, she would assist me. If I needed time alone to write a ballad, she would fend off anybody who might distract me. Unfortunately, neither of us had any idea what was going to happen, and so Iranda could do nothing.

I walked over to where a small, wiry woman was selling scandal sheets, bought one, and walked back. When I returned, Iranda was deeply engrossed in conversation with a grizzled old sea-hound.

"He's been running people out to Eel Island," she said to me. "He takes them out, lets them watch the operation, and brings them back for a flat half-levar fee."

"My boat is safe, clean, and spacious," the sea-hound began. I shut him up by handing him a levar on the spot.

"My friend is going to play for the Eel Island fisherfolk," Iranda said, an explanation that explained nothing. "And maybe for the Zhir divers and sorcerers. Do you think they'd like that?"

"They don't have time for that," muttered the man of the sea. "They're having a bad day, they are. We leave in five minutes."

Just like that, we had our ride to Eel Island. I didn't even take time to kick myself for not dickering. Our co-passengers were four nobles named ola Randiza, just a rich family out seeing sights. I smiled grimly to myself. Maybe one of theirs was the life I was supposed to save. Then, horrified, I felt bitter tears come to my eyes.

Life and death. Life and death. Life and—

We settled onto our benches below decks. The captain gave us his name and that of the boat (I forgot both instantly), told us that we would be half an hour in the traveling, and said with a smile that the bumper-spell on the bow would keep us from colliding with all but the most determined rocks. Hearing this, I felt foolish for a second. The ola Randizas were in no danger. Besides, nobody knew the harbor waters like a small-boat pilot.

But somebody's life and death depended on my trip to Eel Island, and the burden hung heavy over my head.

We'd been on our way not more than five minutes when the old woman who seemed to be the senior ola Randiza asked for a song. I strummed a D chord, cleared my throat, and began "Eel Island Shoals," hoping Iranda would come in on the harmonies. And she did, but her voice was a little shaky, and her timing was off.

If Iranda was convinced that my life wasn't in danger, my life wasn't in danger. But I wasn't going to let her tell me she wasn't worried.

The ola Randizas applauded politely and began to play a game of tatters. That left me free to read the *Cat Street Crier*. Ah, there it was: "Talks between His Scarlet Eminence and the Zhir ambassador to Liavek, Velt, son of Famar, have been halted. Calornen's Stone, still believed to be in a safe aboard the *Praluna*, is ten fathoms deep in water off Eel Island. Velt insists that a sorcerer must be hired by Liavek to raise the *Praluna*. His Scarlet Eminence has said that if the Zhir ever had the Stone and plan no treachery—both of which are in doubt—the Zhir must hire the sorcerer themselves, the better to keep their promise of returning the Stone.

"Meanwhile, attempts at raising the Stone are being performed by the crew of the *Praluna*, most of whom are being quartered on Eel Island for the time being. Your correspondent watches these attempts with interest.

"In the Levar's Council today—"

Then the boat hit a wooden piling with a thud and a scrape, and I realized we had arrived at Eel Island.

My first thought upon sticking my head above decks was that I'd never seen such a rickety dock in my life. Then I took a good look at the island itself and realized it was even worse.

A huge barren expanse of what seemed to be mud mixed with gravel stretched backwards from the dock to the horizon. On the shore side, a motley collection of shacks cluttered up the view. Poor folk indeed must be those who lived in those decrepit wooden buildings! Dirty children played on the beach near the dock. If I'd been a Zhir off the *Praluna*, I'd have let myself drown rather than swim to such a desolate harbor.

Then I climbed a rope ladder to the walkway of the dock and took a better look. Here, a proud new porch stretched forward from a building at least a hundred years older; there, light blue trim marked another building's windows; and—yes—behind another building there was one lone olive tree, recently transplanted, by the look of the ground around it. Maybe my ballad could start with a verse about good fishing, and how the Eel Islanders were spending their new-found wealth.

Iranda climbed the rope ladder and stood alongside me. I smiled. Then something crossed my mind and I clutched at her arm in sudden panic. "Iranda? My being here is a matter of life and death. How do you know I'm not supposed to kill somebody?"

Her eyebrows lowered. "That doesn't seem likely."

"It's His Scarlet Eminence we're talking about! How do I know if it's likely or not?"

Suddenly Iranda had one arm around me and was pulling me toward her. My cittern hung in the way of her other arm. Still, all of a sudden I felt very thoroughly hugged. "I know you're frightened," she whispered. Then she let go, and was suddenly all business. "Come on," she said. "Let's go watch the salvage operation."

We walked to the beach and looked around. What salvage operation? All I saw were two filthy children rolling dice at my feet; three sailors of the Levar's Navy walking erratic beats to my right; an anxious-looking woman with an arm in a sling, staring at the horizon; and, a ways out to sea, a large rowboat with a line over the side. Maybe that was the salvage operation, and maybe not.

The ola Randizas wandered off to the left, where most of the shacks seemed to be. Iranda touched me on the wrist briefly and strolled after them; maybe they knew something we didn't. I was betting on the rowboat, myself. Waves splashed on gravel at my feet as I walked toward the navy guards.

The oldest and tallest one noticed me. "Ho, sailor," I said with a jauntiness I didn't really feel. "May I go out there and play for the Zhir divers?"

"Leave them alone," said the sailor gruffly. The other two stopped their pacing and looked at me curiously. "They have enough problems."

"Beg pardon, Enkis," said another. "Admiral Tinthe said to make sure nobody kept the Zhir from working. He didn't say anything about entertainment."

"There isn't room on that boat for you," said Enkis uncertainly. "Besides, how would you get out there?"

"Maybe I'll just wait right here until they come in for a break," I said. "Meanwhile, it won't hurt anybody if I practice, will it?" I swiveled my cittern around to proper playing position.

> I sing of Calornen, the wizard Levar,
> Sing Tazli, Tenzli, Ozle, and Ben,
> Of history, mystery, near days and far
> And the stone in the circle will not come again—

"Aaaah," snarled Enkis, making an abrupt hand gesture. I stopped playing. "They were singing that all last night. Go on through and talk to the magician. She needs some cheering up."

Magician—oh, the woman with the sling. It had to be. I nodded, thanked Enkis, and walked on past.

She was standing on a little spit of land and staring out at the boat, looking like a mad goddess of the wind. I guessed her age at anywhere from thirty to fifty. I walked toward her, feeling a little shy, not knowing if she even spoke my language. "Excuse me," I said, "but could you use a little music?"

She turned to look at me, and her face showed utter exhaustion. "Companionship, maybe," she said with only a trace of Zhir accent. "Diversion. Anything to ease the waiting."

"What exactly is going on here?" That's right: Get information. And then turn it into a ballad for His Scarlet Eminence. Oh, but I was a sly one! At least she was willing to speak to me.

"There are two wizards," she said, "and we are taking turns." She gestured with her good arm at the rowboat. "Sestin has practice with the usual spell for divers," she said. "Sometimes he casts the spell that binds air to a diver's head, and sends the diver down to scrub barnacles off the hull of the ship. Once we lost a man overboard, and Sestin dived in after him, finally binding air to his head in time to keep him from drowning. But then we had Thung's own time getting the two of them back on the ship." She chuckled, but it didn't sound mirthful. "Sestin casts spells quickly, but they are not very powerful."

Was there a ballad hiding in there? *Sestin the spellcaster binds luck to air, gives life to divers to use as they dare....* There were times I was impressed with my own skill with words and music, but this was not one of them.

She continued, "Sestin has been casting the spells as well as he can, while one of our young sailors goes down the rope in search of the *Praluna*. Every time so far, the sailor has been down only a few minutes before the pressure at that depth collapses Sestin's spell, and we have to pull the sailor up as fast as we dare to keep him from drowning." She blinked, and I realized that her eyes were wet with tears. "I don't know why Liavek won't help," she went on unhappily. "We meant only friendship."

I'd been told that my coming to Eel Island meant life and death. But I didn't see any matters of life and death. All I saw was one exhausted woman, miserable because her people had tried to make a peace offering and had been scorned. How long had it been since she'd slept? (And what business did I have holding her up to ridicule in a humorous ballad?)

"Tell me about your magic," I said. "Do your spells work the same as Sestin's?"

"One is quite similar," she acknowledged. "But most are very different. I know a pathfinder-spell." I must have looked blank. "If I know enough about an object, I can cast a spell that will locate it. In Ka Zhir, I found Calornen's Stone, cast in the base of a brass statue. And you've seen the fording-spell used on rivers?"

Actually, I hadn't, but I knew it existed. She sighed and kept on with her speech. "Or the spell for pushing back underbrush in dense forests, or the spell for parting a crowd so an old or sick magician can get through. They are all the same. The pathfinder-spell to show us where the ship is located, and then the fording-spell to part the waters. I work my two spells. Then Sestin works his. Then I work mine again, and so it continues."

So this was a wizard, and this was spellcraft. Two tired amateur magicians casting spells that didn't work, over and over again, keeping on because there was nothing else to do. "But the sea collapses your fording-spell before it can reach the ship?"

"Exactly," she said forlornly. "It is a more powerful spell than Sestin's; but the Sea of Luck is more powerful than both of us together." She shaded her eyes. "Sestin's waving—it's my turn."

I looked over the sea. It spread, green and uneasy, out to the horizon. Whitecaps rolled in and broke on the shore. Near the rowboat, I could just barely see sunlight reflecting off a partially submerged rock, probably the rock that had sunk the *Praluna*. Yes, I could believe the sea to be powerful.

But all my life I had believed sorcery to be a powerful thing. I had dreamed of being a wizard. Yet here was one wizard—and out on the boat, there was a second—reduced to helplessness in the face of something as natural, as everyday, as the sea.

It's a matter of life and death, Liramal. Life and death.

Then she smiled, or tried to. "I do not mean to bore you with my troubles, minstrel boy," she said, and I could tell she meant it. "Play me a song."

"Gladly. And—could I watch you cast a spell?"

"Magic is not for show," she said. Then she smiled again. "But we shall see. Play for me."

Reflexively, I turned to look for Iranda; a harmony singer could add a lot. She was in sight, arguing with the three sailors standing guard. I could stop talking with the sorceress and go add my voice to Iranda's, trying to get them to let her pass. Or I could play a song.

I could sing better than I could argue. I broke into "The Dry Well of Dondar."

> The caravan road to Tichen
> Has ended at Dondar's dry well,
> But throwing the dice yet again
> May lead us alive out of hell.

My cittern felt alive under my grasp. I could practically feel Dondar's dry well appearing off to my right:

> The meadows of Dondar are dry;
> The wind whistles doom to our sleep,
> And thirst whispers, "Here shall you lie,"
> But earth whispers hope from the deep.

I saw a whirlpool.

It was about twenty feet out in the water, and it was spinning as though someone had poked a hole in the bottom of the ocean. Seaweed and driftwood were pulled toward it. Above it, the air was suddenly hazy.

> First toss gave us meadows of sand,
> And fortune is turned into fear;
> But Navar holds luck in his hand,
> And hope whispers "Water is near."

Suddenly there was no whirlpool. I was staring down, down a dizzying cliffside. Rocks and dried seaweed were visible just for a second; then those were gone, too, and I was staring at bare seabottom. Where the whirlpool had been, a waterfall shot upward, magically upward, to the sky.

Off at my left, my intended audience, the Zhir magician, was staring intently at nothing in particular; her one good hand was moving in a rigid pattern, and her mouth was moving in patterns that bore no resemblance to the ones I was singing. She was praying—no, she was working magic!

Instinctively I drew back. I did not understand what was taking place here, but I knew it was beyond my control.

And besides, all I had to do was take a few steps forward and I'd fall to my death.

Silent and slow gather 'round,
For thirst is a catch in the breath,
And hope is a hole in the ground,
And fear whispers, "Failure is death."

Silent and slow gather 'round—they were doing it. A crowd
was gathering at my right: Iranda, Enkis and the other two
sailors, the ola Randizas, the boat skipper.

For thirst is a catch in the breath—it is the curse of some
singers to feel each word of the songs they sing. Thirsty I was;
I felt the dry mouth of the honestly terrified. Yet I could not
stop to take a drink. The magician's gestures seemed to weave
my song into the whirling water and neither it nor I could
pause.

Once I had met a woman who climbed mountains in the
Silverspine; she had told of deciding she had climbed enough
for a lifetime. Unfortunately, she'd been halfway up a rock
wall when she decided that; she'd had to reverse her decision,
either to climb up or to climb down. Like her, I was trapped—
in the middle of a song.

And hope is a hole in the ground. . . . Or is hope a hole in
the water? I saw plenty of hole. The ground dropped off rapidly
here; deep sea, reef, shoals, and Eel Island itself seemed to
mix in no apparent pattern. The hole was doing nothing but
feeding water to the sky, and showing off the mysteries of the
ocean floor. But— *Glory to the Twin Forces, if the hole gets
big enough, we can walk to the* Praluna *and take the Stone!*

Not only could we do that—if we could get a team of
boatwrights out from Liavek, we could probably salvage the
whole evil-damned ship.

And fear whispers, "Failure is death." Failure at what? I
could feel forces around me so overwhelming that I was dwarfed
by comparison. And I knew that, if I had never played "The
Dry Well of Dondar," those forces would never have been
summoned. So I would simply have to keep playing my song,
contributing to those forces as best I could.

Except—what was I contributing? I wasn't a wizard!

The waterfall was a thick pillar of water now, pointing
straight up into the sky. Yet it didn't seem to go up forever;
somewhere, a hundred man-heights up, it simply ended. Water

was going up into the sky and vanishing—but where was it going?

> The water is lost in the past,
> And time is the master of all,
> But if Navar's magic should last,
> Then time—for a moment—may fall.

Light white stuff began to fall from the sky. I had seen snow once, but it had not looked like this. I let a chord hold for one beat to lick a white patch on my right arm. Salt.

The water was lost in the past—the well at Dondar had given water for one hundred years. And suddenly, I knew where the water had come from. But how much water would the Eel Island shoals have to sacrifice, to give Dondar water for a hundred years?

> So luck hazards time for a throw;
> A new game, with Navar the dice,
> While water waits silent below,
> And time whispers, "You are the price."

His Scarlet Eminence had been right after all. This was a matter of life and death. I knew whose death was involved, too: Navar's.

So I'd come on my mission of life-and-death importance. And by being here, by playing the song I was most likely to play, I had guaranteed that death would take place on schedule. Now, to escape with my own life. And once that was assured, I could go back to searching for my true purpose.

But I had a purpose! I was playing "The Dry Well of Dondar," while magical forces cascaded around me, while water shot into the sky and the past to save the lives of Navar's caravan, while ill-equipped but willing Zhir divers followed a ship's hawser to the captain's safe. . . .

While His Scarlet Eminence waited for me to write a ballad. Well, he might get one, and he might not.

> For death waits on time's other hand,
> And luck wins and loses the day,
> For Navar lies still on the sand,
> And time flows like water away.

I looked out past the waterfall. The Zhir rowboat, beached on a sizable rock, was effectively stranded. Below, at the end of a line that seemed to go on forever, a man in a loincloth stepped gingerly across what had been seabottom, but was now desert. Before him, a small sailing ship, badly holed near the bow, rested at a slight list. The Stone was within reach. And I was going to live.

> The desert will blossom again
> With water, the life Navar gave;
> And we take the road to Tichen,
> And flowers will cover his grave.

And if ever I took the road to Tichen, I would certainly put flowers on Navar's grave. Meanwhile, water was shooting toward the sky in a sheet that seemed to go on forever. Iranda was standing close to me now, near my right elbow; she was watching in amazement. The crowd around us was several dozen strong. The men, women, and children who were the Eel Island fisherfolk, some tired-looking men who had to be Zhir off the *Praluna*, were all watching intently. The Zhir magician, incantations done, was yelling at me, but the sound of the upward-bound waterfall drowned her voice. I put a nice neat ending on the song and listened with all my strength.

"Help me stop it! Minstrel, *help me stop it!*"

The water was no longer disappearing into the air. It was heading toward the sky and becoming storm clouds. Suddenly, the sky was black, as it might have been for yesterday's storm, and it was raining. I felt a sudden flash of panic.

"Play it backwards, minstrel! Play it backwards!"

The rain was falling like no rain I'd ever seen. Lightning flashed, illuminating Liavek like a distant painting. Thunder cracked so loudly I wasn't sure I could hear my cittern. I played it anyway. A minor, E7, D minor—

"Backwards! Please!"

A minor, D minor, D, G, C, A minor—

The storm hadn't stopped, but suddenly the water wasn't shooting up around me any more. I took one sopping step toward Iranda, thinking that she and I together should go looking for shelter. Except all of a sudden she was in my arms, and for at least a minute I didn't think about the rain very much.

Somehow, we wound up in the shack of an obliging fisherman, squeezed in with the Zhir magician and a burly Zhir in his forties who introduced himself as Velt, son of Famar, the Zhir ambassador to Liavek. The fisherman and his wife found us cane-backed chairs and mugs for tea, and we sat and sipped.

"I never thought I could do that," said the magician. She leaned back, looking at me. "Minstrel, do you have any idea what you did?"

"Something magical, I think," I said, still dazed. "Except I don't have any magic."

"No," she said, "not something magical." Rain battered the roof and the fire flickered; I watched her intently. "You just played. And that was enough."

"I played," I said, wondering. I certainly had! I'd never felt so musical, so—I had to say it—purposeful, as I had playing "The Dry Well of Dondar." "But what difference did it make?"

"You told me what to do with the water," she said seriously. "That's the one problem with working spells on the sea, you know. It fights back. It doesn't have luck, the way you and I do, but it has power. The only way you have of fighting it is to find somewhere else for the water to go. Like into the past."

"Or into the sky," Iranda added.

"The sky was an accident," admitted the Zhir magician with a laugh. For just an instant she looked ten years younger. "I was trying to send water to Dondar for Navar and his caravan. Dondar is at least eight hundred feet above sea level, but it was so incredibly thirsty that I managed to send the water there anyway. Then it wasn't thirsty any more, and there was no place for the water to go. I didn't know how to stop it."

"So I played," I said slowly, "and then I played backwards. And that was enough for you to work the spell."

"You played well," the magician corrected. "If you hadn't been playing marvelous music, I never could have focused my luck the way I did." Thunder rolled, accenting her words. "Have you noticed how some spells use verse? Or that some of the best magicians seem almost as if they're dancing while they're casting spells? Art intensifies magic. It certainly makes it a lot easier for an indifferent wizard like me to focus her energy."

"I don't really understand what you did, Liramal," said Velt. His voice was guttural, raspy, thickly accented. "But it seems to me that you and the Lady Rakil together"—he gestured toward the Zhir magician—"might be able to keep the sea divided while we send a couple of boatwrights out to work on the *Praluna*. And then, once we've raised her, you'd be eligible for a large reward."

The Zhir woman laughed. "Not soon, Excellency. I'm as drained as that dry well must have been." She smiled at me. "Whether you can get more work out of Liramal is up to him."

Iranda reached out and squeezed my arm. I was beginning to feel a warm glow, and I didn't think it was the tea.

"And to think," I said reflectively, "I wanted to be a wizard. I guess I still do. But—playing 'The Dry Well of Dondar' with the storm brewing all around me—even as scared as I was, I wouldn't trade that memory for anything."

"You wanted to be a wizard?" said the magician, eyes wide. "I wanted to be a musician! I studied hammered-harp, baghorn, fiddle, and hand-drums. But I had no ear and no rhythm. I finally invested my luck when I realized I had no talent for anything else."

"You wanted to be a musician," I said in helpless amazement. Then, suddenly, I began to laugh, quietly at first, then letting it build up like water pouring over falls. After a few seconds Iranda and the magician joined in.

The Zhir diver showed up at the door just then, drenched in rain water. He bowed to us all and from the waist of his loincloth pulled the biggest diamond I'd ever seen, handing it to Velt. He said a few words in Zhir; probably, "All yours, Excellency," or something like that. Then, to me, in an atrociously accented tongue, "Do you have any friends from Ka Zhir?"

"No," I said. Except for Iranda, I didn't have any friends at all. I looked at him, puzzled.

"You do now," said the diver, and clapped me on the shoulder. I watched him open-mouthed as he disappeared back into the rain.

Iranda and I spent the night snuggled up by the fire, wrapped in the fisherman's best quilt. When morning came, we bade a quiet goodbye to Velt, stepped over the sleeping magician, and tramped through mud and puddles to the dock. Half an hour's wait brought the return of the vessel that had brought us to Eel Island; another half hour brought us back to the Liavek waterfront.

We climbed a wooden ladder to a different dock, long and solid. "Well, Liramal," Iranda said, "do you feel any more purposeful than you did yesterday?"

I pulled myself up, stood on splintery wood planks. I couldn't tell if she was teasing me or not. "Maybe. I guess I just wasn't ready to believe that my purpose was to keep on doing what I was doing already."

She nodded. "When you sing a song, you make it matter, to everyone who hears it. Maybe it just took something really drastic to get you to realize that your music matters to you, too."

We walked up the dock toward the shore, side by side. "So it was Navar's death His Scarlet Eminence was talking about?" Iranda said. "And why did he want you to write a ballad?"

"He said he wanted one that made fun of the Zhir," I said, confused. We were almost to the shore. I wanted to stop and look around, breathe the salt air, see the sights of home: the gaily painted warehouses, the Mug and Anchor, the money-changer's brick house, the camels and pedestrians.

"Ah," Iranda nodded. "If they succeeded, and returned Calornen's Stone, Ka Zhir would have gotten a lot of sympathy from Liavek's neighbors. I guess His Eminence wanted to undercut that."

"But why me?"

"At least," she said, "it's not because he wanted you dead."

"No," I agreed, "not me." Then it hit me like a toppling statue. "Navar!" I said. "May the Twin Forces preserve me, Iranda—I killed Navar!"

Her arms were around me again, warm and strong, and I held her close and shook. My cheeks were wet. "No, Liramal," she said softly. "Navar's dead anyway. He's been dead four hundred years. He was dead before you even learned to play his song."

I had to stop and think about that one. While I was thinking, Iranda continued, "If Navar had cast his spell, and the Zhir sorceress hadn't sent the water in response to his call—if you hadn't helped her—he would have died anyway, and for nothing. The dry well at Dondar would have stayed dry. You saved the caravan, you and Lady Rakil and Navar."

Still thinking, I let go. Iranda smiled at me. Then a footcab approached, so near us it would have been silly not to hail it. Iranda listened in surprise as I told the driver to take us to the Levar's Park.

"I thought you'd go to the palace," she said as we rode

smoothly up Park Boulevard. "His Scarlet Eminence will want to hear about yesterday's events."

"If one of his agents hasn't already told him," I said. "But do you think I'd be let into the palace, dressed as I am?"

Iranda looked me up and down. My blue tunic and white cotton trousers, new two days before, were wrinkled and stained. I continued, "Besides, if His Scarlet Eminence wants to talk to me, don't you think he'll come look for me in the park?"

"Sooner or later," Iranda admitted. "All right; the park it is."

Life and death. His Scarlet Eminence. What did he want?

I tipped the driver handsomely and we got out. I had walked a bare ten paces into the park when I stopped cold.

The tree I called home lay split and shattered on the ground. Black burn marks on the stump bore witness to the flash of lightning that had toppled it. The space where I usually stood while performing was buried under the butt of the trunk.

Iranda said, "He got you out of the park just in time. He saved your life."

I didn't answer. Instead I took her hand and looked at the ruins of the disaster I'd escaped, wondering what sort of world it is when the fate of Liavek is dependent on such a man as that.

Choice of the Black Goddess

by Gene Wolfe

TEV NOEN LAY in his bunk, listening to Ler Oeuni's screams. Something was wrong, he was under some spell. No, it was Oeuni who was under the spell—the spell cast by the surgeon who was taking away Oeuni's right hand. Oeuni was watching the saw blade, her face calm, her eyes screaming, following the saw back and forth, back and forth. How was it, then, that he could hear her screaming eyes? How was it Oeuni never wept?

The surgeon said, "This might have been saved by a spell of healing; healing of a spell might have saved this," and Oeuni screamed again.

"Too far gone. Can't make something too far gone."

The final word ended with a thump; Noen sat up, habit keeping his head from the deck beams. There was a knock at the door. Ler Oeuni's scream became only the shrieking of the block that hoisted *Windsong*'s mainsail, the surgeon's voice the creaking of a pump and the shuffle of the steward's feet on the steps descending to his cabin under the quarterdeck.

No doubt thinking her first knock had gone unheard, she knocked again. "I'm awake," Noen called. "What's the time?"

"Two bells, sir."

Noen swore and swung his long legs over the side of his bunk. "I told you to call me at the forenoon watch." He thrust them into ragged canvas trousers.

"I did, sir," said his steward from the other side of the door.

"You said you were awake, sir." She added meaningfully, "Just like now."

He laughed in spite of his customary resolve to maintain discipline and opened the door. "Well, this time I mean it."

"You were up so late, sir. It don't hurt to sleep a bit extra." She looked at his trousers. "Why don't you wear the ones I've mended, sir?"

There was warm seawater in the wide-bottomed pitcher. He poured some into a bowl and splashed his face. "Because I might need them to go ashore." The shah game he and Oeuni had abandoned when the wind rose was still on the table. Despite their weighted bases, some of the pieces had fallen over. "Put these away," he said.

There was a good breeze, just as he had anticipated from Dinnile's raising the mainsail. Dinnile believed in the slow, implacable heartbeat of the timesman's kettledrums, believed in the sweeps, the enormous oars that could—with the back-breaking labor of four or five sailors at each sweep—send *Windsong* flying over a calm sea like a skimming gull.

"Mornin', sir," Dinnile said, and touched his forehead.

"Good morning, Lieutenant."

"Leak's no worse, sir. Not since I come on. Oeuni said to look for a place to careen her—we got twenty hands at the pumps—but there hasn't been nothin'. I got the lookout watchin' sharp. And seaward too, sir," Dinnile added hastily, noting the expression on his captain's face.

Noen extended his hand, received Dinnile's telescope, and studied the coast. It was jungle, a jungle that looked as solid as a wall, green-robed trees higher far than *Windsong*'s main-mast marching down to the water's edge.

"Deck!" called the lookout at the mainmasthead. *"Deck!"*

"What is it?"

"Looks like a bay, sir. Two points off her bow. I see water past them trees, sir."

Cursing himself under his breath, Noen raised Dinnile's telescope again. It was a bay with a very narrow mouth perhaps—no, a bay with a large island shielding its mouth.

"Out oars, sir?" Dinnile asked happily.

Noen was on the point of saying that he doubted it was worth investigating when the lookout called, *"Flag of distress, sir."*

Noen looked from Dinnile to the bay, and finally at the foam blown from the crests of the little waves. Dinnile was probably right; but Dinnile was too anxious to use his oars, and it would be a pleasure (as Noen admitted to himself) to give his second mate a lesson.

"I don't think so," he said with the calm deliberation suited to a captain who has considered every aspect of the situation. "Strike the mainsail, Lieutenant." He turned to the sailor at the wheel. "See the entrance to that bay, Quartermaster?"

The woman looked. "No, sir."

"I can't either, without the glass. Northeast by east then, until you see it."

With her big mainsail down, *Windsong* was much slower; but she was much handier as well. The foresail and the small mizzen sail—one at each end of her long hull—gave the rudder enormous leverage.

"Sir . . . ?"

Noen nodded reluctantly. "Call gun crews."

A flag of distress was probably just what it appeared to be, the doleful signal of some stranded ship. Yet it was possible (just possible) that it was the trick of some pirate not watchful enough to haul it down at the sight of a galleass of war. Or even of a pirate ambitious enough to try to seize such a galleass.

"Stand to quarters, sir?"

"I said call gun crews, Lieutenant." Oeuni had gotten no more sleep than he had—no, less—and there was a chance, just a chance, that he might be able to get the gun crews to their posts without waking her. If he called all hands to quarters—the order that summoned the entire crew to battle—the midshipman of the watch would pound on the wardroom door to rouse Oeuni and Ranni Rekkue, the third officer.

"Gun crews ready, sir," Dinnile announced.

Noen nodded. "Have them load, but not run out." Running out the quarterdeck basilisks would wake up Oeuni as sure as it would have wakened him. Worse, it might frighten the stranded ship into firing at them, provoking a battle both sides could only lose. He told himself that in trying to preserve Oeuni's rest he was merely acting as any good captain would, then remembered that Rekkue had fought the leak as hard as Oeuni; he had not thought of her until this instant.

It had been useless anyway. There was Oeuni leaping up the companionway with Rekkue, small and dark, at her heels. Noen glanced at the narrow inlet between the island and the mainland, then at *Windsong*'s sails. "Trim up there, foremast!"

Oeuni was hurrying forward to take command of the gun deck; he could count on her to keep the foremast crew on their toes as well. As he watched, she used the iron hook that had replaced her right hand to pull herself up. Resolutely, he forced his eyes back to the island and the presumably inverted flag that rose above its trees. "I'll have a lead in the bow, Dinnile."

"Aye aye, sir." Dinnile, still officer of the watch though Oeuni was on deck now, gave the order.

"Masthead! Are those our colors?"

There was a pause as the lookout made sure. *"Aye aye, sir."*

He had been nearly certain already. Not that it meant anything, he told himself. Any serious enemy of Liavek would surely have its flag in his signal chest.

The leadsman called, *"By the long nine!"*

Plenty of water—water enough for a carrack, and far more than *Windsong*'s skimpy keel drew. Dinnile, sharing his thoughts, grinned and said, "Couldn't improve it without a little brandy."

"By the mark nine."

Yet it was shoaling, as was to be expected. Noen studied the entrance to the bay. Shallows often (though not always) revealed themselves by their color in sunlight and the action of their waves; he could see just such shallows on the seaward side of the island, yet the center of that narrow inlet could not have been a darker blue or more uniformly waved had it been in the middle of the Sea of Luck, far from land.

"By the mark nine!"

Good. Good. Noen trained Dinnile's glass on the flag again. It was the Levar's (the lookout had been right), and judging from its height above the trees, it was flying from a mast a good deal more lofty than their own. A ship seeking shelter from a storm might easily have ducked behind that island, he decided, if her captain knew the inlet was deep enough or simply because he thought she had no better chance. And if a ship that big had managed to enter the bay, *Windsong* should be able to follow with impunity.

"By the long eight."

Weary men clambered from the hold and flung themselves on the deck. That was the pump gang, of course, and their presence meant it was two hours into the forenoon watch. He had been too preoccupied to think about the leak, or even to hear the bell. Yet the leak might grow worse at any time, and their need to careen was as urgent as ever.

"Deck!"

"What is it?" There was a long pause, so long that at last he called again: "Masthead, what do you see?"

"Nothin', sir. I thought I saw somethin', sir, but I must a been wrong."

"What was it?"

Another pause while the lookout decided that refusing to tell her captain could only land her in troubled waters. *"Stone, sir."*

"Stone?"

"Like a tower or somethin', sir." Unhelpfully, the lookout added, *"I don't see it no more, sir."*

Without even considering that the telescope was Dinnile's, Noen thrust it through his belt, jumped down the steps from the quarterdeck to the maindeck, and swarmed up the ratlines to the dizzying crow's nest in the maintop.

"I seen it again while you were comin' up, sir," the lookout told him, "but it's not there now."

"Where was it?"

The lookout hesitated. "Right under the flag, sir."

Noen trained the telescope, trying to steady it against the heaving of his chest and the swooping circle the crow's nest traced with *Windsong*'s every roll. Belatedly, it struck him that his own glass was somewhat better, and that it waited useless in his cabin.

A stronger puff of wind ruffled the leaves of the jungle trees, and he glimpsed a white wall. Squinting and still gasping for breath, he watched the place intently, and when a moment or two had passed he saw it again. "You're right," he told the lookout. "There's a building on that island."

The white stone structure might easily be a castle, or at least a fort; and though reinforced by the gun-deck basilisks, Poltergeist, *Windsong*'s giant culverin, would be no match for even a single small gun mounted on a steady platform and sheltered behind walls of stone.

"I'm glad you see it too, sir," the lookout sighed. "It sort of comes and goes."

"That's the wind in the leaves," Noen told her, and took Dinnile's telescope from his eye.

The instrument gone, his view was no longer restricted to

the little patch of jungle he had watched before. He could see the whole island, including the dark, gray battlements that rose above the foliage and the elaborate, machicolated tower from which the Levar's colors flew.

He clapped the glass to his eye again. The tower remained, a narrow shaft of stone the color of a storm cloud, with a bartizan and a merloned summit. "That was a mast," Noen said.

He had only whispered the words to himself, but in the silence of the crow's nest the lookout had heard him. "Aye, sir," she said. "It comes and goes, sir."

"By the mark seven."

Noen heard the leadsman's cry as he descended slowly to the maindeck, and it decided his course of action. "We'll anchor here, Lieutenant. Break out the jolly boat."

"Aye aye, sir!" Dinnile shouted orders and bare feet pattered up and down *Windsong*'s decks. The jolly boat was slung on davits below the stern gallery, and so could be put into the water a good deal more easily than the big longboat stowed upside-down aft of the mainmast. When the bow anchor had splashed into the sea, Noen bawled, "Steward!"

As though by magic, Oeuni was beside him. "You're not going yourself, sir?"

"Get my sword," Noen told his steward. "My pistol, too. Load it." Belatedly, he remembered to return Dinnile's telescope. "And the small glass."

"Let me go, or Rekkue."

Privately Noen admitted that no matter what regulations might lay down concerning the captain's staying with his ship, he was quite incapable of sending Oeuni into danger while he remained in safety. Aloud he said, "You're not fully recovered, Dinnile's officer of the watch, and Rekkue's not experienced enough yet. That leaves me."

Dinnile put in, "You ought to take the longboat anyhow, sir. That'd give you twenty hands."

"Twenty hands dead," Noen told him, "if there's a gun on that island."

"Pistols for the crew?" Oeuni asked. She was too good an officer to argue.

Noen shook his head. The average sailor was to be trusted with a matchlock pistol only in the gravest emergency. (Not even then, according to some captains.) "Cutlasses and dirks.

I'll have the falconets fore and aft, though. I'll man the aft falconet myself and mind the tiller. Eitha can see to the bow gun."

As he loaded the falconet, taking exaggerated care to keep its smoldering slow match well away from the powder, Noen recalled that moment and regretted it. He was fundamentally a sailor, he told himself, and not a fighter; and even as a fighter he preferred cold steel to the tricky firearms that went off so often when their owners did not want them to, and so often failed to go off when they did.

But the little jolly could not carry more than seven in any kind of sea, and the two swivel-mounted bronze falconets, with their powder and shot, weighed as much as any seventh passenger. Eitha, the cockswain of the jolly, had her gun loaded and ready long before Noen (only too conscious of the eyes of the four men at the oars) had rammed a handful of musket balls down the barrel of his own and fixed the match in the serpentine.

That done, he assured himself that his steward had loaded his double-barreled pistol and that she had *not* wound its wheellock. There would be time enough for that when some actual danger threatened. Or there would not, and he would have to depend on the falconet and the clumsy broadsword he had hitched out of his way. Not that sword, gun, or pistol was apt to be of much use against magic.

The gray stone tower flashed into existence again, only to vanish like smoke. "Cockswain!" Noen called. "I want soundings."

Eitha tossed the lead ahead of the boat, letting the lead line run through her fingers. When the bow was over the lead, she drew it up, counting the knots. "By the half seven, sir," she reported.

"Again," Noen snapped. Could magic deceive a lead weight at the end of a line? Yes, certainly—but not quickly or easily.

"By the half seven, sir."

Plenty of water for *Windsong,* and they had nearly reached the inlet. Noen studied both shores, but particularly that of the island. There should be a sentry there, someone fleet-footed, to tell whoever was in charge that the jolly had come. He saw no one, but perhaps the sentry had already gone. "Cast again," he told Eitha, "when we're at the narrowest point."

A bird circled the island and Noen, fearing it might be of

the carrion kind, trained his glass on it. It was as black as any crow, yet lovely with its long wings and tail and its elaborately ruffled head: not a carrion bird, Noen thought, nor even a predatory one, though he was no student of such things. Twice more it circled, then flew seaward toward *Windsong* and appeared to light in the delicate filigree of her rigging, though when he turned his glass toward her he could not see it. "Smaller with its wings folded," he muttered to himself, then seeing one of the rowers looking oddly at him, cleared his throat.

"By the mark seven, sir." The island and the mainland loomed to the right and left of them.

"Again, when we're well into the bay," Noen said.

Now the castle appeared as solid as the Levar's palace. The rowers were whispering and jerking their heads toward it as they pulled their oars. "Silence!" Noen growled at them.

Rooks circled the tower, and the black muzzle of a gun thrust from every crenel on the walls. Had the castle been real, the entire navy could not have battered it into submission; but Noen felt sure those guns posed no more danger to the jolly than the phantom rooks.

A terrace led from the bay to the portcullis; on it stood two groups of gaily dressed people, some in armor and shouldering halberds or harquebuses. Both groups appeared to be watching intently the two richly dressed figures that stood arguing between them, though occasionally Noen saw someone glance sidelong toward the jolly, then look away at once.

"We'll land there," he told the rowers. "On that pavement." He put the tiller over.

"By the mark seven!" Eitha called triumphantly a moment later.

"*Cut!*" A small man in a shabby tunic stepped from the shadow of a ravelin. "Break, everyone! Rehearsal's over. I think—that is, I hope—we've been rescued."

The gaily dressed actors seemed to relax. They were not really as numerous, Noen saw, as they had appeared; less than a score, perhaps. The two who had been arguing ended their dispute instantly and turned to watch the jolly.

At the same instant, the castle shrank and changed, dwindling to a beached caravel whose canted mainmast flew the inverted flag of the Levar. The white-plumed disputant nudged the other, and together they swept off their hats and bowed low. With a few more oar strokes the jolly's keel grounded, scraped free, then grounded again. "In oars!" Noen ordered. "Get her to shore."

The rowers sprang out, seized the gunnels, and pulled the jolly far enough up the beach for him to step onto the sand without wetting his second-best shoes. "Eitha, see to the matches." Hiking his sword to a more conventional position and throwing out his chest while bitterly regretting his ragged trousers, he stalked up the beach with as much dignity as he could command.

The darkly plumed disputant made a second bow before replacing the hat that bore them. There were flashing black eyes below the broad brim, a great beak of a nose, and a prominent wart. "Welcome, sir!" This in a voice that boomed like a kettledrum. "Welcome, I say again, whomever you may be! I am Nordread ola Gormol, and I've the honor to be—"

"The menace of our troupe," cut in the little man. "That is," he added bitterly, "I hope you are."

The white-plumed disputant favored Noen with a dazzling smile. "And I'm its leading woman." The curtsy that followed this somewhat startling statement involved spreading the tails of a very masculine coat while kicking the wearer's sword out of the way. Noen thought of the awkward fashion in which he had adjusted to his own as he said, "I am Captain Tev Noen of Her Magnificence's galleass *Windsong*."

"Ah," the "leading woman" sighed. (Noen decided the second disputant *was* a woman, though a woman as tall as he.) "I've heard of you. You're the captain who took that big Zhir ship a few months ago. Everyone thought you were going to be simply swimming in gold, but we're not officially at war with Ka Zhir, they say, so they gave it back. What a pity!"

Noen said, "I doubt that my history bears on the situation."

"Oh, but it does! If they hadn't, you'd be at home in Liavek, in your palace, and—"

"I," the little man put in, "am generally called Baldy. I'm our stage manager, and in the absence of our owner and leading man, Amail Destrop, I'm boss. That is, I'm boss when things get bad. That is, when they're not everybody else is, as you've already seen."

"And you are in distress?" Noen asked.

All three tried to talk at once, one booming like a broadside, the other grasping Noen's sleeve and cooing in his ear, and Baldy jumping up and down and yelling until he had shouted them both to silence. "You can bet your luck we're in distress, Captain! That is, we're not actually starving yet, but we can't get off this rotten island, and there're three—"

"We *can* get off in the ship's boats, Captain. But the mainland's ever so much worse! There are—"

"I require transportation to Liavek," Nordread thundered, "and at once! I have myself had the honor of performing at the Palace, and His Scarlet Eminence was so kind—"

"—three wizards," Baldy finished. "And Amail's gone the gods know where. That is, unless something's eaten him."

At that, a silence seemed to descend upon the island.

Noen cleared his throat and clasped his hands behind his back. "Let me establish a few things if I may," he said, raising his voice. "You are shipwrecked. I am the commander of a vessel that has come to your rescue. As such, I can have any or all of you clapped in irons if I judge that to be in the best interest of my ship. Do you understand that?"

The erstwhile disputants glanced at each other, then they nodded. So did Baldy, and so did several of the onlookers.

"I'm going to ask some questions. They're to be answered fully but briefly by the person I indicate, and by no one else. Should anyone else answer—or attempt to answer—he or she will be bound hand and foot by the sailors under my command and thrown into that little boat. You will then be rowed to my ship and turned over to my first officer with instructions to put you in irons and confine you in the hold. My master-at-arms will see that you're fed once a day, provided he remembers. I understand prisoners can keep the rats at bay quite effectively by rattling their chains, at least for the first few days." Noen paused to let his threat sink in.

"Now then." He pointed to Baldy. "I take it you were passengers aboard that ship. Where is her crew?"

"I don't know," Baldy said. "That is, I don't know where they are now, or what happened to them. They disappeared— that is, most of them did, one by one while we were sailing from Cyriesae."

"They deserted?"

Baldy shrugged, his face blank. "I don't think so. That is, we were at sea, and they didn't take the boats."

"Could they have been stolen by the Kil?"

Baldy shrugged again.

"How did you come to this island?"

"With so many of the crew gone, we had to help pull up the sails and so on. That is, we helped as much as we could, but—"

"You weren't sailors, understandably."

"So when it looked like there might be a storm, the captain thought it would be better to get the ship in here. That is, we all thought that, and we did. Only the anchor dragged, and the storm washed our ship onto the beach."

Noen nodded. The bottom of the bay, like the beach, was probably sand. "Where's the captain?"

Baldy jerked his head toward the island, and Nordread coughed.

"You want to say something," Noen told him. "What is it?"

"I wish—I would point out . . . Captain, our captain took the remaining sailors—there were only two of them—and went inland. That was two days ago," Nordread's deep voice laid a heavy significance on the *two*, "and we haven't seen him since."

"He took all the sailors and none of you? Why would he do that?"

"I believe he had some thought of, ah, a hidden treasure, perhaps, or something of the kind. I don't believe he trusted us, Captain. At least, not as much as his own—ah—employees."

Noen nodded and turned to Eitha, waiting with her crew near the jolly. "Go back to the ship," he said. "Tell Lieutenant Oeuni that there's a good shelving sand beach here and no danger. No immediate danger, anyway. Handsomely, now!"

"I wish to point out," Nordread rumbled, "that our sailors vanished at a steady rate of one per night, and that—"

"Shut your mouth," Noen snapped.

That evening Noen told Lieutenants Oeuni, Dinnile, and Rekkue, "That's it. The players know nothing about the white building I saw, or they say they don't. My guess is the captain saw it and most or all of them didn't. As to what happened to their crew and whether it will keep on happening, I'd like your thoughts."

Dinnile said, "We mustn't let our lads and lasses find out about this, sir."

"That's why I made the players stay in the vicinity of their ship and posted the sentries," Noen told him. "But they *will* find out. We can't afford to fool ourselves. They'll probably find out tonight, even if no one vanishes. If they don't, we can be certain they'll know by tomorrow night. If we finish plugging the leak tomorrow and get *Windsong* back to sea, they'll know even faster because we'll have to take the players with us."

Rekkue said, "The storm that washed their ship on the beach must have been the same one that stove in *Windsong*. Sir, do you remember the wind that wizard on *Zhironni* whistled up? Could it have been magic?"

Noen lifted his shoulders and dropped them again. "I don't know, Lieutenant. And I don't know how we can find out, unless we can find the wizard and stick his feet in a fire."

Oeuni used her hook to scratch her head. "You said there were three, Noen. Three wizards."

Noen put a finger to his lips. One of the sentries was coming, his approach made visible by the crimson spark of the slow match in his pistol. As he neared their fire, Noen saw a second figure behind him.

The sentry touched his forehead. "Cap'n, I got a sailor here from the *Lady of Liavek*."

Inwardly Noen berated himself. All afternoon he had planned to examine the log of the beached ship, but he had been so involved in the tricky process of careening *Windsong* without doing further damage that he never had.

Dinnile said, "Is that the derelict, Chipper? I didn't think there was a hand left on her."

The sentry, in more normal times one of the carpenter's mates, shook his head. "He says when the others went off in that pirate they captured, he didn't want to go, sir. So he hid, but then he was afraid the passengers would take it out on him, so he stayed hid." He winked. "I reckon he had a pretty easy time of it, sir. Only now he says he wants to tell about the wizards. They're the ones that make that castle come and go, I guess, sir."

Noen said, "We'll talk to him. Get back to your post."

The sailor who came forward was young and blond, tall but rather slightly built for a seaman. He saluted awkwardly, looked at *Windsong*'s four officers one after another, and at last seemed to fasten on Dinnile as the largest. "Cap'n Noen?"

Dinnile shook his head. "Second mate. That's the captain over there."

The sailor saluted again. "Cap'n Noen, there's somethin' . . ." He seemed at a loss for words.

"Something odd?" Noen prompted. "Something uncanny?"

"Yes, sir. I heard about what them passengers told you today sir, and—"

"I know you did."

"—and I want to tell you some more, sir. 'Cause what that little bald 'un said wasn't the truth of it, sir, not at all, and—"

Oeuni broke in, "Noen, this man's no sailor!"

"Certainly not," Noen told her. "But how did you know, Lieutenant?"

"By his hands." Oeuni paused, suddenly embarrassed. "I suppose I look at hands now more than I used to. But they haven't been in the sun much, and I never saw a hand in my life—I mean a hand's hand—with nails that long."

"I had supposed it was because he said *yes*." Noen was speaking to the imposter, not Oeuni. "Sailors don't say *yes*, because the word's too soft to make itself heard in a high wind. Sailors say *aye* or *aye aye*. Please try to keep that in mind."

The imposter saluted a third time. "Aye aye, sir. I'll try, sir, 'at I will."

"For that matter," Noen told Oeuni, "This man's no man, although the last time I saw her she was dressed like one and playing a man's part. Very skillfully too, I thought. Meet the leading woman of the players."

Oeuni's mouth opened, then shut again.

The player smiled and said in a somewhat higher though still throaty voice, "Since you've penetrated my little masquerade, Captain, may I sit down?"

"Of course. Move over a bit there, Rekkue. By the way, I appreciate your giving my sentry that tale about the pirate ship."

He was rewarded with a dazzling smile. "I thought you would, after the way you stepped on poor old Nordread this morning; sailors are a superstitious lot, I understand. And I want to apologize for playing dress-up; but you or one of your officers must have told those men not to talk to members of our troupe, and I wanted to see you."

"I also told you not to talk to them," Noen said severely.

"For a good reason, which I understood and respected. But what Baldy told you just isn't true." The player paused, pulling off a scarlet bandanna and shaking bright blond hair. "I'm Marin Monns, by the way."

Oeuni said, "What *did* Baldy—is that the stage manager?—
tell you anyway, sir? I was about to ask when Marin came,
and if we're going to have two conflicting stories, it might be
better if all of us knew both of them."

Noen nodded. "I think I can summarize it quickly enough.
Like most theatrical companies, this one has a wizard to provide
appropriate backgrounds for its performances and occasionally
do a magic act as a curtain raiser. Theirs is an old man called
Xobbas, a pleasant, harmless old fellow, according to Baldy,
whose worst fault is that he sometimes produces the mountains
for *The Snow Lover* when the company's supposed to do something else. He also has a hobby of altering his appearance—
making himself taller, turning his beard orange, and so forth."

Oeuni and Rekkue nodded; Dinnile scratched his head.

"Baldy's worked with him for years, and he says he never
changes himself enough to be unrecognizable; but now there
are at least two other people going around looking like him.
They discovered the first on the ship. Baldy had left a wizard—
he thinks the real one—asleep in the passenger's quarters. He
went on deck and saw a second standing in the bow. That could
have been astral projection, but Xobbas had never done it
before. Yesterday the leading woman—Marin here—and Nordread compared notes and found they'd each been talking to a
wizard when their cue came for the second act of *The Prince
and the Piper*. That's the play they've been rehearsing while
they waited for rescue, and in that scene, as I understand it,
they enter simultaneously from opposite sides of the stage."

Marin nodded.

"Furthermore, each got the impression that the person they'd
spoken with wasn't really Xobbas. So that makes three wizards:
the real Xobbas and the two frauds. The problem—one of the
problems, anyway—is that no one has any idea who the other
two can be. The other problem is that Xobbas isn't providing
scenery any more. Baldy started as a stage wizard, so he's been
doing it himself; but he's rusty and the castle comes and goes."

"Captain," Dinnile said, "I've got an idea. Tomorrow afternoon we ought to have the ship patched up. Then we can lighten
Lady as much as we can, take *Windsong* out in the bay, set
both anchors, and winch her off."

Noen nodded again.

"We put a crew, like a prize crew, on *Lady* to sail her back
to Liavek. Well, as these players get on, all three wizards have

got to get on too, don't they? So each time old Xobbas shows his face, we say prove it. He's got to prove he really is Xobbas, or he doesn't get on the ship."

Rekkue said softly, "Dinnile, I think somebody who could disguise himself as a wizard could disguise himself as somebody else too. Suppose there were two Dinniles? For that matter, how do we know the real Marin Monns isn't over there"— she jerked her head toward the unseen bulk of the *Lady of Liavek*—"sound asleep?"

The blond player laughed."I should have known it would come to this. Would you like to hear me recite all my speeches from *Piper?* 'Most noble lords and commoners, have you not seen that when all else sinks, yet the crown swims? When Repartine the Great—'"

Noen raised a hand for silence. "I accept that you're who you say you are, and if I accept it so do my officers. What I want to know is why you said what Baldy told me was false, and how you know it."

"I didn't mean he was deliberately lying to you," Marin said, "but he's wrong. Since yesterday, I've talked to anyone who looked like the wizard anytime I saw him. And I . . ."

"Go on."

"I know him pretty well. He's a kindly old pot, and he still has an eye for the girls. He likes me because I give him a hug every so often, and when we have a cast party sometimes I sit on his lap." Marin paused, staring into the fire.

Oeuni said, "You blush beautifully, Marin. Please go on."

"Did the blood really come up in my cheeks? You sort of hold your breath and try and force the air up, but I've been having trouble with it. Anyway, I *do* know the old man, and that was how I knew the—the wizard I'd talked to while Nordread talked to the other one wasn't real. He was too . . ." Marin made a helpless gesture. "I guess I need a playwright to make up my lines. But Xobbas, the real Xobbas, is old and his mind isn't very clear. He forgets things, and when he feels sorry for himself he says so. Oh, I do, too, and so do lots of other people, but we try to be underhanded about it so you'll feel sorry for us too. Xobbas would just come right out with it like he was talking about somebody else, and this wizard wasn't like that at all. He didn't forget a thing, and I had the feeling he was laughing at me inside all the time."

Noen said, "I understand. What about the others?"

"One was cruel. I know he was! And old Xobbas was never like that. And one was frightened and tried to get away from me as fast as he could. That wasn't like Xobbas either, and Xobbas couldn't have walked that fast, no matter how bad he wanted to. And I think it's important you know that there are three, because what if it's the other two you find, and leave the cruel one? He isn't the real Xobbas either."

Oeuni took a deep breath, looked at Noen, and let it out again. "I've been a little hard on you, Marin," she said. "And I shouldn't have been—you really are trying to help. Is that all?"

The player nodded.

"Sir, is it all right if I take her back as far as the sentry lines?"

"Someone will have to take her back," Noen said. "I don't want her getting into mischief. It might as well be you."

When they had gone, Dinnile wiped his forehead. "By Rikiki, what a looker! And tricky as they come."

Rekkue nodded. "She could be dangerous, I think, starting fights among the crew just for the fun of it and so forth. Are Oeuni and I going to take *Lady* back to Liavek, Captain? If so, I'll try to keep an eye on her."

Noen said, "I don't know why, but I like her."

Dinnile chuckled. "Here's the time I've waited for, sir! The one when I know more than you."

There was a moment of silence, filled only by the crackling of the fire and the call of a jungle bird. Dinnile moved uncomfortably, clearly afraid that he had said too much; Rekkue started to speak but thought better of it.

Superficially impassive, Noen was secretly delighted. A captain necessarily walked a fine line between self-isolation and overfamiliarity with his officers, and he feared lately that he had swung too near the latter. Let them sweat—it was good for them and for the ship! He allowed the silence to grow until he saw his first officer returning, then called harshly, "Oeuni, you're the best judge of character I know. Why'd you change your mind about Marin?"

Rekkue put in, "I was saying how dangerous I thought she was. Was I wrong?"

Oeuni nodded slowly. "Yes, I think you were. I thought so too, at first—all that playacting. But Marin's too fond of showing off to be a real threat; at every moment she wants you to know how completely she fooled you the moment before. And what she said about there being three false wizards..."

Noen cleared his throat. "I thought that was it. You knew she was telling the truth. How did you know?"

"I didn't really know. But—remember late this afternoon, when I went looking for a tree big enough to anchor the winch? This jungle's only thick here at the edge, where it gets sun all the way down. Farther in, there's plenty of space between the trees, and moss and fern on the ground, mostly. I did some looking around while the hands were rigging the winch, and I found a grave."

Rekkue's gasp was distinctly audible.

"At least it looked like one. It was narrow, but long enough for a man, and the earth was fresh. I should have told you earlier, sir; but we were pulling *Windsong* onto the beach, and it didn't seem terribly important at the time."

Noen leaned forward. "We have four missing persons," he said, "though some of you seem to have forgotten it: *Lady*'s captain, two of her crew, and the leader of the players, Amail Destrop. Dinnile, you were talking a moment ago as though we could refloat *Lady* and sail away without making an attempt to locate those people; would you want to be the one to tell Admiral Tinthe we might have left four subjects of Her Magnificence marooned? Now I think we've found out what happened to at least one of them."

Oeuni shook her head. "There was a slab of bark pushed into the loose dirt at one end," she said slowly. "A slab of bark with a letter scratched on it. The letter was X."

As they made their way between the jungle trees the next day, Noen wished he had refused to allow any of the players to come. He had left Rekkue in charge of both ships; young as she was, Rekkue was an able officer, and with *Windsong* and *Lady of Liavek* riding at anchor in the bay nothing remained to do but reload the material they had removed earlier to lighten them. Someone or something, he had argued with himself, had stolen *Lady*'s crew; and if there was going to be fighting, he wanted Dinnile's strength and dauntless courage. As for Ler Oeuni, why, Oeuni was—he winced at his own expression—his right hand. He had brought fifteen steady sailors as well, each armed with a cutlass and a boarding pike.

Then the players had wanted to come, too—the same play-

ers, as Noen had reminded them at length, who had waited
two days on the beach without making the least effort to find
their missing captain and his hands, or even their own missing
leader. But they had insisted, and he had made the error of
permitting Baldy, Nordread (who might actually be of some
use), Marin, and eight more players to accompany him. All
were carrying halberds or swords, rusty yet serviceable; but
Noen strongly suspected that at the least sign of danger they
would drop them and bolt like rabbits.

Besides, he had an irrational feeling that by bringing them
he had brought the three false wizards, too. Once, looking back
through the trees at his straggling column, he had thought he
had actually seen one, a bearded old man in a black robe and
slouch hat. He had called a halt then, inspected the players a
second time, and found no one who in the least resembled the
flitting figure he had glimpsed. After that he had put Dinnile
and two burly hands at the end of the column with orders to
hustle along stragglers and keep their eyes open. They had seen
nothing, or at least nothing they felt worth reporting. There
had been no trace of *Lady*'s missing captain, his sailors, or
Amail Destrop.

Oeuni said, "You'd think it would be cool because of the
shade, but I'd trade it for a sea breeze." Her face was bright
with sweat.

For the hundredth time, he took out his handkerchief, mopped
his own face, and studied the compass. "We should be nearly
across the island now."

"We could have missed it easily enough, sir."

Noen had an uncomfortable feeling that despite her verbal
support Oeuni did not really believe the white-walled building
he had seen from *Windsong*'s maintop existed. He said, "If so,
we'll sweep the seaward side until we find it."

As soon as he had spoken, he realized he had been looking
at it for the past few seconds. That pale blur to the left could
be nothing else—too dim for sunshine, too regular for a natural
rock mass, too light for foliage. Striving to keep any exultation
from his voice and terrified he might yet be wrong, he added
laconically, "Port two points, I think, Lieutenant."

It was a building more impressive for its beauty than its
size, a perfectly proportioned rectangle of white marble sur-
mounted by a dome of the same material. Once its marble walls
had been carved in a tracery as fine as lace. Now pounding

jungle rain had eroded the graceful curves to cobweb; vines clutched at the delicate threads of stone that remained, which bent backward as if fainting in their embrace. Strange letters, angular yet in harmony with the structure, bowed above its dark doorway.

Noen turned to the sailors, who were edging toward the building, curious but still mindful of discipline. "Can anybody read this?"

The hand who stepped forward had been a nomad of the Great Waste before signing aboard *Windsong*. "I can, sir. It's Old Tichenese: 'The Black Warrior Woman, Precious Helper of Men.'"

Oeuni whispered, "I can read something more, Noen. The vines have been cut away so somebody else could read the lettering."

Noen nodded absently, having made the same observation himself. It seemed probable, though not certain, that it had been done by *Lady*'s captain, though— "Pass the word for Baldy, Lieutenant," he said. "No, make that all the players."

As they came crowding up he asked, "Did any of you know your captain well? Could he have read Old Tichenese?"

They looked at one another blankly. At last Nordread rumbled, "I doubt it, Captain. He didn't seem like an educated man. Amail and I dined with him once or twice."

"What about the sailors he took with him?"

"I suppose there's always a chance, but . . ."

"What about Destrop? Could he read Old Tichenese?"

Nordread snorted. "Absolutely not, Captain."

"I see."

Greatly daring, Oeuni said, "Well, I don't, sir."

Noen pointed. "You or I would have cut away enough to discover we couldn't read the inscription and stopped. Somebody's cleared every word. He could read them, so he wanted to see the entire—Dinnile, what the blazes is wrong with you?"

The second mate slapped his leg again and looked apologetic. "Ants, sir. There's a whole line of ants, and I stepped in 'em, sir, not noticing."

"Noen, they're going into the temple."

He nodded, winding his wheellock. "I imagine there's an altar in there, and we're about to find a recent sacrifice on it." He wondered whether it would be a human sacrifice—with four people missing it seemed almost inevitable—but thought it best to keep the speculation to himself. "See that everyone stays here. That's an order."

Three shallow steps led up to the doorway. He paused there to study the dim interior before entering. Nothing moved except the line of ants vanishing into the shadows. There was no altar and no sacrifice, only a statue on a pedestal.

Two more strides showed him that it was, as seemed logical, a beautiful woman carved in black stone. The crest surmounting her helmet was a bird with outspread wings. He moved nearer to examine it, and one of the squares of the tessellated floor gave ever so slightly under his feet.

As he stepped hastily back, his heel struck something that rolled clattering nearly to the wall. He turned to look at it and saw that Dinnile was standing in the narrow doorway, with Oeuni trying to crowd past him. "Rotten stink in here, sir," Dinnile said cheerfully.

Noen nodded. "I think I've just discovered why." He crossed the wide room and picked up the skull he had kicked, then dropped it at once. Despite its tumble over the floor, it was black with ants.

Dinnile took a step and Oeuni rushed past him, the sword she now wore at her right side clutched in her left hand.

"Recent," Noen said. "The ants aren't finished with it yet." He gestured toward two more skulls, clean and white, lying in a corner among a pile of bones. "He—or she—was probably killed last night."

"Aye aye, sir," Oeuni said. Then, "Noen..."

"What is it?"

The point of her sword was probing the back of the skull. "I've seen animals sacrificed. There was a fire, and they cut off the heads and hooves and threw them in, and then the skin and some of the organs. Then whoever had paid for each animal gave part of the meat to the priests and kept the rest. And for magic, when they sacrifice a little animal, don't they usually burn the whole thing?"

Noen nodded. "So I've heard."

"Someone's opened the back of this to get at the brain."

Dinnile had been examining the floor while Oeuni looked at the skull. Now he said, "Captain, here's a crown here."

Noen turned, not sure he had heard correctly. "A crown?"

"Like the one on the shah, in that game." Dinnile looked sheepish at the mere mention of it; he was a poor player, and

Noen, an excellent one, sometimes invited him for a game when Oeuni was on watch. "And next to it's a wizard's hat, sir, and next to that's the warrior's horse."

Noen hurried over.

"See what I mean, sir? It's like the whole place's just a big shah board. Only the only piece left's the black sultana, and that's it over there."

Oeuni kicked aside bones to examine the floor on her side of the room. "He's right, Noen. There are pictures here too, for the white pieces. But the game's already started—some of them have been moved. And the squares move too, a little, when you stand on them. That must be how you invoke the goddess."

Noen stared at her. "Invoke the goddess?"

"Well, this place is obviously a temple, and there's no altar and so on. So what does she want us to do? It must be to play this game, putting a worshiper on each square for a piece. Then she's the black sultana, as Dinnile said." Oeuni paused. "If we did it, maybe she'd help us."

"I'm not so sure we need help. *Windsong*'s patched and both ships are in the water again. As for *Lady*'s captain and his crew, I'm afraid we've found them."

From the doorway, Baldy said, "Maybe you don't, Captain, but we do as long as Amail's missing."

Oeuni added, "And what about whatever took the sailors, Noen? Suppose it's still on *Lady*? I know invoking a goddess is liable to be dangerous, but she must be a good goddess—remember what it says outside? 'Precious Helper of Men'?"

Baldy came into the temple, looking curiously at the statue and the designs on the floor. "If you won't, Captain, we will."

The very impracticality of the idea decided Noen. "You haven't got enough people. You'd have to go back to the beach and get the rest, and even that might not be enough. It would take all day, and I intend to sail with the dawn wind." He turned to his first mate. "All right, Oeuni, I'm no priest and you're no priestess, but we'll try. Get them all in here. Dinnile, you're the tallest; I want you for the white shah. Where's that fellow Nordread? Nordread, you're the black shah. Marin, you're the white sultana—stand there beside Lieutenant Dinnile."

Oeuni said, "One black soldier's been taken, Noen, so we can use the hands for soldiers—there should be just enough. And the players in armor for warriors, and there are four tall women for towers." She gestured toward one of the armored thespians. "Here, you! You're a black warrior. Stand on this mark, in front of the sultana's wizard's soldier. Su, line up those hands on the symbols; I want the other black warrior in front of the shah's tower's soldier. Sir, I need a white soldier three squares in front of Nordread."

Noen nodded and sent a woman over. "I'll play white, Lieutenant. You play black. I must say it looks to me as though white has the better position, besides a lead of one soldier."

"But it's my move, and I'm going to take one of yours, I think. I've got my choice—no, I don't. Captain, you're supposed to have a wizard there by the door, protecting that other white soldier, but we don't have anybody left to play the wizards."

"We have one," Noen told her. "Baldy, you're a wizard. Take your choice of positions."

Baldy walked to the square to the left of the black statue. "If this goddess knows where Amail is, I want to hear it."

When the little temple was no longer filled with the sound of shuffling feet, the silence became oppressive. Dinnile fidgeted and coughed, then pretended he had not.

"Great goddess," Oeuni pronounced. "Black warrior woman and precious helper, I, too, am a woman warrior. I beg you to reveal the fate of Amail Destrop to us and aid us against the slayers of our fellow mariners."

There was no reply. Outside a monkey screeched, swinging away through the trees until it could no longer be heard.

Noen cleared his throat. "I'm *Windsong's* captain, and I'm in charge here. We've done what we think you want. Now we'd like your help. If you want something more, just tell us what it is."

Nothing happened. The statue did not move; no voice was heard in the temple.

"Captain, I'm afraid it's not going to work without—"

"What is it?"

"—the wizards! Noen, don't you see? Everyone kept saying three wizards, three wizards, Marin and Baldy and Nordread and even you. But there *aren't* three wizards, because Baldy's a wizard, too, and that makes four. Four wizards for the shah board! We have to get the other three, and it won't work without them."

A new voice, deep and eerie, seemed to come from everywhere and nowhere, echoing from the bare white walls: "You have one." The tall, black-cloaked man who strode into the temple looked old, his face lined with wrinkles and his long beard gray where it was not white; yet his eyes seemed to glow under his slouching wizard's hat, and he stood as straight as any rapier. Saluting Ler Oeuni with his crooked staff, he took the square beside Nordread.

"Goddess!" Oeuni cried to the statue. "Behold! Aren't two wizards enough? We've given you your shah's wizard, as well as your own."

Nordread stepped forward and touched her shoulder to get her attention. "Three, actually, Lieutenant," the deep-voiced player rumbled, and pointed. A third wizard, smaller than the second but dressed in much the same fashion, stood at Dinnile's right hand.

Noen roared, "Where'd that man come from?"

The burly second mate touched his forehead. "I dunno, sir. I was watchin' you 'n' Oeuni, and then he was there."

"One more," Oeuni said. "If we had the last—"

She stopped because something uncanny was taking place on the square black stone behind and to the left of Syb, the seaman who portrayed Marin's warrior's soldier. A cloud that was black and yet not smoke swirled there, as though a waterspout had somehow formed over the dry floor. Then it was gone, and the fourth wizard grinned at them, rubbing his hands and chuckling.

"Now, goddess!" Oeuni called.

Noen, Oeuni, and Dinnile, every sailor and every player watched the statue; but it did not move nor speak, nor give the slightest sign of magic or of miracle.

As the awful silence lengthened, it brought a sense of hopelessness.

"Maybe we have to continue the game," Oeuni sighed at last. "My warrior there takes Marin's soldier." She pointed to the player in question. "That's you. You go over there, and she goes"—Oeuni hesitated—"outside, I guess."

The player remained where he was.

"You heard me!"

He looked embarrassed. "I did, ah, Lieuteneant Oeuni. But I can't. I can't go."

She stared at him, and Noen asked, "Are you paralyzed, man?"

"No." The player lifted one foot, then the other. "But I can't go over there. When I try, nothing happens."

"Sir . . . ?"

It was Syb, and Noen turned to face him. "What is it?"

"Cap'n, when that wizard there started to appear like he did behind me, I tried to run, sir. Only I couldn't. Just like him."

Noen whirled to Nordread. "You walked over to Lieutenant Oeuni and touched her a moment ago. Do it again!"

The theatrical company's menace nodded, lifted one foot, and put it down where it had been.

"Noen," Oeuni's voice trembled, "are you frightened?"

He was, but he shook his head stubbornly. "Why should I be? We're getting somewhere at last."

"Well, I am. And I'm not afraid to say so. We said we were the shah players, Noen. You were supposed to be white and I was supposed to be black. But we aren't really, or we could move the pieces, couldn't we? Are the real ones good and evil, Noen? Or the Black Faith and the White? Or what?"

Dinnile's wizard said, "It would be better, perhaps, if you were not to ask to know too much." His speech was soft, so low that only the utter silence of the temple made it possible for them to hear him.

"Who are you, anyway?" Oeuni asked. And then, "Why didn't we ask that before?"

The wizard only repeated, "It would be better, perhaps, if you were not to ask to know too much."

Noen said, "We won't ask you any more questions, but I would appreciate your advice. Tell me what to do, and we'll do just as you say."

There was no reply, but Nordread and Baldy gasped. The statue, the black sultana, had begun to move, rocking ever so slightly to the right and to the left, like the pendulum of a metronome that had almost run down.

Slowly it slid from the black square upon which it had stood to the square in front of Nordread, and then to the square beyond that. It was only then that Noen realized the black square where it had been was not a stone at all, but a dark cavity in the floor, a pit or a sunken vault.

There was a sudden cry, unearthly and utterly evil, and some dark thing streaked from the dome over their heads and vanished into the pit.

Baldy and Nordread turned, white-faced, to stare after it. Oeuni, only a step or two farther from the pit than they, threw down her sword and dashed to it, dropping to her knees beside it and reaching inside with both her arms. Her hook emerged with an emerald necklace caught like some shining fish, her right hand with a handful of gold. She reached in again; as she did, a hideous face topped with such a crown as the Levar herself could not boast emerged. It seemed almost a skull, but flames blazed behind the sockets of its eyes, and the fangs of its mouth were smeared with blood.

At once the missing black stone appeared, sliding swiftly from the wall to seal the pit. The hideous face ducked, the crown toppling from its head. Noen called, "Look out!"

He was aware, even as the shout left his lips, that it had come too late. The sliding stone clicked to a stop against Oeuni's iron hook.

At the same instant, the gliding statue reached the wall opposite the door. It seemed to Noen that it must crash into it, crash and perhaps even shatter, for it had been picking up speed, accelerating faster and faster as it moved. It did not. For the black sultana the solid stone seemed no more than a mist. The statue entered that mist and was gone.

He knelt beside Oeuni. The point of her hook was against the edge of the floor, actually driven some minute distance into the stone; the bend was jammed against the slab. Her other arm vanished into the dark crevice that remained, which was about the width of his own hand.

"Noen," she gasped. And then again. "Oh, Noen . . ."

"Let go!" he told her. "That hook could break." Bracing his feet against the edge of the floor, he heaved at the slab with all his strength; it did not move.

"Noen, I can't let go! It's got me, that thing, that devil—it's got my hand!"

He pulled at her arm until she cried out. Across the room, Dinnile raged against the confinement of his square, but neither his curses nor his frantic gestures freed him. Nordread had drawn a rapier, but could not thrust into the pit. Baldy muttered words that sounded like spells—and the reality of the situation altered not at all.

The demon's face appeared at the crevice. Noen fired both barrels of his pistol point blank, the shots deafening in the bare

stone chamber; if he had fired instead into a raging sea, his
bullets could have been no more futile.

"Noen," Oeuni gasped. "It's got me. That *thing!*" Bright
tears filled the eyes that never wept.

The hook slipped. Its movement was slight, and yet Noen
saw it and felt it too, for he was standing upon the slab. The
demon's hand emerged from the crevice, groping for his ankle.
He jumped back, drew his sword, and slashed at the scaly wrist
with all his strength; the wide blade broke like glass, and he
flung down the hilt.

"Now you will die, all of you." It was the voice of the
fourth wizard, of Marin's wizard. "She because she cannot get
away. You because you will not leave her. They because they
cannot leave their squares. But not I. Kakos is mine, you see,
my crowning achievement."

Then voice and wizard were gone, not vanished, but crushed
to a broken doll whose crimson blood splattered Syb and the
unfortunate sailor standing before the player who was Marin's
tower. The black statue had reentered its own temple through
the door like the figurehead of a galley that flies before a gale,
and it had struck him like that galley's ram.

The demon's shoulder followed its arm. Narrow though the
crevice was, it oozed through it like clay through a potter's
fingers. Oeuni cried, *"Noen!"* Her body writhed with effort,
the muscles outlined beneath her thin shirt like cables.

The hook came free. The slab slammed the edge of the floor
as the weighted jaw of a rattrap crashes down when the rat
pulls at the bait, and it left the demon's arm squirming at
Oeuni's feet.

"You all right?" It was Dinnile, panting, sword drawn, leaning over Noen as Noen leaned over Oeuni. Freed from their
squares, the rest, sailors and players, clustered around.

"My hand," Oeuni said, gripped the bent iron socket that
had held her hook.

Noen said, "Your hand is fine," and touched it to prove it.
"But—"

He took a deep breath, feeling that when he had explained
she would want him to explain more, and knowing that he
could not. "When you dropped your sword, it was from your
left hand. But when you reached into there the first time and
brought up that necklace—here it is—on your hook, the hook

was on your left hand. It can't be an illusion, because your left hand couldn't have held back the slab; I don't know what it was."

Nordread and Dinnile, Baldy and Marin and a dozen others were all speaking at once, but Noen paid no heed to them. Leaning close to Oeuni, he heard her whisper, "It's right, what they say. I had to choose. Lose my other hand, or the demon would have killed you and Dinnile and everybody. It wouldn't have killed me—it told me that."

Baldy had taken advantage of his small size to penetrate the crowd. "Let me see it," he said, and examined Oeuni's right arm. "Ha!" He tugged at the iron cup. "This is a prop."

Noen grasped him by the shoulders. "What did you say?"

"It's a prop, Captain. I may not be much of a wizard, but I'm a pretty good stage manager, and the properties come under my jurisdiction. That is, we use one just like this in *The Pirates of Port Chai*. See, the player sticks her hand in it and holds the handle, and it looks like she's lost it. But it comes off. That is, this one won't because it's dented in."

At that moment it did. The hand that emerged from the metal cup was Ler Oeuni's own, slightly larger than most women's and much harder, though by no means so hard as iron. She flexed her fingers and stared at them, laughing and crying at the same time.

"Cap'n?" It was Su; she and another sailor were holding the tall wizard, one at each arm. (Noen suspected there was a dirk at his back as well.) "Cap'n, this 'un's still here. We asked that tower woman if he was the real 'un, and she said she didn't think so."

Noen turned away, sorry to part from Oeuni's joy. "Well," he snapped, "are you?"

"No," the wizard admitted. His voice was as resonant as ever, and loud enough to be heard over the tumult around them. "If my good wife will but remove my hat and my beard (carefully, please, my dearest, though I think perspiration has somewhat loosened the gum), she can tell you who—"

Nordread's sword clattered to the floor. *"Amail!"* Her embrace might have broken the ribs of a bear. Noen looked across the room to the white flagstone where the third wizard had stood beside Dinnile. It was empty, save for a single black feather lying upon the graven symbol of a wizard's hat.

• • •

That night, aboard the *Lady of Liavek,* Rekkue asked, "Was it Amail Destrop who buried the old wizard?"

Oeuni nodded. "He found the body, and he thought if he made himself up as Xobbas, whoever had killed the real Xobbas might attack him. Then when he heard that the false Xobbas was trying to get the players to go inland, he scared them so much they didn't. Only *Lady*'s captain took the wizard's bait." She paused. "We don't usually think of actors as being brave, but I suppose they are, sometimes."

Marin, who had been leaning on the rail listening to them, said, "I think what Nordread did was braver."

"Who was the wizard?" Rekkue asked. "Did the captain ever find out?"

"Not really," Oeuni told her. "Noen thinks he was a Pardoner who'd found the temple earlier and stowed aboard *Lady* in Cyriesae because he saw that Destrop's theatrical company would be ideal for staging the shah game. His pet devil had to be fed every day, but he made it spare the players. Of course he raised the storm that brought the ship to Temple Bay, and made sure she went aground. And now I'd better see . . ." Oeuni glanced toward the quarterdeck, where a midshipman stood watch.

Rekkue wailed, *"Please,* Oeuni! One more thing, or I'll go stark mad. That statue and the game, I don't understand them at all. How—why did it come out of the wall like that?"

Oeuni paused, looking from the sea to the sky, then at the trim of *Lady*'s sails. "Noen and I, and sometimes Noen and Dinnile, play conventional shah, using a flat board with sides. But there's another game; you pretend the board's a cylinder, that it wraps around the whole world, so to speak. Then a piece that goes off one side diagonally appears in the next row on the other, the way the black sultana did. You see, while we thought we were playing conventional shah, the gods were playing cylindrical shah. I think there's a message there, though I'm not sure I know what it means. Anyway, that's why I left the emeralds around the statue's neck—as a gift for the player, whoever that is."

Marin said, "You were right, and you were right about me too, that night by the fire. You see, I often take female roles, and when I saw Captain Noen thought Nordread really was a man, I couldn't resist showing off."

Oeuni took her hands from the rail and started aft. Marin tried to follow her, but Rekkue caught him by the arm. "Passengers are *not* permitted on the quarterdeck," she said sternly. "I, however, am off duty."

Marin grinned. "Hello, sailor. New in town?"

The Ballad of the Quick Levars

by Jane Yolen

———————

(Sung to the tune of "Eel Island Shoals," or, if in an upbeat mood, "Pot-Boil Blues")

'Twas the season of Buds, when the Cat overran
All her banks with a horrible miaou,
That the infamous year of Quick Levars began—
Though to this day no one knows how.

Number one was Azozo the Ancient-of-Days
Who became a Levar as a crone,
And she died the first moment that her antique bum
Touched that cold and implacable throne.

Next Bukko the Baby, still toothless and small,
Whose drools were considered so wise
That even before he had learned how to crawl,
He'd conspired in his own demise.

Then Cruski the Crabby whom nobody liked,
Her unfortunate death no one mourned.
And Denzzi the Deadhead who nonetheless hiked
To a wood against which he'd been warned.

And just a day after, Emmazi the Eager
Was caught in a bedroom that caved

In, and Froz-Factual died of a meager
Supply of the trivia he craved.

Gondo the Ghastly was popped in an oast
As the joke of a baker who drank,
And Hazli Half-hearted choked on the toast
When she tried the same baker to thank.

Oh, the rota is endless; it took a whole year
Of quick deaths and destruction and doom,
Till nary a niche remained empty, I hear,
In the fabulous Levar's Great Tomb.

The bright line of succession by now was quite gray
So the nobles who ruled such affairs
Passed a law that no Levars of less than a day
Could pass on the Great Throne to thier heirs.

"The Ballad of the Quick Levars" was a favorite in the dirty
drink-holes of Ka Zhir for the half century following the unfortunate incidents touched upon in its endless and scurrilous
verses, only eight of which are reproduced here.

The gutteral dialects of Ka Zhir permit no easy rhymes, but
rather a slanting reference to assonances. And, of course, before
the Year of the Quick Levars, the rulers were known as Levars (pronounced *láy-var*), not Levar. The change in pronunciation was suggested by Andrazi the Lucky from one of her
many Shift Dreams as a possible way to manipulate luck. In
order to attempt a more historically accurate translation, I have
used the old pronunciation throughout. Modern readers may
find they have to read a line several times in order to apprehend
the proper scansion. The eight verses translated above have
been tidied up and some of the more base references have been
deleted. (Emmazi the Eager's bedroom preferences, for example.)

To be fair, it must be admitted that all of the Levars mentioned existed and were, indeed, part of the horrible death-
prone year of 2929. However, Azozo lasted for longer than it
took to sit on her throne. She died of heart failure slightly later
on in the long investiture ceremony. Age and excitement were
too much for her. Bukko did indeed die young, choking on his
own rattle, the head of which had been loosened by—some

say—a Tichenese provocateur. The unfortunate Cruski was so disliked that no references to her other than her death have been noted. Denzzi, born vacant-eyed, fell off a cliff in the Endless Woods which are endless only to those who do not stay on the path. But it is a base lie to say that Froz, one of the finest minds of his generation, died of a dearth of information. According to the physicians, his bride-to-be threw a rather large tome at his head and it cracked his skull.

The story of Gondo and Hazli's long and tragic rivalry is better told in the "Tale of a Brother and a Sister" and need not be rehearsed here.

The one indisputable fact in this Zhir mish-mash is that there is, indeed, a law about the length of reign. That is both to our credit and our luck, for we are able to rule on our rulers while the vile and greedy and foul-mouthed Zhir are stuck with their dictator-king.

Pot Luck

by Megan Lindholm

KALOO SQUINTED AGAINST the dazzle of sun off the waves as the little double-ended dory dipped and rose merrily in the waters off Gutters Cove. T'Nar, she knew, had brought her here to lift her spirits. When she had been younger, such tactics had always worked. A day in the sun and salt wind, with little to do but bait her hook and pull in white-fleshed flounders would have erased any gloom from her mind.

"But I am not a child anymore," she reminded herself with a silent sigh. Anyone looking at her might have disputed the opinion. Her face had lost none of its childish shape, nor had her body. But by Liavekan law she was nearly an adult. On some days she wondered if she wanted to be one. Ever since she had begun her search to discover her luck time, and co-incidentally became the apprentice of the wizard L'Fertti, her life had been more complicated. For one thing, there was the sneaking about to get to her lessons. Daril, her foster mother, would have been outraged had she known Kaloo was studying to invest her luck and use the magic it made available. Daril had already planned Kaloo's future. She would help with the running of the Mug and Anchor until she was old enough to take it over and let Daril retire. So Kaloo explained her time away from the inn by inventing a boyfriend... not that any boy would ever be interested in her! Then there was L'Fertti, who made her go so frustratingly slow with her lessons. Had not she just spent a whole month upon the benefits of cooking

159

herbs when used in health potions . . . as if that could be called magic at all?

Discovering her luck time had not been the satisfaction she had expected. It had only filled her with new and more nagging questions about who her natural parents had been, and why they had abandoned her in a ditch beside the Levar's Highway. But worst of all were the strange feelings, half of dread and half of fascination, that gripped her at the sight of a red cloak in Liavek's streets.

"What's his name, anyway?" T'nar's rumbling voice broke in on her thoughts, and Kaloo started.

"Whose name?"

"Whoever it is that makes you stare into space with a look on your face like a sick gull. You've had three bites on your line just now and ignored them all. And look where we are! You said you'd take a turn at minding the oars. We've drifted out past the good fishing. Nothing out here but ratfish."

Kaloo shrugged guiltily. She tossed her hand line to T'Nar, knowing full well her bait was probably nibbled away by now, and stood to the oars. "Time to head home anyway," she replied. "Look at the sun. If we don't go back now, I won't have time to help Daril prepare for the evening rush."

For five sweeps of the oars, T'Nar let her think she had successfully evaded him. Then, "What color eyes does he have, this boy who has ousted poor Roen?"

Kaloo didn't flinch. They had sparred this way too many times before, jokingly when she was a small girl, and more barbedly now that she was maturing. "What makes you think I'm not seeing Roen anymore?"

"I ran into Roen the other day. Down on the docks with another young lady, right after you had left the inn to be with him. Or is that what these moody looks are about? Has he decided that green eyes are more mysterious than flashing black ones?"

"If you want to know, why not ask him?" Kaloo replied sulkily, adopting the attitude of the lover scorned. "He isn't the only fish in the sea, though he may fancy himself the best catch."

"So that's it then, is it?" T'Nar rumbled. "Well, you're right. And I never thought him a fit catch for you at all. No wonder you've been moping about. Well, the first time always hurts the worst, I suppose. And all this time I was thinking you had another young man on your mind."

"Maybe I already do," Kaloo replied in her first burst of near-truth for the afternoon.

"Well, that's the spirit!" T'Nar encouraged her. "And I hope he's worthy of your time."

She made no reply to that, but kept her eyes on the beach and leaned into the oars with a will. If you only knew, she thought. How would he feel to know that the man who fascinated her was Count Dashif, the bloody right hand of His Scarlet Eminence? Oh, not with the silly romantic notions T'Nar imagined filled her head. No. But it was true he was handsome. He had eyes near black as his character, and hair to match that hung in ringlets to his shoulders. His red cloak and white silk shirt drew eyes to him, eyes that were quickly cast down. But it was not his appearance that drew Kaloo, but something else. A power. But even that didn't describe it. More like an echo of something she once knew and couldn't recall. A feeling for him. She wished she knew if it were love or hate.

That question was still on her mind as she and T'Nar slogged up to the front door of the Mug and Anchor, their catch heavy in a tub lugged between them. But all thoughts of Dashif vanished suddenly. "By Rikiki's nuts!" T'Nar blasphemed softly, too overcome for volume.

The wide doors of the Mug and Anchor that stood open to weary seamen in all but the most vile weather were firmly closed. More shocking than this was the crudely lettered board tacked across them. CLOSED. NO BUSINESS TODAY. NO FOOD SERVED.

"Daril!" hissed T'Nar.

Daril had never closed the inn before, not when she had fallen down the steps and broken her ribs, not even on the day that T'Nar had put Kaloo, a squalling, dirty, abandoned baby, into her ample lap. Wordlessly they hastened down the side alley. At the back door they dropped the tub, and T'Nar shouldered Kaloo aside to be the first one to face whatever disaster was changing their lives.

The shutters were closed, the room darker than Kaloo had ever seen it. But it was another change that took her breath away. The kitchen fire had died away to mere coals. The pot-boil in its blackened kettle was not bubbling and murmuring as it released today's variety of fragrance. The pot-boil that had simmered there for one hundred and fifty years was being allowed to cool and congeal. A dark figure huddled on the bench before it.

For an instant Kaloo did not recognize Daril. The keeper of the Mug and Anchor seemed to have shrunk. Only yesterday she had come home from visiting with her hair braided and coiled upon her head in a ridiculously youthful style. A friend had helped her stain her gray hair into a carroty parody of the auburn tresses of her youth. T'Nar had professed to like it, but Kaloo had been appalled. In Daril's present posture, it looked even gaudier, and, if possible, more foolish, like new yarn hair on a worn-out rag doll. Her arms were wrapped about herself as if to ward off a chill. She did not turn at their entrance, but continued to stare at the darkening embers of the fire.

"Daril?" T'Nar moved swiftly to put his hands on her shoulders.

"It's gone bad," she whispered hoarsely as she turned a tear-streaked face up to him. "More than one hundred and fifty years gone rancid. Oh, T'Nar, what's to become of us?"

He had no words of comfort for her. Kaloo stood frozen by the door. Never in her life had she heard such hopelessness in Daril's voice, nor seen T'Nar stand mute and helpless in the face of any problem. He did not even curse. Kaloo tried to grasp the magnitude of the disaster. Pot-boils were a tradition in Liavek—the savory, simmering pot of meat and vegetables kept bubbling over a fire. No two were the same. As fresh ingredients and new spices were added daily, each pot-boil moved through a spectrum of delectability, yet kept its own special identity. Daril's was one of the best. No one in the city would have argued the point. And now it had gone bad.

"Are you sure?" Kaloo asked.

"How dare you ask her a thing like that?" T'Nar snapped. But Daril accepted her question even if T'Nar did not.

"Rancid," she whispered. "And I can't for the luck of me understand why. Just before you left, I finished chopping the day's vegetables and fish. I slipped them in, and crumbled in my herb mix, and left it to simmer. Just as I've done every day of my life since I was tall enough to stir a kettle. But when I came to taste it, it was..." Suddenly she bowed her head into her hands. She sobbed silently, her broad shoulders shaking. T'Nar's callused hands patted her trembling body.

Kaloo took a deep breath. "Daril, we can't just close the inn. I can put the meats to roast over the mainroom fires. I can make up a chowder from today's catch, and the breads were fresh-baked this morning before I left. While the inn is closed, we have no income. And a lot of sailors have no place to eat. Let me take down the sign and—"

"And let all the town know our shame?" Daril asked incredulously. "Some little snit from the *Cat Street Crier* has already been here rattling at the latches and wanting to know what was wrong. I told him we were remodeling our mainroom, and couldn't serve customers until it was finished to our satisfaction. If I open the doors now, they'll know it's not true. And the first time someone asks for the pot-boil and we have to refuse, the truth will be out. No, Kaloo, it's the end for us. We'll have to close the Mug and Anchor and do—I don't know what . . ." Her voice had gotten hoarser and hoarser as she spoke, and she again dissolved into tears. T'Nar shot Kaloo a despairing glance, then bent to talk to Daril softly.

"Let me take you up to your room. You lie down for a bit and I'll rub your back and we'll think together. It can't be as bad as it seems right now. Kaloo will stay here and look through the vegetables and meat supplies. And if she finds someone has sold us tainted meat or bad produce . . ." His words trailed off and the muscles in his shoulders and arms suddenly knotted. Gently he urged Daril to her feet.

Kaloo stood for a moment in the darkened kitchen, listening to their slow heavy footfalls as they ascended the stairs to their living quarters above the inn. Suddenly the strangeness of that familiar room scared her more than any spook story T'Nar had ever told her. She leaped to fling open the shutters and let in the warm afternoon sunlight. Next she moved to the fireplace and put more wood on the dying coals. Pot-boil or not, she would need a fire to fix something for them to eat tonight. Cautiously she hooked the fire-blackened kettle toward her and took a sniff, ready for the foul odor of meat gone rotten.

There wasn't any. Kaloo frowned and, taking up a wooden spoon, stirred the congealed pot-boil carefully. Still no stink; it didn't make sense. Turning from the pot-boil, Kaloo dug hastily through the garbage tub of vegetable ends and meat scraps that they saved for a local pig farmer. It looked fine to her. Oh, the spiny heart stubs had begun to brown a little, and the bits of fat had softened in the heat of the day, but there was nothing there to make the pot-boil go bad. Kaloo hesitated, unwilling to place her judgment over Daril's. Then she swung the kettle back over the heat. She stirred it as the rich gravy began to loosen and simmer again. The scent of the Mug and Anchor's famed pot-boil began to fill the kitchen. Kaloo put a dollop into a bowl and ventured a taste. As familiar as she was with it, it was still delicious. The hunger that had built up from her morning's fishing suddenly demanded satisfaction. She filled the bowl and cut the crispy heel from one of the new-baked loaves. She ate it standing at the hearth, at first tasting each chunk of meat and vegetable carefully in search of some taint, but soon devouring the whole bowl.

"T'Nar!" she called up the stairs. "Come eat!"

"A moment!" he replied, and she soon heard his heavy boots. He came into the kitchen sniffing like a dog on a scent, and wordlessly took the heavy bowl Kaloo pushed into his hands. He took the first mouthful and turned incredulous eyes on her. "How did you do it?" he demanded. "It tastes just like the old pot-boil!"

"It is the old pot-boil. I just heated it up, that's all. T'Nar, there's nothing wrong with it. It tastes wonderful, just as it always has."

He took another mouthful, more cautiously, and then a second with relish. He motioned for bread and she cut a slab and passed it to him. He finished the bowl rapidly, and as he set it on the table, he demanded, "Why didn't you call and tell us right away?"

"Same reason you aren't shouting for Daril. I don't want to be the one to contradict her about her own pot-boil."

"What is that stench?" demanded a voice behind them, and they both turned guiltily as Daril entered.

"What stench?" Kaloo asked, becoming aware of it as soon as she spoke. It was a dreadful odor, one part charnal house to one part fresh sewage. Daril strode forward to hook the kettle away from the fire. As she moved the simmering mixture, it became obvious that it was the source of the stink. She turned to Kaloo and T'Nar, her hands on her hips.

"Which of you had the marvelous idea of heating up that hopeless mess?"

"I did," Kaloo admitted before T'Nar could speak.

"But it smelled fine at first. Tasted good, too," T'Nar added.

Daril glared at them. "I suppose it will be my luck that you've both poisoned yourselves and I can nurse you while trying to figure out how to save my business? Hasn't either one of you a nose or a tongue? Just the smell of it is making me sick. I'm going back up to my room. You two can clean up your own mess. And don't go stinking up my kitchen any worse than it already is."

Kaloo and T'Nar had both backed up against the kitchen table in remarkably similar postures during her lecture. As the door swung shut behind her, they exchanged glances. "Get a tub to dump it in," T'Nar instructed Kaloo. "She's probably right. We'll both of us be sick tomorrow."

But as Kaloo started to tip the kettle into the tub T'nar held, she froze. At his questioning glance, she sniffed loudly several times. He copied her, then pulled the tub away as she righted the kettle. "It smells fine now," he said. "Damnedest thing I've ever seen."

"Or smelt," Kaloo added wryly. "T'Nar, something about this makes no sense."

"Nothing about this makes any sense," he corrected her gravely. "Unless . . ."

"Unless what?" she demanded, alarmed by his solemnity.

"Unless someone's fooling about with our luck. What could be worse for our inn than for our pot-boil to go bad?" At Kaloo's blank look, he went on. "For it to be good one moment and bad the next. For us never to know if a customer is going to get a bowlful of Daril's pot-boil or a bowlful of slop. That's the kind of reputation that puts a place out of business."

"So where does that leave us?" Kaloo asked impatiently.

His dark eyes met hers without hope. "In a mess."

Kaloo pushed L'Fertti's splintering door open, leaning on it as it scraped across the floor. "I wish you'd fix that," she said petulantly to the old wizard.

L'Fertti didn't look up from the herbs he was sorting on the table. "And I wish you'd learn to be on time. Come and tell me the proper names for these, and what each is good for. Then I've a shopping list for you to fill. Put on the kettle before you sit down."

Kaloo didn't move from where she stood. Her eyes, dark and bright as a raptor's, stared at him as if seeing him for the first time. He was not an inspiring sight. No majesty or mystery clung to him. L'Fertti was just a stooped old man in a tattered robe. His white hair and beard were unkempt and the single jade earring in one ear gave his head an unbalanced look. Yet she had been witness to the magic his luck could provide when he put his time and wits to work.

Recently, as part of her instruction, he had begun working small daily magics for her edification: the lighting of a candle, levitation of small objects, making a copper disappear from the table (My copper! she recalled), and souring a bowl of milk. At the remembrance of the last example, she frowned. It struck a bit close to home. Still. . . .

"Just how good are you, really?" she demanded.

"Good enough to make ladies weep in the morning when I leave."

Kaloo flushed. Lately he had taken to making jokes of that ilk, and she suspected he took a secret pleasure in flustering her. But she hadn't time to be peeved with him today.

"I mean at magic, at manipulating your luck. If someone came to you with a real problem, could you do anything about it? Something worse than a belly ache or an infected hangnail?"

He turned to stare at her imperiously. Moments of silence ticked by, and then Kaloo was suddenly assailed with a furious itch in a place not scratchable in public. "You crude old pig!" she shouted, and it ceased as suddenly as it had begun. "I come to you, for once, with a real problem, with something that could ruin my life, and all you do is make nasty jokes. I don't know why I bother with you!"

"And I don't know why I bother with an apprentice so thin-skinned that she makes an insult of a jest between friends. You insinuate that I am a fraud, and then shout at me when I prove your allegations false. If one wishes to consult a wizard, it is customary to start by stating the problem, not insulting his credentials. Sit down!"

The last was such a roar of command that Kaloo sat, not in the chair he indicated, but in a heap on the floor. Then, much to her own dismay, she burst into tears. This seemed to distress L'Fertti as much as it did her, for he made no comment on it. She buried her face in her hands and wept helplessly, while he magicked his kettle to a boil and brewed kaf. He nudged her with a sandaled foot, and as soon as she looked up, put the steaming mug into her hands. There was enough apology in his face that Kaloo surrendered her grudge.

"Someone's cursed our pot-boil. Or something. Maybe the whole inn. I don't know. T'Nar and I came back from fishing, and Daril said the pot-boil had gone bad, but it smelled fine to us, so we ate some, and then she came in and took it off the fire and it was all rotten. T'Nar says it will ruin our trade if the food isn't dependable, and Daril says we will have to close the place and find another way to make a living, and it's breaking her heart. And stupid T'Nar doesn't know what to do, and he's supposed to know what to do when things like this happen. What will we do if Daril closes the inn? She doesn't know anything but cooking and putting out beer, and all I know is how to help her. So I don't know what will happen to any of us, and then when I come to you for help—"

"Enough!" barked L'Fertti, and Kaloo stopped as suddenly as she had begun. "Now be attentive and try to answer my questions carefully. First of all . . ." He paused to consider. "If I help you with this, what's in it for me?"

She should have known. "I don't know. If I told T'Nar I wanted to hire a wizard, he would either not approve, or not let me be the one to do it. He's very suspicious of any kind of wizard, anyway. He and Daril have the same attitude: 'Work done today will show tomorrow, but magic's only as reliable as the wizard that makes it.' My friends' parents don't think like that. But T'Nar and Daril both act like training your luck can only lead to abusing it."

"I see," L'Fertti replied. "Very provincial attitude. How unfortunate. Well, what can you lightfinger for me out of it?"

"I don't steal from my own people!"

"It's not stealing. What's a bowl of pot-boil for free on a cold day when I happen to drop by? Or a cold beer on a hot day like today? That's all I'm talking about."

Kaloo could see the problems inherent in such an arrangement, but her anxiety overrode her natural caution. "It might be arranged, just between you and me. But can you fix it?"

"One step at a time. How can I fix anything until I know what's amiss? Now. Who would have an interest in seeing the Mug and Anchor go out of business?"

"No one," she replied instantly.

L'Fertti rolled his eyes. "Fascinating. A business that prospers, yet has no rivals, is not in a location that anyone else would desire, and does not take customers away from any other business. Now try again."

Kaloo knit her brows. "Liana perhaps. Once Daril caught her trying to smuggle a tureen of our pot-boil out of the inn. Daril was sure she was going to have a wizard figure out our recipe. She dumped the bowl over Liana's head, and said that was the last taste she would ever get of our cooking. Kenuki is furious with T'Nar and Daril since they stopped buying crab from him. Daril paid him for a basket of live crab, but after he left, we found half of them were dead and going rotten. He wouldn't make it good, and told everyone on the docks that he'd get even with T'Nar for spoiling his reputation. Or Dori. She runs a slop shop off a houseboat near the canal. Whenever she drops in, she brags that with a location like ours, she could do twice the trade we do. As soon as she leaves, T'Nar always comments that with food like she serves, we could do no trade at all. Or . . . L'Fertti, this is impossible. There are too many people who might wish us ill. But I can't believe that anyone would really do something like this."

"You are too young to imagine half the things that people will do. Go on. And while you are at it, call to mind sailors who have been ushered out of the inn for brawling, and those who owe you money, and those to whom you owe money. Think of those you owe favors, as well. But most of all, think of those who you believe should be grateful to you. In my experience, those are the ones who most often do their benefactors ill."

"You have a low opinion of people, don't you?"

"Just a realistic one. One you would do well to acquire. Now begin."

It made her feel sick and old inside to sit and methodically list all the people who might possibly wish her family ill. Never before had she stopped to realize how many there might be. Out of such a multitude, how would L'Fertti ever find out who had done it, and what they had done? A more immediate worry came to her abruptly. "Will you have to come to the inn to find out what the curse is?"

"Of course!"

"But you can't get in. Daril has locked all the doors and let it be known that we are remodeling. She barely lets T'Nar and me in and out. No stranger will get into her kitchen."

"Leave that to me. And remember, when next you see me, that you do not know me," he added theatrically.

The last of the day was fading into dusk. Kaloo watched the sky tinge with pinks from her bedroom window. Usually she enjoyed the spectacle of the white towers and graceful arches of Liavek taking on the tints of the sunset. But tonight it was too much of a contrast with her bleak mood. She rolled from her bed and jerked the curtains closed. She was about to fling herself down again when the rising quaver of an old man's voice split the quiet of the street.

"Please, aid! Will no one come to an old man's aid?"

There was a heavy thud against the front doors of the inn. Kaloo was halfway down the stairs when a shirtless T'Nar passed her. He drew the bolt and threw the door open, tearing loose Daril's sign in the process. An emaciated old man fell into the room at his feet. His blue robe was tattered and stained, and a rusty streak in his white hair bespoke an injury. T'Nar moved swiftly but gently as he raised the old fellow and brought him to the comfort of the hearth cushions. "Kaloo! Get the door, and then fetch me some cool water. Quickly!"

By the time she brought the water he had arranged the frail old man on the hearth cushions and given him a light covering. T'Nar eased him to a sitting position and put the cup to his lips. The old man sipped, choked, and then managed a long drink of the water.

"Thank you," the oldster sighed, and Kaloo flinched at L'Fertti's voice. As he drew himself up and managed to sit without T'Nar's aid, she stared into his face, wondering how she had not recognized him. His features were not so changed, but his carriage and facial expressions were ones she had never seen before. He ignored her stare, smoothing the covering over his legs as if glad of its warmth.

"Can you tell us what happened to you?" T'Nar asked gently.

"In a moment. I feel so weak, and I must try to pull my poor old mind together. It has been . . . I don't know how long it has been since I last ate or drank, or knew the comfort of being without torment."

T'Nar, sensing a story that would bear many repeatings, leaned close to the old man. "Kaloo. Fetch a little of the good brandy, and see if you can stir up something for him to eat. A little broth, perhaps."

"Or something more solid, if you would not begrudge it to an old man. A slice of yesterday's roast, a bit of bread, some sausage or a wedge of cheese or a morsel of smoked fish. Whatever bits there are left in your kitchen that you can spare. I feel so hollow and faint." L'Fertti let his voice trail off as his eyes sagged nearly closed.

"Don't stand there, child," T'Nar snapped at her. "Fix him a plate, and not yesterday's scraps. I'll never have it said that the Mug and Anchor was stingy with a man in need."

In the kitchen, Kaloo clattered cutlery and dishes savagely as she slapped together a meal for the old miscreant. Lying to T'Nar! Of all the low tricks! She picked up the pepper sauce and was going to tip a spoonful of it into the noggin of brandy when her common sense triumphed. So she didn't approve of his methods. Well, at least he had gotten himself into the inn, and found a way to get T'Nar's ear.

She backed through the swinging door to the common room in time to catch part of L'Fertti's tale. ". . . and when I refused they threw me into the hold and left me there, without a scrap of food or a drop of water. And all because I would not curse that poor man's boat for them. No doubt they would have beaten me more severely, but I was able to use my luck to shield myself from the worst of their blows."

"Why didn't you blast them with your magic and be free of them?" T'Nar demanded in a voice choked with emotion. The mere notion of a curse on any kind of sea-going vessel was enough to rouse blind fury in any sailor in Liavek.

"Have you not listened to me, young man? Do you think all who invest their luck only abuse its power? No, I preferred to withstand their ill treatment until I could make my escape."

"Then at least tell me who did this, and I will see that they receive their dues," T'Nar growled.

"I told you. They came at me from behind, stole me from my own doorstep, and always kept their faces masked. I have no idea who they were, and as for the boat, well, when I managed to batter my way out of the hold, I found it was just a hulk, beached and left to rot. Yet even if I did know their names, I could not tell you, for I would not permit the kind of vengeance you are considering."

T'Nar grumbled and chewed his lip. Kaloo set the plate on a low bench beside L'Fertti, and approved of his inventiveness. One story had established him as a wizard, a gentle soul, one who knew that there was nobody lower than one who would curse a boat.

L'Fertti sniffed the brandy appreciatively and tossed it off. He attacked the plate with an interest that reminded Kaloo that she had not done the shopping for him that day. But if T'Nar saw anything unusual in his appetite, he made no mention of it. The embers seemed to fascinate him and he stared into them, seemingly lost in some puzzling of his own.

Kaloo felt a sudden and savage itch on the top of her head. She shot L'Fertti an angry glance as she scratched it, but he was rolling his eyes upwards and making tiny jerks with his head toward the ceiling. At first she could not fathom what he wanted, but at last she deciphered his hint.

"Why didn't Daril come down?" she asked T'Nar.

"Sound asleep," he replied, not even glancing at her. "Cried herself out, and fell asleep exhausted. It would take a tidal wave to stir her."

"Ah," L'Fertti sighed gently. "I feared as much. Yet I hoped I was wrong."

"What do you mean?" T'Nar asked in a soft growl. "What did you fear?"

"I thought I had the strength to take myself back to my own home, but as I passed the Mug and Anchor, I was overcome by a weakness and a sense of dread, of magic used to selfish and evil ends. I feared then that there was a curse upon your inn. Yet you let me in and treated me so kindly that I could not imagine you had any troubles of your own. For is it not said, 'Many a man is charitable until his own pocket is less than half full'?"

"Meaning?" Kaloo asked.

"Why, that only a fool asks help of someone who already has his own troubles. What folk enduring an unjust curse would have the time or charity to help a battered wretch like myself?"

"Ones who remember Liavekan hospitality." T'Nar accepted the compliment with only a hint of pride in his voice. Kaloo knew T'Nar well enough to sense the uneasiness that made him pause. "You . . . are a wizard, you have said."

L'Fertti met his question with a grave smile. "Yes. And one of great perception. I would like to use my skills to repay your kindness, yet I can feel that you are uneasy about all who use their luck, even those who would use it to your benefit. So let it be put to you this way: By the old laws of Liavekan hospitality, I ask you not to make this guest uncomfortable. Do not send me away with a debt upon my shoulders, but let me lighten your burden as you have lightened mine."

Kaloo let out a sigh of amazement. Perfect. T'Nar would never have been comfortable accepting aid, but L'Fertti was asking a favor.

"I doubt there is much that can be done for us . . . even by one with skills as sharp as yours. But if you really wish to try. . . ."

"I do. And my perceptions . . . wait . . . the pot-boil. Something about the kitchen and the food . . . it comes to me through the mists . . . the food is both good and bad by turns . . . the pot-boil seems most affected . . . I must follow my luck . . ."

L'Fertti rose with a creaking of knees, his eyes near closed in his seeming trance. His long graceful hands lifted from his sides, seemed to float before him and lead the way as he was drawn to the kitchen. Kaloo and T'Nar looked after him, she in disgust at his theatrics, he in confusion. But after the doors swung to behind the wizard, Kaloo heard T'Nar mumble, "I would swear I know him from somewhere. I am sure of it."

"Perhaps you have just seen him here and there, about Liavek," Kaloo suggested hastily. "Let's see what he's doing in there."

L'Fertti stood in the center of the kitchen, eyes tightly closed, hands fisted at his sides. Strange symbols had been chalked on the clean wood floor in a circle around him. Herbs Kaloo did not know were smoldering before him in one of the best saucers. They stank. He was working, finally working, Kaloo told herself. And about time, too. There was a sheen of sweat on his brow, and the concentration that shut him off from the rest of the world when he was actually calling on his luck. Kaloo knew that this would take some time. His was a slow and thoughtful sort of magic, and she didn't expect this to be as easy as lighting a candle or boiling a kettle of water.

Nor was it. The stars filled the clear skies over Liavek and still he stood. It wasn't until T'Nar left the room to relieve himself that L'Fertti seemed to snap out of his trance. Kaloo was sitting cross-legged on the floor, waiting patiently, when he suddenly expelled a breath as if coming up from a deep dive. "Not here," he told her succinctly. "The food is fine, the utensils are fine . . . have you any idea how many spoons there are in this place? The water is fine, the pots are fine. . . . Oh, let it go, and let me tell you that every object in this kitchen, right down to each brick in the oven, is as it should be. No curse, no magic, nothing with even a sniff of wizardliness about it. Are you sure your foster mother isn't having an off day? Change of life, perhaps? Does strange things to women. I once knew a lady—"

He stopped at the look of fury and insult on Kaloo's face. "Why don't you ask T'Nar about it?" she suggested in a small, cold voice. "I'm sure he'd be happy to discuss all the intimate details of Daril's physical condition."

"Sshh!" he hushed her as they heard T'Nar's boots in the common room. "Don't fly into a snit again. I was only trying to be thorough."

"Has he found anything?" T'Nar asked as soon as he saw that L'Fertti's eyes were open.

"That which troubles you is not within the kitchen, yet in the kitchen is where it does its mischief. Stand still a moment, both of you."

L'Fertti sank back into his trance. Kaloo and T'Nar exchanged shrugs, but complied. After an eternity of silence and waiting, L'Fertti said, "No, it's not on either of you."

T'Nar narrowed his eyes. "Why would either of us bring bad luck into our own inn? You don't make sense. Perhaps that knock on the head has damaged your faculties. I knew I should have looked at that wound. Let me see it now."

Kaloo coughed to cover her breath catching. There was a subtle change in T'Nar's attitude toward L'Fertti. Was it only his normal distrust of wizards or was there more to it?

"My head is fine now, thank you. I have seen to my own healing, since your generous meal gave me the strength to do so. No, I did not mean to imply that one of you had cursed the kitchen, only that you might unwittingly . . ."

The kitchen door swung open and Kaloo saw the reason for T'Nar's change of heart. It's all going to be my idea now, she reflected sourly. Daril stood in the door.

"Allow me to present the proprietor of the Mug and Anchor," T'Nar said. "Daril, this is the fellow I told you about when I discovered you had awakened. This is . . . beg pardon, I don't believe you gave me your name."

"Laf," the wizard said. "Only poor simple Laf, waylaid by evil men, starved and beaten, and trying now to repay the generosity of one who had helped me to recover from such treatment."

His words made no impression on Daril. "What is going on in my kitchen?" she demanded, glaring alike at chalk marks, scorched saucer, and wizard.

Kaloo matched her. "He's a wizard, Daril. He's trying to find out why the food is sometimes bad and sometimes good.

We . . . he thinks perhaps there is a curse on the inn."

Daril's mouth sagged open slightly. Then her face was contorted with an anger such as Kaloo had never seen. "Fools! The one thing I don't want done, and you do it! Tell someone of our shame! Why not proclaim it to all of Liavek? Can't you accept what has happened? Isn't it bad enough without dragging some old fool in here to make it worse? I don't know what you mean by 'the food is sometimes bad and sometimes good.' It's all bad! Rotten, stinking, gone rancid, spoiled! Do you think I'd have it changed by magic? And liable to be bad again as soon as the spell wore off! The Mug and Anchor is *my* inn, and the pot-boil served here is *my* pot-boil. Not some wizard's version of what it used to taste like, or ought to taste like! What is the matter with you two? Have you no respect for my feelings at all?" Suddenly the anger went from her eyes, her shoulders slumped, and she dropped heavily to the bench beside the hearth.

Always, always in Kaloo's life, Daril had been strong and unshakable, knowing all things, from how to cure a stomach ache to how to save jam that wasn't jelling. She had never been one for weeping or ranting. She had faced troubles and made the best of them. But this business with the pot-boil was drowning her. She sat on the bench, looking wounded, and tired, and aged, like the old women Kaloo saw on the street. Like she wished someone else would fix it, for a change.

T'Nar was the one who had hugged and tossed and tickled Kaloo when she was small, the one who teased and joked and comforted. Daril was the one who advised, ordered, made rules, and taught lessons. Kaloo could not remember when last Daril had hugged her, or kissed her. She did not remember Daril ever saying she loved her. It was a very long walk across the kitchen, to sit down on the bench beside Daril and put her arm across the older woman's shoulders. She noticed that T'Nar could not look at either of them. Even L'Fertti was embarrassed. He was staring fixedly at the ceiling, his eyes closed to slits, his hands clenched at his sides.

Kaloo's voice came out husky. "Daril. We didn't mean to upset you. We only wanted to help set things right. And the food has been bad and good today. When T'Nar and I ate some of the pot-boil, it was fine. Then when you came in and stirred it, it smelled awful. And now. The kitchen smelled fine for a while, and now . . ." Kaloo put a hand to her nose. The odor of something rotten was close to overpowering. Daril rose and stalked over to the counter. She lifted the lid from the cooled pot-boil and the rank stench filled the air.

"I thought I asked you to dump this out!" she wailed, as if the evidence of their misfortune was more than she could bear.

"No!"

They all started at L'Fertti's roar. T'Nar opened his mouth to put him in his place, but a wave of the wizard's hand silenced him before he could speak. "It's not the pot-boil. No, the pot-boil is fine. But . . . I feel a spell working here. I shall have to try an experiment. Mistress, if you would be so good as to step out of the kitchen?"

"Please!" Kaloo begged. "What harm can it do, Daril?"

"Spread our shame all over Liavek. We shall be the laughing stock of the whole town," she muttered, but she retreated, leaving the room with such a push of the swinging door that it slammed against the wall behind it. Kaloo turned anxiously back to L'Fertti. His eyes were closed again, his face screwed up in concentration.

"I once had a deckhand who looked like that, right before he got sick all over the galley. What's the matter with him?"

"Sshh! He's just concentrating. His magic takes time and effort."

"You seem to know a lot about it all of a sudden," T'Nar observed in a harsh whisper. Kaloo bit her tongue, wondering what was going through T'Nar's head now. Trust him not to miss a slip of her tongue.

L'Fertti gave an awakening snort suddenly, and spoke. "It's tied into the kitchen," he announced, smiling proudly.

"Didn't you just say it wasn't in the kitchen?" Kaloo asked. He wasn't getting anywhere. Her bringing him here had only upset Daril, and now T'Nar was on the trail of where she was really spending her spare time. Things couldn't get worse, and her wizard was contradicting himself.

L'Fertti said smugly, "You saw it yourself, and yet didn't see it. The food was fine when you and T'Nar ate it. Yet when Daril came into the kitchen, it was rotten. Sniff the air now. What do you smell?"

Kaloo sniffed and then shrugged. "Nothing."

"I smell a rat," T'Nar remarked in an undertone that didn't carry to L'Fertti.

"Exactly," the wizard agreed with Kaloo. "Nothing. Nothing

is rotten in this kitchen when Daril is not in it."

"If you are trying to say Daril is at the root of this, you had better say something else instead," the fisherman growled.

"Not exactly." L'Fertti stepped back from T'Nar and held up his hands. "I'm not saying Daril is doing it. Quite the contrary. Someone has done something to Daril. I thought at first it was a spell on the kitchen that was triggered whenever Daril entered it. But that's not quite it. There is a spell on Daril that is triggered when she enters the kitchen. So you don't have that serious a problem. Just keep Daril out of the kitchen and have Kaloo do all the cooking."

"No problem at all. She'd just make half of Liavek sick."

Kaloo was outraged. "Is that really how you propose to solve this? Just keep Daril out of the kitchen forever? Maybe we should try something simpler, like building a new kitchen that won't trigger the curse, or moving the cooking hearth out into the common room! Maybe we should just move the whole Mug and Anchor!"

"All perfectly good alternatives to my suggestions." L'Fertti's tone was acid.

"I thought you could solve the problem, not just find ways to sidestep it. Don't you understand, you old camel? You're talking about taking everything away from Daril. How'd you like to lose your magic? That's what it would be like for her!"

The comparison seemed to move him, and L'Fertti considered a moment. "I must speak to the lady and determine the source of the curse. Has she received a gift of jewelry lately? A new garment? Clothing we can burn in the hearth if it is the source; spelled gems I shall bear away with me to a place where they can no longer work their mischief."

"I bet you will," Kaloo mumbled under her breath.

"Let me have a word with her," T'Nar suggested. "She is difficult sometimes, and reluctant to have much to do with magic. It can be a fickle ally. I feel much the same. Someone very dear to me was once lost through too much contact with the deadlier side of luck. I wouldn't want to lose another." His voice took on a graver note as he spoke, and he looked at Kaloo. Kaloo stared back innocently. He nodded, as much to himself as to them, and exited to the common room.

Kaloo glowered at L'Fertti. "He suspects there's something between us," she hissed. He only shrugged his shoulders at her. In a moment T'Nar's voice reached them. "Kaloo. Wizard. She'll hear you out now."

Daril was waiting for them on a bench drawn up by the hearth. Her red curls were incongruously brave above her set face and wary eyes. T'Nar stood behind her, one hand on her shoulder. Her eyes flicked to Kaloo, then gripped L'Fertti's.

"No one has given me jewels. And the clothing I wear is that I have sewn myself, from cloth purchased several months ago. I'm a simple, honest innkeeper who makes good, clean food for working sailors and runs a clean, honest inn. So don't think I'll be buying magic from you to change this misfortune, because I won't."

L'Fertti stood the outburst well. "I ask nothing of you, except that I be allowed to examine your aura."

"And I won't be touched by any wizard, either!" Daril would have stood and fled, but T'Nar's hand restrained her.

"Everything will be fine," he said. "If it isn't, I'll beat the luck out of him."

"No need for violence," L'Fertti quailed.

"No. It's not your way, is it?" T'Nar grinned meaningfully.

Muttering in his beard, L'Fertti stooped to draw with chalk upon the common-room floor. There was a moment of indecision when he had to ask T'Nar to move out of the figure he was making around Daril, but at last they both co-operated. When she was enclosed in three circuits done in six different colors of chalk, L'Fertti seemed satisfied. He crouched to draw a smaller figure about himself, decorated with symbols at each angle. Then he stood, crossed his arms on his chest, and closed his eyes.

After a bit, Kaloo's legs began to ache. She quietly seated herself. Daril sat very still, her eyes sagged almost shut, her breathing even and very deep. She looked like a weary innworker taking a nap after a busy day. L'Fertti was a different matter. Sweat shone on his face; there were lines gouged deep in his brow. Damp circles were spreading under the arms of his robe. His eyes were clenched shut, and he stood motionless save for the spasmodic twitching of his fingers. At one point Kaloo left the room and returned with two hot mugs of kaf. As she handed one to T'Nar, he spoke very softly to her. "At least Roen was closer to your age."

Kaloo flinched. No use pretending now. "That's not how it is, T'Nar."

"I know," he said gravely. "If I didn't, do you think this Laf would still be standing? Yet I'd almost rather it was an affair of the heart between you than what I suspect it is. I know you're nearly a woman now. There's no way I can forbid this. All I can hope is that his motives are the same as yours."

"Think what you like," Kaloo flashed. "But as you say, I am near a woman grown. I don't have to explain this to you. And I won't."

"Then I won't ask you about it." T'Nar's voice was cold with finality. She knew he meant what he said. "But I hope you'll be careful. I hope—"

A heavy thud turned their heads. L'Fertti was sitting flat in his figure, trembling. Daril stirred and lifted her head.

"Stay back!" the old wizard hissed as T'Nar and Kaloo started forward. Dragging moments hung, and then the chalk figures on the floor melted into a meaningless smear. "Now," he gasped. "Do I smell kaf? Fetch some for both of us."

Kaloo hastened to bring it as T'Nar moved to support Daril. When she returned from the kitchen, the wizard was slowly shaking his head. "It was almost too subtle for me," he explained, taking the mug from Kaloo. "Whoever did it paid well for that strength of magic. And if it was done by the one who specializes in such spells, I'll wager he didn't take money as payment. He has other hungers. A subtle spell. Yet, in the end, it could not elude me. Mistress, I am forced to ask a personal question. Is your hair . . . natural?"

Daril sat a little straighter. Red flushed her cheeks as she put a hand to her coiffed locks. "Why? Does it look that bad?"

"On the contrary, I find it charming," L'Fertti assured her, earning a glare from T'Nar. "Even bewitching," he added in an undertone.

"I wasn't sure of it at first, but Dori insisted."

"Dori with the slop shop on the houseboat on the canal?" L'Fertti broke in. He shot Kaloo a superior look.

"Well, yes, but you shouldn't call it a slop shop. She makes very good bread, and her soup—"

"Is the best kitty stew in Liavek. When her customers sing the 'Pot-boil Blues,' they do it with feeling!" T'Nar interjected.

"T'Nar, don't be unkind. She does very well, considering what she has to work with."

Kaloo snapped out of her silence. "Doesn't she owe us money?"

"A levar or two," Daril admitted.

"Or three, or five," T'nar added in an undertone.

But Daril had heard him. She rounded on him. "Well, I'll

not say it's paltry to us, but it's a far greater sum to her. She has her moorage fees to pay, and her trade hasn't been brisk. . . ."

"But she does owe us money. Has she paid any back lately?"

"Well, no. Kaloo, what's come over you? When did you start to care about such things?"

"Exactly how much does she owe us?" T'Nar asked. His dark eyes went from Daril's to Kaloo's. His quiet was dangerous.

"Well," Daril hesitated, flustered. "I suppose I'd have to figure it up to be sure, but . . ."

"That much, hm? When's the last time she spoke of paying it back?"

"She had promised to pay back part of it on Windday. I wasn't even thinking of it when I stopped by to see her. But she got flustered when she saw me, and was close to crying when she told me she didn't have it."

Daril began to relax and spoke as volubly as if L'Fertti were a customer. "'What's a few coins between friends?' I told her. 'A few coins to you,' she said, 'but I know you could take my boat for it. But you wouldn't understand. You've never had to lie awake and worry about losing your business and home.' On and on like that, she was, caught between anger and crying. I didn't know what to say."

Daril glanced anxiously around her circle of listeners to ask sympathy for Dori. But T'Nar's face was stony. "People like that are always the same. They think we don't have problems because we don't howl them all over Liavek. And they'll always twist it around so that their misfortune is the fault of those who do well, and not the result of their own foolishness."

"Well, but then she calmed down and apologized for being so rude. I told her it didn't matter, but she insisted on doing something to show how she felt. 'I'm going to fix your hair,' she said. 'Not as payment, but just as a token of how I feel about you. A well-to-do innkeeper like yourself should keep up her appearance. It's not like you can't afford to look nice.' Well, I didn't see it that way at all, but as I'd always told her I admired her way of fixing her hair, I couldn't very well say no. She got the curls to stay, which I've never been able to do. And she even used up the last of the special herbs she had that put the gloss of youth back on your tresses. That's just how she said it. Though I don't think it's quite the color I had when I was a girl. And when I came home and T'Nar admired it, I felt better. You don't know what a mercy it is in this hot weather, to finally have it up off my neck and forehead."

L'Fertti had been nodding steadily. Now he turned to Kaloo. "A large tub or basin. Soft soap, warm water, and plenty of vinegar. Quickly. Some of those herbs can be irritating to the skin, to say nothing of the magic mixed with them."

It was done quickly, a chagrined Daril sitting with her head bowed over the basin as Kaloo soaped and rinsed. Two ewers of vinegar and three of fresh water were used before L'Fertti was satisfied. T'Nar set the tub of polluted water outside to be dumped later, on the beach where the ocean could disperse the magic. As he opened the door, Kaloo was surprised at the gray flash of dawn he let in.

"Morning already. And we've not started the breads for the day, nor renewed the pot-boil," she sighed.

"We won't be opening today anyway," Daril reminded her from under the towel she was using to dry her steel-gray mane. "Remember that I told the *Cat Street Crier* that we were re-modeling. I'll have to change a few things before we open again, or they'll know that we've been doing something else."

"What about Dori?"

"What about her?" Daril turned away, but not before Kaloo had seen the hurt in her eyes. "Just be glad you don't have to live with her conscience."

"But why would she do it?" Kaloo puzzled.

"Misery loves company, they say. Perhaps she thought my life undeservedly easy."

"What if she tries something else?" T'Nar asked gruffly.

"I know her better than you. She'd only have the courage once. When next she sees me, I fancy she will know I'm not as big a fool as I looked. No, let it go, T'Nar. And I don't want you meddling in it either, Kaloo. Now." She took a deep breath and changed the subject. "Kaloo, what do you think of new hangings for the wall? I saw some red and yellow ones in the Market yesterday."

"If I may be allowed to speak, why spend money for new cloth, when it would cost you less to have me magically alter the appearance of the hangings you have now?"

Daril withered L'Fertti. "I thank you for what you've done, wizard. But the Mug and Anchor is an honest inn. If I put up new hangings, then they're new hangings, to last until they wear out. If you put a spell on the old ones, then they're still the old ones, no matter what semblance you give them. And the old ones are what my customers will see when the spell wears off, or some cart runs over you. I'll have none of your magic about here."

"Nor I." T'Nar broke in suddenly, speaking more harshly than the subject seemed to warrant. He stood. "Daril, the matter of new hangings will keep. There's another matter that needs discussing." He locked eyes with L'Fertti. "Exactly what's going on between you and Kaloo, and how long has it been going on?"

Silence swallowed the room. L'Fertti gaped like a fish and Daril gasped as the meaning of T'Nar's words reached her.

"But I thought you had brought the wizard in?" Daril glanced in confusion from one face to the next.

"I assure you, mistress, I am but a wandering—" L'Fertti began.

"Too late," Kaloo cut in, disgusted. "No, Daril, I brought L'Fertti into this."

"What have you to do with wizards and the like?" Daril was incredulous. Her face was as unbelieving as if Kaloo had announced she had been dallying with His Scarlet Eminence.

Kaloo glanced from Daril to T'Nar. She made a quick gesture asking for L'Fertti's silence. "I'm studying with him. I intend to invest my luck."

Daril sat down, the damp towel falling from her hand. She gave Kaloo a look of dumb anguish.

"I wouldn't mind so much, if she knew what she was doing. I blame you, wizard, not the child." T'Nar spoke bitterly.

"I'm not a child. And I do know what I'm doing. It's not as frightening as you've led me to believe, T'Nar. Look what magic has done for us this night. Was that a dark and dangerous thing? If it weren't for L'Fertti's magic, we'd be out of business."

"If it weren't for magic in the first place, there wouldn't have been a threat to our business," Daril countered. "Kaloo, child! This luck investiture is not a thing for folks like us. It's fine, I suppose, for folks who can't or won't work, or for a girl who has no other prospects. But not for you. Why, it goes against all that you are. For generations, our family has run this inn, putting out an honest meal for an honest price. Perhaps it isn't exciting and glamorous, but it's nothing to be ashamed of, either."

"Your family, not mine. Who knows what my family has been doing for generations?" The cold words hung in the air, and it took Kaloo an instant to realize that she had actually spoken them aloud. "I mean—" she tried to amend, but the damage had been done. T'Nar's eyes blazed at her. Daril's were wide and empty. This, coming in the wake of the pot-boil curse, was too much for her. She dropped her face into her hands. Kaloo was guiltily grateful that she did not have to see her foster-mother's expression.

"I really must be going," L'Fertti quavered, stepping lightly toward the door.

"No stomach for what you've wrought?" T'Nar snarled, his hands resting on Daril's shaking shoulders. "Stay, wizard. This is going to be settled."

L'Fertti froze obediently. T'Nar transferred his stare from the wizard to the girl. Blood darkened his face. He aged before her eyes. "If I had known this day would come," he said, voice shaking, "I wonder if I would have bothered with you."

"T'Nar!" Daril gasped in rebuke. "Don't say such things!"

Kaloo unclenched her jaws to speak. "Well, you needn't bother any longer. If you can't accept that I have to be whatever it is that I am, then there's no place here for me. I'll go. I'm old enough. I can manage on my own."

"Fine! Get out, then!" T'Nar snapped, but Daril shrieked. "T'Nar, no, oh no, don't say that. She mustn't go. Kaloo, you can be whatever you wish, do whatever you like, but please don't go!" Daril's voice soared up the scale as she gripped T'Nar's arm pleadingly. "Don't let her go! Make her stay. She's all I have. And she's all you have left!"

Daril was shaking, her eyes and nose running, her face mottled red and white beneath her damp gray dangling hair. Kaloo had never seen her so distraught, nor suspected her stolid manner of masking such intensity of feeling. She had thought her foster-mother was immune to the kind of emotional storms that wracked Kaloo's own heart. With sudden guilt she realized that her thoughtless remark had struck very deep to unleash these hidden things.

"Please!" Daril begged suddenly, standing and opening her arms. "If you go away, there's nothing left!"

Kaloo was undone. She did not know how she crossed the room, but she was hugging Daril tightly, weeping for the pain she had caused and would never be able to erase. Daril clutched the girl, staring defiantly at the two men. "Arrange it!" she commanded T'Nar shrilly.

The man stood frozen and torn. With a cry, he brought both his fists down on top of a table, making it shudder and skip over the rough floor with the impact. The wizard yelped and cringed, but T'Nar shook his head like a baffled bull. Putting his fists behind his back, he took a deep breath.

"All right," he conceded savagely. "All right. But it will be on my terms. You, wizard, will come here for these 'lessons.' I'll not have her dangling about Wizard's Row, consorting with the gods only know what. If she must be taught, teach her well. I'll see that you are paid for your time, so be sure that my money is the only thing you take in payment." He looked at the wizard with cold and knowing eyes. "Do we have an understanding?"

"We do! We do!" L'Fertti assured him frantically. He turned and vanished through the inn doors like a rabbit darting into its burrow. The dark look T'Nar gave Kaloo frightened her, but Daril only gripped her more tightly.

"She's mine, T'Nar. Mine. And it's going to be all right. You'll see."

"What have I done to you?" he asked in a stricken voice, and slammed his way into the kitchen.

Kaloo wondered which of them he had been speaking to. Daril gave a ragged sigh and wiped her hand across her face. She freed herself from Kaloo awkwardly and glanced about the inn as she shook out her skirts and patted at her dangling hair. "Yes," she said, her voice still unsteady. "New hangings will make a world of difference in here."

"Perhaps blue," Kaloo said, clearing her voice to cover the break in it.

"Yes, blue would be lovely," Daril immediately agreed. She tried to meet Kaloo's eyes, but it was too soon. "Don't worry about T'Nar," she spoke softly to the old hangings. "He'll come around. It's harder for men to see their daughters grow up. Makes them feel old and useless. Well," she added in a suddenly brisk voice. "Will you look at me? I'd best get upstairs and fix myself. You'd think I'd been through a war!"

"Grown up," Kaloo muttered to herself. The empty room made no reply. Well, she'd won. Daril knew she was old enough to make her own decisions now. She was going to study with L'Fertti and invest her luck. The pot-boil was safe, and the inn was going to have new blue hangings. She should be happy; everything had turned out so well.

"He's never going to take me fishing again," she said softly. She stared at the dead embers in the fireplace and hugged herself against the chill.

Show of Faith

by Gregory Frost

THE CATTLE HAD appeared on the Farmer's Road near dusk, precisely as Jolesha had heard one of the granary guards predict. By then a harsh wind had risen from the direction of the Sea of Luck, a briny, gritty wind. It snatched away the sounds of the men she watched below, erased the clamor of the approaching cattle. In the last light of day, she peered into the cul-de-sac and watched the guards and the herdsmen work the pulley system that opened the gates on the chutes and let a river of grain pour into the feed troughs. One of the guards jumped up to straddle the trough and began raking the grain along it. Jolesha looked across the ridge and saw Urgelian waving, his signal that now they could be about their business. As she scurried across the open space to the nearest of the three wells, she silently gave thanks to Roashushe, god of the surf, for sending the wind; surely, when their work was done, the guards would remain down in the cul-de-sac, where the stinging wind could not bite.

Wide capstones marked the three subterranean silos like three dolmens. Once there had been silos above the ground here, but those had been burned down in the Saltigan Wars as, very nearly, the city of Liavek had been; so, in a very real sense, the capstones were markers of another time.

Jolesha crouched in the shadow of the capstone, her eyes alone marking her position, glittering like two new stars in that nocturnal face. She watched Urgelian come boldly across the flat toward her, while her other companion, Klefti, appeared silently from the next capstone along. Urgelian had a rope slung over his shoulder. As he crouched into the shadow beside her, he shrugged and the rope slid down his arm.

"Loop it around one of the supports before you tie it to yourself," he whispered to her.

"I know," she replied peevishly. Urgelian always tried to dominate his two comrades. It was his single characteristic that irritated her; otherwise she loved him very dearly in secret. But because of his need to be first, her pride would not allow her to say so, while his pride would have made him reject her advances in any case.

She tied the rope securely around her middle and tugged on it to satisfy herself that the knot would hold. Her hands were sweating. For a moment the wind shifted, buffeting them with the sound of lowing cattle. Klefti handed her the two sets of saddlebags she was to fill. He touched the base of his palm to his forehead, then drew his hand down with the fingers curled— his way of telling her to have strength against her fear of heights. Klefti, who could not speak, never doubted she would triumph. After all, the silo lay underground.

Jolesha reached up and pulled herself over the edge of the storage well. Balanced on it, she patted the dark in search of the second wall, called the spoilage wall, that kept the earth's moisture from reaching the precious grain. The distance between the two walls was a matter of inches, but enough that she could imagine herself accidentally slipping between the two and dying there, wedged in place. Angry at herself, she banished the image and recklessly swung her legs toward the middle of the wide well. For a second the rope failed to support her and she almost screamed. Then it jerked tight at her waist. She gritted her teeth and let go of the lip of the inner wall.

Klefti and Urgelian played the rope out slowly as she descended into utter darkness. Earlier she had looked into the silo, and she knew that somewhere below her lay a walkway where the farmers stood while emptying their sacks into the well. She tried to guess how near she was to the walkway and stretched her toes to touch it. Finally, her feet brushed the boards. She realized then that she had been squeezing her eyes shut and opened them. The difference was negligible.

She groped for the railing on the walkway, found it, and climbed over, then let the rope take her again, down into the pit. This final descent seemed to expand into hours. Then quite abruptly her feet crunched into the top layer of grain and the rope began to go slack. She sank up to her knees before the kernels compressed enough to buoy her. Refusing to give in to her fears, she made herself let go of the rope: she sank no further. Quickly, she unslung the saddlebags and opened them, then began scooping grain into the bags. She kept her thoughts on the plan, the plan to make money. This grain would do that for them. Klefti knew the secrets of making Dragonsmoke. All it would take was one more trip down, four more bags of grain. It would not be the best Dragonsmoke perhaps, but how often did anyone on the way to Ombaya get *any* kind of potent drink? Herdsmen, just paid for delivering their cattle, would be free-wheeling with their money if approached properly. This plan, this glorious plan, had been most carefully considered. None of them were thieves by nature, only by circumstances. And who would miss a few small bags of cattle feed?

She drew the bags closed, then tugged on the rope. She was jerked out of the pile, loose grain hissing off her clothes. Some kernels trickled into her boots. Jolesha began to rock back and forth and had to keep one hand out for the walkway. She bumped up against it sooner than she had expected, but climbed the rail easily. She pushed herself off from the railing with a bit too much zealousness, as she discovered a moment later when she smacked against the wall. After that, she merely clung to the rope and let the other two do the work.

At the top, she stretched herself across the two walls and heaved the bags over to Klefti. Urgelian remained holding the rope. The bags had cut into her shoulders with their weight. Klefti took them and gave her two more sets of empty ones. She realized suddenly that the wind had shifted again, that she could hear the mooing cattle and the shouts from the men. They seemed angry, but she knew she was nervous and not given to reason at this point. Klefti vanished almost silently. The rope tautened as he rejoined Urgelian beside the capstone. Jolesha took a breath, then pushed herself backward into the well.

Down she went for a second time into the pit. The smell was cloying now and the dust tickled her throat. She went off the railing like an experienced climber, soon settling into the grain again. She filled the bags and strapped them on, twisting the strap of one and cursing as she fiddled with it in the dark. Her collarbone hurt. One good tug and she ascended—for the last time, she told herself. It was all well and fine to pretend

bravery but quite another to perform so boldly. Next time Urgelian insisted on showing his skill, she would let—

The rope went slack. Jolesha found herself holding onto
nothing. She turned, clutching for something to support her,
cried out, and shot headlong back into the grain. She hit with
a smack. Tiny kernels poured into her nose and mouth, crackled
in her ears. She kicked and flailed like a Kil in a whirlpool,
clawing through the grain. Its dust gagged her and she thought
she would suffocate. She could not tell if she were digging out
or burrowing in and realized in a panic that she might be burying
herself. Wildly, she pushed up out of the grain into darkness,
spitting and choking on the noise she made. Air filled her
greedy lungs and she began to calm down, to consider what
had happened.

Had the rope broken? She tugged hard and found it still
strung up in the air. Something scuffled above. A misty light
appeared, illuminating a face—a dark face encircled by a white
cowl. It was the cowl that somehow glowed, creating light.
The face saw her but instead of registering surprise it cracked
a smile, then threw something down into the grain beside her.
Instinctively, she dug her fingers into the kernels until she felt
the softness of leather. She pulled out a small but heavy bundle.
As she fondled its shape, her rope came spilling down on top
of her. The light vanished.

Voices echoed in the well, phrases strangely warped by the
wind. Jolesha heard anger in the voices. She crawled her way
across the grain until she lay against the cold stone wall. She
lay very still and tried to understand the shouting. Light suddenly appeared overhead, above the walkway, which both
blocked her view and hid her in its shadow. A voice said, "This
is the one he ducked into. He must have thrown it down here,
Count Dashif."

"I should do the same to you," answered a much deeper
voice, "for allowing him so much freedom in his escape. I
suppose your men have killed him?"

"Well, I . . ." The voice faltered. The light retreated.

Something unforseeable had occurred, Jolesha knew, and
Urgelian and Klefti had been forced to flee. She understood
that. The problem was how to get out of here before the grain
did suck her down. She banished the image of ghoulish hands
reaching up from the depths.

Flickering light appeared above the walkway again. The

same voice that had addressed Count Dashif spoke again. "He says it's our fault the priest is dead."

"'Course he does," came a reply, followed by a grunting, wheezing, then the creak of wood, and, shortly, a thump. "You don't think he's going to tell the likes of Resh that *he* bunged the beggar, now do you?" The voice was getting louder; Jolesha realized with horror that the man had lowered a ladder and was descending. She wriggled down into the grain, all but her head. "Hey, what's that rope doing down there?" Footsteps tread the boards above her. The torchlight pushed the shadows toward her.

"How should I know? Probably some sod of a farmer dropped it. You couldn't pay me to go down there and get it. Probably full of rats."

"Well, you won't have to, will you? You know what he said? He said that he doesn't care if we have to empty all *three* wells and how dare we put the importance of cattle feed above the Regent's satisfaction. That snooty bastard."

"Better not say that around him. There's a rumor he killed a girlfriend for crossin' him. And I know he killed a camel once that annoyed him."

"I'd believe anything about Dashif. Anyway, we might as well go down the other end and watch it pour out the chute. There's no artifact lying around down here. If that nasty priest threw it in, it's going to be halfway to the bottom. Did you see the muscles on him?"

"Yeah. But, look, Habig, it's not even Fog—you any idea how many herds are going to come needing this between now and Flowers?"

"Plenty," replied Habig on his way back up. "But none of them needs it like Dashif needs that stupid artifact. Tell you, I hope it's right at the bottom, 'cause I don't care to freeze *my* arse off kicking through this grain."

"Got worms in it."

"Bugger!"

The voices and light faded away but Jolesha had learned all that she needed to escape. Around the wall above her, struts hammered in between the stones supported the walkway. She scooped her way to the nearest one, then pressed herself up the wall until her fingers touched the wooden beam. She shook off the bags, then hung from the beam and walked one leg up the wall and over the strut. Ignoring the splinters that stabbed her hands and legs, she inched up the strut like a caterpillar, gripping it with both thighs while she got a hold on the edge of the walkway. Finally, she dared to let go of the strut and swung herself up by degrees, onto the boards. They creaked with her weight as they had with Habig's. She lay flat, ready to drop out of sight again if necessary. Nobody came. The wind skirled in under the capstone. She got to her feet and stood poised, listening intently, but nothing could be heard above that wind.

Jolesha felt her way step by step around the walkway until she bumped up against the ladder they had lowered. Emptying the silo would take hours; she hoped they would not be back for their ladder before then. Cautiously, she climbed up to the lip of the well. From there she scanned the plateau outside. It seemed utterly stark. There were no trees there to capture the wind, nothing for anyone to hide behind except rocks. No one moved out there, no torchlights could be seen, and she could see in every direction. Not too far away a pale shape lay on the ground. She saw movement there and, with a sick premonition, climbed over the lip and then scurried low across to it.

The face lay in shadow, but the cowled robe proved that this was the same man who had smiled down upon her in the well. He had been a priest of the White Faith, the ones who called themselves the Church of Truth, denying all empyrean promises of all other faiths, just as all other faiths denied everyone else's. He was dead, however—the motion she had seen had been the wind picking at his robe. A flower of blood decorated the center of it, just above the sash. He might well know the truth about the afterlife now, she considered, but he would not be passing it on. Her fingers traced the heavy object tucked into her tunic.

She moved away from the priest, her attention on the edge of the hill where at any moment she anticipated a torch would appear. In looking away she did not see the second body, and she stumbled and sprawled across it. Her head hit the ground beside his. The marksmen had been less decorative in targeting Urgelian. They had shot off half his face.

Jolesha crawled, then ran, then fled from the horror of what they had done, but it pursued her like a ghost through the dust devils.

•   •   •

Two cords bound the leather pouch. They unknotted easily and Jolesha rolled the artifact into her hand: a cylinder, twice the width of her palm. The surface looked like highly polished gold worked into interlocking strips, a gridwork pattern, around the central core. She held it up to the morning light but the black glass or gem beneath the gold remained absolutely opaque. Why was it so heavy? She could not figure it out.

Klefti tugged on her shoulder.

"Oh, I'm sorry. Here, see it for yourself." She handed over the artifact. He turned it over and around, his fingers following the weave of the gold. He looked at each end, where the cylinder was slightly larger in circumference. His dark face screwed up in perplexity. Finally, he shook his head and gave the cylinder back to her. She was about to wrap it up again when she noticed the iridescence of the inner leather surface. She rubbed her fingertips on it, felt its waxiness. None of this made the purpose of the object any clearer. Magic was something she had little knowledge of; she considered it a dangerous subject and stayed as far away from it as she did from the roofs of tall buildings. "I think we should take it to the Levar," she told Klefti. "If it *is* magic, she'll know what to do with it better than we will."

Klefti shook his head and pointed to his temple to indicate madness.

"Perhaps, I don't know. But maybe we can get money, Klefti."

He brooded on that, nodded with the greatest reluctance. She pressed her hand to his cheek. He had pursued her from the silos and held her while she cried. She had fallen asleep crying, not needing to tell him what she felt. Klefti knew her so well. He knew a great many things that no one would have suspected of him, like the process for making Dragonsmoke.

She got up and pulled Klefti to his feet. Here they were, two homeless thieves who would gladly have been anything else had the world offered alternatives. Orphans held little hope for better things.

They set off, walking, to the city, to Liavek, and Jolesha let herself fantasize about riches and opulence as she tucked the wrapped cylinder back inside her heavy tunic and rubbed her arms against the morning's chill.

Once there had been a better life for her. Until she was six, she had parents whom she thought were in love and loved her.

Then her father showed her how wrong she was by assaulting, killing her mother, then turning on Jolesha. By then the noise had brought neighbors and soldiers. Her father was prevented from harming her, was beaten and dragged away. She remembered people standing over her like trees, recalled the twisted way her mother lay in death beside her, and one of her father's teeth where it lay on the dirty floor. Someone in that towering crowd told her that her mother had taken a lover and her father had killed him first and now would have to go live on Crab Isle. She supposed that he, too, must be dead by now. No one lasted long on Crab Isle.

Independence had been forced upon her after that. By the time she was nine she had the self-reliance of an adult. At the Hrothvek orphanage, she met Urgelian and Klefti. Urgelian's parents had died when their tavern burned. Klefti, like her, had been orphaned by his parents, specifically by his mother, who had gone mad from some addictive drug. They became an inseparable trio at Hrothvek, capable of protecting themselves because they were three. Finally, they escaped together.

That was three years ago; they had lived on their wits ever since. Winters were the hardest, even along the warm coast. She remembered a night last Snow, when the temperature had suddenly plummeted, catching the beggars who slept outside unawares; she could still see the soldiers carrying away all the stiff, frozen bodies the next morning. So many drunks and addled beggars had perished that, for a time, things had been easier in Hrothvek, hardly any competition. But more always came. Equality, like everything else in the world, belonged to those who had money to buy it.

These things concerned her as she walked beside Klefti that day. She remembered her adventures with him and Urgelian. They all seemed fantasies now, as though someone else had told them to her and she had made up the pictures in her head.

The nearer she and Klefti got to the city of Liavek, the more people they saw. People herded sheep and pigs; two fishermen discussed the amazingly good season over on Minnow Island, one trying to convince the other to go there. Jolesha lifted a dried fish from his supplies. She and Klefti ate it greedily while watching a man in a tent booth beside the road trying to convince passersby—and he had a good crowd—to "invest" their money in his business, the specifics of which seemed more than a little vague. The salesman made a great joke of playing on all the meanings in that word, invest: "Magic, my friends, is what you'll think it is when you see your money triple, quadruple even, before next Buds and Flowers. Invest in me, let me invest for you, and we'll all be rich together. And, to show my good intentions, my good faith, in return, these wonderful implements can be yours. Invest ten levars and receive this hand-crafted mug for your kaf; twenty levars and you'll walk away in these handsome sandals, absolutely free." He went on showing people all the gifts they could receive. Many in his audience began fumbling for coins. Jolesha and Klefti moved through them, scavenging dropped pieces of copper and silver, but no gold.

"Why didn't we ever think of so obvious a ploy?" Jolesha asked Klefti as they left the crowd. "People will believe anything if they think you'll make them richer in the bargain." She heard herself say that and wondered if she were any different, really, with her fantasies.

They wandered along Market Street and spent most of their coin on meat pies and kaf where that road met up with the Levar's Way. It was dusk when they reached the Levar's Park. Musicians played, acrobats leapt over flames, and more booths sold steaming food. Among the shops that lined Gold Street they found hostelry for the night, paid for with the last of the money they had scrounged.

Just before dawn the two of them left the hostel and went across the park toward the spires of the Levar's Palace. They had gone perhaps halfway through the park—Klefti again scrutinizing the artifact—when Jolesha stepped off the path and pulled him after her into the bushes.

In an open area where three of the paths intersected ahead, two men stood back to back, each with a matchlock pistol held up beside his cheek. Three others looked on, their backs to Jolesha and Klefti. The two armed men began to stride away from each other, their steps smooth, slow, rhythmic. One was lost to sight behind the foliage. Abruptly, the other man turned, lowering his pistol. Before he could fire, there came a loud shot and he suddenly spun around and slammed to the ground. One of the three onlookers went calmly to the body and knelt there. Klefti suddenly clutched Jolesha and she assumed the spectacle of the duel had overwhelmed him, but he tugged harder and she glanced over at him to find him bathed in light thrown off by the artifact. The blackness beneath the gold had

turned pink, the intensity throbbing. A whispery voice issued
from it; "Marakele, Marakele, I fought for you. Marakele . . ."

The strange, susurrant voice faded and the color dimmed
in the cylinder. It was a wonder to Jolesha that Klefti had not
dropped it. He stared into her eyes and there was so much
distress in that look that she could not answer him.

One of the onlookers placed a blue cape around the shoulders
of the surviving duelist and they turned away from the scene.
The onlooker grinned like a father proud of his son and said,
"Now the girl is yours—even her parents won't interfere if
you want her. I envy you." The duelist grunted and sneered to
his companion. Jolesha could smell him as he passed.

Klefti still held out the artifact. She took it from him and
wrapped it up again. Somehow it had let them hear a dead
man's voice, of that she was certain. The sooner it belonged
to somebody else, the happier she would be. Even getting
money for it had become of minor importance.

At first the two Scarlet Guards insisted that the Levar saw
no one, being far too busy with preparations for the End of
Wine to hear some beggar's tale. Then Jolesha explained that
she had a religious artifact to deliver to the Levar, an artifact
belonging to the Church of Truth. The guards fell silent then,
eyeing one another with something akin to wonder. One of
them said, "You'd best come with me then," as if to his com-
rade, but she knew he was speaking to her. Klefti started to
accompany her but the other guard grabbed him by the scruff
of the neck. "Not you. You stay put, whelp." Jolesha went
back and calmed him, saying, "Wait for me here. I'll be fine.
If it takes long, you go to where we saw the duel fought and
meet me there. Okay?" She smiled to show him things would
be fine, but she was hardly inclined to believe that herself. She
shot the guard a hard look but he did not seem to notice. The
other one said, "Girl?" and she backed a few steps, then turned
and followed him.

The guard led her past neatly trimmed bushes and up wide
marble stairs. They went inside, where it was warmer, she saw,
because they had come in near the kitchens; she caught a glimpse
of vats hung in the back, a spitted pig, and a table piled with
fresh loaves of bread, all different colors and textures. The
guard marched at a steady pace along the halls, oblivious to
the tapestries, murals, and sculptures that adorned them. Jo-

lesha slowed and stared at every one of them, touching an enormous marble Kil rising from a waterspout, the eyes fitted with emeralds; she was completely awed by a painting of the Levar that was mostly gilt-work, and by a mural of farmers irrigating their fields, which rose up the height of two floors. She had to run to keep up with the guard. She was breathing wealth and power the likes of which she had never seen; they rode the air like the smell of baking bread.

The guard brought her to an anteroom of woven rugs, floor-length curtains, and intaglio woodwork. "You wait here now and I'll get Count Dashif to hear your case." As he retreated, he was grinning at her as if at his favorite food, but Jolesha hardly noticed. The name . . . the one who had stood above her in the silo, who had been responsible in some way for Urgelian's death. She had stumbled into a terrible trap. She thought to run back through the Palace but was certain the guard would spy her, and even if he didn't, she knew she would never be able to retrace her steps.

The curtains at the far end of the room opened onto a high window that showed her a view of a courtyard two stories below. She backed away from it dizzily, her eyes squeezed shut. Soldiers had been drilling down there, and across the yard she had seen the kitchen chimneys and so knew where she was. In no way could she make herself look below much less climb out and escape. But the guard must think she had done just that. She steeled herself enough to reach out and throw the window open. In the anteroom again, she searched for a place to hide and noticed immediately that the woodwork had been designed to conceal the cupboard doors that lined both sides of the room. Jolesha tried two before she found one she could squeeze into. She dragged the door closed, then listened against it.

She hid in that cramped place so long that she thought no one would be coming back. Then someone ran into the room. "She's gone," the guard exclaimed.

"I shouldn't be at all surprised if she weren't even corporeal," said the voice she had heard in the silo.

"Lord?"

"Forget it. I'm surrounded by fools, and worse still, fools of my own picking. Now I'll have to . . ." He fell silent as slow, measured footsteps entered the room.

"Your Eminence," Dashif said. The tone of his voice had

changed completely. "The urchin would appear to have fled."

The measured tread continued without interruption past the cupboard. At the curtains the footsteps did hesitate for a moment, but continued on to the window. "Out this window, down to the yard," said the new voice, and she could hear tension in it; she realized suddenly that this person shared her fear of heights but had made himself deny them just now. The window scraped shut and the footsteps came back. "Someone should be looking for her, hmm?" Now he sounded tired or bored.

"Uhh—right away, Your Eminence." The guard clattered out.

"Dashif," said His Eminence. "As things stand, the Faith must pay for the loss of an entire well's worth of grain that was destroyed . . . effectively in pursuit of four saddlebags and a length of rope."

"Eminence, I—"

"Furthermore, word of this device has at last reached the Levar and she wants it for her own in order to communicate not only with her dead parents but also with her first regent. There are important questions she wishes answered, some of which she has voiced to me. Must I explain to you the possible consequences of such a discourse with my predecessor? Is that clear?"

"Eminently, Your . . . Eminence."

His Eminence sighed deeply. "Her agents are seeking it even now. Neither they nor the heretical White priests must gain it. *I'm* no longer concerned with having it. I'd prefer it were simply destroyed along with anyone who knows of it. That is all." The footsteps of His Eminence strode away, followed shortly by Dashif's hurried tread.

Jolesha's mind whirled with all that she had overheard. She stole out of the cupboard and crept to the door. People milled about in the hallway; any one of them might have been Dashif. She decided that she would climb down from the window. His Eminence had her fear and if he could master it, so could she. She closed the curtains with sweaty hands. The latch had been fastened tight and she had to struggle with it, finally flinging the window open. She found herself hanging over a wide ledge that led all around the palace at this level. She got up into the window. Her head seemed light and sound took on a strange hollowness. She tried to step out on the ledge without looking at it and was reminded of the feeling of stretching her toes for the walkway in the silo. This was different and much, much worse. She might have touched the ledge or not—by then she could not say. The curtains had reached out for her by then and dragged her back, wrapping her up in thick darkness.

She awoke because the sun was baking her. She was lying on the floor below the window, part of the curtain trapped beneath her. The artifact still lay in the folds of her tunic. The window hung open.

How long she had been unconscious she could not guess, but it must have been some time in order for the sun to swing around and strike her. She left the window open and went through the anteroom. The hallway contained fewer people now and surely none of them would have been the one called Dashif. She began walking in a direction she hoped would take her back toward the kitchen. Some of the people eyed her with mild curiosity, but she was hardly the strangest sight walking along those halls. At one point she passed what she thought was a tall man in dark leggings and a cloak. She was going to ask him if he could direct her to the kitchen, but when she looked into his face she saw the strangeness of his eyes, like cat eyes, and knew that she was looking at a Bhandaf, something that seemed utterly impossible. He smiled, no doubt amiably, but she could not find her voice or slow down. She hurried on, searching for the statues, that same mural, something to guide her, to show her the way out. Soon, she began pausing at doorways and, when no one was looking, opened them carefully in the hope of finding an exit. In one such room a man turned and saw her, then waved her in. He gave her a green silk cloak covered in embroidery and told her that he needed it by that evening. She backed out the door with the cloak. She went down one hall, holding it out in front of her like a maid, but then put it on to disguise her less fashionable attire.

When at last she found an exit from the palace, the guard at the door stiffened up and called her "Mistress" as she passed. He held the door for her. She pressed her fingertips to her forehead and fought down the desire to run. The guard closed the door behind her. She was outside. No one bothered her as she hurried across the yard.

Jolesha circled the perimeter until she neared the entrance where Klefti had stayed behind. He was no longer there, and she crossed the road immediately to set off for the park.

In the clearing where the three paths met, she waited. At sunset he had still not appeared. Jolesha could not bear to think what that meant. She sat on a stone bench across from where the duel had been fought. Not one trace showed where the dead man had fallen . . . the man whose soul they had heard escaping.

She took the artifact from her tunic, unwrapped it, and studied it again, turning it over so that the last light of day played scintillas off the gold. With a deep sigh, she murmured, "Klefti, Klefti, where are you?"

The artifact grew warmer. Its black depths began to glow, first a dark vermilion, but brightening in moments to pink as it had done once before. A strange voice stirred the air around her, calling as if from a vast distance, "Jolesha, Jolesha." She had never heard that voice before, because he had not had a voice, but she knew him as she knew her own skin.

A sharp, stabbing knot caught in her throat. "Klefti. Where are you?"

"Gone. Free. They took me away, Jolesha, a man with long curly black hair ordered my torture. Where were you and where the cylinder? they asked me, as if I could tell them. So much pain, all gone now. Much peace now."

Tears fractured her vision of the park. "Oh, no, Klefti, what do I do now?"

"Avoid the palace people, the Red Faith. They're wrong, all of them—even the ones who fashioned the cylinder, all so wrong. So much beauty, texture, color. Not like life at all."

"Klefti!"

"It hurts to talk with you, but I have a *voice*. You can hear me. I love you, Jolesha. Urgelian, too, he's here. He'll talk a time if you call him. Must go now. The color's closing. I can see you! I can see you! Call, I'll answer again. Jolesha. . . ."

The artifact grew cold and dark. Jolesha clutched it to herself, doubled up with her head on her knees, and shook with grief. The sun had set.

The traffic on the Saltigos Road in the month of Wine was heavier than most other months of autumn due to the travelers who came for the End of Wine Festival. The warmth of Kil Coast at that time of the year attracted many of the nomads with their booths and tents, hawkers with everything from sex to shoes for sale. Even the investment broker had moved his show there from the Farmer's Road.

Among them all, one small striped tent was erected, offering communication with Ghostside for the price of a five-levar piece, rather a high price for a spiritualist—especially one stationed this far outside the city—but no one had yet gone away dissatisfied.

The interior of the tent was kept dark and the woman with the ancient voice kept her dusky face concealed behind a veil. But she had very young eyes.

The various faiths lumped her in with all the others they decried, denouncing all as one. What could such vagabonds know of the afterlife, asked the faiths, when the truth of it was so clearly written down and spelled out—depending, of course, on which god and belief one followed? Despite their condemnation, the spiritualist did an exceedingly good trade, and her growing fortune kept her there longer than she had intended while word of her practice spread further than she would have chosen.

One cool Luckday morning, a tall, thin man with a scarred face and curly black hair to his shoulders entered the dimness of the tent. Jolesha had not intended to open the tent for business that morning, so the man caught her off-guard, tending a brazier, her face exposed and colored by the glowing coals. She quickly veiled herself but knew that he had seen her face clearly. Leaving the brazier, she went and sat behind her small table. The man smiled grimly as he seated himself on the stool across from her. She knew she had fear in her eyes, and lowered them.

"What price for a communication?" he asked.

"I'm giving none today," she said in an old woman's voice. "I'm leaving here today."

"Undoubtedly," he agreed, and the sound of his voice chilled her; finally, they were face to face. Almost. "However," he continued, "not before you and I complete a small transaction."

She could not help glancing past her left shoulder, where an exit lay hidden in the folds of the tent. He rapped on the table to draw her attention back to him. "There really is nowhere for you to go," he said. "I have soldiers outside who have stopped the man you paid from loading your belongings aboard the wagon you purchased on Windday. Shall I tell you where you intended to go? On which vessel? You see, I know much about you. You've done well for yourself in so short a time— too well, one might speculate."

"You're Count Dashif," she said, no longer bothering to disguise her voice.

He leaned across the table and pulled free her veil. "And

what would your name be, girl?" When she said nothing, he pressed, "I've spent considerable time and money seeking you. I'll have your name now."

Defiance lighted her eyes. "Jolesha."

"Jolesha. And the rest of the name?"

She shook her head. Dashif sighed. "Very well, child. I'll have the artifact now, and please, no tales or fabrications. I bore easily."

Jolesha dug into the layers of robes she wore and brought out the leather pouch. She placed it on the table between them. Dashif reached for the object almost reverently. He weighed it in his palm, turned it over, then set it down. He took off his gloves to untie the leather. It unfolded and the artifact was revealed. He stared at it, Jolesha thought, with something almost fearful in his gaze.

"How does it work?" he asked in a whisper; even so, the sound of his voice warmed the blackness of the crystal to maroon.

"You call a name," Jolesha said. "Your voice draws the spirit. If you like, I'll call up someone for you. Perhaps you'd like to speak with the former regent."

He looked up at her in narrow surprise. "What do you know of that?"

Instead of answering, she ran her fingertips across the knurls of gold. "Or perhaps you would rather speak to . . . Erina?"

The color seemed to drain from Dashif's face and into the artifact as it flickered with pink candescence. Light, feathery sounds emanated from it. Dashif stood suddenly, kicking over his stool. Jolesha picked up the artifact and came around the table. Dashif backed away. "Here," she said to him, "you have only to call her as I have done on numerous occasions in order to speak with her. Just say her name: *Erina*." The light from the artifact burst over them like the sun emerging from behind a cloud, casting an enormous shadow of Dashif that hung vulturously over him.

From the artifact a susurrant voice spoke. "Who calls? Who calls me back?"

"No!" Dashif cried. He flung himself away into the layers of thin material that hung across the doorway; the cloth seemed to wind around him with intent and he struggled wildly to escape it, tugging his way out into the safety of the misty morning light.

Jolesha said, "No one calls now, Erina. Go back. I'll speak with Klefti . . . in a moment." She set down the artifact. The light it threw began to dim as the spirit of Erina retreated from the border between worlds. Klefti had brought her to speak with Jolesha the first time; the dead knew unfathomable secrets. The dead knew, perhaps, everything.

Pushing back the entrance curtains, Jolesha emerged, veiled once again, to hear him order his men away. She called his name, saw him stiffen before he turned, a waxy smile on his face. She went toward him. "Here," she said and held out her hand.

Dashif flinched and put up one hand to fend her off. For a moment she could not understand; then, just as quickly, she saw what he saw: he thought she was pushing the artifact upon him again, instead of his leather gloves that he had left lying on her table.

His expression of fear blossomed momentarily into anger. Jolesha turned away before he could threaten her with words. She sensed that he had not finished with her, that he would try some other way to get to her and to destroy the artifact—now because it could destroy him.

The sound of the soldiers' horses regaining the road followed her into the tent, where she dropped the curtains on the murky day and stood with just the light of the dead and the weight of her aloneness in the world of the living.

An Act of Trust

by Steven Brust

As the scion of the county once called Dashforth walked along the Levar's Way toward the palace, he became aware that he was being followed.

He did not reach for the documents he carried inside his scarlet cloak—documents recently stolen from a Tichenese agent in Hrothvek—but he thought about them. He didn't know exactly what they were, except that they involved a good-will gesture from Ka Zhir, and that they had had to be removed from Tichenese hands before causing what His Scarlet Eminence called "an incident."

Dashif had taken them from the agent, and was now only a few score paces from returning them to his master; mission accomplished.

And he became aware that he was being followed.

It is not difficult to follow someone if he doesn't know he is being followed. Avoid standing out *too* much in a crowd, and if the person being followed doesn't go places that are *too* deserted, he will probably never notice.

On the other hand, if one suspects one is being followed, it is almost impossible for the person doing the following to remain hidden. Dashif always half wondered if he were being followed. And, certainly, he was. He was followed by the ghost of Erina, the lover he had betrayed and later slain; he was followed by the memories of all he had done in the service of His Scarlet Eminence, the Regent of Liavek; and he was followed by the fearful looks, almost tangible, of all who beheld

him and stepped aside, some because they knew him and some
even though they did not.

On this occasion, however, he became convinced that he
was being followed by someone real, corporeal, and able to
be questioned. He dealt with ghosts by denying their existence;
he dealt with memories by denying their validity; he dealt with
others' fear by ignoring it. He dealt with the individual following him by stepping into an alley, drawing and cocking one
of his double-barreled flintlock pistols, and waiting.

At that, he almost missed her.

It was one of those chilly mornings that Liavek manufac-
tured in the fall, with patches of fog hiding behind the corners
of buildings as if to pounce upon unsuspecting travelers, or
sometimes moving with a stray wind to embrace the pedestrian
and keep him company for a few paces on his errands. When
she emerged from a fog-patch his grappling hand and his pistol
hand were too high, as she barely came up to his chest. But
she was more surprised than he was.

That part of his mind that he allowed to control his actions
at such moments took over and told him that fear would suffice.
He grabbed her throat, pulled her into the alley, swung her
against the hard, graying brick of the empty hotel that had once
boasted a view that no one had wanted.

Fear, erupting from her eyes and stifling her scream, fed
into him as he held the pistol up to her head. "What is your
name?" he asked quickly, before she could decide what not to
tell him.

"Kal—" She stopped, fear having closed the mouth that
shock had opened.

"The rest." He gave his voice no special emphasis, for he
needed none.

"Kaloo," she said.

"Kaloo," he repeated. "Why are you—" And then it came
back to him.

It was shortly after the Massacre of the Gold Priests that he
had received an anonymous gift; a pair of jade and gold earrings
wrapped in hair that was apparently from the head of a Farlander. It could have been an attempt at an assassination under
the guise of an assignation, or a signal he hadn't been told to
expect, or a mistake on the part of someone's agent, or a trick,
or, possibly, legitimate.

He had chosen to gamble, and worn the earrings in public

exactly once. On that occasion, walking through the Market, he had been the victim of some sort of massive unbinding spell. The earrings had fallen from him. One had been snatched up by a scurrying squirrel or something, the other by a small, dark girl who had locked eyes with him for a moment before being lost in the crowd.

Now he locked eyes with her again.

He smiled.

"Well. I've been looking forward to meeting you."

She stared at him like a fish lying in the bottom of a boat after it has stopped flopping but before it has stopped trying to breathe. "Perhaps," he said, "we should go somewhere comfortable to talk. We aren't far from the palace. Have you ever seen the palace? There are many things I'd like to ask you."

He released the hammers of the pistol, put it in his belt. He gripped the girl firmly around her skinny arm and propelled her out of the alley. He had just stepped out when he heard a voice behind him. "Hello, Count Dashif."

Keeping his grip on the girl, he spun around. "And good-bye," continued the voice, and he threw himself one way and the girl the other. He heard something go *wheet* past his ear just as he heard the *shhk-chuk* of a crossbow releasing a bolt. He had a glimpse of a woman dressed in green holding a crossbow, about forty yards down the alley, but she was gone before he had his pistol out and leveled. He did, however, have enough time to recognize her, and cursed.

The girl, Kaloo, was gone, too, even her footsteps having faded.

Whoever the urchin was, she was quick. Dashif wondered if the girl and the woman could be working together. He thought about Kaloo as he considered it. She had a pleasant face. It reminded him of someone. He stood up and brushed away the thought with the dirt on his cloak; he didn't believe in ghosts. And now that he had her name, it was only a matter of time before he found her again.

He resumed his walk to the Palace.

The Eminent Pitullio, tall, cheerful, and talkative, leaned back in his chair so its two front legs were off the floor. Dashif had been waiting for years for him to break his chair and fall in a sprawling heap, but he hadn't yet. Pitullio was, perhaps, the only man in the city to see His Scarlet Eminence, the

Regent, on a daily basis. Dashif supposed cheerfulness to be
the only way to survive the Regent's morose abruptness.

Dashif gave him the documents.

"He'll be pleased," said Pitullio. "Everything went smoothly,
I take it?"

"Smoothly enough," said Dashif. "It seems I should have
killed the agent, though. She followed me back here, and almost caught me with a crossbow on my way to the Palace."

"Why didn't you? Kill her, I mean."

Dashif chose not to answer, though he wondered, briefly,
himself. Why? Because there was no need to. But then, when
had that stopped him before? He put the question out of his
mind.

"I'll give these to him," said Pitullio. "And how is the great
search coming?"

Great search? Oh, the waif who had the White priests'
artifact. Dashif looked up at him and looked away. He debated
not answering, just to be perverse. But then, His Eminence
probably wanted to know, and Pitullio was easier to deal with
than the Regent. "We'll have her in a few days. She has been
working as a spirit medium, claiming to communicate with the
dead."

Pitullio laughed. "I imagine a more successful one than
most. *He*"—Pitullio gestured with his head toward the other
side of the wall—"was having fits for a while, when it looked
as if someone might get the artifact to the Levar. He'd be more
than a little embarrassed if the Levar was able to speak to the
spirit of his predecessor."

Dashif didn't answer, although, in fact, His Scarlet Eminence had as much as admitted the same thing to him.

"You'll have her soon, then?" said Pitullio.

"Yes. We know where she has been practically every day
for the past month. We know what ship she has arranged to
take her to her next destination, where she bought a wagon,
and approximately where she is. Another day or two should
see it done. I will attend to the conclusion personally."

"Good. I'll tell him."

"I need something else."

Pitullio cocked his head to the side. "Hmmm?"

"A girl named Kaloo. About twelve or thirteen, with—"

"Going after the young ones, eh, Dash—"

That was as far as he got. Dashif crossed the three feet that separated them and took Pitullio by the throat, staring at him. He felt Pitullio tremble and read the fear in his eyes. "Sorry, Dashif," Pitullio said mildly, managing an even voice, and Dashif let go of him and stalked out of the room before he did something irreversible.

He touched the pair of vertical scars that ran down below his eyes and didn't think about what had just happened.

Dashif did not, then or ever, wonder why Pitullio's words had so enraged him. To say that there had been a measure of truth in Pitullio's jest would be much too simple. Dashif had, in fact, very little interest in romance of any kind since his wife had left him, and Erina, whom he had deserted to marry the rich vavasor, had contrived to destroy his luck-piece in such a way as to destroy his luck forever, and he had killed her.

But she, Erina, haunted him. She haunted him, most of all, through other women with smooth, flowing dark hair. He had, in large part, adjusted to this, although the adjustment had once led to the massacre of nine helpless priests and to Dashif's latest scars. He had adjusted so well, in fact, that he wasn't aware of it when he met someone who really *did* very closely resemble his lost Erina.

He went about his business.

A few months before, the priests of the Church of Truth had either discovered or invented an object that allowed one to commune with the dead. Typically, instead of using it, their only thought was to get it to the poor, mad Levar, for whatever damage it could do to the Regent, whom they hated. Dashif had foiled the plan, but the object had disappeared and a great deal of effort had gone into tracking down the girl who had come up with it. He had spent much time and effort on this and now almost had her. He was awaiting only the last few pieces of information to tell him exactly which tent set up along the Saltigos Road contained the right spirit medium.

This allowed him some time to relax, and his method of relaxing was to wander through the Levar's Park at dusk hoping that the Tichenese agent would make another attempt on his life so he could stop her.

Just as the morning had been strangely chill, the evening was peculiarly hot. It was a thick, humid heat that brought sweat that refused to evaporate. On impulse, before the sun set behind the trees that hid the market from the park, Dashif approached the old woman overflowing an octagonal stool beneath a date tree.

A woman with braided white hair was speaking to the old woman. The former turned to look at Dashif, scowled, and tap-tapped away.

"Good evening, Asie."

Asie Blackfinger stared up at him, her eyes curiously bright through the film of age. "Come for your picture, sweetie? I haven't done you since you got the scars. They're rather fetching, y'know. Just sit down and—"

"Be still. I need a picture of a girl, about twelve years old. Very dark hair, straight, below her shoulders, parted in the middle. Her face is long and thin, with a cleft chin. No, hollow out the cheeks more . . . not that much . . . right. Now . . ."

He paid her a levar and went on his way, studying the picture. It shouldn't take long to find her. He continued through the park, staying alert to anyone who might be following him for one reason or another.

He went through his usual haunts then, showing the picture to various contacts. It was a thing he liked; from the Wall to the docks; from the Market to Mystery Hill.

He was smiling a little as he began the walk from the Street of Rain to the canals. She had probably taken to her room after this morning's encounter, and hadn't been seen since. But why was she following him? And, speaking of following, was he being followed now, by the Tichenese agent? He listened and looked as he walked, and decided that either he wasn't, or she was very good.

Well, best give it a try, anyway.

He slipped into Fortune Way near Narkaan's Skull, and made another turn into an alley that had only one exit. A thin young man was going through a pile of garbage, but Dashif was otherwise alone. He kept his hand on a pistol.

When no one showed up, he started to walk out.

"Don't move, Count Dashif."

The voice came from above him, behind him, and to his right. He silently cursed himself. Of course she knew her business; she had climbed to a rooftop.

On the other hand, she hadn't yet shot him. Without turning, he said, "I don't have the documents anymore."

She said, "I don't have the trust of my master anymore.

Soon, you won't have your life anymore."

Dashif laughed without humor. "You're going to have to learn not to take these things personally." He heard the hiss of indrawn breath, and wondered what his chances of diving behind a pile of garbage were. Not very good, he decided, but better than no chance at all.

But she said, "My master was entrusted with those documents by the Ambassador. He trusted me. I take everything personally."

The garbage-picker was staring back and forth between them, his eyes wide. Dashif turned his head and addressed him. "What do you think? Will she kill me quickly, or a piece at a time?"

The other stared at Dashif, then shook his head and limped away.

"Do you suppose we can work something out?"

"Surely," came the voice from above him. "I'm willing to convey your funerary wishes wherever you'd like."

"That wasn't what I had—" and he jumped for the garbage pile, twisting and reaching for a pistol. He heard the sound once more, and the smack of the quarrel hitting the building wall. He crouched in the trash heap and cocked the pistol, but she was gone, and the sun had set, and it would soon be too dark to follow her.

He stood up and began walking back to the Palace. He had no intention of seeking this Kaloo child while smelling of trash.

Before dawn the next day he received a note giving the location and description of a tent along the Saltigos Road. He allowed himself a small smile of satisfaction. The medium had been found—he would soon see the end of this annoyance. He washed himself and donned fresh garments. He adjusted the collar of his white blouse, ran a soft brush over his hair, checked the charges of his pistols, and pulled on his gray gloves.

He rounded up eight of the Scarlet Guard and procured horses from His Scarlet Eminence's stables. For himself he chose a white mare, picturing himself on her, his red cloak flying in the wind. This was to be the end of a long project, and Dashif wanted to look his best.

As they turned into Widow's Road, with her once-elegant houses now dilapidated but often hidden by new white façades, Dashif wondered if the Tichenese agent was following him.

There was nothing to be done if she was; Dashif wasn't about to ride through the streets of Liavek looking over his shoulder. It was only after they had passed through Soldier's Gate and left the city behind them that Dashif checked his pistols once more. He felt the soldiers behind him glance at each other. The sun was just rising.

When they reached the first of the tents set up to exploit those who had come for the End of Wine Festival, the sun had traced only a small fraction of its daily journey. They kept riding until they came to the tent that had been described. There was a wagon a little ways away and a man carrying a chest to it. The wagon might have to be searched later. Dashif dismounted, hobbled the mare, and quickly stationed the guards, save for one he sent to stop the man who was loading her wagon. He walked around the tent once, spotted the rear entrance, and made sure there were two guards there. Then he checked his pistols once more and entered.

The inside was fairly bright, as the tent was thin. In addition, there was a single brazier which was being tended by a small figure whose back was to Dashif. She turned as he entered. Her face matched the description, if one discounted the makeup. Her gaze seemed to affix itself to the matching scars below his eyes, and she hastily veiled herself.

She sat down on a stool behind a thin square table rough with knots. He sat on a matching stool opposite her. She dropped her eyes. She held her hands together in her lap, probably to keep them from trembling.

"What price for a communication?" he asked. He didn't know why he needed to play with her; perhaps only because she had led him so long a chase.

She stuttered and stumbled and muttered and mumbled, and at last spoke in what she must have thought a good imitation of an old woman's voice. "I'm g-giving none today. I'm l-leaving—"

"Undoubtedly. However, not before you and I complete," he paused and smiled, "a small transaction."

She glanced over her shoulder toward the exit. He rapped on the table and shook his head, mocking sorrow. "There really is nowhere for you to go. I have soldiers outside who have stopped the man you paid from loading your belongings aboard the wagon you purchased on Windday. Shall I tell you where you intended to go? On which vessel? You see, I know much about you. You've done well for yourself in so short a time—too well, one might speculate."

"You're Count Dashif," she said in a normal tone.

He quickly pulled her veil from her. "And what would your name be, girl?" She didn't answer; she seemed too stunned to speak. "I've spent considerable time and money seeking you. I'll have your name now."

Her eyes narrowed, and he could almost see her stiffening her spine. "Jolesha," she said, as if the word could banish him.

"Jolesha. And the rest of the name?"

She seemed to be done answering questions. "Very well, child," he said. "I'll have the artifact now, and please, no tales or fabrications. I bore easily."

Without a nod or an answer of any kind, she placed the leather pouch on the table between them. So easy. He set his gloves on the table, picked up the pouch, and removed the gold-traced cylinder from within. A link to the past. For the first time, it occurred to him that it could be a link to *his* past, as well. He stared at it. He heard himself asking how it worked, and heard her suggest he call a name. One came to his mind, but not to his lips.

But she was still speaking. He heard her say something about the former regent and looked up sharply. "What do you know of that?"

She reached out and touched the cylinder. "Perhaps," she said slowly, "you would rather speak to Erina."

He stared at her. How could she know? How? No one knew. If she knew that, then she might know everything about him. In one instant, he was closer to panic than he had ever been in his life. He dropped the cylinder and began to reach for his pistols—

He felt her.

His muscles turned to water and he stood dumbly. The girl was still speaking, saying something, but Erina was there, too. His dark-eyed witch from Minnow Island whom he had loved, betrayed, been betrayed by, and finally slain.

Finally? Could there be a finally? Would it never end?

"Dashif?" It was her voice, her presence, from her lips. He smelled the scent from her hair and felt the strands upon his face. Tears he hadn't known he could shed came to his eyes, and with them, knowledge of his own weakness. "I forgive you. . . ."

"No!" he cried, throwing himself backwards out of the tent. He emerged into the full light of day, and the heads of four of his guards snapped to look at him. He forced the semblance of calmness over his features, and made his voice remain even. "Let them get on with their business," he said. "She has nothing we want after all." He let a hint of a smile come to his lips so they would think there was more going on than they knew.

He heard Jolesha call his name, using her old-woman voice again. She approached him and held up her hand. He saw she carried something. The artifact? He felt the rush of panic again as he raised his hand to ward it off. Then he realized that she was only holding out the gloves that he'd forgotten in her tent. He took them, and they locked eyes for a moment.

He made his way to his horse. Behind him, he heard her walking back to the tent. He had to think, to plan, to decide how to deal with this. He had to decide *now,* before the chance got away from him. But one thing was certain; no one who knew that much about him could be allowed to live.

He turned back to the tent, speculatively, feeling his pulse and breathing return to normal. Perhaps the best thing to do would be to walk in and kill her now, before she could speak to anyone. But no, that wasn't enough. He had to find out where she had learned about his past. Ghostside itself? Maybe. But he would question her. And he couldn't have anyone else around when he did it.

"Go back to the palace. All of you."

He waited for them to leave, keeping his eye on the tent. He didn't know what to do about the artifact, but the girl, Jolesha, would die now.

When the guards were out of sight, Dashif walked back toward the tent. The wagon was still there, but the man was gone. He was completely unobserved. He drew his pistols. If necessary, he would leave the artifact on the floor. Perhaps, if he waited, it would be safe to touch it again. But Jolesha would have to—

He was walking past the wagon when a crossbow bolt hit his left leg just below the knee. One half of his mind screamed from a physical agony almost as sharp as the mental agony he had endured moments before. The other half considered. She was a good shot, therefore she must be quite a ways away. Therefore, he would have time . . . He became suddenly aware that he couldn't move. He looked down and found that the shaft of the bolt was protruding from his leg, and the head was sunk into the wagon's wheel. A freak accident? He quickly turned in the direction the bolt had come from, raising his pistol. He had a glimpse of green, then—

He screamed and dropped one of the pistols as another bolt caught him in the left arm, pinning it to the side of the wagon. He was now caught by his left arm and left leg to the wagon side and attempting to turn caused such pain that he nearly screamed again. He forced himself to hang on to the other pistol and try to shut out the pain enough to think. If only he had his magic. Magic. Erina. No! Think, idiot! The agent hates you; she wants you to suffer. She'll probably go around behind you and taunt you; why else would she play with you like this? You have time, now *think*. Ignore the face in front of you, it isn't the agent, just another illusion. *Think*.

He held on to the pistol as a drowning man holds on to a log, but all he could think of to do with it was to kill himself before he could be subjected to more pain and humiliation. The face on the illusion was showing pity, which was bad enough, but now it was looking like a younger Erina. He shook his head, but it wouldn't go away.

"Count Dashif?" said the illusion.

He focused on her for the first time, and found himself face to face with the girl, Kaloo. She was peering up at him from under the wagon.

"Are you really going to die now?"

That was enough to convince him it was an illusion. She was still staring up at him. She said, "Should I find a City Guard?" He shook his head but no words came forth. "Why don't you use your magic?" she asked, and he nearly wept.

"Dashif!" came the voice of the Tichenese agent. And yes, she was behind him; only four or five feet, judging from the sound of her voice. He had his pistol, but it was useless unless he could turn to aim, and two crossbow bolts prevented that. He felt himself getting dizzy and he started to sag, which sent jolts of profound agony through his arm and leg.

"Kiss it goodbye, Dashif. Any last words?"

He stared at the girl who had called herself Kaloo, realizing suddenly that his body concealed her from the Tichenese agent. How could she be here? But, dammit, she was *real*. Could he count on a stranger, a child, and one who looked like . . . "I forgive you, too," he muttered.

Hardly moving, he cocked both barrels of his remaining pistol, reversed it in his hand, keeping it before his body so the agent couldn't see what he was doing. Over his shoulder, he called, "Yes. One question." He handed the pistol down to Kaloo. She took it. Her eyes were wide, her mouth forming an O as she stared at it, then at him. He felt himself start to faint again.

The agent responded. "What is that, Your Scarred Eminence? Or is it now Your Scared Eminence?"

"Do you really think you can last in this business if you take everything so per—"

Kaloo held the gun in both hands, stepped out in front of him, and fired both barrels at the Tichenese agent. There was a scream, the sound of a bolt releasing, and the sound of a body falling. Then there was the sound of Erina sobbing. No, someone else. Dashif discovered to his amazement that he had closed his eyes.

He reached over with his good arm and drew the bolt from the wood, leaving it in his arm. A gasp of pain escaped him. He reached down and retrieved his other pistol, which had somehow not gone off. He turned, but the Tichenese agent was gone. He found himself staring into Kaloo's red, tear-filled eyes.

"I didn't kill her," she said.

"Good," said Dashif without understanding why.

"Here, I'll help you."

And she did. Together they got him free from the wagon wheel, and he collapsed onto the ground. He struggled to stand again.

"Rest," said Kaloo.

"Can't," said Dashif. "Have to get up."

"Why?"

"Have to kill—" He stopped, finding that his wounded leg wouldn't support him. He collapsed again, onto his back, and found himself staring up into her face. Why? she had asked. He lay there panting. The face above him faded in and out. "Erina," he called, or maybe he only thought it. Her hair tickled his face and he smiled.

Dashif stared at the place on the bed where the lower half of his left leg should have been. The Eminent Pitullio sat by the bedside.

"He says he will keep you on anyway, Dashif."

"I'm surprised."

"Yes. What about the artifact, though?"

Dashif paused. Yes, the artifact. He thought about Kaloo. He thought about Jolesha, and those last looks they had exchanged. Yes, she was smart enough not to return. "I've taken care of it," he said at last.

Pitullio looked at him quizzically, then nodded. "I'll tell him."

"How did they find me?"

"An anonymous message, saying you were injured. Most of the words were spelled wrong, if that's any help. I've saved the note. You can see it when you're feeling better. You'd been very crudely bandaged, too; otherwise you wouldn't be alive."

"Such as I am."

"Such as you are. Are you smiling?"

"If he's going to keep me on, I'll want as good a wooden leg as you can find. And don't let anyone know about this."

Pitullio nodded. "Of course."

Then he left the room, leaving Dashif to try to adjust to this new current life had asked him to swim through, or against, or with. He stared down at the spot where his leg had been and wondered. He had felt something, while the girl was looking at him, and helping him, that he hadn't known he could feel. Dead areas inside him were waking up, and that hurt almost as much as his leg did.

Dashif wondered if the pain, both kinds, and even the loss of his leg might have been a fair exchange for what he had gained. He couldn't—yet—understand that by asking the question he had answered it.

Ishu's Gift
An Ombayan Folktale

by Charles R. Saunders

———————

IN THE MORNING of the world, the Mother's skirt spread across the sky. And the sky hung closer to the ground. Luck fell like rain from the clouds and gathered the elements of wind, water, earth, and iron about itself. And the luck became the inisha: *the gods and goddesses who shaped the land until it was time for the Mother to shake Her skirt and end the morning. . . .*

Ishu sat in the midst of a meadow of green and gold grass that stretched farther than his eyes could see. Newly-made antelope gamboled nearby, chasing each other, testing the speed built into their long, slender legs. Bright-colored birds wheeled through the sky. They carefully avoided brushing their wings against the hem of the Mother's skirt. Ishu looked up and called one of the birds down to him.

Flame-feathered, long-legged, hook-beaked, a flamingo angled down to land delicately at the feet of Ishu. Cocking its head to one side, the bird spoke to the *inisha*.

"What do you want of me, *inisha?*"

A short silence passed before Ishu replied. The *inisha* was a lank, angular being composed of the darkness of shadows and midnight. Sunlight could not penetrate the surface of his body. Yet his features shone like stars as he replied to the bird.

"A single feather is all I ask."

"Easily done," said the flamingo.

It snapped its wings once, and a lone flame-red plume floated before Ishu's eyes. The feather hung easily in the air, without falling to the ground.

"What use will you make of my feather?" the flamingo asked.

"As yet, I am not certain."

"It is said that the Mother has called all the *inisha* to the World Above because she has made a new thing for the land," the bird persisted.

"That is so."

"Is that why you want my feather?"

"Perhaps."

Angrily, the flamingo snapped its wings again and began to ascend with awkward grace. As the bird rose into the azure sky, its voice drifted downward: "I will never understand the *inisha!*"

"Neither will I, my friend," Ishu murmured as the flamingo joined its companions and dwindled in the distance.

Ishu rose. He seemed to flow to his feet rather than unbend. The feather rose with him. Ishu reached out and trapped it between the thumb and forefinger of one ebony hand. Then he balanced the quill of the plume atop his smooth skull. It remained upright and motionless even as Ishu's long legs stretched and began to carry him away from the meadow.

Green and gold grass melted into a blur beneath him. He moved swifter than a bird's shadow across the ground. Yet for all the *inisha*'s speed, the flamingo feather remained upright and unwavering until Ishu reached his destination: a broad river that flowed along a serpentine track through groves of trees with leaves that burned like emerald fire.

When he arrived at the riverbank, Ishu stared into the clear water and called to the *inisha* who dwelt there.

"Yemiyi! Are you prepared to answer the Mother's call?"

In reply, the surface of the river began to whirl until it lifted into a column that rose high above Ishu's head. Fish, frogs, and crocodiles complained loudly, but there was nothing they could do other than cling to the banks or swim downstream.

Slowly the water in the column coalesced until it took the shape of a tall, long-limbed woman. Although the water remained clear, Yemiyi's features were delineated by the sunlight that shone through her. Strands of emerald weed fell past the middle of her back. Her feet barely disturbed the surface of the river as she gazed at Ishu.

"Why do you carry that feather, Ishu?" Yemiyi asked. "Do

you think that is what the Mother meant when she asked us to bring gifts to the World Above?"

"I see no gift in your hands," Ishu retorted.

"The Mother's creations will see it."

"Then let us not keep Her—and them—waiting."

Without further words, Ishu mounted the air and ascended into the sky as though climbing an unseen stairway. Yemiyi followed, leaving a fine mist behind her. Rainbows marked the passage of the two *inisha*.

The Mother's skirt hung in bright blue drapes around the assembled *inisha*. Above Her skirt, She was a vast ebony mass speckled with stars. Her arms encircled the moon and the sun, and Her face could not be seen. She was the source of all the world's luck, and the *inisha* were Her first children. Now, She was preparing to unveil Her new children. . . .

The *inisha* were gathered around two long bundles wrapped in palm leaves. The bundles rested in a fold of the Mother's skirt. Ishu and Yemiyi were there, as were all the others who had enfolded their luck in the elements of the World Below.

Ushin, *inisha* of the winds, was there. She appeared only as a vague outline, a dimly discernible turbulence in the air. When she spoke, breezes stirred the leaves on the bundles.

Oshuni, *inisha* of animals, was there. Oshuni's shape changed constantly: now a lion; now a shrew; now the form of a creature that existed only in the *inisha*'s imagination. He never retained a single shape longer than a few moments.

Esanyin, *inisha* of herbs and plants, was there. Of all the children of the Mother, Esanyin's appearance was the most remarkable, for he had only half a body—one eye, one arm, one leg. His skin was covered with nodules of crimson, blue, and yellow. Between the nodules, his hide was like the bark of a tree blasted by lightning. The luck Esanyin represented was chaotic, unpredictable.

Ugon, *inisha* of iron, was there. Her shape was massive, blocky, and gray, as though the ore from which she had been formed was poured into a mold made from the side of a mountain. Ugon's thunderous voice shook even the folds of the Mother's skirt.

Of all the *inisha* present, only Ishu openly displayed his gift. To the amusement of the others, Ishu continued to balance the feather on his head. Together, the *inisha* awaited the time when the Mother would strip the leaves from her bundles.

At last, the Mother spoke. Her voice was a vast, warm whisper.

"My children, I have created something new for the World Below—something greater than the birds or animals, but far less than you inisha. *Their names are Ekinrun and Ibinrun, and the future of the World Below will be theirs.*

"Although you have not yet seen my new children, I have asked that you bring gifts to them. When I awaken them, I will ask them to choose one of your gifts. That gift will hold their destiny."

The moment the Mother stopped speaking, the palm leaves disengaged themselves and spiralled slowly out of the sky. And Ekinrun and Ibinrun were revealed to the *inisha*.

Ekinrun was masculine in form, like Ishu. Ibinrun was feminine, like Ushin and Yemiyi. But the *inisha* were elementals; their gender was inconsequential to their true being. The man Ekinrun and the woman Ibinrun were flesh, and that flesh contained the essence of the male and female imperatives that would shape the fate of the World Below.

How frail these two appeared to the *inisha!* The dark envelopes of skin that covered them were fragile, vulnerable to injury and age. There was scant strength in their limbs. Their eyes were closed, and their breasts showed no movement of breathing or heartbeat. To the *inisha*, the Mother's new children seemed more artifice than real.

Then the breath of the Mother wafted down from Her mouth and steeled on the faces of the woman and man. They began to breathe, and their eyes opened. Blinking, staring, they sat up. Then they helped one another to their feet. Wide-eyed, they gazed at the *inisha*, who impassively returned their stares.

In addition to life, the Mother had granted knowledge to her children. Ibinrun and Ekinrun knew who they were and what their place in the World Below was to be. Still, they longed to remain in the World Above with the Mother, secure in the immense folds of Her skirt. But the knowledge She had given them included a sad awareness that they would never live in the sky. . . .

"Are you ready to choose?" the Mother asked gently.

Ekinrun and Ibinrun nodded.

"My children, it is time to present your gifts."

Ugon was first. She held out a blunt-fingered hand large enough to close around the bodies of the woman and man together. From her fingertips, a double-bladed iron axe emerged. The axe matched Ekinrun's height.

"With this, you could split a mountain in two," Ugon rumbled. "Nothing would be able to stand against you."

Yemiyi was next. She cupped her liquid hands before the eyes of Ibinrun and Ekinrun. A milky, sweet-smelling fluid pooled in her outstretched palms.

"Drink this, and you will be able to live beneath the water and share my domain," she said.

Ishuni appeared in the form of a great ape of the forests. In one outstretched hand he held a large, round fruit, its purple skin beaded with moisture.

"Eat of this, and you will be able to speak with all the animals of the World Below, and none of them will harm you," the ape grunted.

Ushin was still all but invisible. A gust of air eddied in front of Ekinrun and Ibinrun.

"Breathe this," Ushin whispered, "and the winds and rain will be yours to command."

Esanyin hopped toward them, his maimed body moving with surprising grace. Balancing easily on his single foot, the *inisha* lifted his hand. From its palm a green vine grew, lacing between his gnarled fingers.

"With this vine in your hands, you will never know hunger," he said.

Ishu was last. The dark *inisha* removed the feather from his head and offered it to the couple. He said nothing. For the first time, Ekinrun spoke.

"What is the meaning of your gift?" he asked.

"If you accept it, you will learn," the *inisha* replied.

The Mother spoke then: *"You may now consider your choice."*

Ibinrun and Ekinrun faced each other uncertainly. From the knowledge the Mother had given them, they were aware of the value of all the gifts—except, of course, Ishu's. To have mastery over the animals or the wind . . . to gain the ability to split a mountain with a single blow . . . to live underneath the river . . . to be free from hunger . . . with any one of the *inisha*'s gifts, Ekinrun and Ibinrun would become almost as *inisha* themselves. Any one but Ishu's. . . .

The woman and man continued to talk until the voice of the Mother interrupted them.

"Choose," She commanded.

After an exchange of glances, Ibinrun reached out and took Ishu's feather.

While Ishu smiled, the other *inisha* stared in disbelief. Their gifts vanished, leaving no trace behind. And the disbelief was superseded by anger.

"Why did you choose the feather?" the Mother asked.

"The axe is too large for me to lift," said Ekinrun.

"I do not want to live underwater," said Ibinrun.

"We will have more to say to each other than to animals," said Ekinrun.

"The wind and rain belong to their *inisha,* not to us," said Ibinrun.

"We will be able to find our own food," said Ekinrun.

"Ishu said that if we accepted his gift, we would learn," said Ibinrun. "He did not say we would merely learn why he offered us a feather. He said we would *learn. . . ."*

"You have seen it," the Mother said proudly. *"The gifts of the others would have given you power, but no luck. Ishu's gift grants you luck, but not power. It will be interesting to see what you make of the consequences of your choice."*

With that, the Mother shook her skirt, and Ekinrun and Ibinrun were gone from the sky.

In the World Below, the first woman and man huddled on an open plain while a driving rain drenched their naked bodies. The wind whipped tall grass against their legs. Beneath their feet, the ground rumbled and quaked. In the distance, the growls of lions and leopards could be heard. Further away, a river overflowed its banks and began to creep across the plain.

Of Ishu, there was no sign other than the sodden feather Ibinrun clutched in her hand.

"Why did you choose that cursed feather?" Ekinrun complained. "What good is it doing us now? Where is this 'luck' it was supposed to bring?"

"We chose it," Ibinrun reminded him.

The incipient quarrel hung between them like a door that could be opened or closed with a single word. Ekinrun said the word that ensured that the door would remain open, though not always wide.

"Yes."

He placed his hand over hers, touching the feather.

"We cannot rely on Ishu," Ekinrun continued. "We must rely on ourselves."

"Then we had better begin," Ibinrun said. "Those growls are getting closer."

Hand in hand, they headed for shelter.

As time passed, the woman and man did learn, even as the ire of the inisha *subsided. They learned how to do for themselves many of the things the* inisha *would have bestowed with their gifts. And they learned how to harness the luck Ishu had given them.*

The Mother drew her skirt further away from the World Below, and the inisha *spent less time there. Ekinrun and Ibinrun had many children, and the children of those children became Ombayans. To this day, many Ombayans invest their luck in ebony statues adorned with red feathers. And women rule in Ombaya because the children of Ibinrun have never forgotten that it was she who accepted Ishu's gift.*

A Cup of Worrynot Tea

by John M. Ford

THE OBJECT ON the roadside looked like a bed, as much as it
looked like anything. Two young people, a dark and muscular
boy and a slim fair-haired girl, were climbing over it with a
sort of exhausted good will. The girl, whose everyday name
was Reed, said, "It's no use at all, Kory. The spring's broken
and the hub is bent."

The boy, Kory, crouched next to the wheel of the light
wooden landsailer and looked across the Saltmarsh in the direction of Liavek. It was no-longer-early afternoon in late Wine,
the breeze off the marsh already turning chilly, and they had
been no more than halfway from Hrothvek to Liavek when a
gust sent the spidery wind-car off the road. If they started
walking now, it would be very late when Reed got home. Very,
very late. Unconscionably late.

And you were no doubt thinking—oh, *shame* on you.

A two-horse coach appeared from the south. Kory said,
"Look, there's someone. Maybe they'll give you a ride to the
city. I'll walk the 'sailer back."

"You'll never get it back before night."

"Then I'll tent the sail over it and sleep inside. I've done
that before, hunting dawn spooks. I've got all the stuff for an
overnight."

"You do, huh? You didn't tell *me* that."

"Aw, Reed—"

"And what about me? What if I don't choose to risk my
life with the first stranger to come along the Hrothvek road?"

"Reed," Kory said desperately, and then she laughed and hugged him. "I'd better, uh, stop that coach. Before they decide we don't want to be rescued."

"You said it, I didn't," Reed said, and kissed Kory on the nose.

The coach pulled rather suddenly to a stop. It was painted a dark maroon color, with polished brasswork; well-made and well-kept without being flashy. The driver was a big man in a long coat of blue leather. Kory looked up at him and blinked. The driver's face and hands were a shade of blue only a little paler than his coat. He was bald except for a line of bushy white hair around his temples, like fur trim on a collar. "Good day," he said, in an accent unlike any Kory—who had grown up on Bazaar Street—had ever heard, flat and unmusical.

The side window opened and another man leaned out. This one looked like a Liavekan, with sun-bleached hair above an ordinarily dark face with bright blue eyes; he wore a black quilted gown with a high wing collar. He was smiling.

"Are you in need of assistance?" the passenger said, in perfectly proper Liavekan. He looked past Kory to the car on the roadside. "Mechanical difficulties?"

"Yes, master. I'll get the car home all right, but my ... friend must be back in Liavek before dark. We were wondering if you could—"

"I'll ride on top of the coach, sir," Reed said, stepping in front of Kory. She looked up at the driver, who had not moved at all. "Or on the back will be fine," she said, in a less certain tone.

"There's room for both of you inside," the passenger said. "And for your vehicle on top, I should think, if you and Jagg can lift it without doing it any more damage. Jagg?"

The driver looked over the landsailer and said, "The car folds?"

"Yes," Kory said, surprised. "I built her jointed, to carry and store."

"Plenty of room, then," the driver said. He climbed down. Kory glanced at the passenger, who was looking at Reed. There was something Kory didn't like about the way the man looked at her—but he supposed he was just annoyed. If the travelers had anything bad in mind, they were going to a lot of effort for it. Kory went to the landsailer and began pulling the hinge-pins that held it rigid. It folded up tightly, the side spars bracketing the pedal-drive cables. Jagg began folding the linen sail expertly.

In very short order Kory and Jagg had the car folded down to a square bundle of spars and a stack of wheels. They began to lift it onto the coach roof, when another hard gust came in off the Saltmarsh. The coach rocked slightly. Kory's grip slipped.

The bundle did not fall. Kory looked through the coach window. The passenger was smiling at him. *A wizard,* Kory thought. *So what kind of luck has this been?* He got the covered bucket with his and Reed's catch and handed it up to Jagg. "Please see that doesn't turn over," he said, and Jagg fastened a strap over it.

The coach got under way. Kory and Reed sat on red cloth cushions, facing the light-haired wizard. He seemed to be in early middle age, whatever that meant.

"My name is Ciellon," he said. "My friend is called Jagg."

"Is he a Farlander?" Reed said.

"From a far land, yes. And whom have I rescued from the Saltmarsh?"

"I'm Korik Li. I'm . . . I trade and transport. People call me Kory."

"I am Cadie ais Ariom, called Reed. My father is Dyelam ais Ariom, of the Liavek Society of Merchants, and the Levar's Council."

"Korik Free-Fortune and Ariom's White Heron," Ciellon said. "Kory and Reed. Happy to meet you both." He paused, then said, "Ais Ariom is a Hrothvekan name. But you are both Liavekan?"

"Kory is," Reed said. "I was born in Hrothvek, but we moved to the great city when I was four. My father's trading business was prospering, and he needed to be near the centers of commerce."

And society and politics, Kory thought without saying.

Ciellon nodded. "I know your father's name, though I regret I do not know the man himself. I am Hrothvekan by birth as well, you see, but that was—oh, a long time ago."

After a brief silence, Reed said, "Have you returned for the celebration, then? The End of Wine?"

Ciellon said nothing for a moment, as if considering his answer. "Yes. I have come for the End of Wine." He reached inside his black tunic, took out a small silver flask, sipped from it. "Forgive me, an indulgence. I have juice of apples and apricots if you are thirsty, and I think a little cold milk left."

Reed accepted a glass cup of apple juice. Kory said, "I'm not thirsty, thank you," which was not true.

Ciellon poured himself a cup of apricot nectar, adding to it a little golden liquid from his flask. "May I ask why you were on the road? Visiting friends in Hrothvek?"

"We were hunting marsh crabs," Kory said. "The small ones, with the red patterning, called clawfires. I . . . trade in them, with Thomorin Wiln the apothecary."

Ciellon nodded. "Is it profitable?" he said, in the tone of any serious business discussion.

Kory relaxed a little. "Worth one day a week," he said casually. "It really depends on the size of the crabs, you see. Thomorin Wiln uses a small fluid sac from inside the crab, and the rest goes for animal fodder—or to a couple of inns in Old Town, which I can name for you."

Ciellon laughed. "My arrangements are made, thank you. So the apothecary pays more for big crabs, then?"

"That's what you'd think," Kory said, pleased with the question, "but it's just the other way around. He wants them tiny. He's said that if I can find one no bigger than my thumb, he'll pay me . . ." Kory thought, then doubled the figure for effect, ". . . half a levar."

"Extraordinary," Ciellon said. "But why is this?"

"I believe," Kory said, and gave his best guess, "the fluid in the sacs becomes less potent as the crab grows."

"That is logical," Ciellon said, nodding. "Though it is also a possibility that what the apothecary desires is not the fluid but the sac itself, and the skin of the sac must not be too stretched."

Kory felt himself flush. Reed grinned. Kory said, "Excuse me, sir. I did not know you were an apothecary."

"Excuse me for embarrassing you," Ciellon said. "And I am not an apothecary . . . though I do require the services of one. Do you recommend this Thomorin Wiln?" he added gently, "In your informed opinion."

"Very highly, sir. He does business on his boat, *The Vessel of Dreams,* which is anchored at Canalgate. I'd be pleased to introduce you."

"That would be most satisfactory!" Ciellon said. "It is true what they say, that a kindness is always returned with profit." He pointed out the window. "And look, you can see the city wall already." He took another sip from his silver flask, then put it away. "I am staying at the Sea Eagle; we'll be passing it very shortly. Would you have a cup of tea with me before going on?" Ciellon looked at Reed, and once again Kory found something to dislike in the wizard's expression.

Reed said, "I am expected at home."

"By dark, you said, and there's plenty of light left. And look, you're both all over salt and sand; you'll look better for homegoing after some water and a towel. And you will have tea?" Kory was not sure it was a question.

"Yes, certainly we will, sir," Reed said finally, and Ciellon nodded. Kory noted something in Ciellon's look like . . . well, disappointment, though that made no sense.

The Sea Eagle Inn was built on the seashore at the farthest southwestern reach of Liavek, beyond Minnow Island in the quarter sometimes called "Nearer Hrothvek," almost against the city wall. Despite its location, it was not a new inn but a very old one, with an ancient reputation as a smugglers' landing and place of unrefined pleasure. Then the city had rolled, like an incoming tide of respectability, up to its doorstep; now the Sea Eagle was considered a Quite Proper Place with a Colorful Past.

The innkeeper, a former captain named Zal najhi Zal who still shaved the right side of her head, came out on the portico to meet the coach. Kory saw her stiffen at the sight of Jagg helping Ciellon to the ground. Her lips moved in the First Prayer to Bree Amal, Goddess of Keepers of Disorderly Houses: *May These Events Not Involve Thy Servant.* Kory looked at the blue-gray driver and knew what the innkeeper was thinking: her guest really was ridden by a troll.

Ciellon leaned on a black-ash walking stick and said, "Blessings on this house you keep, my friend. I am Ciellon; you received my message?"

"Of course, master. The room you requested is ready."

"With a view of the Saltmarsh? I do insist on that."

"A splendid view, master, from the topmost floor."

Ciellon leaned heavily on his stick. "Everything has its price, I suppose. No matter."

"Your baggage, master . . . and your message mentioned only two persons—there *is* a surcharge—"

"My man will carry the baggage." Kory thought he heard the hint of a threat in that. "And my friends are pausing only briefly. You will, please, have hot water sent up? And tea, for four."

"The Sea Eagle," the innkeeper said with formal pride, "has hot water in all rooms, heated by the sun in our roof cisterns, which also provide safety from fire."

"Lovely idea," Ciellon said, smiling.

"And the master's tea . . . what blend would be preferred?"

Ciellon said innocently, "Do you have Worrynot?"

Zal blinked, startled at the sudden mention of the contraceptive leaf. Kory chuckled to himself. It was not the sort of thing that ought to startle an innkeeper. "Why, of *course*, master . . . but the *tea* . . ."

"Just what I meant," Ciellon said. "No matter. We'll take Tichenese Gunpowder. Unless you've got Prince Fyun's Folly."

"I'll . . . see, master."

"Good, good." Ciellon turned to Kory and Reed. "Shall we?" As they went up the stairs, Kory noticed that Ciellon bore down on his cane as if an enormous weight rode his shoulders.

Whatever sorts of things were in the wizard's mind, Kory thought as Ciellon poured tea, he had been right about washing up. He and Reed looked a hundred times more presentable now, as if they had just been feeding doves in the Levar's Park. Not, of course, that Reed's father would believe that. Dyelam ais Ariom seemed to suspect Kory of everything short of treason with his daughter. More than once Kory had wanted to demand that ais Ariom accuse him directly—though if he proved his case to the merchant, what would he do? Challenge ais Ariom to a duel over Kory's wounded honor? Not very likely. He sometimes wished that Reed had some other suitor. One chosen by her father, one that Reed detested, and she wept on Kory's shoulder for horror of marrying. One he *could* challenge, and settle things once and for—

"I was just thinking," Ciellon said, pouring more tea into Kory's cup, "how admirable was your concern for your friend, there on the marsh. It would have been a cold night for Wine, and very lonely."

"I . . ." Kory said, "that is, we . . ." He wondered if the wizard had been reading his mind.

Reed said, "We met when Kory was employed as a courier for important documents. My father has a great deal of respect for Kory. He himself started as a small trader." She took Kory's hand.

Ciellon said, "And therefore he understands how difficult it is to be a successful solitary small businessman." He sat back, holding his teacup in both hands. "It is bad enough to fear failure when one has only oneself to suffer for it. But to bind one's failure to another—that is difficult. And to see it happen to one you feel love and responsibility toward—that is sheer torture."

Reed said, "Do you have a wife, Master Ciellon?"

"I—" Ciellon stopped, smiled faintly. "No. I just talk too much." He set down his cup. "Now, I think, I should send you on your way. Jagg?"

The bulky blue man was standing against the door, cup and saucer looking absurdly fragile in his hands. "Master?"

"Hire a pony-trap and take the Lady ais Ariom home. Then, Master Li, if you will guide Jagg to *The Vessel of Dreams*, I shall be indebted."

Kory said, "The master will not meet with Thomorin Wiln . . . ?"

Ciellon said, "Jagg knows what to ask for. I am certain that Thomorin Wiln will have no difficulty. Oh." He reached inside his quilted black gown, held out his hand again, and pressed a coin into Kory's palm. "For your recommendation." Kory knew the coin by touch, but checked it with a glance anyway; his fingers closed over a silver half-levar.

"A pleasure," Kory said, and then almost started giggling, "doing business with you, master."

"Not at all." Ciellon stood up slowly and went to stand by the room's large window, which gave a truly excellent view of the Saltmarsh stretching out of sight to the southwest.

"If there is anything else. . . . I happen to know that Thomorin Wiln can provide a much finer grade of Worrynot leaf than any . . . other establishment in the city."

"Kory," Reed said.

Ciellon turned from the window. "I thank you, Master Trader, but that was just a small joke. Mistress Reed, did your mother never speak to you of Worrynot tea?"

"Sir? No, sir. I have never heard of it. The tea, I mean."

"But you are Hrothvekan."

"My natural mother was, Master Ciellon, but she died when

I was five, soon after we came to the city. My stepmother is Liavekan."

"Ah. I am sorry. Truly sorry. Please forgive my lapse of tact, and taste."

"Of course, master," Reed said, puzzled.

Ciellon said, "I have one last request of both of you. I hope it does not seem . . . odd."

Kory tensed. Jagg was still barring the door; no way past *him*. Through the window it was four floors to the beach.

The wizard said quietly, "I would rather that my presence in Liavek not be made known for a little while. I don't expect anyone to ask you, and I don't ask you to lie; only not to speak. Will you agree to this?"

Kory said, "Of course, master."

Reed said, "Why, sir, if you are here for the End of Wine?" and Kory's heart skipped three beats.

Ciellon said, "That's a reasonable question, my lady. The most reasonable answer I can give is that I am an acquaintance of His Scarlet Eminence the Regent of Liavek, and I do not wish politics to complicate my visit to this most beautiful of cities, at least not yet. Do you understand?"

"Of course, sir," Reed said. "I will tell no one. If you will have your man take me to the apothecary's as well, then Kory can take me home, and there will be no need to explain your man's presence."

Ciellon laughed. "How can any businessman fail, with such a reason to succeed? Good day to both of you now, and please call upon me again if I may be of help."

The Vessel of Dreams had its anchorage in the hazy region between the raucous Old Docks, the even older but newly fashionable Canal District, and the south end of Wizard's Row, when Wizard's Row decided to be there. The *Vessel* was a flatboat with a catamaran hull; the hulls were snow-white, coated with something that barnacles and worms couldn't bear the taste of, and the superstructure was dark blue with a spangling of stars on the deck and the roof. Its masts were removable, and stayed in storage except for two months of the year, when Thomorin Wiln took *The Vessel of Dreams* out onto the Sea of Luck, to trade in faraway ports and fish in strange waters.

The trap pulled to a stop before the *Vessel*'s gangway, less than a bowshot from the posts of Canalgate. Kory and Reed jumped down from the back of the cart as Jagg hitched the horse to a post. Jagg wore gloves and a raised hood, which kept his appearance from drawing attention.

Kory looked toward the docks; he saw a familiar figure in green, but before he could be sure it was Ghosh, the person had vanished. Which meant it probably was Ghosh.

Jagg tapped Kory on the shoulder and pointed to a sign near the gangway. It read, FREEHOLD BY LIAVEKAN LAW. "I don't understand," he said in the strange, atonal accent. "Are not all ships so?"

Reed said, "The last Levar created Thomorin Wiln a landed noble. He's really Vavasor of *The Vessel of Dreams*. But whatever you do, don't call him that."

"Why?"

Reed smiled, said, "The Levar wanted Thomorin Wiln to serve on his Council. But he couldn't be bothered, and never put his name in for election by the Merchant's Society; so the Levar made him a noble, and the chancellors appointed him."

Jagg nodded. "Rulers have a way of getting the things they want."

"Oh, but that's not the end of it," Reed said primly. Kory bit his lip. He knew the story, too, but hearing Reed tell it, with the calm manner of a counting-house clerk, was priceless. "The rule is that noble councilors can send a representative. Thomorin Wiln sent a message saying that, since he couldn't serve, he was sending another chemist, of proven ability."

"Yes?"

"He sent a civet cat," Reed said, voice still even. "It got *very* upset. Do you know what a civet cat smells like when it gets upset? The Council had to meet in the Levar's Park for three weeks while the Chambers aired out." Then she laughed.

Jagg scratched his cheek. His expression might have been a smile, or anything.

Reed looked up. "I see someone I want to talk to," she said. "I'll be right here when you come out." Jagg bowed slightly and followed Kory aboard *The Vessel of Dreams*.

Thomorin Wiln's boat was tightly packed, the shop front no exception. There was a narrow counter with a cased set of balances, and a strongbox built into the countertop itself; there were wall racks for glassware and pottery herb jars; there were lockers with brass catches and extensible lamps and, in a corner, tin buckets with fresh material brought in that day; Kory set his bucket near the others. And there were drawers, hundreds, thousands of little drawers in ranks on the walls, each with a tiny white label describing its contents. Thomorin Wiln did not seem to need the labels; he just went to a drawer and pulled it open. It always seemed to be what he wanted. Kory imagined that if he leaned over to read the labels, they would all read, THINGS (ASSORTED).

Thomorin Wiln came in from the rear. He was tall and quite slender, with straight black hair streaked with gray; he wore it long, bound with engraved lead rings. He was wearing a rust-colored gown, somewhat ragged, covered by a heavy leather apron. "Kory," he said, and touched a hand to his forehead; he stopped, sniffed the hand, which was stained strange colors, and shrugged. "What were you out after? Spooks?"

"Clawfires. Got some smaller than your palm, too."

"I've got big palms. Wish it had been spooks, though. There's a— Oh, excuse me, master." He bowed slightly to Jagg, indicated Kory. "This gentleman is one of my suppliers."

Jagg pushed back his hood. Thomorin Wiln cocked his eyebrow slightly. Jagg said, "I am acquainted with Master Li. He recommended your services to my master." Jagg took a folded paper from his blue coat. "Can you make these preparations?"

"The sign says 'apothecary,'" Thomorin Wiln said. As he unfolded the paper, he added, "I won't make Universal Solvent, though. Not on a boat."

"I meant, master, have you the materials."

"Apology acc—" Thomorin Wiln stared at the paper. "Do you know what this says?"

"I do, Master Drugsmith."

"I mean, do you know what it *means?* These concentrations—excuse me. Kory, do you need your money now, or can it wait?"

"I'll be back tomorrow," Kory said, desperately curious but taking the hint. "Jagg, may I pick up my 'sailer tomorrow morning?"

"Certainly, trader."

Thomorin Wiln's eyebrow went up again. Kory smiled and went out.

Reed was on the dock, and Ghosh was with her. Kory waved and ran down the gangplank.

Ghologhosh said she thought she was the same age as Kory

and Reed, though she wasn't sure, and she looked older. She was very dark, with short, straight black hair and startlingly black eyes in an angular face that had been hit until it was no longer pretty. She was a little shorter than Reed, and even thinner, but incredibly strong for her build; Kory had seen her bend the iron bars of a window grille enough to slip through, then straighten them again when she had what she was after. She was wearing a leather collar (it would turn a knife and stop a garrote, and Kory knew she kept a set of lockpicks inside it), a coarse green tunic bloused above a wide belt, and matching loose trousers.

"If you're going to do business in the nice parts of town," Kory said, "you've got to put on shoes."

"The cheap kind are noisy and the quiet kind wear out too fast," Ghosh said. It was their greeting, like a handclasp or a hug; you didn't touch Ghosh. "So you all made it back again with your virtue intact. I swear I don't know what you two do all that running around for; it makes ais Ariom just as mad, and you sure aren't getting anything out of it."

Reed said, "We just like the sight of each other, Ghosh."

Ghosh nodded, spat over the edge of the dock. "Asie Black-finger'll do your pictures for a copper each, and you can stare all day. Kory, you mind if I sleep on your floor tonight? One of the regulars 'round my place cut a noble outside Cheeky's, and there's a couple of Guards waiting to see if he's stupid enough to go home."

"Sure, Ghosh, come by when you want." Ghosh's "place" was a block of abandoned Old Town buildings, sometimes called the No-Copper Bazaar, or Gizzard's Row. It looked like living hell, but in its way it was safe enough—there was nothing there to steal.

"I don't believe you're having this conversation in front of me," Reed said in mock horror.

"If you were going to fight me over the Merchant, you'd have done it a long time ago," Ghosh said. "And if anything was going to happen between him and me, it would have happened already. But you aren't and it ain't, and *that's* what I don't believe."

Ghosh turned sharply, apparently at nothing: Kory saw Jagg coming out of *The Vessel of Dreams*. He was not carrying any parcels. Kory said, "Thomorin Wiln *couldn't—*"

Jagg said, "It takes some time to prepare. I will expect you tomorrow, Master Li. Well faring to you. And you, mistress. And—"

Ghologhosh," Ghosh said, looking narrow-eyed at Jagg.

"Mistress Ghologhosh." Jagg pulled up his hood, boarded the trap, and drove away.

"Friend of yours?" Ghosh said.

"Tell you about it later," Kory said. "I'd better take Reed home now."

Ghosh said, "You really do ask for it every chance you get, don't you? Look, I'll see Reed gets home all right. Anybody asks, she gave me a two-copper as her bodyguard."

Reed said, "I'm quite able to walk myself home, you know."

Ghosh bowed low. "Oh, Lady not want to go there, Lady meet terrible fate, worse than death, maybe even better." She straightened up. "Besides, I've got to go over that way anyway."

Kory scratched his head. If Ghologhosh had business in a quarter of wealthy merchants' houses, it was better not to ask what it was. "All right. Knock when you come in."

Ghosh nodded. "Well?"

Kory said, "Well what?"

Reed said, "Well *this*," and kissed him.

Ghosh said, "I didn't think you'd finish that before dark. Come on, Reed, let's go make some pretty boys cry."

They started up the canalside path. Ghosh, who never moved without looking in all directions, saw Kory just standing by the *Vessel*'s gangway, looking in no particular direction.

"So is there any hope for the two of you," she said to Reed, "or are you just going to keep on mooning and strolling until Dyelam finds someone rich enough to bring into his business, with you as the splice?"

"Kory will be rich enough . . . or maybe he won't. I really don't care. And my father isn't the kind of man you seem to see him as."

"Wouldn't know. All I ever see is money. Is Dyelam just gold-plate, then?"

"What do you know about anybody?" Reed said, almost angry. "You don't love or care about anyone but yourself."

"You give me too much credit," Ghosh said quietly. "Hey, don't get mad. You cry and streak up your face, we'll have to explain it to your family."

Reed said, "And you couldn't do that, could you? You don't know how to cry."

Ghosh could tell she wasn't angry any longer, which was good. Reed was smart and funny, good to be with—like Kory. If Ghosh had been either of them, she probably would have spent as much time as possible with the other. Which was exactly why this courting game of theirs was so Gholdamn dumb. There was a Bree Amal proverb: *The line between wealth and poverty is as thin as a half-copper. The line between life and death is as thin as the edge of a knife. So why waste time drawing lines?*

They were passing the Levar's palace, which glittered in the late-day sun. The canal was alight. Caught between sparkle and shimmer, Ghosh felt suddenly grubby. "Hey, stop a moment," she said, and took a black cloth bundle from her pouch. She unwrapped a pair of black kidskin slippers, pulled them on. "You see? Some of your boyfriend's advice is worth taking." Reed laughed. Ghosh wiped her face with the cloth, shook it out, and wrapped it around her head, tucking in the ends.

"Here," Reed said. She plucked at her clothing, and held out a small silver pin with a green-enameled olive tree.

"You'll want that back," Ghosh said. "Don't give it to me."

"No. Father had a lot of them made when he bought the grove. So no one will think it's stolen, either."

"Can I call you if I ever need a judge?" Ghosh pinned her turban. "Forget it. An honest judge is something I'm never going to need."

"Ghosh, I . . ."

They were at the bridge across the canal. Across it, the Levar's Park spread out to the right, the expensive houses fronting the Levar's Way to the left. "Not now, hey? You don't want people to think you know me, not this close to home."

The ais Ariom house was of gray stone with black ironwork, with decorative castings of sugarcane on the exterior walls. It had belonged to a sugar merchant, before Dyelam ais Ariom moved to Liavek and needed a fashionable old address. As Reed knocked, Ghosh slipped into the shadow cast by the doorframe. A Tichenese in eggshell-colored silk, carrying a butler's rod of black wood, answered the door. "Pleasant evening, Mistress Cadie."

"Hello, Xochan. Am I awfully, fearfully, dreadfully late?" Xochan smiled. "Not so late as that, Mistress. The master your father has had business all this day, and a private guest for noon meal, and has had no time to notice your absence."

"Happy birthday, Reed," Ghosh muttered.

Xochan leaned forward. "Is that Mistress Ghologhosh?" She slapped her rod into her palm.

Ghosh moved out of the shadows. "Night breezes blow you sweetness, O Source of Order."

Xochan's grin showed polished white teeth. "And may the moon favor your labors with her darkness, O Mover of Property. I would shower you with riches for the safe return of my willow mistress, but sadly I am only a poor servant. . . . However, there is warm apple pie in the kitchen."

Reed said, "Why does *she* get apple pie?"

Xochan said, "Because it is not yet the mistress's dinnertime."

Ghosh slipped inside. "Tell her the truth, Xochan. If you rob the house of a person who's fed you, you spend ten thousand years of the afterlife as a plum tree."

Reed snorted in a most inelegant way and ran up the curving, carpeted staircase.

Ghosh said, "And with the pie, might there be cream?"

"There might be cream, for speakers of truth," Xochan said. "Was she truly with Master Korik?"

"I'm the only one you saw her with."

Xochan nodded. Her eyes narrowed. "A *plum tree?*"

"Liavekans," Ghosh said lightly, "will believe anything."

A twentieth-watch later, Ghologhosh sat in the outer sill of a shuttered window, licking pie crumbs from her fingers. She reached down and wiped her hand on night-damp grass, then dried it on her shirt. She took a pair of thin gloves from her pouch and tugged them on. She started to take off the kid slippers, then thought better of it; she could cross the rock garden wearing them, then slip them off and leave no track inside.

Her contractor wanted a small brass mask set with yellow opals. Junk by itself, he said, only valuable to a collector. That was what contractors usually said; sometimes it was true and sometimes it wasn't. Ghosh could almost always tell how much an object was really worth, but she was never tempted to scout for higher bids. Unlike Kory's businesses, her trade didn't have much room for private initiative.

She slipped to the ground. The earth was cool, the air quite crisp for late Wine. There was a little low fog, and almost no moon. Fine thieving weather.

Ghosh crossed the rock garden without any sound. The garden was poorly tended, overgrown, rocks turned over. It had been the hobby of the house's last owner. Dyelam ais Ariom didn't have time for such things, and as the garden was not visible from the street, there was no social reason to maintain it. Ghosh's foot stirred a pool of mist. She suddenly remembered a rumor that the prior owner, ruined in the sugar trade by some Ka Zhir intrigue, had gone into his garden and cut his wrists. *Interesting story,* she thought. *When I get wealthy, I must remember not to keep a garden.*

She came to another shuttered window, listened at it. Silence. She took a thin tool from her collar, slid it between the shutters, lifted the latch. No click. Very slowly, she opened the shutter. Only a whisper of sound. Praising fine craftsmanship, Ghosh examined the window beyond. There was no curtain. It was entirely dark within. Her contractor swore, whatever that was worth, that this storeroom had not been opened in years—perhaps not since Dyelam had moved in. It contained, he swore double, only some of the sugar trader's old trivia, not worth displaying or selling.

Ghosh wondered why he had told her that. Reassurance that the mask would not be missed? Or that she would not *really* be robbing ais Ariom? If it was starting to get around that she and Reed—well. She'd have to worry about that later. There was enough to do now.

She undid the window latch. The window swung inward with a faint groan. *Stay dead, Sugarman,* she thought, *you can't spend it now.* And then she was inside.

There was a faint rumble of conversation from the far side of the room, probably through a door, though it was too dark to see. That was just fine. If no light leaked through to this side, none would shine out. She took a tiny spirit lamp from her pouch, unfolded it, scratched flint on steel. The light was small but steady and sufficient.

She could see that the contractor was right: the room was cluttered with small objects on shelves, all of them dusty, untended. That meant the need to move carefully, not leave too much written in the dust. She kept her slippers on; they were less distinctive than footprints.

She saw the mask. It hung on the wall, on a strip of leather with several other items of oxidized brass. She reached gloved fingers around it. There was a simple hook. It came away easily, went into her pouch with no protest at all. She turned. One of the voices beyond the door was raised. She moved to go. Her business was over. Dyelam ais Ariom's voice said, "—kill the Regent." Ghosh stopped still. She moved to the door. Spying was, she reasoned, only another kind of stealing.

Dyelam was talking with another man. Ghosh did not know the voice.

Dyelam said, "—but I *don't* want him dead. Only removed. He's a bad influence on the child."

"You mean Her Magnificence, the Levar," the other voice said. There was an accent, familiar, not quite placed.

"I mean a flighty child, impressionable, who in not many years is going to have outrageous responsibilities. But keep this quite clear, wizard"—Ghosh bit her lip— "this is not an attack upon the Levar. It is a measure to save her from a man with only his own ends, his own interests, in mind."

He could be talking about Kory and Reed, Ghosh thought.

The other man, the wizard, said, "It can be done without killing. And far safer to do it so, of course. I know certain . . . potent facts about His Scarlet Eminence, which can—"

"I don't want to know," Dyelam said.

"Customers so rarely do." There was a clink of porcelain. "It is necessary that it be done on the End of Wine, in Hrothvek."

"A magical reason?"

"You don't want to know." Ghosh knew the accent now: it was faint, but it was Hrothvekan. "The Regent may be reluctant to attend your celebration, but you will find a way to persuade him. After all," the man said, with acid irony, "his position isn't so *very* secure."

"His man, the Count—"

"Dashif will be elsewhere occupied. There is no extra charge. May I have some more tea?" The cups clinked again. "Oh, and speaking of which, I need to pay a chemist. One hundred levars will be sufficient."

"Do you think in amounts smaller than a hundred levars?" Dyelam said, frustration audible in his voice. There were heavy footsteps, a drawer being pulled open, the sound of coins. Ghosh could tell ten-levar gold by its clink.

The wizard said smoothly, "Have you never heard the aphorism, 'One must pay an assassin three times: once to come, once to kill, once to go away'? After all, merchant, if this scheme fails, you will have no further use for money. While if it succeeds..."

"If it succeeds no one will ever know!" Dyelam almost shouted. "I grew up in a warehouse. I know the price of doing business. If it succeeds, no one will—*what's that?*"

"This little light? One of the things your money goes to buy," the wizard's voice said calmly. "Protection from spies."

Ghosh had once been told that all trap spells contained a loophole: something about balance of luck. You always had one chance to escape.

She looked up and saw glowing eyes, suicide's eyes, staring at her from the window. She froze for an instant. And her chance slipped past.

The two points of light rushed at her from the mist. Ghosh held up a hand, reaching for her knife with the other. A moth-mote whirled around her wrist: it trailed a streak of blue-white light that tightened suddenly and hard. She felt it burn. The other light bound her knife hand to her side. The motes spun round her knees, pulling them together; she fell. The lights continued to whirl around her, wrapping, constricting, searing. She couldn't move. She couldn't breathe. She opened her mouth to gasp, and the traces gagged her tongue; she heard spit sizzle. She felt the wire wrap her throat, and then she felt nothing.

The midnight watch had gone by, and Kory was still awake, wondering about Ghosh. She often worked all night, but since she had asked for a place to stay, then presumably tonight... well. Ghosh was not the most predictable soul on earth.

Kory stood up, chewed on a piece of apple, walked from one end of his room to the other. It only took a few steps. It was a basement room in a ship chandler's, in Old Town near the docks. The only air came from a tiny window near the ceiling, but it was cheap and fairly private at night, and he had the off-hours' use of the shop to work on his landsailer, which was built of broken spars and odd brasses bought at cost. He wished he had the 'sailer now. He could work on the spring and hub. It would be better than pacing. He looked out the window, getting a rat's-eye view of the street: nothing.

Ghosh didn't want to be owed anything, she had a funny way about debts, but Kory felt he owed her something. Kory had been tempted toward thieving more than once; it seemed so easy, the overhead was so very low. But Ghosh was good at it, very good, and you couldn't call what she had a good living. It wasn't exactly a debt, but—

There was a tap at the door. "Ghosh?" Kory said. There was no answer. Kory went to the door. "Ghosh?" Still nothing. Kory loosened the broad-bladed knife that hung near the door frame. He opened the door.

There was no one there. A folded paper lay on the steps. Kory looked around; there were a few lights, a few walkers, that was all. He picked up the letter, shut and latched the door.

The room was furnished with a bed and a table and a chair and a lamp. Kory turned up the lamp and unfolded the paper, which was unsealed. He recognized Reed's handwriting at once, and as he read his hand began to shake.

Beloved Kory,

Father has finally done it. He plans to marry me off to some horrid Hrothvekan, so he can make sure he doesn't lose control of the old part of the business.

I am to have no say in this matter, of course. The Hrothvekan is, I am told, "not a horrid man." I suppose this means he is abominable.

I will not be property. But I will be yours, if you will have me, without goods or dowry. The wedding is to be announced at my father's celebration in Hrothvek, on the End of Wine. There is so little time. Please, tell me what we shall do.

I love you.
Reed

Kory read the letter, and read it again, and again. *The merchant has finally done it,* he thought, *finally challenged me to a duel.*

He did not sleep that night, and never noticed that Ghosh never came.

Ghologhosh hovered in darkness, immobile, feeling pressures against her bones. Her normal senses were all useless:

she could not move, but did not know if she was bound, or held, or . . .

Then there was the clear touch of a hand to her face. "You're strong, dollikin," said a voice out of the nothing. It was the wizard's voice, the Hrothvekan—

The hand slapped her, hard. "Yes," the voice said. "I am that one. You don't know my name, though, do you? No. Good for you that you do not. Good for both of us. You can be of use to me, dollikin, but I have to lock some things up inside you for a while. And I couldn't take chances of something as potent as a name slipping out."

The hand stroked her face, then slid down her body, cold flesh on cold flesh. "What a misused little dollikin you are. All scars. All the pleasure used up. I could mend you, of course, and start *all* over—but there's no time. We must take such enjoyment as we can."

The hand brushed her hair back from her forehead. The fingers spread out on her brow.

The pain was like the edges of seashells scraping across her naked brain, the salt sea flooding in upon the wound. She did not scream. She did not cry. At least, she did not think so. The voice had said she would live. How? she thought. She wondered, if she did live, how she would ever again imagine hell.

Ghol, oh Ghol, make me a plum tree for ten thousand years—

Ghosh felt herself bathed in coolness. Her head hurt, and her wrists. She lay on something soft. Something struck her, but gently, gently. She opened her eyes.

There was a ball of spiky silvery filaments crouched a hands-breadth in front of her face, filling her whole vision. It stretched a pair of fibers toward her: on their ends were tiny, bright blue eyes. Ghosh smiled idiotically.

Then a foot kicked the dawn spook away and a hand touched her shoulder. She looked up at the sky and a figure dark against it: a broad-faced man with a strange fringe of white hair around his head. His blue head.

"What is it, Jagg?" another man's voice called, and the blue-gray man pulled Ghosh to a sitting position. Another wave washed around them. Ghosh looked around groggily: they were on the beach at Liavek's far southwest, down by the Sea Eagle Inn, almost to the Saltmarsh.

"Half-drowned lady," the blue man said in a weirdly flat voice. "Friend to the pair we met yesterday. Saw her with them at the drugsmith's barge."

Ghosh remembered him then, the one who had spoken to Kory. She turned to look at the other man. He was of average height, just passing middle age, with light hair and eyes. He wore a high-collared black tunic and rolled-up gray trousers; his feet were big and blue-veined and pale. He leaned on a black stick.

"How ever do you come to be here, mistress?" the blond man said, in a voice that said something else was on his mind.

Ghosh thought. She couldn't remember. She saw the blue-gray man, she walked Reed home, there was apple pie—then nothing but a feeling like pain that had passed by, the memory of an infected tooth. And she wasn't about to tell these two about it. "I sleep on the beach some nights," she said, which was no lie.

"Below the tide line?" the blond man said. "Careful you don't sleep too late. . . . Jagg, help the woman up. My name is Ciellon. Do I understand that you know Kory Li and Reed ais Ariom?"

"Yeah . . . yes."

"We met them upon the Hrothvek road yesterday. They were gathering—what was it, Jagg? Oh, yes, crabs, for the apothecary Thomorin Wiln. But Kory's windcar had a slight accident. We drove them home." Ciellon smiled. "Does that establish our acquaintance? I could show you the landsailer, but Kory came for it very early this morning."

"I . . . uh, pleased to meet you, Master Ciellon. Master Jagg. I'm . . . Ghologhosh. Call me Ghosh."

"Good morning to you, then, Ghosh. We were just going for a walk to the Saltmarsh edge to have a little breakfast. Pleased to have you share it with us, if you've nowhere better to go."

She didn't know whether she did or not. But it wasn't far. And she did know she was hungry. "Happy to join you, Master Ciellon."

"Splendid! You meet the nicest people by accident here."

They sat on the rocks, eating smoked fingerlings and spiced toast with kaf, tossing the scraps to the sea eagles, who caught them on the fly. Ciellon talked on, explaining that he was a wizard, born in Hrothvek but long gone from there. Ghosh was wary of all his talking. People who started off with so much talking usually thought they were paying in advance for something.

In one of the pauses, Ghosh said, "Ciellon isn't a Hrothvekan name," and was surprised at herself for saying such a dangerous thing.

"No. It comes from a Farlander myth. Ciellon is the herald who leads the Brightmetal Gods when they go forth at the end of time, for their last battle with the Gods of Rust and Sand. Bit pompous, I suppose. Ciellon isn't even very smart, for a god. He's the first to die, of a Rusty arrow through the heart. . . . Look, there's Crookneck Zal." He pointed at a cormorant, taking off from the reeds. "Our innkeeper's name. Excuse me; names are a hobby of mine, but I don't know yours. Can you tell me the meaning of 'Ghologhosh'?"

Ghosh blinked. She had been calling herself that ever since she was small, and no one had ever asked why. "He's a god too," she said. "The God of Throwaway Curses, the ones people don't really mean. He's not much of a god now, but every time someone says 'Kosker and Pharn!' or 'by the Red Faith, from pole to pole!' he gets stronger."

Ciellon's smile was absolutely joyful. Ghosh wondered suddenly if she had given up part of her soul to the magician, by giving up her name. "But that's wonderful!" the wizard said, and began to laugh. After a moment he stopped, wiping tears from his eyes, and looked across the Saltmarsh.

"Come walk with me a little while longer, Ghologhosh," Ciellon said, his voice again preoccupied and faraway. "Jagg, go on back. We'll be all right."

Jagg left. Ciellon stood up and gestured with his cane. Ghosh supposed they were headed for a nice sloppy tumble in the marsh. That was all right. She'd paid more for breakfast.

But all they did was walk, and talk. Ciellon seemed to know everything about the marsh: the names of fifty kinds of reeds, "all slender, all supple, like your friend Cadie"; where to turn over rocks to send outlandish creatures scuttling toward the safety of the sea, how to get seven skips from a flung flat stone.

Ghosh found herself forgetting the loss of last night. All she wanted to know was what she could not ask—what did Ciellon want?

She thought, just maybe, she knew. Maybe he just wanted to talk. Maydee Gai at the House of Blue Leaves had once told her that many of the customers wanted nothing more, and paid for nothing more. Ghosh had never met anyone like that. She had certainly never been touched by one.

Ciellon said, "Oh my. We must head back, or we'll miss the noon meal."

Ghosh looked up, startled to realize it was past midday.

"You will take lunch with me? After we've both cleaned up a bit."

No sense in missing a meal. "Certainly, Master Ciellon."

"Honored, mistress. Damned honored. There's one for both Ghologhoshes." He paused. "Ghosh . . . do you have a place to stay tonight?"

Well, she thought, finally. "No, master."

"Ciellon will do. Then, I would be pleased to guest you this evening. Our room's big enough for a regiment."

"I—"

"Don't answer me now," Ciellon said. "I warn you, I shall insist on taking afternoon tea with you. It's my inflexible custom. Decide then."

Wrapping a borrowed linen robe around herself, Ghologhosh came out of the bath into Ciellon's room, which was in fact enormous. Ciellon was standing by the picture window, looking out at the Saltmarsh, as a man who has lost something precious into the sea will stare at the waves, knowing they give nothing back.

"Your clothes are rather far gone," Ciellon said. "Somewhere in that trunk there must be a shirt and pants that will fit you, with a little judicious sashing. You don't wear shoes, I take it?"

"No. But I don't—borrow things."

Ciellon said, "Then it isn't a loan. Though your things are where you left them." He pointed with his cane.

Ghosh did not refuse gifts outright. She found a black blouse of heavy fabric—winter was coming—and green trousers similar to her old ones. Her belts and gear did not appear to have been touched, her knives all in place.

Jagg came in then with lunch, and Ciellon began to talk again, and then suddenly it was the end of the afternoon.

"Tea," Ciellon said. "Shall we take it downstairs, in the parlor? I need a small change of scene. And then you may leave, or not."

Ghosh saw Zal the innkeeper look up as they entered the parlor, running fingers over the bald side of her head. As they passed, Ghosh heard a few words of the Second Prayer to Bree Amal the Great Madam, which is: *May These Events Not Cost Thy Servant Money.*

Zal najhi Zal showed Ciellon, Ghosh, and Jagg to a table with a sea view. "Tea, master?" she said, with just a little too much deference.

"Tea, innkeeper," Ciellon said. "I think the Incense of Fair Memory."

"I would have you know, master," Zal said with pride, "that at great expense we have procured a small quantity of the rare Tea of Worrynot."

Ghosh stared.

Ciellon said, "That's very nice, innkeeper. But I've made my own arrangements about that. I suggest you save it for the appropriate occasion."

To Ghosh's surprise, Ciellon did *not* talk during teatime. None of them did. Ciellon looked at Ghosh with an unreadable expression, Jagg looked at Ciellon in an even blanker way, and Ghosh tried to look out the window at the declining light.

Ciellon said, "Well, Ghologhosh?"

More from curiosity than anything else, she said, "I would be honored, mas—Ciellon."

The wizard nodded, waved Zal najhi Zal to the table. "Innkeeper. Please add the surcharge for an additional guest in my rooms."

There was only one bed. Ciellon slept in it. Jagg took a heap of silks and furs from a trunk, and another for Ghosh, and they slept curled up in those, all quite far from one another in the enormous room, its picture window silvery with faint moonlight off the sea.

Ghosh slept as she had never done in her life. Until the dream came. The voice, and the hand—

Her eyes snapped open. She did not stir. The dream—she could not remember the dream.

There was a black shape against the silver window. It was Ciellon in his nightshift, leaning against the sill as if a weight were crushing his shoulders. Ghosh could hear his voice, very faintly, speaking in rhythm. A ritual spell? She wondered, and then she heard the song:

Call to thee, Harmony, Saltmarsh's daughter,
Drink to our faith in a cup of salt water.
Come to me, Harmony, promise unspoken,
Follow your faith where the marsh reeds lie broken.
Never be, Harmony, healed or forgiven,
Salt in the wound where the promise was riven.

Ciellon turned away from the window. Ghosh held entirely
still: she could feign sleep for a long time. It had saved her
life more than once. Her knife was naturally at her fingertips.

Ciellon leaned over her. He touched her hair, ran his fingers
through it. He knelt. He spoke some words she did not understand. He kissed her on the temple. Then he stood up slowly
and got back into his bed.

Ghosh lay very quiet in her sleeping bundle. She was entirely
awake. She was more than awake. She was beginning to remember. First a trickle. Then a stream. Then a flood. Ais
Ariom's house. The Hrothvekan wizard. The Regent. Kory.
The pain.

She opened her mouth in a noiseless scream and stood up
in the silks, slashing herself free, and before Jagg or Ciellon
could move, she was racing down the hall, down the stairs,
away from the Sea Eagle and into the twisting alleys of Liavek.

Kory woke to a hammering on the door. He drew the sheath
knife, stepped to the side, and opened the door: Ghologhosh
half fell into the room. She was wearing new clothes and her
knife was out.

"Plan," she said, "remember, stop." She twitched like a
puppet on strings. "You, letter, they, plan, chemist, kill, *wizard.*"

"What's happened to you?" Kory said. She was jumping,
whirling her knife wildly.

"Spell," she shouted at him, "spell-spell, *spell.* Wizard.
You, plan. *Kill-not-kill.*"

"Calm down," Kory said. He put out his hands, saw the
knife he held, dropped it. Ghosh dropped hers. "Sit down,
Ghosh. Be calm. Sit-down-on-the-bed."

Ghosh sat, calmer but still shaking.

"Who did this to you?"

"Wizard," she said, and shook her head violently. "Nuh-
nuh-name. No-name wizard."

Kory understood then. It was a gag spell: Ghosh was under compulsion not to speak the name of the wizard responsible. "You said 'kill.' Kill who?"

"No-name-kill. But not-kill. No-name-not-kill."

This was getting complicated. Kory had a sudden awful thought. "Who am I, Ghosh?"

"You. You-you-*youyouyou!* No-name-you. No-name-*any-body.*"

Kory let out a breath. The compulsion extended to the names of everybody and everything. This was going to be very difficult. What else had Ghosh said? "You said 'letter.' Letter from—oh, sorry. What kind of letter?"

"Love letter," Ghosh said quite clearly, and looked surprised.

"Reed's letter?" Kory shouted. Ghosh spread her hands in a desperate gesture.

Kory thought. "Maps," he said suddenly. "I'll get my maps." He brought out the small stack of maps he used for courier work and unrolled them on the table. Ghosh staggered over, squinting in the lamplight. Kory pointed at the location of Reed's house. "Letter from here?"

Ghosh opened her mouth. She strained. There was only a squeaking sound. She held out her hands, but the fingers curled up.

This was getting serious. Apparently she couldn't even act to betray the—*Conspiracy?* Kory thought, and thought of the letter.

Ghosh had taken Reed home. Reed must have given Ghosh the letter. Then Ghosh had been grabbed right off the street—only the kidnapers missed the letter—

Some horrid Hrothvekan, the letter had said.

Some horrid Hrothvekan *wizard.*

Kory shuffled the maps until he found his chart of the southern roads. He spread it next to the city map. He pointed to Hrothvek with his left hand, with his right to the Sea Eagle Inn.

Ghosh gabbled and choked and kicked the table over. Kory barely saved the lamp as it fell.

"That's all you had to say," Kory said.

The shadow of *The Vessel of Dreams* still reached to the wharf when Kory pedaled his landsailer to the gangway. Leaving Ghosh still fidgeting in the passenger seat, Kory ran to the boat and pulled the FOR MEDICAL EMERGENCIES ONLY bellcord.

Thomorin Wiln appeared in a cloth coat tossed over his nightshirt. "I'm certain there's an explanation for this," he said.

"The man I brought in the other day—the blue one. Where are the things he ordered?"

"What business is that of yours?" Thomorin Wiln snapped, and looked at the end of the counter, where a small paper box sat. More mildly, the apothecary said, "Did he hire you to fetch them?"

Kory tensed. Ghosh had managed to choke out "One hundred levars." If the payment was due now, he was out of luck. "Yes," he said. "Sorry about the hour. He insisted."

Thomorin Wiln nodded. "I hardly blame him. Well, there it is. It's in glass, so be careful."

"I will."

Kory reached for the box. Thomorin Wiln caught Kory's wrist in his discolored hand. "I mean *be careful,* Kory-of-All-Trades. I used up all the prepared rapture flower in Liavek for that bottle, and it'll be ten days to ready more, plus the distillation time." He released Kory. "The other wasn't so hard. I just don't get much call for it."

"I'll treat it well," Kory said.

Thomorin Wiln said, "I'm sure you will. Sorry, Kory. Too early."

"Sure."

"If you're going to start rising at this hour regularly, I still need some dawn spooks."

"Tomorrow."

"Fine. Off. Tell the man a happy End of Wine, will you?"

The box wedged between his hip and Ghosh's, Kory drove up the canal to the first bridge, crossed, and pedaled back to the seashore, to an empty dock. He got out of the car, lifting the box; Ghosh sat quietly. Kory looked out at the water, the sails of the fishing fleet off Minnow Island. He opened the box. Inside were a slender flask full of pale golden liquid and a jar of blue-black leaves. The jar said INFUSION TAXALIN AZI-FLORA (WORRYNOT TEA). The bottle was not labeled, but Thomorin Wiln had said enough. Rapture flower was the most potent narcotic Kory knew of. He remembered the wizard, the addict, slurping from his flask.

"Kill-not-kill," he said to Ghosh, who looked at him with

unfocused eyes. Kory grasped the delicate flask, cocked his arm to throw it into the bay.

Ghosh moaned and struggled. She fell out of the car.

Kory lifted her back in. "We go to Wizard's Row next. I hope I can afford—" Suddenly he had a better idea than smashing the bottle. He went to the edge of the dock, pulled the ground-glass stopper, and poured the yellow liquid into the water, being careful to avert his face from the fumes. He hoped it did not poison the fish.

He refilled the bottle. Fortunately, it was not too large. Then he pedaled along the shoreline, almost to the Sea Eagle. "Wait here," he told Ghosh, who opened her mouth uselessly. "Back soon. With money."

Zal najhi Zal told Kory that Ciellon was on the beach walking. When Kory reached the shore, Jagg was standing soldier-like on the sand, watching the wizard, who stood some distance away, alone out in the Saltmarsh.

"Jagg," Kory said, and the blue man turned. "I've brought Ciellon's preparation. From Thomorin Wiln. I had some other deliveries, and I thought—"

"The master will thank you well," Jagg said. "But your friend, the small dark one? Ghologhosh. The master must see her."

"I'm sorry," Kory said, trying to choke down rage. "I don't have any idea where she is."

"The thing is important." Jagg turned. "Master! The master Korik Li is here!"

Ciellon looked up, waved his cane, started toward them.

"I have other deliveries," Kory said. "It's medicine, it won't wait," and he shoved the white box into Jagg's hands and ran, waiting for his heart to be stopped, lightning to strike him; but nothing happened. When he got back to the 'sailer, Ghosh had gotten out, and dragged herself along walls almost forty paces. Kory led her back to the car, half-carrying her. She seemed about to explode, like a gun stopped at the mouth.

"I'm sorry," Kory said to Ghosh. "I've brought what money I have. It'll have to do."

They drove to Wizard's Row—or rather, they tried. Wizard's Row was not there.

"Damn street's never around when you need it," Kory said. He spun the landsailer hard. Somebody dropped a parcel and swore at him. Someone else was interrupted in the middle of a pickpocketing; Kory saw the victim draw a pistol on the thief and he pedaled on hard, not listening for the bang. A few blocks on, he turned—and clearly saw the signs and rooftops of Wizard's Row.

"Happy birthday, Ghosh," Kory said, executed an illegal U-turn (knocking over a rubbish bin, which rolled into a one-legged beggar, who unfolded his other leg from his cloak and sprinted away), and pedaled for all he was worth.

There was no corner to turn. No signs, no rooftops. The Row was gone again. Kory looked at Ghosh, who looked miserable and furious. Kory pedaled on for a block, and got out of the car. "Wait," he said, and sprinted back toward the place where the street had been.

And still was, signs, roofs, dustbins, everything.

Kory stamped back to Ghosh, sighed. "That's a damned comprehensive spell. Is he a magician or a lawyer?" He looked at the sun. It had become terribly near midday. "I have to meet Reed, right away," he said.

Ghosh struggled. Tendons and veins stood out on her flesh. Her clothes were drenched in sweat. Kory reached out, cautiously, to her forehead. It burned. "I'll kill him," Kory said. "I don't care if he is a wizard. I'll stuff his luck right down his throat, and then I'll kill him. . . . I've got to get you home first. You'll be safe there. Ciellon doesn't know where I live."

Ghosh shivered and sweated.

By the time they reached Kory's room, Ghosh was too weak to walk. Kory carried her down the steps, kicked the door open, put her gently on the bed. He fumbled at her clothes, then let go and drew the blanket up to her chin.

She grabbed both his wrists, lifted her head. "You wrote letter," she rasped, *"You wrote her letter?"*

Kory nodded. "They're leaving for Hrothvek just after the noon meal for Dyelam's party. Reed'll have everything all packed. But there's a slight change in plans: she's going with me. To Saltigos. The marriage will be Liavek-legal, and too late for Dyelam ais Ariom. And Company."

"Not her!" Ghosh said and fell back on the bed.

Kory was suddenly sad. "Always her and no one else but her," he said slowly. "I'm sorry you never understood, Ghosh." He backed away from her. "We wanted you to come to Saltigos with us, be our first witness . . . but . . ."

Ghosh's head rolled.

"We'll tell the City Guard where to find you. Ciellon—they'll take care of him, or I will. I—goodbye, Ghosh."

The door closed behind him.

Ghologhosh tried to rise, to run after him, but her arm would not lift, not a finger. The spell was like a wire snare: the harder she fought the more tightly it bound her. She could not even think the names of things now, could not even pray.

The snare would choke her before she could break it. But maybe—if she could relax, stop fighting—she could slip it. Just enough to breathe.

The wheels of Kory's 'sailer chirped by the window and Ghosh tensed again, and felt the sensation leave her feet. *Be still,* she thought. *Still. Calm. Nothing.*

Her right arm rolled off the bed. She felt her knuckles strike the floor. *Yes. Fall. Do nothing. Let what falls, fall.* Her right heel hit the ground. *Fall.* Her head tipped over; she saw the floor, her limp hand. There was blood on the scraped knuckles. *Scrape. Pain.* Her other hand moved. *Pain for him. He wants pain. Give him pain.* She clawed her hand around the bed leg, feeling the corners of the wood dig into her flesh. *Not against his orders to hurt.*

She pulled herself off the bed, landing with a thump face down. She got her hands under herself and pushed. *Follow the pain where it leads.* Like a disjointed doll, she got to her knees, shuffled around, grasped the door handle, pulled herself upright by the pain in her joints.

On the other side of the door, she knew, were three impossible stairsteps up to the unimaginably long street. She could not do it. She could not live so long.

You must live, said a voice inside her head. *You're doing fine. You're doing right. Think of nothing. Think of sand, sea, sky, all empty.*

"The hurt . . ." she said.

Here is pain enough. Something flowed through her, something cold as mountain water. She knew that it was someone else's pain, feeding the invisible hunger that the caster had put inside his spell.

She knew whose pain it was.

Sand, sky, sea . . .

"Sand, sky, sea . . ." she said, wondering at the rushing cold pain, wondering how anyone could live adrift in such a cold sea of agony. . . . "Sea, sea-sea, *Ciellon!*"

The door flew into splinters. Jagg stepped through, held out his blue hands to Ghosh.

No, Jagg. Let her do it herself.

She took three firm, straight steps toward him, and then she fell, but he caught her easily. He thumbed open a vial and made her drink; she felt better at once.

"Ciellon," she said, "Jagg, Ghosh," drunk on the sound of names. "How, Jagg, Ciellon, Ghosh, find?"

Jagg reached into her hair, drew out a tiny, shiny object. Ghosh tried to focus on it. It was a golden louse, tiny hooks along its legs. "Ciellon put this on you," Jagg said. "He tracked it."

Ghosh nodded. "Nice Ciellon bug." She struggled to think. "Track. Kory track Reed. Track Kory!"

Yes. Jagg, take her to him, quickly.

The ais Ariom house was surrounded by plenty of bustle, more than enough for Kory to hide among. Baggage was being moved, wagons loaded. Dyelam ais Ariom himself stood in the middle of the confusion, trying to look in charge.

The rock garden, Reed's letter had said. *It's invisible from the street.* It was exactly the route he would have chosen. He knew for the ten-thousandth time that he loved her.

He sidled up the alley that led to the garden. The old iron gate was open. Good; less noise—though galloping horses might have been lost in the caravan out front.

Kory paused at the gate. The day had become cool and damp, Fog coming early, and there was mist filling the garden. "Reed?" Kory whispered.

"Here, Kory," Reed's voice said from the mist.

Kory took a step. He looked up. A pair of glowing points stared back at him.

A spinning dagger flew past his head, toward the floating lights. It sailed between them; there was a long spark, and the lights were gone.

Jagg, the wizard's servant, stood in the gateway. In one thick arm he held Ghosh, limp as a rag doll.

Kory yelled and ran, drawing his knife. Ghosh's head bobbed up. "Kory, stop," she said.

"Let her go," Kory said.

"Yes, Jagg," Ghosh said. Jagg released her. She stood unsteadily.

Kory moved next to her, holding his knife level on Jagg. "Now, you're going to—"

"No time to argue," Ghosh said, and Kory looked at her just in time to see her fist knock him cold.

Thomorin Wiln closed his bag. "That's no substitute for rest," he told Ghosh, "but it should keep you on your feet." He looked at Ciellon, who sat up in bed against pillows. "I've given you the strongest pain medicine I have, if you won't let me put you to sleep—"

"I will be fine, thank you," Ciellon said in a thin voice.

Thomorin Wiln started to speak, then shut his mouth. On his way out of the inn room, he turned to Kory and said, "The next time you decide to go into the apothecary's trade, see me about an apprenticeship."

Kory stared at the floor as the door closed. "I don't understand—the caravan was just leaving; I saw it."

"An illusion, waiting for you to trigger it," Ciellon said. "The real party left early in the morning."

"But I had Reed's letter."

"Show it to me."

Kory unfolded the paper and held it out.

"Ghosh, read it," Ciellon said.

"'My father wishes me to marry against my will. Let us flee.' It isn't Reed's handwriting."

"What do you mean? It says right here—about the Hrothvekan—"

"It doesn't even mention Hrothvek," Ghosh said, and Kory looked shocked at the coldness in her voice.

Ciellon said, "Mirage ink. The writer draws the intent of the message, and the reader's mind creates the text and handwriting. Only wizards can use it, but many chemists can make it. For a high fee. Now, you must go to Hrothvek, and quickly. Reed's life may depend on it. The Regent's certainly does."

Kory was still staring at Ghosh. "I don't know why—I guess I thought that—"

Ghosh turned away from him. She said, "What are they going to do to His Eminence?"

Ciellon's face was rigid for a few moments. Then he sighed. "Look out the window."

Ghosh opened the curtains. A storm was forming offshore—unnaturally fast, clouds boiling black, stabbing lightning. It was racing toward the shore.

Ciellon said, "Resh—His Scarlet Eminence—has a fear of high places, and of storms. A very strong fear."

Kory said, "Now even I understand. He was a sailor, wasn't he?" He looked outside at the dark mass. "And if he should funk in front of all manner of powerful people—he'd never be able to hold power, once that got about. But what does Reed have to do with it?"

Ciellon was silent for a moment. He put a hand against his abdomen and pressed. Then he said, "What only Resh and a few Hrothvekans know—myself, and apparently this wizard of Dyelam's, among them—is that the storm at sea was the second storm. It was the first storm, when he and I were your ages, that drove him to the sea, and me to the Farlands, and the young woman—her to the Saltmarsh on the last night of Wine, and to wherever the marsh hides its dead."

Ghosh said, "Harmony."

"That was her everyday name, yes." He shut his eyes and breathed shallowly. Tendons bulged in his neck. "And jhi Hisor means to play the tragedy out once again, with Reed in Harmony's part . . . poor Resh."

Ghosh thought, *Now there's a word for His Eminence I'll never hear again.*

Ciellon said, "And now you *must* go. Jagg will drive you. Jagg, if you must kill the horses, then you must."

Kory said, "The landsailer's faster." He pointed at the storm. "Especially running before that."

Ghosh went to Ciellon's side. "The other wizard. You used a name. Do you know him?"

"Phris jhi Hisor. He was only an unkind little boy when I knew him. I would never have believed him determined enough to succeed in investing his luck, but I've learned since. . . . Oh, I am sorry, Ghologhosh. I removed the spell he laid to bar your memory—you fled before I was quite aware of the second spell beneath it. I was never . . . a very clever wizard. Go now, quickly." His eyes closed and his back arched with his pain, for which there was no medicine in Liavek—Ghosh knew there had been none since Ciellon had given the last diluted drops of it to Jagg, to give to her.

She said, "Why are you here? For Harmony? Or the Regent? If you knew about the plan—"

"But I didn't know, Ghosh. Nor was I told. It just happened—things do sometimes. Go. Go, before the wind rises too high."

"Why did you come back, Ciellon?"

"You know that already, Ghosh. Kory, take her and go. I can't concentrate enough to stop the storm."

Kory put his hand on Ghosh's arm. She shoved him away. She looked at Jagg, pointed at the storm clouds, which seemed about to crowd through the window into the room. "You see he doesn't try to stop it, understand? See that he's quiet, if you have to sit on him! We'll be back."

On the Hrothvek road, night had come hours too early, and the sky howled, and the lightning tore down the black walls of air with ragged-nailed hands, showing the Saltmarsh blue-white and the sea blue-black. Wind threw gravel across the road like grapeshot, and the first cold rain was falling hard.

In the landsailer, which was built for pleasure cruises on fair days, Kory held the sail, Ghosh the tiller and wheelbrakes, pumping them, with showers of sparks from the pads every time the car began to slew in the wind.

Ghosh knew that Kory kept snatching glances at her, his eyes wide, as if he were trying to decide what she was, what she had become.

No wonder he didn't know; she didn't know herself. Reed had been saying for a long time that Ghosh didn't understand love. She had a sickening feeling that Reed might have been right after all.

"Look!" Kory shouted. There was a line of wavering lights ahead. A lightning stroke showed them as pavilions set up on the Saltmarsh edge. Dyelam ais Ariom's party. *See the End of Wine out with ais Ariom,* Ghosh thought coldly. *See His Scarlet Eminence the Regent out on his ear. But you never thought to see your only daughter out in the storm, eh, Master Dyelam?*

If only she were weaker in the arms. If only she had drowned in the sea. She had taken the first false letter to Kory, and then, at total war in her mind with the unhardened magics, staggered to the docks and jumped in. But she was a strong swimmer. She could swim in her sleep. If she had drowned that night, not washed up alive on Ciellon's beach, this all might still have happened, but safe in hell she would never have seen it. . . . *Make me a plum tree for ten thousand years, and all my plums will be poison.*

"Hold on!" Kory shouted as a sheet of rain hit the 'sailer. Ghosh leaned on the tiller and the brakes, and the car flexed and skidded off the road. Ghosh rolled into soft wet coldness, tasting salt that might have been marshwater or blood.

"Kory?" she yelled.

"Here—here, Ghosh." He had gotten a lantern alight some-how. "I'm all right. You?"

"That letter of yours—did you tell Reed to meet you *in the city,* or just to meet you?"

"I—just to meet me. She set the place—I mean, the letter I got said—"

Ghosh pointed marshward of the pavilion, to seaward. "Then Dyelam's sure to have seen your note. If you don't find her, you'd better just keep going."

"Ghosh—" He stared at her. The rain swept his black curls down his forehead. "Luck, Ghosh," he said, and turned his lantern and headed into the darkness.

"Damn luck," she said, and hoped her god was stronger for it. She started for the pavilion.

There were guards at the entrance to the huge tent, but they looked at Ghosh, stamping in from the storm, and made no move to bar her way. She looked around. The whole scene within was frozen into tableau, all the elaborately dressed guests staring at an open flap that looked out on the Saltmarsh. Staring, Ghosh knew, after Cadie ais Ariom. Ghosh wondered what the wizard had put in Reed's mind, to send her walking into the storm; Kory, probably.

Dyelam ais Ariom was dripping jewelry and sweat, biting his knuckles. *You should have stayed in your warehouse, merchant,* she thought. *You didn't know the price of doing assassin's business.*

She saw the red-robed figure of His Scarlet Eminence the Regent of Liavek, his hands loose at his sides, staring out into the night. He was taut as a bowstring, ready to snap.

We need a diversion, Gosh thought. *Thieves and pickpockets know all about that. Basic street work.*

"Hey-*yo!*" she shouted. Heads turned. "Hey-yo, hey-yo, my masters and mistresses, why so mum? 'Tis time for merry mischief! Ring bells! Sing songs! For is this not the last night of Wine, and we'd better celebrate before the Wine runs out?"

She did a handspring past the Regent, coming up right under his moustache. "Your Eminence! Oh, excuse me." She knelt at his feet, looked up at him. "Now I see what they mean by eminence."

Someone giggled. The Regent looked down, his face rigid.

Ghosh said, "Don't you get scared of heights, with all that eminence?" She nodded, winked. The Regent nodded slowly.

Thomorin Wiln's drugs singing in her blood, her heart screaming on the edge of despair, she danced around the pavilion, tugging beards, punching playfully at bulging bellies, sipping at guests' drinks. "Whooo! What is that, shrimp cocktail?"

She looked back at His Scarlet Eminence, who had a small smile. Ghosh wondered how much he knew about this. Well, he would know a lot more very soon.

Ghosh pirouetted over to a table loaded with pastry. "And now, the centerpiece of tonight's entertainment, a masterwork of mystery, a syllabus of surprises, an astonishment of artifice—but first, I need a volunteer from the audience. Would that prince of conjurors, that most eminent sorcerer, that offspring of a Ka Zhir camel, Phris jhi Hisor, please show his owl-dropping of a face?"

It wasn't hard to spot him. She just watched for the blush. Ghosh took a cream pie in each hand and flung them, and that was easy, too—she pretended they were knives.

Jhi Hisor gaped and grabbed instinctively for a silver button on his gown. The pies struck him in eruptions of berries and cream. Ghosh cartwheeled toward him, slamming both feet into his breastbone. He groaned and went down against a side table, which buried him under an avalanche of sliced fruit.

Ghosh tore the silver button from jhi Hisor's coat, pulled his jaw down, and rammed the button down his throat. He swallowed involuntarily, and his face went slack as his luck went free.

"That was one of Kory's best ideas," Ghosh said. "If you've any luck left, you'll choke to death."

There was a disturbance at the other side of the tent. Ghosh looked up. It was Kory. He was carrying Reed. They were both soaked, but they were both alive. Dyelam ais Ariom went running to his daughter and inevitable son-in-law.

And the rain had stopped.

Ghosh stood up slowly and went to the tent flap. The storm mass was splitting in two, peeling back from a cut as straight as a knife could make, exposing blue-black sky specked with a few hard stars.

"No," she said in a small voice. "Ciellon, no, you don't have to, we're all right—"

"The wizard," Dyelam ais Ariom said. "She freed the wizard's luck, and the storm broke." Dyelam beamed at Ghosh. "My dear young woman, I—" He stopped when he saw Ghosh's face, and he took a step backwards, and another. Ghosh looked at him for a long moment, thinking any number of things, which all boiled down to one.

"No," she said, "you live, to pay."

She turned and went to His Scarlet Eminence, who looked so stately and reserved that no one could have imagined him any other way. Ghosh spoke a name, and His Eminence gave her his hand, and in a moment they were aboard his coach and away up the road toward Liavek, as fast as horses could run.

Zal najhi Zal was just about to hand over the desk to her night clerk when there was the screech of a wagon braking, and the front doors of the Sea Eagle were thrown open by two men of the Levar's Guard. She promptly spoke the First Prayer to Bree Amal. Then there entered His Scarlet Eminence himself, and with him the short dark woman that the wizard had entertained the night before; he looked terrifying and she looked like a drowned rat. Zal spoke the Second Prayer.

The Regent and the soggy girl were met on the stairs by the wizard's ghastly blue servant, who actually looked like he might send His Scarlet Eminence away, though he led the pair upstairs instead. Zal najhi Zal stood at the desk for the next three hours, staring at the immobile guards at her still-open doors, being fed kaf and dry toast by the night clerk, until the Regent and the blue man came downstairs again and the blue man really did seem to send the Red priest away. The guardsmen shut the doors, and the blue man went upstairs, and only then did Zal najhi Zal utter the Third Prayer to Bree Amal, which is *May These Events Leave No Trace of Themselves in Thy Servant's Memory.*

"Prop me a little higher, Jagg," Ciellon said. "So I can see the Saltmarsh. I'm not going to have my last sight on earth be a plaster ceiling."

Jagg adjusted the pillows and said, "I believe the master intended to tour the Dreamsend Hills before his death."

"Did I? If a road were paved with intentions, Jagg, where would it lead? Come closer, Ghologhosh. I want to see you, too."

"Damn you," she said.

"Stop praying and come closer."

"You're a *magician*. Magicians live for centuries."

"Some of them do."

"Why not you?"

Ciellon gasped, exhaled slowly. "Because . . ." he said faintly, then coughed and said in a stronger voice, "Because of birthdays. Do you know what every magician must do on his birthday?"

"He has to reinvest his magic, in his luck-charm."

"And has no use of it 'til he does. That's why, yes, some of us last for a long time, but not forever. Because on your birthday, you revert to your actual age. Investiture is very trying, without the added burden of being three hundred years old when you try it. . . ."

"But aren't there charms—bound things—"

"Yes. But another must make them, and they cost the binder his or her entire luck, all magic for the rest of the maker's life. And I was offered it—I think we all are, at some time. A reflection of our power. A test of what that power has done to us. I found the cost much too high.

"It is the nature of my disease—which is itself partly magical—that a spell can repress it, but not destroy it. So I could live without pain—until my next birthday, when the pain would arrive so suddenly and in such great measure that I would never be able to reinvest. So there was the choice: one year free from pain, or several with it. The choice is straightforward, but not, I assure you, simple. In the event, it has been about eight years. I went many places in those extra seven years, saw many things. I think I did some good. I think I chose . . ." His face tightened and he twisted against the pillows.

Ghosh said, "But last night you did the magic. You took away the pain. So you could stop a storm you didn't have to stop, so . . ." She clenched and unclenched her hands. "And now you're hurting again. That means today's your . . . birthday."

"I was born on the first day of Fog, a little after dawn. My mother was in labor some four hours. I am told that is a very bad pain, to have suffered with for four hours."

"Then you did come back just to die."

"I had to die somewhere," Ciellon said patiently. "Not in Hrothvek—you can't really go home, not that way—but in sight of the Saltmarsh." He looked at the closed window. "Though I've been struggling all night with the question of purpose. Was I brought here? What a grand thought, to be needed, and a terrifying one, to be summoned. . . . Well. I was here to do the good thing, and now it's done."

"Done? And nothing else matters, not me, not Jagg—"

"Please. My precious Ghosh. Don't break my heart."

"Why not?" She put her hands to her eyes, but she did not cry; she really did not know how.

"Jagg," Ciellon said, "open the windows."

"It is cold out, master."

"Of course; that's the marshmist. I want to smell it. Open them, Jagg."

Jagg did so. Streaks of dawnlight ran across the Saltmarsh, turning it the color of iron in the forge. The mist was rising, smelling of reeds and salt. There might have been no storm at all. Jagg stood by the window, in the cold marsh breeze, as still as a cedar tree.

Ciellon said, "The girl's name was Seva sei Varun, but she was called Harmony. Resh didn't think I would remember. He told me, before we both went away, that I would forget. But I didn't forget. I never forget names. The girl's name was Seva sei Varun, and things went so terribly wrong, and she never came back. Resh and I thought we'd never come back either . . . but we did. And . . ." Ciellon turned his cloudy blue eyes on Ghosh. "You see, Harmony, I did remember. And I heard you call, and I came."

Ghosh said, "Will you have tea with me, Ciellon? Worrynot tea?"

Ciellon smiled. "So you learned what it—" His body went rigid. He made a strangling noise. Ghosh leaned over him, put her hands on his shoulders. "Fight, why won't you fight? What do you want dignity for, without any life to—no *life*—" She felt the breath leave him. She let him go, took a step backwards and bumped into the door, sagged against it. Outside the window there was a flutter of white wings, and Ghosh turned her head and stared—but it was only a white heron, only a cadie flying; and then a golden cormorant was flying with the heron; and then both birds were gone.

Jagg closed the window. He went to Ciellon's side, reached into his collar, and drew out a small pendant on a cord. He put the luck-piece on Ciellon's chest and folded the wizard's hands over it. He looked at Ghologhosh.

She said, "He didn't babble at the end. He didn't think I was anyone else. There was never one moment when he wasn't sane and wise and—Isn't that right?"

Jagg nodded silently.

"He just wanted me to know he was happy. I wish to Ghol-whose-curse-doesn't-count he hadn't been so happy."

Jagg said, "I must wait now with him 'til midday. So no other spirit can enter his body. It is my land's custom."

"That's a good custom. Show me where to wait with you."

There were four of them in the Sea Eagle parlor, taking afternoon tea: Korik Li and Cadie ais Ariom called Reed, Jagg, and Ghologhosh.

"We're going to live in Hrothvek," Kory said. "Reed's dowry is the old part of the ais Ariom business—but we won't be part of Dyelam's company."

Reed said, "We like Hrothvek. It's quieter than Liavek, but near enough that we can visit when we want."

Ghosh thought but did not say that it was very generous of the Regent to let Dyelam's children visit him in his house on the Levar's Way, since Dyelam's house would certainly be a kind of prison for the rest of his life. Dyelam would not suffer a hundred thousandth of enough, but he would suffer. And his heirs were good. Ghosh was satisfied.

Kory said, "We've got a big house . . . there's plenty of room for you. For both of you."

"I thank you, no," Jagg said. "I like your country, but it is not home to me. Any place was home when the master was alive . . . but now no place, 'til I find it again."

Reed said, "And you, Ghosh?"

"I'm going to help Jagg find his place," she said. "He's going to help me find a new name, too."

"Harmony?" Kory said.

"No, not Harmony," Ghosh said, gently because Kory didn't know any better. But he was learning. They all were. "Don't try to find my new name." More firmly: "I mean that. Don't try to find me."

Ghosh waved to Zal najhi Zal. "Innkeeper, I believe you said the inn had procured some Worrynot tea. Would you bring it, please?"

As Jagg filled the cups, Reed said, "I wondered about

Worrynot tea. Ciellon was always talking about it, and calling it a Hrothvekan joke. So I asked someone at the End of Wine party, and she explained it."

"And?" Ghosh said.

"The way she told it—well." Reed imitated a matron giving out the story over teacakes. "The leaf, you know, the child-preventer, it's usually chewed, but one can make a tea of it, if one knows how. And mothers, you see, in the *older* parts of Hrothvek, their children would be going out, and no use to say 'Be careful,' because at that *certain age* one's quite deaf to such words, of course. But Mother could say, 'A cup of tea with me, before you go,' and that they'd hear, and that they'd do. You see, my dear?" Reed chuckled. "And I did. Worrynot tea is a care you don't know you're taking—a favor you do someone else that's really a favor to yourself."

"And," Ghosh said quietly, "the last cup of childhood, the first cup of responsibility." She reached over to the teacups; Jagg had filled five. Ghosh took one and poured it in the earth-pot the followers of Herself used for libations. "For Ciellon." She raised another cup. They all did. "For all of us."

"For all of us."

They drank.

"Gods, it's bitter," Kory said.

The Well-Made Plan

by Emma Bull

THE YEAR WAS waning graciously, as years will in Liavek. Out of a jewel-box of seasons, late autumn brought a rich cascade of topaz mornings, carnelian afternoons, and opulent sapphire-blue evenings. On just such an evening early in the month of Fog, Lir Matean Koseth ola Presec, Margrave of Trieth, was strolling south on Park Boulevard, bound for the Tiger's Eye.

He was full of contrary, contradictory urges, and they fascinated him. His pace, for example: He had no appointments and the twilight was pleasant, almost narcotic. Yet he had to shorten his step constantly, or he would have been striding down the wide street, his embroidered black coat swirling around him in a self-made breeze.

The whitewashed walls of the Tiger's Eye were aglow with the last reflected light of the sky, its two front windows and open door golden with lamplight. The sight conjured its own set of contrary impulses, and these, too, he examined. Here was his destination, and it called to him as his own townhouse never did. Yet he also wanted to turn and saunter away, to come back tomorrow, perhaps. Now, why? Simple contrariness, perhaps, the desire to prove his independence to himself. But if that was all, why was there a school of darting minnows in his stomach?

At the door, he smelled a rich waft of jasmine, and envisioned suddenly what he might find inside—the shop's proprietor, back from her long buying trip, unpacking perfumed oils and incense and stacking them neatly on shelves. Her hair would still be bound in a scarf to keep the road dust out of it, but a strand would have escaped into her eyes, and she would brush it aside with the back of her wrist. . . .

Koseth stepped into the doorway and saw, with a wave of irritation, nothing of the kind. Thyan, the shop assistant, was scooping dried jasmine from a jar into a cone of paper. There was none of the commotion and clutter that attended a return from a buying trip, and, most telling, no proprietor.

"She's not back yet?" he asked, to be sure.

Thyan frowned judiciously at the level of jasmine in the cone, producing two neat creases in the brown-black skin between her brows. "Hullo, Your Grace. You mean Snake?"

"Yes, I mean Snake."

"Not yet, but I expect her back any day."

"You've said that since last Rainday." Then it was his turn to frown. "She's not overdue, is she?"

Thyan looked at him oddly and twisted the paper cone closed. "No. She's doing a route through the Waste, and there's a lot that can come up."

He knew that, of course. He had spent years in the desert that lay between Liavek and Tichen, before his title came to him and he had to return home and tend it. What he felt, he decided, was restlessness brought on by the season's change, the loose-ended feeling of being between the End of Wine and Festival Week.

"Hullo!" called a large, rough-edged male voice from the back of the shop. The back door boomed, the cotton hanging on the back wall swept aside, and Silvertop, the young wizard who tutored Thyan, poked his head in. Silvertop seemed never to have grown into his voice; he was small and slender, white-skinned and pale-haired, with narrow shoulders and features as delicate as a court lady's. But his voice, at least, was a magician's.

"*Most* people use the front door," Thyan scolded at him, but she smiled, too, and dropped her gaze to the countertop. Her hands fluttered suddenly like dark birds, at odds with her usual neat movements. Koseth was amused. Surely he'd never seen Thyan shy with anyone else?

Koseth could tell nothing from Silvertop's behavior, but then, he never could. Away from his magics, Silvertop never seemed to know where to put his hands and feet. Now he shrugged and said, "I was coming from Cat Street, so the alley was closer. Your neighbors are having lamb for dinner."

"Well, I'm having sausages, so if you want to eat here, get that wistful note out of your voice," Thyan replied.

"Oh, good. I let the stove go out again at my place."

Thyan rolled her eyes, and Koseth coughed to hide his smile. It was no use to suggest Silvertop get someone in to keep house for him—he would complain that strangers got in the way of his work. And—Snake had told Koseth the story—the cookshop a few doors down from Silvertop's lodgings refused to deliver his meals anymore. Thyan, as Silvertop's emissary, had explained that the elephants had only been an illusion, and a mistake at that, a spell that Silvertop had forgotten to undo that had been brought to life when the door was opened, and the hall light met the light from the window. But the cookshop would not deliver.

And when, Koseth wondered with a start, *did I grow so close to these people?*

Until he'd coughed, Silvertop hadn't seemed to notice him, or at least, hadn't noticed that he was Koseth. Now he turned his pale gray gaze up and said, "Glad you're here."

Koseth raised his eyebrows.

"That is, I was going to come to see you tomorrow. About . . . about clothes."

"Clothes." Koseth had never seen the least sign that Silvertop thought about clothing, beyond recognizing that he should wear some.

"Yes. I wanted to ask you, um, where you get yours made."

Koseth opened his mouth to ask Silvertop what in the name of luck he was playing at. Then he remembered Thyan's sudden shyness and stopped. Romance had a way of changing one's habits, and it wasn't impossible that Silvertop should want to impress Thyan with his elegance. And Silvertop was regarding him with such a curious mixture of intensity and dread.

"A lot of places, actually," Koseth said at last. "But not many that are . . . moderately priced."

"What about Bright Needle?" Thyan spoke up. "And they're not far from you, on Street of the Dreamers."

Silvertop shot her a quick, blind look, as if he'd forgotten she was there. "Maybe," he said, turning back to Koseth, "if I could . . . describe the coat to them. Do you mind if I, well, study it?"

Koseth blinked. No, this was all too odd to be put down to

young love. Silvertop was up to something. But whatever it
was, Thyan was clearly not in on it. Better, perhaps, to pry it
all out of Silvertop out of her hearing. He nodded, and Silvertop
stepped around Koseth to stand behind him.

"You've got something in your hair," Silvertop said. "Hold
still."

Koseth felt something stir the hair at the base of his skull;
then Silvertop came around his other side and handed him an
olive leaf. Koseth raised an eyebrow. The young magician's
eyes met his, but not comfortably.

"I'll see you tomorrow," Silvertop told Thyan, heading for
the door.

"But you just—I mean, dinner!" Thyan wailed.

Koseth, too, made for the door. But once in the street,
Silvertop had begun to run, and Koseth didn't care for the idea
of chasing him like a City Guard after a thief. He turned back
into the Tiger's Eye.

"If he does come back tomorrow," Koseth said sternly, "tell
your young man that I'd like to speak with him."

"My young man?" squeaked Thyan. She cleared her throat.
"He's no young man of mine. I mean, not if that's what you
mean. He's a bubblehead. And I wouldn't have him if he *was*
interested. So there." She turned, abruptly, to fuss with the
contents of a shelf.

He smiled. "There's an old S'Rian proverb: A long 'no' is
the surest 'yes.'"

She shot him her fiercest scowl.

"All right, I'll go," he laughed, and raised his hands as if
to ward her off. "If Snake comes back, tell her I was here."

He strode out and back up Park Boulevard, humming softly.
The stars were out, thick as frost on a mountain meadow, and
the wind was fresh. He paused just inside the Levar's Park to
listen to two women playing cittern and wooden whistle, and
to leave them a few coins. The path along Lake Levar was
empty and silent, and for a moment he felt a wary itch between
his shoulder blades. He ambled around a blind corner, faded
quickly back into an oleander hedge, and waited. But he heard
no footfalls, and saw no shadows moving but those of the leaves
that tossed gently on the sea wind.

He shook his head and smiled at himself. He'd spent too
many years as the Desert Rat, it seemed, to settle easily into
the peaceful life of the Margrave of Trieth. He walked the rest

of the way to his townhouse, just off Gold Street on the Boulevard of Summers Past. His butler opened the door before he reached it, his coppery face pleated with a hundred wrinkles by his smile.

"Welcome home, Your Grace," he said, and pressed his palm to his forehead. "There is a gentleman to see you."

It was late, but not unconscionably late, for company. "Has he been waiting long?"

"No, Your Grace, only a few minutes. I made him comfortable in your study."

"Thank you, Maseka. Will you bring us tea there, please? The Crown of Suns blend?"

"Certainly, Your Grace." Maseka touched his brow again and left him, crossing the courtyard to the kitchen archway with a stately tread.

Koseth shook his head and smiled. *There's more gracious nobility bred into Maseka's big toe than into all of my scruffy self*, he thought. The leathery leaves of the sweetbay rustled over his head, an appreciative audience. The night sky was blue-black, and the three sides of the house and the front street wall made it a square-cut dark jewel splashed with stars. *Scruffy or not*, he smiled up at the sweetbay, *I wouldn't change places with anyone in the world tonight.*

The study was on the ground floor of the left-hand arm of the house, with windows on the street and the courtyard. The latticed inner shutters had been closed over all of them for the evening, and the room was rich with the light and smell of the lamps burning scented oil.

The man who rose and bowed deeply to him was in his early twenties, his bearded face very dark. He wore a long cinnamon-colored robe, drawn up and tucked under his sash on one side for easier walking. Beneath that were full black trousers, tied at the ankles on the outside of his soft, low-heeled boots.

Koseth returned the bow. "You bring grace to my home," he said in the shared language of the watering places in the Waste. "I am the Margrave of Trieth. How may I serve you?"

The young man gave a little shake of his head; then he crossed the floor quickly, took Koseth's hands, bent, and pressed his forehead to them. He looked up, smiling. "Great Lord," he said, "you already have."

Koseth laughed and slid back into Liavekan. "Unless you're

not what you look, there are no great lords in this room." The young man looked startled. "Sit, and tell me your name." Koseth dropped into an ebony chair, and the young man sat carefully on its mate.

"My name is Hama, Great L—I am sorry, Your Grace, is it?" Koseth nodded. "And I think you will always be a great lord to the clans of the northern Waste."

Koseth studied his visitor's face more closely. Yes, his features showed the mixture of clan and Tichenese blood that was sometimes found on the northern edge of the Great Waste. But shared blood was no symbol of peace there. Tichen claimed much of the Waste for its empire, and it was the northern clans that most often brought the opposing viewpoint to the provincial governors, usually with fire and steel.

Hama looked down at his twined fingers, then turned his solemn stare on Koseth. "I was fifteen when you led the Casoe and Longfinger clans against the garrison at Well of White Flowers."

It was a pretty name when translated, as Hama had, into Liavekan. Koseth had once thought it pretty in Tichenese, too. "I don't know what seven years of songs have done to the truth," Koseth sighed, rubbing the space between his eyebrows. "But that was not a night of heroism and honor."

Hama looked startled again, before his face closed up completely. "My father died that night."

"I'm sorry for that. He had a lot of company. The garrison commander treated the clans like a horse he meant to ride to death. Once the clansfolk were inside the fortifications . . ." Koseth found his eyes drawn by the flames in the grate. "They had too many scores to settle," he finished softly.

There was a gentle knock at the study door, which made Hama jump.

"My butler," Koseth said, "with tea."

Maseka brought the tray in and set it on a little round table between them. The pot and handleless cups were the pale azure-green of a summer morning's sky. When Maseka had gone, Koseth poured for his guest.

Hama accepted the cup and sipped hesitantly. "Whatever may be the truth of that night, I and mine have owed you a debt since then. I came here only to tell you that I will pay it back."

"A long way to come to pay a debt."

"The turning of luck has only now brought me to Liavek. Could I have come sooner, be sure I would have."

Koseth smiled. "You owe me no debt. Or if you do, pay it by getting rich and helping your people."

"Perhaps," he said, almost to himself. He set down his cup and rose gracefully. "It is late. I am trying your hospitality sorely."

Koseth shook his head, stood, and bowed. "Come again as your heart bids or luck wills it," he said in the trade language of the Waste.

The young man bowed and left.

Koseth sat for what seemed a long time, staring into the fire, before Maseka knocked and came into the room again. "Olduv has your dinner ready, Your Grace."

"Thank you, Maseka." Yes, easier to be the Margrave of Trieth. No one would have waited dinner for the Desert Rat. "I'll eat in here."

"Very good."

"Oh, and I won't be going out again tonight. Tell the staff to take the evening off."

Maseka beamed and touched his butler's rod to his forehead. "Thank you, Your Grace. I shall."

Koseth woke the next morning to wholesale discomfort and the conviction that he didn't know where he was. For a moment he wondered if he'd fallen asleep on the low couch in his study.

Then he realized he could see the ceiling above him, and knew he was nowhere in his townhouse. Olduv would have taken his own life before he let a cobweb reach such a size. And Koseth was sure that no one in his household would keep a rather plucked-looking stuffed peacock hanging upside down from a crossbeam.

He felt—not weak, precisely, but fragile. He reached to rub his eyes and stopped, horrified, when his hand came into view.

It was the wrong color.

He sat up, and a wave of dizziness made his vision fold in the middle like a sheet of paper. He clutched the edge of the— probably—cot he lay on, waited for the vertigo to pass, and dismissed explanations as quickly as he thought of them. Drugs, illness, madness—none of them could explain the sight of his hand made small and slender and pale as milk. Pale as . . .

He looked down at himself, stretched out on a cot, covered

with a worn wool coverlet. He pulled that back. The body that reason said was connected to his head was also small, slender, and pale, with a surprising quantity of white-gold hair on the torso and legs. He took very little comfort from knowing that he was still male. In fact, it only fed a growing suspicion.

This time he sat up slowly and swung his feet onto the floor. With each minute that passed, he was less wobbly and ill. But his body felt like a bad fit; every motion reminded him of it.

The room before him also fed his suspicion. It was in the most complete disarray Koseth had ever seen, and he had seen a caravan encampment after a bandits' raid. Much of the mess seemed to be paper—bound books, scrolls, single sheets—piled on the long work table in the middle of the room, and on chairs, the floor, and any relatively flat surface. There were dirty dishes; old clothes; two shiribi puzzles, both dismantled; a pectoral of beaten copper and coral; an assortment of glass bottles with various colors of murky liquid in them; and other things that made Koseth want to rub his eyes. None of the other things, inconveniently enough, was a mirror. But he saw what looked like a polished tin tray on the seat of a chair. He stood up slowly and made for that.

It reflected his image well enough for what he wanted. For a moment he stared at his suspicion proved true. Then a white-hot fury mastered him and he began to curse aloud, until the sound of Silvertop's voice speaking Koseth's words, the sight of Silvertop's face twisted with his anger, made him trail off into befuddled silence.

He sat staring into the bottom of the tray until he realized that his stupefied expression didn't sit well on Silvertop's features, either. He put the tray down.

The little bastard had done it in the Tiger's Eye, of course. Walking all the way around him, the touch on his hair—had he only touched him, or had he left something there? Koseth reached up to feel the back of his head and realized only as his fingers touched the fine pale hair that this was, of course, the wrong head. That prompted another fit of cursing.

So, he decided, once he'd started thinking again, *if I'm in Silvertop's body, then is he in mine? For his sake, I hope he is. If he's in any other body, I'm going to break its arms.* Then he looked down at Silvertop's delicate hands and realized that arm-breaking was not one of his options.

He thrust his hands through his hair, found the wrong hair once again, and went, muttering, in search of clothes.

• • •

Koseth's heart plummeted at the sight of his townhouse. It was neat, quiet, and two of the Levar's Guard were posted at the front door. He found two more at the kitchen entrance. What *had* Silvertop done? Koseth had been sure, at first, that this was just another of Silvertop's experiments, done purely in a spirit of magical inquiry. Had Maseka spotted the imposture and called the Guard?

He started up the low stone steps to the front door, and the two gray-clad guards drew together before him. The one on the right, a lean woman with broad shoulders, nodded. "Pardon, master, but may I ask your business?" She was polite, but not conciliating, and Koseth scented trouble.

"I wish to see"—he couldn't help it; he stumbled over his own name—"the Margrave of Trieth."

"I must ask you why."

"I have something of his I'd like to return," Koseth smiled. He wondered what effect a Silvertop smile had, and hoped it was reassuring.

"Wait a moment, please," the guard said with a frown, and turned to wield the heavy bronze knocker. Her companion kept his eye on Koseth.

Maseka opened the door, and Koseth saw the expression that usually met his guests. Or, at least, something close to it; Maseka was gracious and dignified, but there was a canted look to his brows and the slightest air of hopeful appeal about his features. This dissipated as soon as his gaze fell upon Koseth.

Before he could speak, the lean guardswoman asked Maseka, "Is this man known to you?"

"No, mistress."

"You're certain? You've never seen him before?"

"Not to the best of my knowledge." Maseka turned to Koseth and touched two fingers to his forehead with grave politeness. "May I be of assistance, master?"

"Not now," the guard said firmly. "We'll want to ask this man a few questions." At this, the second Gray Guard detached himself from the doorpost and took Koseth, as politely as possible, by the arm.

Maseka cloaked himself in the icy and impenetrable dignity that he employed only in the face of the most awful transgressions of etiquette. "The gentleman has come seeking hospitality of the Margrave of Trieth. Which of you will tell His Grace, when he returns, that you mauled his guests on his very door-step?"

Returns? thought Koseth.

"Do you think we're standing here for the air?" snapped the guardswoman. "Damn it, man, we're dealing with a *kidnaping!*"

"We're dealing with a what?" said Koseth, and the second guard's hand tightened on his arm.

The woman turned and scowled at him. "The Margrave of Trieth was kidnaped last night, and if you don't stay out of this, I'll arrest you out of sheer annoyance."

"Maseka, is this true?" Koseth said.

Maseka blinked. "Your pardon, master?"

Koseth remembered that he didn't look like anyone Maseka knew. "May I come in?"

"No!" said the guard, and "Certainly, master," said Maseka.

Koseth looked at the guard. "I . . . may have some information that will prove useful."

"Then you can give it to me, here or at the nearest City Guard post."

Koseth frowned. It would be a daunting look on his own dark features, but he suspected it wasn't of much use on Silvertop's. "Maseka, *I'm* Trieth. I'd prefer not to explain it here. How can I prove it to you?"

The guard protested, but he paid no attention. He was watching Maseka's face, where disbelief and hope chased each other across the copper-colored features. The butler drew a deep breath, let it out, and studied Koseth. At last, he said, "If you really are His Grace . . . tell me in what object His Grace has invested his luck."

Koseth stood stunned for a moment before he found his voice and roared, "I'll see us all in jail first! I'd as soon print it in the *Cat Street Crier* as tell it to these two lumps of dung—and it wouldn't do you a damn bit of good, since I've never told it to you!"

The change that came over Maseka was astonishing. He beamed, he glowed, he seemed close to weeping. "Welcome back, Your Grace," he cried, "oh, welcome back!"

Surprise seemed to root both guards to the stone steps and loosen the grip on Koseth's arm. He stepped through his front door, and Maseka closed it firmly behind him.

When they stood in the cool tile-paved front court, Koseth asked, "Maseka, what, by the Levar's future . . . womanhood, possessed you to ask me that?"

Maseka's air of pleasant dignity had returned; he nodded and smiled gently. "I am sorry, Your Grace, but I could not be certain we shared any . . . privileged knowledge. I could only ask a question that would elicit a characteristic response. And if you will forgive me, your response was very much characteristic."

"I . . . see," said Koseth. "I think. Now, where was I kidnaped from?"

Maseka raised his eyebrows. "Then you *were* kidnaped, sir?"

"This is not an illusion, Maseka—it's someone else's body. I'm assuming the someone else has mine. I'd like it back. If he, and it, are not here, then I have to start looking for them somewhere."

"Yes, Your Grace." Maseka looked taken aback. "Well, you were . . . he was . . . the kidnaping occurred in your bedchamber."

On the way up the curve of stairs to the second floor balconies, Maseka added what he knew. He had, as instructed, given the staff the night off after dinner, and retired to his own quarters behind the kitchen. He'd sat down to work on the household accounts. All he could remember after that was the popping sound of pottery breaking, and scraps of a succession of ugly dreams. At dawn Maseka woke slumped over his writing table, his ledger stopped in mid-entry and ink dry on the pen. When he searched the house and found Koseth missing, perhaps three-quarters of an hour ago, he called the Guard.

"How did you know I hadn't simply left the house early?" Silvertop, after all, would never have thought to tell the servants he was going out.

"I'm familiar with your wardrobe, Your Grace—you'll pardon me if I say that it is not extensive. All that was missing was your dressing-robe."

No, not even Silvertop would have left the house in a dressing-robe.

The bedchamber, the rearmost of the rooms in Koseth's private suite on the second floor, was undisturbed, except for the unmade bed. There was no sign of a struggle or a search.

If it hadn't been for Maseka's familiarity with Koseth's clothes, the disappearance might not have been recognized until hours later.

"Have the City Guard brought in a magician yet?"

"Yes, Your Grace. The magician came immediately; the inspector has not yet arrived to do a physical search."

"Find anything?"

"Unfortunately, the trail seems to be rather cold. The magician could tell that magic had been used both here and in the servants' quarters, but could not identify a spell or its maker."

Not, then, any great outpouring of magic, such as rendering Silvertop—or Koseth—immaterial and whisking him out through a second-story wall. That would leave a trace that could linger for a day or more. Koseth doubted that he could do better than a Guard magician, but he had to try. "Maseka," he said, "brew some kaf for me, would you?"

Maseka looked startled for an instant, then nodded. "Yes, Your Grace." He touched fingers to his forehead and went away. Koseth waited until he heard Maseka's steps on the stairs. Then he went to the marble-topped washstand near the bed and opened a drawer.

For an instant he felt a disorienting lack of something. Then he realized what it was, and a drowning terror seized him. His luck was gone. He felt for its hiding place anyway, but without hope; he was well within three paces of where his invested object should be, and there was none of the comfortable resonance he'd grown used to, his particular manifestation of the bond between magic and its owner. Could the kidnapers have known what his luck was invested in, and taken it, too? But if they thought they had Koseth, they would have done better to leave it where it was, much too far away for their victim to draw upon it. Unless they'd destroyed it. . . .

At the back of the drawer, in its crevice, his fingers met the soft leather of the coin pouch that held his invested luck. He pulled it out and stared at it. It was the same one: thin, glossy black leather, a little scarred with use, drawn closed with a red silk cord. He could feel the weight of the polished ball of rose quartz inside, but he could feel no magic. He rolled the tassel between his thumb and forefinger—

His pale-skinned thumb and forefinger.

The thing was brimming with invested luck, ready to be tapped . . . but not by Silvertop, and not by Koseth in Silvertop's body. Perhaps he could use Silvertop's invested object, but finding it in that disaster that passed for Silvertop's living quarters would have meant playing a grown-up version of Hot and Cold for hours.

Koseth tucked the pouch into his heavy cotton sash and began to examine his bedchamber. Perhaps familiarity would give him an edge that the Guard, searching later, would lack.

The grillwork over the window was painted wrought iron. He looked for scratches in the paint or flakes of rust on the sill, and found none. They hadn't taken the grill off, then, and hadn't gone in or out that way. The bedclothes were rumpled, but clean. Nothing had been taken from the dressing table or the ornate cedar-lined clothes press except, as Maseka had said, his dressing-robe.

There was no sign of a struggle, which probably meant that Silvertop had been drugged. Maseka's account indicated that *he'd* been. Maseka had also said that he'd heard crockery breaking. Koseth left his chambers, went to the top of the stairs, and shouted, "Maseka!"

The butler popped out the arched red door from the kitchens. "Yes, Your Grace?"

"You said you heard something breaking last night?"

"It seemed so to me, Your Grace—not a shattering sound, but a sort of pop, like a cup breaking."

"Did you find anything broken this morning?"

Maseka shook his head. "I looked, Your Grace, after I called the Guard."

Koseth went back to his bedchamber. It was a maddeningly tidy crime, difficult enough to solve without the raveled end of his and Silvertop's identity switch. Had the kidnapers intended to take Koseth? Or had they intended to take Silvertop in Koseth's body? His only route to the kidnapers' identity was motivation, and without knowing who they thought they were kidnaping, he couldn't determine that, either.

Since they hadn't come in the window and hadn't used any great magic, they must have gotten in downstairs and come in the sitting room door. Koseth sighed and got down on hands and knees to study the polished ebony floor and the carpets. He followed a straight route to the bed, ranging a few feet to either side in his search. When he reached the bed, he lifted the nearest bed curtain and shook it out, then raised the bed skirt. Nothing on the floor under the bed. Then his eye was caught by a reflection in the folds of the hanging on the other side of the bed. He scurried over and lifted the other bed curtain.

What rolled out was a piece of broken stoneware. It seemed to be a rough cross-section fragment of a jar, with some lip on one end and base on the other. The outer glaze was a glossy green painted with the outlines of clouds and birds in black and gold. Koseth cupped it in his hands for a moment, then, very delicately, sniffed the inside surface.

The smell, faint as it was, was associated in his mind with being dizzy and falling down, and he was a little surprised when the floor didn't tilt beneath him. Oil of green satinbark, mixed with some volatile liquid and sealed in a breakable jar, would produce a sort of narcotic gas bomb. A very small spell could make a patch of window immaterial, just long enough to levitate the jar through. When the magic was withdrawn, the jar would fall to the floor and break, and the vapors would do their work quickly and be gone, and leave no clue. One in Maseka's room, to keep him out of the way, and one here— then the kidnapers could gather the fragments, and leave nothing behind but a mystery.

But here was the piece of jar. Koseth scowled at it. Had he been meant to find it, or had the kidnapers really overlooked it when they gathered up the rest of the fragments? The chemists and apothecaries of Ka Zhir used such jars, stoppered with porcelain and sealed with melted wax, to hold volatile liquids and oils, and herbs that deteriorated quickly in air or sunlight.

Koseth was not certain how he came to the resolution, but he acted on it at once. He pulled a large square of silk from a drawer of the dressing table and wrapped the bit of pottery in it. Then he went headlong down the stairs and into the kitchen.

Maseka raised his eyes from a neatly arranged tray and blinked. "Yes, Your Grace?"

"I may have found something. Tell whoever shows up from the Guard that they should meet me at the Tiger's Eye."

"Very good, Your Grace," Maseka sighed. As Koseth swung out the back door, he saw Maseka shaking his head over the pot of kaf.

The ride to the Tiger's Eye was neither long enough nor fast enough to work the fidgets out of his horse. The chestnut was inclined to make the entire journey sideways. Koseth was past the Levar's Park before he remembered that the horse thought he was a stranger—and he felt like one. Silvertop's thighs began to ache almost immediately from their unaccustomed grip on the saddle, and his slender hands threatened to blister under the chestnut's nervous pulling at the bit. When Koseth slid out of the saddle at the door of the Tiger's Eye, his legs quaked with weariness.

He was inside the shop before he realized that Snake was home.

She was surrounded by bales and baskets of things, very much as Koseth had imagined she would be. She was not, however, still in riding clothes. Her hair was freshly washed and still damp. It was pulled back from her face and bound high on the crown of her head with an enameled gold ring, from which it fell to her shoulders in a cascade of tiny black braids. One long gold earring hung from her right ear. She wore a sleeveless calf-length tunic of persimmon-colored wool that pleated and draped from a beaded yoke as if it were no heavier than fine linen. Beneath the tunic she wore a tight-sleeved blouse and narrow trousers of heavy bronze silk. Her slippers were black leather painted with morning glory vines.

She looked up at him and smiled, her face full of gentle amusement, and he realized that he'd been standing dumbstruck since he'd seen her.

"Don't tell me," she said in that kaf-with-honey voice, sharp and sweet at once. "You came to elope with Thyan, and my presence has sunk the whole scheme."

"What?" he said finally. He had outbargained the Tilandre horse breeders, but the sight of this tall, elegant woman in her shop reduced him to unprecedented stupidity.

"It was a joke," Snake said patiently. "Hello, Silver. What can I do for you?"

"I'm not Silvertop," he said, and his words sounded bald, foolish, and completely unbelievable. "I'm Koseth."

Snake nodded and stroked the bridge of her nose thoughtfully. "And I am His Scarlet Eminence."

"Blast it, Snake, it's true!"

"Is this Thyan's idea?"

"It's the sort of crack-brained thing Thyan would think up, but she gets no credit for this one. I'm not joking. It's a vile tangle, but I *am* Koseth."

Snake propped her elbows on the lid of a waist-high basket, and her chin on her knuckles. "I may be over-cautious . . . but

I've lived with Thyan for six years, and it's ruined my disposition. Prove it."

Had he been thinking coolly, he would have been able to summon up any number of more temperate ways to prove himself. As it was, he stalked scowling over to Snake, took her face in both his hands, and kissed her with ferocious intensity.

When he drew back, he was certain for an instant that she'd boxed his ears; he felt as disoriented as he had when he woke in Silvertop's body. Snake blinked and gave her head a quick shake.

"Well!" she said, a little gruffly. "I'm convinced."

"You are?" said Koseth.

Snake grinned. "It didn't feel at all like you, of course. But you're the only person on this side of the Sea of Luck who would do that and expect me to leave his skull intact."

"I seem to have a lot of . . . singular characteristics. I must remember to thank Silvertop when I see him."

"How is it," Snake said with a tip of her head—a question mark personified—"that you haven't seen him, if you're wearing his skin?"

Koseth flung himself down in one of the wicker chairs that Snake kept by the hearth for guests and leisurely customers. "A fine question. I woke up this morning in Silvertop's body, in his rooms. I assume he woke up in my body. Some poor fool certainly did."

"You haven't checked?"

"I tried. Someone seems to have kidnaped me."

Snake's dark eyes grew round as half-levar pieces. Then she frowned, bit her upper lip, and said, "Why?"

Koseth nodded; it was like Snake to ask the most important question first. "I don't know. It depends on whether they thought they were getting me, or Silvertop in my body."

"Why would they think that?"

Koseth shrugged. "The body-switch was Silvertop's doing. If I knew why he'd done that, it would be a help. Could he have known that someone planned to carry me off, and thought, for some luck-bereft reason, that it would be better if they got him instead?"

"No," said Snake after a thoughtful moment. "Not Silvertop. His sort of silliness is in inaction: forgetting to eat, or not coming in out of the rain. Active silliness is not his style."

"Silliness? To leap heroically forward and take a blow meant for me?" Koseth clutched at his chest. "I'm wounded."

"Silly for Silvertop to do it. Now had it been me, instead . . ."

Koseth warily raised an eyebrow.

"Well," said Snake with a bat of her lashes, "they'd be shocked, wouldn't they, to find that their victim *could* fight his way out of a flowerbed?"

"May your linens mildew and your glassware crack."

Snake grinned. "Start at the beginning, my dear, and tell me the whole of it."

He did, trying to be thorough. When he was finished, Snake said, "Show me the piece of the jar."

"That's partly why I came here," Koseth said, gesturing vaguely at the collection of ceramics on one wall. He pulled the parcel out of his coat pocket, unwrapped it, and handed it to her. She carried it to the window and peered at it closely all around, rubbing her thumb over the inner and outer surfaces and holding it up to the light.

"It's Zhir work," Koseth offered.

"Umm. The shape and the ornamentation are unique to Ka Zhir." She looked up, frowning. "But that isn't where this was made."

"But if it's unique—"

"Come look," Snake said, and he obeyed. "See the footring on the bottom? Zhir potters cut the footring on their pots with a square-edged tool, and you get a sharp angle where the foot meets the pot. This was cut with a rounded edge. Liavekan potters sometimes cut the footring like this, but the ring is usually thicker when they do, and much higher."

Koseth shrugged. "A Zhir pot with impure foreign influences?"

"I don't think so." She put it in his hands and pointed. "Look at the spots in the interior glaze, where the oxides in the clay have leached through. Zhir stoneware is very clear, almost as clear as porcelain. The combination of this and the footring suggest that this pot is Tichenese."

After a moment, she said, "You're staring again."

"Tichenese?"

"Probably."

"Fascinating. Tell me, why would you suppose I found a piece of a Tichenese forgery of a distinctive Zhir jar on my bedchamber floor?"

Snake's eyes got wide again. "Because you were supposed to?"

"No—because whoever searched my bedroom after I disappeared was supposed to."

"What I meant."

"And whoever found it wasn't supposed to know it was Tichenese."

They stared at each other over the fragment for a few long moments. Koseth knew that Snake was fitting the facts together in her mind; it was, after all, what he was doing.

"Tichen would love to see Liavek and Ka Zhir hacking pieces out of each other again," she said. "I'll wager they weren't pleased to see Calornen's Stone returned so peacefully."

"And the apparently Zhir kidnaping of a Liavekan noble would certainly toss a cat into the henyard."

"Do we go to the Guard with this?"

Koseth scrubbed his face with his fingertips. On Silvertop's face, it was more distracting than refreshing. "When the inspector from the Levar's Guard gets to my townhouse, Maseka will direct him here. Whether he'll come straight here or not, we don't know." Koseth drummed his fingers on the window-frame. "Damn! If the kidnapers find out they only have half of me, what are they likely to do? How much danger is Silvertop in?"

"That depends. Half of you is quite enough to rouse Liavek against Ka Zhir."

"Unless they don't mean to hold him hostage at all."

Snake understood him immediately and paled. "Let's go after them, then," she said quietly. "I'll roll Thyan out of bed and tell her to tend the shop. I won't tell her about Silvertop; better she should have her hysterics when we bring him back."

"We can't go after them. Which direction would we go? They could have gone anywhere, curse them, including out to sea." He paced the short distance the crowded shop allowed. He'd been wrong the night before, it seemed; his life as the Margrave of Trieth was going to be remarkably like his life as the Desert Rat. He remembered his visitor, Hama, and the memories the young man had forced upon him of the battle for Well of White Flowers. Chaos and butchery, revenge in the name of justice. The twisted features of garrison commander Iesu . . .

And the way they mingled with the features of the commander's clanswoman wife in the face of their son, barely come to manhood, beardless then. What had Hama said? *"My father died that night."*

"Get ready to ride," he said to Snake. "I know where they've gone."

He looked down at the fragment of pottery in his hand. It was in two pieces now.

Snake's possessions did not include a fast horse, so they rode double back to Koseth's townhouse and he provided one from his stables, a big black gelding with an ugly head and long, powerful shoulders. Koseth gave Maseka their probable route, and told him to direct the Guard after them.

They rode as quickly as they could through the streets above the Levar's Park and out the Drinker's Gate. Then they turned north and east, onto a road that ran through the bleak western foothills of the Silverspine. Once, when they'd stopped to rest the horses, Snake asked, "If they're bound for Tichen, why this route? Why not through Trader's Town?"

"Too well-traveled. Hama is no cold-blooded professional, to drive a wagon at a leisurely pace down the highway with his captive tied up in the back. He's a young fool bent on revenge. He'll be on horseback, with his captive thrown over the saddle bow. Harder on the captive that way, too. So he'll have to stay on the byways until he gets to the Waste."

"And then?"

Koseth shot her a bleak look. "If he gets that far, he can take any damn route he pleases. We'll have lost him."

"Well, then," Snake said, getting to her feet and pulling her ash-gray cloak around her. "We'd best not let him get that far."

The only comfort he had, he realized as they rode, was that if Silvertop opened his silly mouth and convinced Hama that he wasn't Koseth, Hama almost certainly would let him live. It was Koseth that Hama wanted, and he wanted *all* of him. And the young codhead wouldn't realize that killing Silvertop would be the best revenge of all: Koseth would be tormented with guilt for a friend's death, and cursed to wear the friend's body to keep the guilt fresh.

At least, Koseth *hoped* that Hama wouldn't realize that.

The sun was setting wound-red in the dusty air over the plains when they sighted their quarry.

Snake shaded her eyes with a gloved hand. "Four horses,

three with riders, what looks like badly-made panniers on the fourth. That would be our wandering lad." She looked at Koseth. "They've turned west, toward the Waste."

He swore gently and flexed Silvertop's cramping hands. "They must have discovered that I'm not all there."

"No surprise for your friends."

"I *gave* you that one."

"Just because it's free, I should turn it down?"

Koseth grinned reluctantly. "Well, now it's a matter of the quality of our horses against the quality of theirs."

Snake checked the thong that tied her caravaneer's whip to her saddle. "We've been traveling at a harder pace than they have."

"Mm. But if those are the same horses they rode south on—and they are, if he's bent on secrecy—then they weren't well-rested to start with."

"Let's find out." The black gelding leaped forward, and Koseth gave the chestnut his head.

They gained several yards undetected, simply by staying among the brush and scrub trees along the road. When they broke out into the sparsely grown lower foothills and into the sight of the Tichenese, they were galloping.

The rearmost rider of the party turned in the saddle, then shouted something. The Tichenese horses began to run.

It seemed to Koseth that he had been stretched out along the chestnut's lathered neck for hours. The thundering of hooves might have been the noise of a waterfall, or his own blood roaring in his veins. The chestnut's nose drew even with the last Tichenese horse's flank. Koseth slid his saber from its scabbard.

Then Snake's whip curled out with a sound like the sky tearing, and the Tichenese horse shied. The battle-trained chestnut leaped forward at a signal from Koseth's knees and hands, and slammed against the other rider's mount. Koseth's saber rang against the blade of the Tichenese woman.

She was a smart and savage fighter, and Koseth thought later, when he could turn his attention from wielding Silvertop's untrained muscles, that she might have been recruited from the Tichenese cavalry. She would not return to it. Her weary horse stumbled, her guard fell for an instant, and Koseth took her in the throat.

He turned to see the second Tichenese, his lance falling from his hands, yanked from the saddle at the end of Snake's long whip. He landed hard and lay still. Snake rode toward the fallen rider, coiling her whip.

"Desert Rat!" Hama's voice spat out, and Koseth wheeled his horse.

Hama had ridden his smoke-tailed gray up to the packhorse and held it there with his knees. In his right hand he gripped the man-shaped bundle by its wrappings at what looked to be the head. His left hand held his long Tichenese blade. The steel was gory red, and for a moment Koseth stopped breathing; but it was only the reflected sunset.

"Killing in cold blood won't please your father's ghost, Iesu Hama."

"Keep well back, and keep your companion back, too— more than the length of her whip."

At the corner of his vision, he saw the black gelding sidle nervously, back and to the left.

"If you kill him, Hama, we'll tear you to pieces and water this slope with you."

The young man grinned fiercely. "Ah, but I will have had half my revenge. What will I have if I surrender?"

Koseth shook his head. "That's the wrong half of your revenge. The fool who let your father die is in this body."

Hama's eyes narrowed. "You think I will believe you did not want my father dead?"

"I wanted justice done. I was twenty-six years old, Iesu Hama, and if possible, even more of an idealistic idiot than you. The Longfinger and Casoe clans had been treated like domestic animals for a generation, yet I thought they would be wise and noble human beings if I only put freedom in their hands. No, I did not want your father dead."

Hama was silent, watching Koseth. The Tichenese sword continued to press against the wrappings of the packhorse's burden.

"At least my country never used my idealism as yours has," Koseth went on. "How did they find you, Iesu Hama? Who came to you and sharpened your hate like an arrow point? Who set you in his bow and fired you at Liavek, with no more care for your life than a wealthy archer cares for a lost arrow?"

Hama's face warped in a snarl, and his right hand twisted in the cloth wrappings. At precisely that moment, Snake's black gelding reared and she slid sideways in the saddle, her whip hand low.

In the space of scrub before the packhorse, something flicked out from behind the black gelding, hissing and twisting through the sand in serpentine curves. The packhorse screamed and plunged forward. Hama's tightened grip on his captive yanked him out of the saddle.

Koseth dug his heels into the chestnut. As the horse leaped over the fallen Tichenese, Koseth flung himself off, onto Hama's chest, and swung the hilt of his saber down on Hama's temple.

Silvertop's remaining strength was not sufficient to knock Hama unconscious, but he was dazed enough to lie still when Koseth kneeled all of Silvertop's weight on his chest.

"You had it backwards, damn you," Koseth panted down into Hama's face. "It was I who owed a debt to your father, not you. I will pay it now."

A little tongue of fear flickered in Hama's eyes, before his jaw clenched and he stared bravely back.

"Idiot. At Well of White Flowers, I learned a bitter lesson in human nature. I also learned that blood makes bad currency—the rate of exchange is lousy." Koseth backed off him slowly, holding the tip of his saber to the young man's throat. "Stand up."

Hama did, though he looked a little dizzy.

"Now," Koseth continued, "you're going to get on your horse and ride toward Tichen. We're going to stand here and watch until you disappear over the horizon. If we ever see you again after that, you'll get to find out what we really think of you."

Snake was coming toward them, leading the black gelding and the packhorse and shaking sand out of the coils of her whip. Silvertop sat unsteadily in the pack saddle, wrapped in Koseth's crumpled dressing-robe, clutching the tiedown horns in front of him. Looking at himself in a mirror and seeing Silvertop had been disorienting; watching himself riding toward himself made him want perversely to laugh.

"I'll take care of his assistants," Snake said and stalked off, a length of thong in her hand.

Hama looked at Koseth, then jerked his head toward Silvertop, in Koseth's body, on the packhorse. "Yes. This pale little body would fit that one."

"He's a good man. His death would have lessened both of us." Hama looked down. "Mount up," Koseth said finally.

They watched as Hama rode north, his back very straight.

His surviving henchman rode with him, swaying wearily, his hands tied to his saddle bow; the woman Koseth had had to kill lay over her saddle, wrapped in the cloth that had bound Silvertop.

The Tichenese were only a dark blur when Koseth said, "Silvertop, I hope you have an explanation of rare beauty for all this."

"Gently," said Snake.

Silvertop shook Koseth's head. "No. I mean, this shouldn't have happened. Not the kidnaping, though I suppose that shouldn't have happened either—that we switched bodies, I mean."

Koseth found it very odd to hear his own voice through someone else's ears. "And what should have happened?"

"I . . . what it was . . . listen, I'd rather not say, all right?"

Koseth swung around and rested his fist rather firmly on Silvertop's knee. "No, it is not all right. I have had an unpleasant day, Silvertop, and while I realize that yours has not been particularly restful either, I will consider it an insufficient penance. Unless you tell me something to change my mind."

Silvertop's blush tinted Koseth's sharp features. "It's . . . it's not even really a spell of transference. It was supposed to duplicate in me some of—" Here Silvertop descended to mumbling.

"Speak up."

Silvertop gazed at him rather desperately. "You . . . know so much about the world. And the way you talk, and move, and the way you think fast when you have to—I thought if I could do some of that"—he stared hard at his hands on the pack saddle—"then Thyan would like me more," he whispered.

For a long moment, Koseth and Snake stared. Then Snake turned her face against the black gelding's side, and her shoulders began to shake. Koseth covered his eyes. Finally he looked up at Silvertop, who was turning Koseth's face alternately pale and flushed. "That was all you wanted? You codhead. Snake, tell him."

Snake rolled over against the horse's flank. She was speechless with laughter, and tears rolled out the corners of her eyes and cut through the dust there. At last she gasped, "Too late! She already loves you!"

"She does?" Silvertop gaped unattractively.

"Only for as long as I've known her," Koseth said sourly.

"Why should I have thought you would have noticed?"

"Oh," said Silvertop.

"'Oh,' indeed. Do you think you could switch us back?"

"I'm not sure. Something interfered with the spell I did, so I don't know how big a job it would be to straighten it all out again. And I don't have my luck object, anyway."

"It wouldn't do you any good," said Koseth. "In your body, I can't use my invested object. But it may be that in my body, you can." He pulled the black leather pouch, heavy with the polished quartz ball inside, from his sash and handed it to Silvertop.

Snake gave him a long look, and he shrugged. "It's almost my luck day anyway."

"Hah," she said.

Silvertop held the pouch for a moment, then shook his head. "It doesn't work. I don't feel anything."

Koseth groaned and Snake patted him on the back. "Happy birthday, Koseth," she said.

"What's happy?"

"This," Snake said, and pulled out her own coin purse and jingled it at him. "I may have enough money to pay The Magician to switch you back."

Koseth looked rather sadly at the coin purse. "Surely someone a little cheaper would—"

"—be able to undo Silvertop's work?" Snake spared a wink at Silvertop. "I wouldn't bet money on it."

"The Magician explained what had happened after he got us back in the right bodies," Silvertop told Thyan, who was listening raptly. They were all, Koseth and Snake, Silvertop and Thyan, sitting in the second-floor living quarters of the Tiger's Eye, watching evening settle over the City of Luck. "I'd put my spell on Koseth, which was supposed to work slowly over the course of the night. Then the Tichenese fellow used a spell that would serve as a sort of beacon for their magic, just in case Koseth discovered them and tried to misdirect their spells. A spell of association, y'see, works as a sort of binder on the physical body—"

"Get on with the story, and give me the theory later," said Thyan, but she was smiling.

"Huh. Anyway, the two magics mingled, since mine was still in flux when the second one was laid on, and instead of getting some of Koseth's characteristics, I got his whole physical self, and he got mine."

Koseth leaned over to Snake and said softly, "We've heard this before. Want to go sit on the roof?"

She pursed her lips. "Colder up there."

"Snake . . ."

"All right," she grinned.

As they climbed the ladder, they heard Thyan say, "The only thing I don't understand is, why did you put the spell on Koseth in the first place?"

Snake murmured, "I can't bear to watch," and hurried up the last few rungs.

The sky was clear, and the moon, though waning, was still close enough to full to wash the flat roof with silver. Snake kept a little garden here: an acacia tree in a huge tub, some fancifully trimmed flowering shrubs, a collection of late-season vegetables and herbs. Koseth sat on the edge of the acacia's tub and Snake sat on the wall.

"So do you forgive him?" Snake asked.

"I think so. He's got blisters, saddle sores, aching muscles, and sunburn. That seems like enough revenge."

Her laugh was strong, and seemed to bubble up out of her like clear water. Koseth shivered.

"I was waiting for you to get back," he said. "Silvertop's and Tichen's little interruptions distracted me."

He saw her head tilt to one side, and imagined what he couldn't see in the dark—her eyebrows raised, her mouth a little puckered. He reached out for one of her hands, and stroked the long calloused fingers.

"I've decided to ask you if you'd marry me, you see. Don't fall off the roof, in the name of luck!"

She steadied herself by taking his hand in both of hers. "Why, pray tell, do you want to marry me?"

"What do you mean, why? Haven't I ever told you that I love you?"

"Yes, of course, but you told me that for the first time two months ago. What's different about it now?"

"Do you suppose it would help if I gave you a good shake?" sighed Koseth.

"No, I'd fall off the roof. I can't marry you, dear. You're the Margrave of Trieth. It would make my mother deliriously happy."

"Oh, luck forbid you should make your mother happy."

"Well, that's what I thought. I'll keep the Tiger's Eye, you know."

"I should hope so. I need something to fall back on after I run heedlessly through my inheritance."

Snake made a rude noise. "You never spend anything. I tell you what—I'll make you a partner in the business. With my knowledge of buying and selling and caravaning, and your money and familiarity with the Waste, we'll have the largest piece of the northern trade in all of Liavek."

"Snake, I'm proposing a marriage, not a merger."

"Same thing." She leaned forward and kissed him, long and intoxicatingly, on the mouth. "I adore you, Lir Matean Koseth ola Presec."

"So what," he grinned, and drew her closer.

Fantasy from Ace fanciful and fantastic!